Sky Tracer

The Fungal Realms Book One

Hayden Moore

Vraeyda Literary

Edited by Lis Goryniuk-Ratajczak
Cover by Sapha Burnell
Chapter Illustrations & Maps by Hayden Moore

ISBN 978-1-988034-26-3 (eBook)
ISBN 978-1-988034-25-6 (Paperback)
ISBN 978-1-988034-27-0 (Hardcover)

Vraeyda Literary sends authors to events, virtual events, Book Clubs & interviews. For promotional consideration, large-volume orders, please contact ambassador@vraeydamedia.ca.

From the time we danced into each other's lives, my heart found harmony...

MUSHROOM
CLUSTER

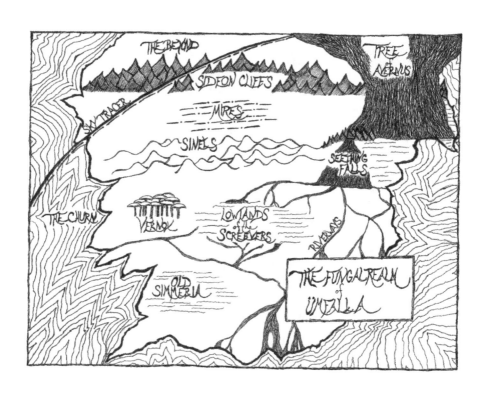

Part I

What's Beyond the Dark

I T WAS THE WIND forcing her to look down, always looking down, at the gloom to come. Had she the strength to raise her head, she would have seen the cobalt sky and peerless sun that reigned. Mighty birds of prey played deadly games with murmurations, elegant in their multitudes, articulating emptiness, only to fall back into a cluster and remake, with fewer birds than before.

It was a beautiful game played for time-eternal, an ethereal dance of death, boundless, unlike the carriage tracing its predetermined course over the spore cloud. Muffled screams would have driven the Weir mad, but for her Whispers in the wind.

Just before the dark carriage left behind the blue, an errant gust blew the Weir's skeletal face up. Windmills spun atop a world of branches, as daunting as mountaintops, where cloud ponds and Labyrinths and the tangled road loomed. The Weir's black hair undulated like black waves in the wind, along her bound body and beyond her ruined feet. Wind found its way back down and her head followed, to witness the oncoming murk.

In the grim embrace of a windless realm, all settled into quiet. Her eyes grew pronounced in the darkness, while her Whispers to the cloud only made them shine brighter. Spores danced darkly in her gaze, wild and thoughtless, acquiring touches of crimson from the Weir's unblinking eyes. Dew dappled her skin, thinly covering her bones, good for nothing but accepting ropes holding her body to the carriage's foremast. Her bones resonated her Whispers and the spore cloud bulked at the magic.

Droplets sustained her as she Whispered on, yearning for death, while her spirit diminished, orbit after orbit, around the same old sun. Spores constituting the darkness were her source and her Voice was the only thing keeping the spore cloud over the Fungal Realm of Ümfalla. Through the tilt of the carriage, she was left staring upon the Sinel Hills.

Muffled screams reinvigorated the carriage, on in its arching way back down, down into the winds over The Churn. The Weir heaved at the screams, sending the vessel into manic bursts of speed. Her lips kept moving, in spite of her torment. Through grim magic, the spore cloud bulged through replenishment.

Her need to scream remained unrealized, a primal force contained, feeding her Whispers. The sea hissed at the carriage's approach and the Eternal Storm claimed the horizon through swirling thunderheads. Balance was restored, just as it would be in the days to come, through an unchanging ritual. The only difference would be in the Names of the ones ferried back.

1

OF SPORES AND MEMORY

I N THE GLOOM OF the Fungal Realm, a burst of iridescent spores resembled colors dreaming of something more. This kind of spore-sparkle was rare, in a land where darkness reigned. Waist-deep in black water, Mēna let the moment take her, allowing beauty to overcome her pain. As the spores faded in their descent, before vanishing in the crowded spheres of puffball mushrooms—fungi tall enough to dwarf a giant—Mēna's *need* took hold again. Her keen eyes re-adjusted to the darkness of her world.

Then she saw her.

Things fell from the perpetual darkness of the all-encompassing spore cloud. Owls dropped their prey and greater mushrooms toppled over, only to rise again. Mischievous scavengers tossed gnawed bones from on high and Night Skimmers dropped shrill cries, far more jarring than any other sound in the world of Ümfalla. Light would never break through the gloom, but Mēna never witnessed a human fall from such heights.

Vital urgency banished wonder. She stepped out of the thick water and her boots found one bundle of moss after another, as she bounded towards the fallen figure. In stride, she covered her face with a mask of her own making, before spores found her airways. If the mycelium mask failed, her swift-footed journey into the Mushroom Cluster of Vernox would be her last.

Aromatics from home remained in the mask, a home where countless orbits of thoughtful toil gave rise to the glory of Filigrees Mushrooms. From sparkling cap to mycelium, the lush fungus fed, clothed and healed her people. Now the mask on Mēna's face was all that remained of the lost art. A somber death threatened her, an easy kind of death, mercy she did not deserve. She was facing the fundamental truth, once again: *Spores always found a way in.*

Her left arm numbed, while her right one ached beneath the adamant mechanical, allowing function in her limb. When she spotted a crumpled figure in the mushroom cluster, she leaped over a fallen stipe, where she gathered the body in her arms.

On the uphill journey back, Mēna's eyes were near bursting, while her heart raced along with her legs. Just as the world was growing dim, she fell to her knees and let the body roll from her bare arms. When she pulled off the mask and heaved, she marveled at the distance she covered. If spores fooled with anything, it was Time.

"*Take me back.*"

The voice startled Mēna back into the moment and a pair of eyes met her own. An utter lack of ocular luminescence told Mēna the young woman had fallen into a darkness of her own. Where Mēna's eyes possessed an inner-light, through lenses deciphering secrets of the dark, the other stared back through sunborne eyes, *darkly*.

She wore nothing but a slip of silk and her skin was smoother than a day-old mushroom cap. When she reached up to touch Mēna's mechanical, Mēna pulled away. The fallen one's eyes drifted in the darkness, in search of meaning.

"I know you're not the Goddess," Mēna said, eyeing her peripheries.

"Are you certain?" the fallen one said. "Maybe I am the beginning and the end, the origin of words."

"Someone as soft as you would never create a world like this. Where did you fall from?"

"Up there," she gestured with her chin. "Didn't go as planned. Need pushes one beyond reason," she groaned, as she sat up slowly.

"That's not possible. Nothing reaches that high but the Sideon Cliffs to the north. And you should be a pretty corpse after landing in the Vernox. Maybe I'm still confused from the spores. *You* exist. I carried you this far. Unless I'm imagining this... No," she clenched her jaw. "I haven't built Hexes from spores since I was a youngling. This is no hallucination. Hexes never create illusions with weight."

"Your eyes. You see beyond the dark. I never—"

"We have to keep moving. Can you stand?"

"I think so. But I—"

"Take my hand, or you're food for the feeding earth."

"My name is, Ruthy," she said, reaching up her hand.

"Mēna."

In the midst of Naming herself, Mēna took hold of the first hand of anyone else in orbits. Marking pale flickers to the west, she kept hold of Ruthy's hand and headed east, where the Sinel Hills stretched all the way to The Churn, the raging sea, embracing the entirety of the realm. Ruthy held onto Mēna's hand and stepped from one bundle of moss to the next. Mēna resisted instinct, to let go and carry on, alone. But instinct had nothing to do with what was Good and Just. When Ruthy stumbled, Mēna halted and glanced back.

"Your legs still function?"

"Yes," Ruthy heaved. "Can't..see much in this gloom...but your eyes. Slow down a bit... The fall didn't wound me, but—"

"Good. Save your breath. Follow my lead and don't drag your feet. *Do not* let go of my hand. *Listen* and trust me. Forget about putting trust in your eyes. I can see the way," Mēna winked, urging Ruthy on, with a squeeze of her hand.

Mēna was unaware of her swift-footed gift, not unlike a bird in flight who never admired its own grace. Her life was one of the solitary Wanderer. Her feet were sure and her eyes saw into the yellow, a depth and range of sight, escaping most. In a sunless realm, most were left to earthy blues and purples, on their way into endless grays. For Mēna, the Fungal Realm contained colors yet to be named, since only she perceived them.

With a sunborne woman in tow, every step was uncertain, but Ruthy was remaining upright and her body was at a tilt, as if her nose were leading her, since her eyes were almost useless. In spite of her sunborne eyes, her ears were finding a way to hear the sure steps of her guide, while Mēna's hand in hers *spoke* through squeezes and turns.

Mossy terrain was merciful to Ruthy's bare feet, even if her steps sank a bit with every footfall. Mēna imagined herself in Ruthy's situation and decided she would have crawled back to the Vernox and let the spores take her away.

After countless stumbles and falls from Ruthy and curses Mēna had not spoken to the air in orbits, Mēna shifted her gaze, in search of a place to rest. In a handful of moments, the toll of the heavy murk and ruthless pace would be too much for the stranger holding her hand. Nightfall was near and the many glows of mushrooms ahead would only bewilder Ruthy when thick darkness was upon them.

In the murk of the ubiquitous spore cloud, a pale light drifted across the sky. The nauseous knot in Mēna's stomach told her Sky Tracer was passing overhead. As the pale light slowly made its way over the Fungal Realm of Ümfalla, Mēna stood in absolute stillness. Through her dark-bright eyes, she traced its course, never blinking, while her drifting head appeared subject to Sky Tracer, like a moon to its ruling world.

She whispered, *beautiful*, in the midst of the ritual.

In a moment, the spot of light vanished in its slow ascent into the bulk of the spore cloud, before reaching somewhere beyond The Churn, far to the east. Mēna's nausea passed with the pale red light. She turned to Ruthy, who was still holding fast to her hand, but heaving for breath, after crossing the sharp hills of the all-encompassing Sinels.

"There is…one…less…passenger…in that thing," Ruthy heaved. "I need a—" Ruthy fell to her knees on the receiving moss, but Mēna held fast to her hand, keeping her upright. Ruthy clenched her eyes shut and took a few heaving breaths, before she stood back up, while her legs quivered. "Sorry for that."

"The body follows its own course," Mēna muttered to the ground. "You were a passenger? You mean you fell from Sky Tracer?" Mēna asked, suddenly aware of Ruthy's hand still in her own.

"Sky Tracer?" Ruthy grimaced. "Is that the Name?"

"No. *I* Named it. Nobody will carry it on. But even the abysmal light deserves to be Named. Sky Tracer makes me feel as if my navel is consuming me, whenever it passes. I could never keep calling something so strange, 'it'. But I can never help myself from looking at Sky Tracer. *So beautiful.*"

"I promise you, it's not."

"Sky Tracer is from down here. Cmon. I'm about to lose you to sleep."

"Can't cross any more hills. My feet are almost as weary as my eyes. Everything's dark ruin."

"For your sunborne eyes. But no more hills. I just need your arms. Look up."

"All I perceive is a gray bulk, like a tree from my nightmares."

"*Trees?*" Mēna leaned closer to Ruthy.

"Yes. Trees are everywhere where I come from."

"Climb onto my back. We're going up and you're going to tell me everything."

"We're going up this?"

"Yes. But hold your breath. This is the most poisonous shroom in Ümfalla."

"*What?!*" Ruthy cried.

"You must have jokes where the sun shines. Just seeing if you sensed this one," Mēna grinned. "Breathe as much as you want. Just don't let go."

"You are beyond reckoning. *Thank the Goddess I didn't die,*" Ruthy muttered to herself.

"Speak fuller," Mēna said.

"Nothing. Just a quick prayer."

"Nobody's listening to prayers anymore."

Ruthy climbed onto Mēna's back, crossing her ankles up front, while Mēna pried her fingers into the stipe of the towering Hydra Mushroom. Considering the unsure handholds, Mēna was thankful for Ruthy's lithe form, as she made her winding climb towards the spherical cap of the fungus.

Powdered clumps of stipe fell as Mēna's dextrous fingers found the surest holds, along the way. Taut strands of supporting fibers beneath the surface of the stipe were the surest way not to fall. The trick was finding enough of the elusive strands beneath the pliant surface to reach the top.

Mēna climbed countless Hydras in her life, but never with another body in tow. Having the stranger on her back was turning into a daunting lesson, inculcating the overwhelming responsibility of having another life dependent on her choices.

Mēna's heart beat faster, while her hands made doubly-sure they were finding the best holds, before the slightest tinge of vertigo intruded, in sympathy with Ruthy clinging to her back. The moment another soul came into her care, Mēna felt vulnerable, when she was supposed to be the strongest.

When Ruthy took a halted breath and sneezed from the spore-thick air, the suddenness threw off their collective balance. Had it not been the last push before they reached the top, Ruthy's hold on Mēna would have failed and left her falling to a sure death.

On the undulating surface of the crowded caps, Ruthy slid from Mēna's back and released her embrace. Ruthy's arms were shaking, as she marveled at countless mushrooms glowing and pulsing across the inky world, as far as her sunborne eyes could fathom. Shapes she never imagined, in luminescent colors beyond language, appeared as if from a beautiful nightmare, tantalizing ciphers from the unknown.

Her legs gave out and Ruthy was comforted in her fall by the pliant ground of the Hydra's caps. She looked up to the glow from Mēna's eyes, when a melon-sized mushroom dropped at her feet, a species unlike the Hydra in shape and pockmarked texture. Mēna gently stomped on the mushroom, evoking a deep green glow, soothing, through the gentle warmth it exuded. Ruthy detected tinges of cedar, evoking windswept memories from sunlit days past.

Through the glow, Mēna stood in a revealing light. Far more than the sheathed sword on Mēna's back pointed at *warrior*. There were battles imprinted in her gaze, an inner-strength, no less remarkable than her physical form. While she was more than a head taller than Ruthy, Mēna loomed like a mighty oak dreaming of the warrior, especially from Ruthy's seated position. Through the light of the lantern mushroom, the shadow Mēna cast turned Ruthy's silk slip a sparkling silver-green.

"You'll be dreaming soon," Mēna said, running her fingers through her own wild black hair, hanging down her long back. Sweat from the toil of the ascent poured down the sides of her head—where her hair was cut to little more than a stubble—before trickling across her powerful jawline.

"Where did this light come from?" Ruthy asked, staring at the glowing mushroom.

"Shrooms never exist alone. The ones you fell on were full of beautiful death, noxious spores, a species helping to keep balance in the realm. Life feeds on death, too. This lantern shroom holds bright secrets, secrets the shroom keeps. That goes on and on. Lantern shrooms like to grow on Hydras and Hydras are grateful. Now we share the light, upon a place removed."

"So strange. So *beautiful*. Even this dark realm, that's so..."

"Go ahead and sleep. When you return from that shattered realm of dreams, stay close to the lantern, so we can see each other speak."

2

Both Sides of the Light

W HAT SOUNDED LIKE SOMEONE peeling wet bark from a tree greeted Ruthy's
ears, before her eyes opened back up to the darkness. In the glow of the lantern
mushroom, Mēna was seated with her back to Ruthy, directing a gleaming knife along her
left temple, while short hair fell to the soft surface of the mushroom.

Running along the middle portion of her head, Mēna's pitch black hair reached for the
dark sky, making her appear taller than she already was. Veins and streamlined muscles in
her arms were dancing beneath her skin, as she slowly shaved her right temple. Lying next
to Mēna, a sheathed sword, as long as her arm, was pointing to the darkness beyond.

An exquisitely crafted ring of adamant metal clung to Mēna's upper arm, where her
armpit was congruent with the lowest portion of shoulder muscle and deltoid met tricep.
A custom loop-shaped band of metal secured the ring through connecting screws, along
the front of the shoulder, completing its parabolic journey on the opposite side. Alternate
strips of metal, no broader than a finger, ran down the bicep and tricep and connected
at the nexus of the mechanical on the warrior's elbow. There, hidden mechanisms of
silent-working gears and levers took over, where Mēna's arm failed, partly visible, through
small holes encouraging airflow.

From there, an X—black leather interspersed with silk threading, both renowned for
their immunity to rot and capacity to withstand tremendous force, in cases of forceful
pulling and striking—ran from the mechanism at her elbow, down to a band around her
wrist, with a thin rod further connecting the wrist ring to the elbow mechanism. Tiny
screws lined the band of metal at the wrist, where four adamant knots marked places
where the X's connected, able to be tightened and loosened, according to Mēna's needs.
X's of leather-silk on alternate sides of her forearm were tightened to the degree of a
bowstring.

Ruthy was unable to discern the finer details of such an instrument of torture. The mechanical was silent in its workings and of an art Ruthy had never seen. Something had to be done about what was festering beneath the mechanical. Nothing mattered but the warrior on the other side of the glow, not in a sunless world.

"How much can you see beyond the lantern?" Mēna asked, without turning, as she shaved the short hair at the top-edge of her hairline.

"I see you have eyes in the back of your head," Ruthy muttered. "I love your hair. So free. Mine isn't," Ruthy said, holding her thick braid of red hair that reached across her waist and into her hands on her lap. "Why do you shave your head in such a way?"

"To mark passing time. To remember."

"Remember what? You look so—"

"*How much can you se*e?"

Ruthy pretended to look thoughtfully into the darkness, behind her, "Glows in the darkness. The rest is black."

"Fuck," Mēna grunted, as she flipped the knife in her left hand and returned the tool to one of the many sheathes on her waist.

"I'm sorry."

"Stop saying that. We can't be blamed for our own bodies."

"Oh? Look at you. You were born for this."

"Not really. Nobody is. If I were, I wouldn't be here with you," Mēna let her head drop to her chest. She mumbled to her sternum, in a voice far deeper than before.

Ruthy cringed to witness the murmurs, but crawled towards Mēna, out of need. The spongy surface made her legs tremble along the way, while she imagined the monstrous mushroom cap she was upon, gobbling her up at any moment. Another few crawls brought her to Mēna and she reached out her hand to touch the mechanical. The acrid stench of rotting flesh made Ruthy's eyes water when her fingers touched the metal. Mēna swatted away Ruthy's hand and faced her with raging eyes, glowing with silver light.

"Never touch me without reason!" Mēna seethed.

Ruthy fell back, but quickly leaned towards Mēna, "I'm sor…You're the only thing that seems real here. After the madness of falling, I thought I was dead. Your eyes are the brightest thing I've seen. So alive. You're *real*. But I've smelled something like that before. Too many times. You have the rot. If the skin turns black, you'll lose your arm at best. If you take the mechanical off—"

"*Never*," Mēna said, shaking her head. "Not out here. Not now. Only when I sleep in a place removed from danger."

"Will you try? Just for a moment. I owe you my life and if a look is all I can do, that's still something. We must be safe up here. I doubt many people can climb like you do."

"There's always someone stronger. *Always*. And the stipe of this shroom can be felled in a few sword strokes, from below. I—"

"Please," Ruthy whispered, as she crawled closer to Mēna. "You helped me, *a stranger*. Let me try to help you. I've seen something like this before and your skin needs to breathe, even if this air is like breathing underwater. This will only grow worse. I have a better view."

"A bootless woman with sunborne eyes, coming to my need," Mēna said, as she reached below the hem of her dark sleeveless shirt where her ribcage began. The material stretched, while droplets of water trickled out, before dropping beside her, renewed in appearance. The way the dark shirt settled beside Mēna made the garment look like it was breathing.

"I should give you some..." Ruthy muttered, turning her face away.

"What was I supposed to do?" Mēna said. "Ask permission before I offended you?"

"*No*. I'm not offended. Envious, perhaps. Wasn't sure of your ways. I've been bound by rules made mostly by men. So much is dictated by what we can't do. But you're so...confident and free."

"That's rich-earth coming from you. All that covers your body is a bit of spider silk."

"This is nothing but an undergarment. Where I come from, our clothes are...more realized"

"You seem free enough in what you're wearing now. I doubt your words. You won't last a few turns out here if we don't find you good celium to wear. Silk is lasting in beauty, but you need the strength of mycelium-weaving, like mine. The Sinel Hills might be soft underfoot but you'll be worn to the bone without proper boots. You wanted to see my shoulder. How would you accomplish this with celium in the way? I don't ask permission for what's necessary."

Ruthy looked back with a flushed face, "Never mind what I said. I need to learn to be more like you. *Stronger*. We just met, but your strength is undeniable."

"You are surely not the Goddess. And yet I keep expecting the Goddess to return, as if I were some lost child looking for her mother. She's dead and gone," Mēna laughed to herself, in her raspy voice, while she loosened a screw on the mechanical at her wrist. "*Skin needs to breathe*," she muttered.

"May I touch you? Lean a little to the left...so I can catch the lantern light. I need to feel—"

"Go ahead," Mēna winced from the strain of turning the screw on the mechanical on her elbow, loosening one of the bands, forming an X on top of her forearm. The shrill squeak made Ruthy cringe.

"What happened here?" Ruthy traced scars undulating over the muscles between Mēna's shoulder blades.

"What are you talking about?"

"I'm worried this is the rot, too," Ruthy whispered, running her fingers down Mēna's long back. "*No...* I never knew a woman so strong,"

"You know little of me."

Ruthy's fingers reached the skin where Mēna's deftly woven black pants began. "Men claim the swords where I come from."

"Not much different here," she said. "How bad? It itches...feels like dead lichen. I might tear my skin off and relish the pain."

"So powerful," Ruthy whispered, as she let her fingers linger on Mēna's exposed hip bones. "You're like a beautiful dream in a nightmare."

"Desperation makes us imagine depths in the shallows. I don't need your *seeming* envy," Mēna alternately and deftly turned small levers on the wrist-portion of the mechanical to loosen the X's on both sides of her forearm. With unseen actions of her left fingers, on the underside of the wrist and elbow portions, she grunted, "*Got it.*"

Ruthy's hands dropped to her sides when the mechanical was pried loose, where the device dropped to the fungal cap in a clump and impressed on the gray surface, betraying weight neither meagre nor extreme. The warrior clenched her bright eyes shut, turning away from her exposed limb.

Mēna's right arm hung limply, like some kind of magic caused the bones at the elbow to part ways, leaving only useless sinews and powerful muscles without a united guide. Only fidgeting fingers showed any signs of life. In places where the mechanical's pieces were removed, grooves and scars marked many orbits of wear. Wind carved shapes into the world over an Age and Mēna was a being who weathered countless storms, bore scars and markings to prove it, like hard-earned rings in a tree.

Nevertheless, the life of a Wanderer's struggles left the crippled arm a testament to the limitless wonders of the body, how the mind united the unfinished limb with a metal construct and resulted in a crowning achievement of breathtaking musculature. Even though Mēna's build dwarfed Ruthy's, there was no vanity in the dazzling form, a body bereft of the vane bulk male warriors sought in Ruthy's realm.

The way Mēna moved through Ümfalla was something far more devastating in grace. Such gifts were apparent at first sight, just as a bird passing in flight showed its skills in a passing glance. In the midst of her reverie, Ruthy tried to suppress her need to turn away when the stench overtook her. But she remembered beauty might smell like anything, even death.

"You're as green as the lantern shroom," Mēna said, wiping sweat droplets from her brow, with her functional arm.

"Must be the light," Ruthy eyed the green light of the lantern shroom.

"*Funny,*" Mēna half-smiled, as she ran her left forefinger along the time-worn grooves of the inner-side of her festering elbow, where her skin bore a burst of bright-red, a cipher of fever. "While my skin breathes, tell me about Sky Tracer."

"I didn't see much," Ruthy said, swallowing hard. "That's why I fell. I panicked and I broke through."

"Where did you come from?"

"I came from the Thunder Cliffs. They are the three islands to the west."

"You mean you live in The Churn?" Mēna asked, leaning closer. "Nobody crosses those waters."

"Yes. I lived there. The Eternal Storm rages on the horizon and never leaves. Wind always blows and the sun reigns. Three Sister Moons keep watch over the night, where the stars battle for space in the heavens."

"*Three moons*? I thought there were only two," Mēna half-smiled, with a knowing wink. She adjusted her limp arm with her good hand. "Nobody crosses and yet here you are. That means Sky Tracer reaches there. A lucky fall... I would be as lost as you, if I fell upon the Thunder Cliffs and was faced with the naked sun."

"So you've never seen the sky?"

"The sky is all around. We breathe the sky, pass through, until we return to mud."

"What I mean is...you've never seen beyond whatever keeps this place in night? Is it always like this?"

"*Always.* This is the only way. And this realm is not always night. You lack the faculties to sense the changes of a turn. Sun-born eyes call turns, days. I know that much. I've come along a few who were born in the sunlight. And yes, the spore cloud is ever-replenishing."

"How much can *you* see?"

"I can see into the yellow. Some say the Goddess sees into the white."

"What does that mean?"

"You perceive the glow of the mushrooms in the black. All the light you receive is borrowed. My eyes light this world from within. I marvel at the multitudes of mushrooms on the ochre Sīnels all around us, without any need for the mushroom glow. I admire blues into the purples of the moss on the hills, the vibrant orange-ness of Puffball Mushrooms. I revel at indigos into the yellows of the sky all around us. I mark the owl watching us, just behind you and the slugs lurking on the edge of this shroom. I discover creatures yet to be Named. Only the zenith is dark. Most others in Ümfalla see into the blue. Blues and purples and into the gray... Others find me strange for my eyes, but I can't imagine another way. Their life is one of the half-light. But they can look into fiery minerals. I cannot. I am a Simmerian, *the ones who dream*, if you believe in the importance of Names. We were gifted with a light within."

"Why are you alone? Where are your people? I recognized the look. I see longing, even though your eyes are made of light."

"My people lost their Name. They became a dream. I'm searching for something to bring their Name back," Mēna said, before mutterings took back over. She cleared her throat and shook her head, "I've distracted you long enough. I form habits, unnoticed, until another sees them. Wanderers acquire strange workings, along the solitary way, or so I'm told," she laughed. "I never believed I would. Speaking at length is odd. It feels... Ignore my ramblings. Have a look, if you're going to. I have no skill in the healing arts. Nothing beyond maintenance," Mēna said, looking away from Ruthy. She furrowed her brow, "What am I going to do with you?"

Ruthy pretended she failed to hear Mēna's last words before she found her own, "What happened to your arm? I mean...before the mechanical?"

"An exchange of memories? I understand," Mēna half-smiled. "I was born this way. Had I been born to another mother, I would have been fed to the ground, in infancy. But my mother was good. Good and brave. She spent ten orbits looking for someone who had the skill to make something like this," Mēna frowned, looking at the mechanical.

"Who made the mechanical?"

"I don't know. She never told me. All that matters is the mechanical's existence. It allows me to move, but comes at a great cost. I've been having trouble with the screws. Don't you smell it?"

"Yes," Ruthy whispered.

"Why were you on Sky Tracer? You're avoiding the focus. Your words become air."

"What is 'your words become air'?"

"Noise upon the air. *Meaningless.*"

"Does the wind ever blow here? Even a breeze?"

"No. Air moves when things do. Air moves through deeds. Hot breaths of mating. The wing-blown air from Night Skimmers inspires air when I run, or jump from a height. Understand? Your words are air. Why were you on Sky Tracer? How can you ride a light?"

"Sky Tracer isn't a light… but a vessel. Nobody I've come across knows where Sky Tracer goes, or why. Nobody returns. Women my age, often younger, are there one day and gone the next. I'd never seen Sky Tracer, up close, not until I was taken. All was quiet, except for the terror inside me. Inside was pitch black, so I clawed at everything…kicked and found a weakness. I fell, fell to live, even if the deed should have been my death. My words feel thin in this thick air… When I struck that mushroom cap, I saw stars and thought I was dead. *So beautiful, the sparkle…* Time was gone, mercifully. Poisoned thoughts, I suppose. But most things are poison, in the end. That moment in the sparkles of the mushroom made me experience something real, even if illusion ruled it. Before I fell, I lived under people who used me for …an instrument for their ambitions. I had no will of my own. Not anymore, not here. I'll *fucking* speak as I choose. To hell with manners."

"Manners?"

"Doing things to please others. You should forget such a word. It's meaningless in such a place as this. You're free. Now, let me look closer at you."

"I want to learn more," Mēna winced, when Ruthy's forefinger touched the crook of her elbow. "Words only have meaning in the stream of life. To live in a narrow and dry channel is a living death. Perhaps the wind is at fault where you come from."

"That's truer than you realize. Wind shapes more than trees."

"Words are free here, if you can find the person to listen. You've had a life of pain and there's not a scar on you. How is that possible on a grown woman? Your body is perfect."

Ruthy tried to ignore the veiled compliment, while she traced stigmatic streaks of purplish-red on Mēna's bicep. The presence of such strength, bereft of a functioning nexus, twisted Ruthy's mind more than the abysmal streaks did along Mēna's skin. Scars marked Mēna's chest, arms and all over her back, from histories of violence Ruthy would never fathom. Mēna's heaving chest accentuated her torment. Ruthy realized those heaving breaths were not out of pain, but out of anxiety to have someone so close to her.

"Well?" Mēna gasped, "Will I live?"

Ruthy looked into Mēna's shining eyes and spoke, calmly, "Not if we don't get you help. How long since you saw—"

"*Shush!*"

Ruthy looked over her shoulder, in correspondence to Mēna's fierce glare. By the time Ruthy turned back around, Mēna already pulled her shirt back on, slid on the mechanical and was in the midst of aligning and retightening, at triple-pace. The sheer speed of Mēna's actions made Ruthy's heart race.

Mēna's muscles aligned in her arm and the veins pulsed in battle-readiness, throughout. When the top wrist-screw was tight—the one responsible for clasping and unclasping the ringed piece on her wrist—and the X's on both sides of her forearm were taut, Mēna slung the sheath across her back, drew her gleaming sword with her left hand and struck the lantern mushroom at its center. Bifurcated, the pale light flickered out and everything went dark.

All Ruthy perceived were Mēna's dark-bright eyes, staring into the gloom, haunting the refreshed darkness.

Mēna pulled silk line from her hip satchel and staked it in the Hydra cap. Without warning, Ruthy was in a free fall, while Mēna held onto her, tightly. When Ruthy sensed the ground drawing near, they slowed to a stop. She pointed her feet down and found the ground, before Mēna released her. Mēna tugged at the lifeline and it fell. She gathered the line and took Ruthy by the hand.

"You have to do exactly as I say," Mēna whispered. "They're closing in."

"Who?"

"Reapers."

3

CHTHONIC

Beyond the glow of mushrooms, only Mēna's dark-bright eyes were distinguishable, whenever she glanced back. Now thick night was taking hold, the confined light of fungi all around made the darkness palpable. Beyond the glow was nothing but oblivion. Ruthy's nightmares paled at such a scene.

Her bare feet suffered with every step, but the guiding hand never let go. Rich aromatics, earthy and magical, were too entangled to be anything more than a distraction. The thorough dampness of the land softened Ruthy's feet to the point where even the spongy embrace of mosses and decomposing mushrooms were an assault on her soles. But she had not fallen, after many moments of stumbling flight. Behind her, three pairs of glowing eyes were staring back at her.

'Rak-ak~Rak-ak-kak'

Shrill cries from their pursuers sent a chill through Ruthy. The spore-thick air was supercharged, as if an abysmal storm was rising. She wanted nothing more than to fall to her knees and scream, except for the strength of the warrior holding her hand. A lonesome soul was risking everything for a lost one, so Ruthy refused to give in.

If there was anything in the world to hold onto, it was Mēna's hand, a palpable reason to stumble through life through to the end. But Mēna's tangible fear quickened Ruthy's own. A warrior, with strength beyond reason, was running for both their lives. Without warning, Mēna halted and pulled Ruthy close.

"We'll never outrun them," Mēna whispered. "You mark the glow of that shroom cluster behind you?"

Ruthy nodded, breathlessly.

"Tuck yourself in there and don't come out, no matter what."

Ruthy fell into the amber glow of the cluster, a dense network of mushrooms, with caps resembling clenched fists, standing taller than her cowering head. By the time Ruthy tumbled into the midst of them, they already ceased to sway. Their rich amber glow prevented her from seeing what was unfolding in the darkness, beyond. Dank earth smelled of rotting wood and owl shit, but mushroom aromatics soon took over, a perfume reminiscent of citrus and burning moss.

She tried to block out the boot-stepping horror from approaching predators, but there was no sense in shutting her eyes. All was amber glow. Darkness kept its secrets, but her ears were seeing for her. Steel sliding along leather told Ruthy Mēna's sword-hand was *full*. Just as the glow of mushrooms settled into her sunborne sight, a glimmer from the blade in Mēna's hand found Ruthy's eyes. Mēna's eyes grew brighter, as Ruthy's breath quickened. The rapid thumping of footsteps approached like an abysmal song.

Thump/thump...thump...thump/thump/thump

After a guttural breath from Mēna, something heavy fell beyond Ruthy's limited field of vision. A dull thumping brought a severed head rolling into the cluster, within arm's reach. Glowing eyes stared up at Ruthy, before they dimmed like stars at dawn, until they were out. When Ruthy turned away, the strain left her mouth open to receive streams of blood from another slaughter at the periphery of the cluster.

A Reaper cut from crotch to chin, fell like a human husk and left Ruthy gagging a mouthful of blood. As she coughed, another stream of blood splattered on her back. Ruthy stifled her scream as the intrusion of blood curdled her saliva. Childhood tales of glorious battles were spat out as lies, along with blood. Ruthy dropped to her chest and held onto the soft earth, digging her fingers into thick mycelium, as if the spore cloud were sucking her back up.

Ruthy's fingers clenched just below her breasts, working themselves beneath the moss and humus. As they did, her fingers found inner-workings in the network of mycelium, the infinite entanglement constituting the brain of the Fungal Realm. Intricate aromas of the realm filled her senses, hyper-complex, as seductive as they were overwhelming. Her fingers warmed at the mycelial touch and her heartbeat slowed.

Secrets of the earthen deep seeped into her hands and revealed their Names. Air was articulated in its fungal aromas, becoming known, all at once. Time leaked out of the world and a primordial *hum* coursed through Ruthy. She found courage through mycelial entanglement, a hidden song. Pain was gone and the metallic aftertaste of blood vanished.

She sensed the wordless language of chthonic brains, countless threads, constituting a Singular Mind.

Ruthy received and *spoke* through her fingers. Something Whispered back... Through the exchange, greater mushrooms, towering darkly all around the area, suddenly flickered with silver light, before going dark. A Reaper's voice screamed Ruthy back into the moment.

"*Nyctá!*"

After the Reaper screamed, quiet followed. The body fell with a dull thump, and nothing remained but the trilling of insects. Mēna's heavy breaths slowed when her battle-bright eyes peered into the glow of the mushroom cluster. At the sight of Ruthy, Mēna turned away. A throbbing force in Ruthy's hands left her pinned to the ground.

When she managed to tear through clumps of mycelium and crawl out, Mēna was standing a little ahead, stock-still, with her blood-dappled sword in her left hand. Her eyes were too bright to look at directly, while Mēna muttered to herself in the same guttural voice she had back on the Hydra Mushroom. Ruthy listened, but the sounds were so rapid and intertwined, the result was noise from a broken language.

When Ruthy took a step towards her, she slipped on the gore, but stumbled back into a standing position. As Mēna continued to mutter beyond the moment, Ruthy followed her voice, until she reached Mēna's distant face, before the warrior lowered her forehead and pressed against Ruthy's. Blood from Reapers dripped from their bodies and gathered in a little pool between them.

Mēna's broken language was soothing in its deep resonance, while Ruthy pressed her head hard into Mēna's. The warrior's heartbeat was so fierce, the air between their chests was disturbed. Ruthy waited for Mēna to look up, but writhing agony from another's nearness never came. Mēna's mutterings slowed, until they were breaths with no words. Mēna raised her head and rested her chin on Ruthy's blood-soaked head.

"Reapers," Mēna said, barely in a whisper.

"Yeah. *Reapers*. What are they?"

"Bodies without a soul."

"They still scream as if they had one... So many blades clashing, the sparks, the blood... Chaos with teeth of steel. But *you* emerged. I have no words... And I can't get the grime of blood out of my mouth."

"I know a shroom to fix that. Just give me a moment."

"Would this work?" Ruthy held up a wilted mushroom between her face and Mēna's, no larger than her thumbnail.

"*How do you know that?*" Mēna whispered, still catching her breath.

"I pulled this mushroom up when I was in the cluster. Smelled like the sea, so I thought—"

"Chew until the shroom goes soft and spit it out, while I gather my breaths. Then we carry on."

After vigorous chewing, Ruthy spat out the remains and looked back up at Mēna, "Why did someone shout, *Nyctá,* as if they were calling out to you? I've only heard that word in old tales."

"Why do you ask?"

"A Reaper shouted, *Nyctá*, distinctly. Names are important to me, too."

"It's a Name from the Ancients."

"Where I come from, Nyctá, means, *the long night.*"

"A lot of good the word did the Reaper. They live in the chaos of another Age, such beliefs that devour the soul. Nyctá also means, darkness. Darkness and evil. Fear. Nyctá is: *fear the night.*"

"*Nyctá.*"

"Never mind Reaper chatter. They disturb the air to create fear. It's their grim asset. Even soulless bodies scream in the face of death. Ruthy?"

"Yeah?"

"What the *fuck* did you do during the fight?"

"I stayed down in the cluster, what you told me."

"Speak *fuller* and tell me: *How did you light up the greater shrooms?*"

4

A Gathering of Hexes

With Ruthy's hand in her own, Mēna strode on in silence. She sensed vibrance in Ruthy's hand, tinges of a hidden truth exuding from her embrace, through soft fingers that turned the darkness bright, if only for a blinding moment. Even the battle with Reapers seemed ordinary after such an event.

Reapers were known to prey on Wanderers, but never in such numbers and risk. If not for the distraction through inexplicable lights—exuding from surrounding mushrooms—the Reaper who screamed, *Nyctá*, would not have missed with her blade.

Greater mushrooms towered over the land, darkly. Only a mighty stroke from a sword on the greater mushroom's stipe produced a glow, maybe a flicker, but never a silver shine. Ruthy's ecstatic hand was growing stranger with every step.

"If you're not going to tell me what you did, at least tell me who you are," Mēna said, glancing back. When she caught sight of Ruthy, she was chewing with vigor. "Have you smelled your way into more luck?! Show me what you've got in there!"

"I'm fine—"

"What's in your mouth, now?!"

"*Nuwt blood any-moooor,*" Ruthy muttered, with a mouthful and a smile. "This one called out to me from within."

"Spit it out!"

Ruthy stopped walking and opened her mouth. Only her tongue and glistening teeth showed, before her jaw went slack and her eyes drifted.

"I haven't eaten in days...I suppose it's *turns* now," Ruthy said, with vacant eyes.

"Even younglings know better than to trust their noses."

"These mushrooms are *so* good, makes my nose twitch. A secret reached out through the glow. They *begged* me to eat them. Didn't want to bother you. My mouth is still watering. The texture is a song. *So earthy,* I want more—"

"Why would you do that?! And you ate more than one... You can hardly see beyond your own hands!"

"I followed my *inner-nose*. Things are starting to make sense. Getting my hands dirty does that. Battle makes a person really hungry, right? You were unbelievable back there! The *terror* of Ümfalla. These Reaper boots make me faster," Ruthy muttered, gawking at her newly acquired boots. "I *am* faster. Don't you think? But I'm still not putting on that headless Reaper's clothes. Not until we wash them. How *do* you wash things here?! Huh? Everything's so murky. *But the air is so loud.*"

"That's your voice. This is fine, might even be good. We can get beyond your seemings and into the truth. Nobody within screaming distance. Well," Mēna half-smiled. "At least you picked a good spot. We both need a moment. You're lucky those weren't the mushrooms that 'make your nose twitch,' a little ways back. You'd be as pale as their caps and stone-dead. I've never come across *luck* like yours."

Mēna leaned over, brushed her fingers through the glow and picked a wrinkled mushroom at her feet. Unlike the others, the species lacked bioluminescence, while the shriveled cap resembled puckered lips on an elder. When she chewed, the bitter earthiness reminded her of the first time she gathered Hexes, a lifetime ago, when her sister guided her through the illusory world. As soon as Mēna swallowed, the tell-tale warmth down her throat told her to settle in. There was no distinction between past and present, nothing but the elongating moment, stretching through heartbeats.

"*I can't believe you did it, too!*" Ruthy almost sang.

"Nobody should Hex alone... Follow me and settle in... Time is about to leave us."

"The darker dark? Sure. Darker than the darker dark. Dark—"

"Cmon. The Goddess...I haven't

done

this

in............................

Mēna and Ruthy were tucked away in an overhang of the
Sinel Hills. Lying beside each other, the visual world

of hard and soft dissolved. Hexes began to form, like liquid light, in their corresponding perceptions. Where Hexes were bright for Ruthy, they were dark for Mēna.

Hex mushrooms were one of many manifestations from the Singularity running throughout Ümfalla, the entanglement of mycelium. The one was many and the many were One. These words were heard but not spoken to Ruthy, in a voice not unlike the one she 'heard' through the mycelium during the battle. That voice was the undercurrent of all that followed, the hidden chorus.

—Mēna?

—Ruthy?

—Your name tastes like dark fruit.

—Naturally.

—You're pretty devastating with a sword for a *Wanderer.*

—I follow the blade. It's not me. Something else moves the sword.

—Epic. Does your sword have a name?

—Slender.

—Slender? That's it? Not mysterious at all? Mist—eerie—us. We're lying in mist in an eerie world, us.

—How could you?

—What?

—Do that to the word. Must be the dryness of your world.

—You might be right…Wait a moment…which one of us is talking?

—You.

—Okay, good. Whoa! I just threw light! Just a little glowing mushroom and whoosh.

—You're doing pretty well for your first time.

—Do all of your people shave their heads on the sides like yours?

—No. I began shaving on the turn I chose not to use the blade on myself. I make that choice every time I put the blade to my head.

—Oh. Well…that's fucking grim. Grim and dark. I bet your choice terrified the Reapers, seeing a hawk-haired warrior, cutting them to pieces.

—If my hair is that distracting, take a piece. Here…

—You tied the lock in a knot for me. Even your hair is strong, like a silk rope. I'm braiding this lock into mine…

—It's just hair, Ruthy… What are those little brown dots on your shoulders?

—Tell me what you dream.

—You wanted to ask me that for a while.

—It's a way to get to know this *wandering* warrior beside me.

—A voice haunts the air, speaks from a deeper dream, to *me*. I am myself and another, at once. I have blood on my hands and desire more. That voice bids me to carry on, but I never hear the rest. Screams and I wake up. Every time I dream, this happens. Every time.

—That's a nightmare. Maybe this prepares you for threats like those Reapers. What are you searching for, Mēna? Look! Those Hexes are epic!

—Yup… Almost twenty orbits ago, I fell.

—So you were a child?

—No, just a little younger.

—You're joking?

—My words are my own, carved in truth. After a fall from the Sideon Cliffs, I awoke inside a Pitcher Mushroom. On the way back home, I realized a tremendous amount of time had passed. Everything replenished itself, beyond recognition. Just before I made it home, a horde of Reapers raided the Simmerian village and we lost our Name.

They followed me back. Reapers were only a rumor before my fall. My family was slain, along with many others, while the rest were taken. Seeing my sister's aged face, even in death, I realized I fell into a Kronos Mushroom, an eater of time. I took my family's bodies back to the Kronos Mushroom cluster and put them inside. Their bodies are waiting.

—That hurts my heart for you. But…they're dead, Mēna. Nobody comes back from that darkness.

—Their bodies are whole. If a Kronos can stop time, then tales of Resurrection Spores might be true. Maybe your luck will rub off… Look at that arrangement of Hexes.

—I can't believe we're both seeing the Hexes! Dancing liquid-light of warm-crystals.

—That's pretty good.

—How do you tell time here? By the length of your hair? The sun and moons are hidden.

—Lesser mushrooms wilt, alongside greater ones shedding their skin. Night Skimmers scream, from high above…a woman falls from the sky. *Ruthy*… How did you manipulate mycelium back there?

—Still don't know what you're talking about.

—You didn't luckily find these Hexes, just as you *knew* which shroom would clear the taste of blood from your mouth. You played the helpless victim before, but you have powerful secrets. Lesser mushrooms reveal light. Greater ones hide their glow, within. Every greater shroom in sight went bright. *I* didn't do that. Lucky I spotted my next thrust, before the light blinded me. I noticed your fingernails when you stood up. Even the blood on your hands couldn't hide mycelium beneath.

—I reached into the earth and discovered warmth. Then I started to hum because the ground was humming, too, a

silent song, singing inside me. You've never felt that
before?

   —Never.

   —My mother had a gift, or so I was told. I don't remember
her. I used to imagine what kind of gift… I loved the
secret. I was somebody else before the fall, somebody
less real. Your fall was an accident, but I chose this.
Twenty orbits asleep, or a fall…change comes. We have
that in common. I'll have to go back. I'm so close… The
only way is up. Up, into the leafy embrace where wind—

Hexes vanished and reality rushed back in. When Ruthy turned to Mēna, her eyes were
half-shut and her body was covered in sweat. Mēna's eyes were in the back of her head,
casting a dim glow, revealing streaks of black on her ailing arm, before Mēna fell into
violent convulsions.

   Ruthy shuffled out of the overhang and stood in the darkness. She imagined her
sunborne eyes distinguishing dark from utter darkness, scanning the void, until she was
dizzy enough to sway. Air seemed unbreathable and the soft notes of chirruping insects
were horrors. When she turned around, she spotted more than a dozen lantern shrooms,
floating along. Her voice was on the brink of letting itself loose on the darkness, but the
threat of more Reapers kept Ruthy's mouth shut. She looked back to Mēna and made her
choice:

   "HELP!"

5

FIVE HANDS OF SILK

Pleas for help were met with silence, while Ruthy stood alone, in a sunless realm. When the lanterns drew near, Ruthy squinted her eyes at the green glow, before distinguishing their leader's grizzled face. As soon he spotted the quality of Ruthy's silk, he promised her a turn's worth of service for five hands of cloth. Before Ruthy finished telling the russet-bearded man calling himself, Dorian, of Mēna's plight, around two-dozen followers were already making camp.

He demanded the silk, at once, so Ruthy pulled off the garment and tossed it to Dorian. While she stood still in her booted nakedness, Dorian sniffed the silk and grinned at the reek of blood. He laughed as Ruthy cursed in the green glow, while she put on the clothes Mēna took from the Reaper corpse. An old woman's voice turned Ruthy around.

"Leave her to me," the old woman said. "Try and move her and she's finished. Death is already making her cradle in here. Go make yourself useful and stay out of the way."

"I'm *not* leaving her," Ruthy said, putting on the blood-crusted celium shirt. It reached just below her sternum. "She's my partner in life...we are united."

"Of course, you are. Blinder than a worm, with an accent something finer than can be traded for," she said, narrowing her bright eyes. "*No*...those are sunborne eyes. The name's Ībeka."

"I'm Ruthy. And this is Mēna. We—"

"Sure you are," the old woman laughed, as she descended into the overhang, with her layers upon layers of tattered garments, swaying along with her. Her eyes were almost as bright as Mēna's, giving Ruthy enough light in the gloom to distinguish the contours in the wrinkled face.

"Tell me you're not going to kill us both just to take our wares."

"That's always a possibility," Ībeka laughed. "But Screevers have a code, a double-faced one, but a code. Sort of like parasites that don't kill the host. Everyone follows the other, believing somebody believes in our leader. I'd be dead, otherwise. But deathly things do happen," she said, as she touched the mechanical on Mēna's arm, with her crooked fingers. Her matted gray hair brushed along Mēna's heaving chest.

"The mechanical comes off. If you just—"

"*Easy*," Ībeka sighed, having already managed to loosen the screws at the wrist, before it unclasped and she pulled off the mechanical and into her gnarled hands.

"How did you do that, so quickly?" Ruthy muttered in wonder.

"Patience. Listen, *Ruthy*...I'll talk to you til' my heart loses its rhythm, but I need you to take this abominable contraption to the stream and wash it until your fingers bleed. Don't worry about its integrity. Things like this are made to withstand an Age. You got that?"

"I can't see the way."

"Take the lantern," the old woman said, as she inspected Mēna's swelling arm with black stigmata, throughout. "It'll light the way."

"But how will you see?" Ruthy said, taking the shroom-lantern.

"Because I've got eyes like hers," she grinned, through a toothless mouth.

"Where's my daughter?!" A woman cried, from afar.

"Who was that?" Ruthy asked, looking back at the darkness.

"That was nothing. *Out*. Now."

"How will I find—"

"You'll hear the stream. It sounds like a drunk taking a piss. You're just another *briar* in my side, if you catch what I mean. Oh! And wash those celiums you're wearing. They reek of Reapers."

When Ruthy returned with the gleaming mechanical under her arm and bloodless clothes back on her body, she found Ībeka leaning over the unconscious Mēna, with her ear to Mēna's muttering mouth. Crimson glowworms, no bigger than an eagle's pupil, were doing their work on Mēna's festering arm. A sliver of translucent mushroom gills covered her nostrils, trembling with every faint breath. From Ruthy's perspective, Ībeka had fallen upon a strange fish. Through subtle mutterings from the old woman, Ībeka betrayed a sense of recognition, as to the tangled language Mēna was whispering.

Ībeka lifted her weary head and turned to Ruthy, "Even a spirit asleep is hard at work and helping to make something of this broken world."

"Tell me she'll live," Ruthy whispered, placing the lantern down, where she sat next to Mēna. "You were talking to her just before. Do you understand her mutterings? They sounded like Weir. Or was she—"

"It *was* Weir Whispers. Haven't encountered this since I was about your age, not like the ones she's muttering.. *The Goddess*...I had a face on me would topple the Sideon Cliffs."

"Tell me about the Goddess you believe in. Mēna thinks the Goddess left us, as little as she's spoken of her."

"Belief tells us this land was shaped by the single Word of the Goddess. The Sinel Hills and the Vernox, the Sideon Cliffs that reach far above the murk, even this hole, all was shaped by formative sounds of that single Word. Hard and soft sounds and everything in-between."

"I was never told this tale."

"*Good*. Don't believe a bit of it. Goddess be damned, here or not. We're all the same for it. Any Weirs you saw are shadows of what they used to be, ambitious tricksters. But the old Weirs were a people from before the Ancients. They held a bit of that Word within them and how to move *through* the Word. Such powerful articulations are too slippery to be spoken. *They must be Whispered*. The trick is, getting the story right. Slip up and those lips trying to Whisper, close forever. Whispers can move hills, as surely as they can bewilder a mind. Powerful stuff...very terrible and powerful. Only met a few, when I was around your age. Rare around here, even in those times. I picked up a little of it. Figured the few who remained were gone."

"Is Mēna a Weir?"

"Haven't had the chance to ask her," Ībeka grinned. "But she certainly encountered one. Probably even loved. I thought you would know, considering you two are—"

"Friends. Mēna is my truest friend. But my heart belongs to me and nobody else."

"Never mind that. What I was saying... The Whisperings are passed from one to the next, takes something more than *listening*. But learning the Weir language means nothing unless you *inhabit* it. Know what I mean?"

"I do. *More than you could believe*," Ruthy muttered. "Shouldn't we be doing something more for her?"

"Sure. Have any suggestions?" Ībeka laughed, licking her thin lips.

"I thought *you* were the Healer."

"Time heals, as surely as it eats away at us. So go ahead and dream. You shouldn't go out to the camp," Ībeka said, with a look of disgust. Ībeka leaned closer to Ruthy and sniffed her braid. "Nothing masks tree-scent from that abominable place."

"You *cannot* tell *anyone*—"

Ībeka silenced her with a raised forefinger, "*You* encountered many Weirs, as sure as you miss the sun on your face. Never mind the lying wind. Don't worry your pretty red head. I won't tell your *friend*. Won't tell her you're looking for something beyond mere survival. Sure won't tell the poor souls in camp. Seen many things in my days and turns and I recognize a pretty little liar when I see one. Lies aren't bad. Lies are lies and they keep us living, as surely as they can kill us and all the rest. I won't tell them only the Chosen, *up there*, could ever wear that silk you were wearing, or grow their hair like yours and have skin like a Goddess. I won't even begin with the hidden things behind those eyes of yours, *Ruthy*. Name sounds familiar...like a piece of a greater one I've heard before. Your eyes tell me you're learning to listen and respond to a new Name. Better keep practicing. Your other *Name* is still listening," Ībeka trailed off.

"Where's my daughter?!" The same woman from before cried out, from the darkness. "Is she—"

"Ignore her," Ībeka said, as she closed her bright eyes and began to snore, shortly after.

On the following turn, Ruthy woke to discover no change in Mēna, who remained unconscious, while Ībeka continued to snore beside her. Feeling vulnerable, she scanned the knives on Mēna's waist and chose the smallest one with a cross-guard. With a weapon of Mēna's tucked into a sheathe on her Reaper pants, Ruthy felt less alone, *stronger*, even if her skill with a blade was confined to theory. She picked up the lantern and muttered a jumbled prayer over Mēna's damp forehead, before heading out to the Screever camp.

Lantern shrooms of various colors and sizes were set throughout the camp. Wagons small enough to be pushed by hand sat on their rears and were cluttered with wares too tightly packed for Ruthy to recognize. From the looks of the wagons, they were built to float, as well. No more than thirty souls were gathered, ragged in appearance, focused on nothing in particular. Nobody spoke or made eye-contact, as if they grew tired of waiting for death and were pretending to be ghosts. At the far end of camp, illuminated by a cluster of lanterns, Dorian was stroking his thick crimson beard. When he caught sight of Ruthy, he waved her over.

"Your time is short!" Dorian laughed, in a guttural tone. "Everything has a cost in Ümfalla, especially time."

"Hasn't been that long," Ruthy said, while Dorian looked her up and down.

"Your keeper has weapons that'll buy you a turn longer, a piece. I'll give you seven, if you hand over that bastard sword of hers."

"How did you—"

"Oh, I have eyes everywhere. Never would have made it this long, if I didn't."

"Nobody touches anything of hers. And she's not my keeper."

"Not your keeper? Ahahahaha! So you're leading the way with your sunborne eyes? Not your keeper. I'll tell you what, 'not being kept', give me some time with your insides and I'll give you another turn. Never seen a girl as fresh as you."

"If it comes to that, it won't go the way you imagined," Ruthy said.

"That's the fun of it," Dorian winked a pale eye. "I'll start with your tits and work my way down. Give me a good suckle and buy you a turn. Turn after, I'll find out if your cunt's made of silk, too. Then I'll—"

"Where's my daughter?!"

A skeletal woman, no older than Ruthy, was stumbling behind Dorian and looking manically at the darkness of the horizon. Her hands were clenched together and the rags she wore were covered in the muck of the Fungal Realm. She stopped and stared at Ruthy, wild-eyed.

"Have you seen my daughter?!" She muttered, as tears streamed down her face.

"I'm sorry," Ruthy said. "Haven't seen much of anything."

"Are you sure?" the woman cried, walking towards Ruthy. "She was here before...*right here*," she pointed at the ground. "The dark took her...they took her for—"

"Oh, for fuck's sake," Dorian grunted. "I told you not to follow us anymore, you loon cunt!"

As she drew nearer, the woman's skeletal form obscured Dorian from Ruthy's perspective. Just as she reached out for Ruthy's hand, her head fell from her shoulders and her body dropped to the ground, with a thump. Dorian stood, with a short sword in his hand. The blood gushing in torrents from the headless corpse was the only sound between them. Ruthy looked back up at Dorian and stifled her scream.

"I told that bitch to keep away from us," Dorian said, staring at Ruthy. "Reapers take children, way of the world. Now she's found her fucking daughter. Time's getting short. Don't make me come and take it."

Ruthy clenched the lantern shroom in her left hand and it brightened. She walked away, breathless, in a waking nightmare.

When Ruthy returned, pale-faced, Ïbeka was frantically whispering to Mēna. Ïbeka's eyes were so bright, Ruthy had to look away. The air around them was energized, making Ruthy's red braid dance at its tip. She wanted to run, but there was nowhere to go. Ïbeka's spirit was somewhere far from the hole in the ground, somewhere Ruthy hoped was summoning Mēna's spirit to return. But as quickly as everything turned eerily ecstatic, a dark calm fell and Ïbeka groaned deeply, as her eyes returned to their silver glow.

"Just seeing if I still had it in me," Ïbeka chuckled, through a violent cough.

"I need Mēna back, Ïbeka," Ruthy whispered, staring at Mēna's soaked face.

"She's right here," Ïbeka said, swatting away the words. "You shouldn't have gone out there."

"Yeah, too late for that... I could kill that piece of shit, Dorian. I've dealt darker things than death."

"I believe you, whatever your Name *really* is."

"We both have secrets. I just hope yours help bring Mēna back."

"You'll be dead without her."

"That's pretty *fucking* clear, Ïbeka...Why are you with the Screevers, huh? Are you aware what happened with the poor soul looking for her daughter?"

"Same kinds of things happen all over Ümfalla, all over everywhere. I'm far too old to shave my head and strike out on my own. In my youth, I traded my body *and* my craft to carry on a little longer. I embraced that horror. If she dies, you'll have to make a choice, too. But look at you, *Ruthy*. Nobody makes it to your age looking like that. You traded something. I see it in your ambitious eyes and smell it on your coddled body. You *reek* of magic. And you know of the Weirs and the Wind, as surely as you miss the strength of trees, long for leaves rustling in the wind. Don't carry on trying to trick an ole' trickster like me. You're from Sky Realm, as sure as wind blows above the darkness."

"If you tell Mēna, I swear to you, I'll show you the darkness within me. Sometimes it takes a fall to realize the place you really need to be was the place you leaped from. But I had no choice. Change is messy."

"Failed to kill yourself, did ya'?"

"A worthy risk. I never imagined Mēna finding me first. Good thing she did. I fell too far from the place I intended. But I'm *so* close... Every word of this is secret, Ïbeka. You never made it this far without knowing when to keep your mouth shut."

"Listen to your *regality*. Bet that feels real good to fall back into character. You'll be in charge someday, eh? You could move mountains with that tone. Bet you never spoke like that to your new friend," she laughed. "Been playing the weak and desperate soul, in need of a hero, have you? This Mēna and you have as much in common as the Fungal and Sky Realm. Leave her alone, *Ruthy*. Let Mēna be and find another way. All she needs is Ümfalla. There are few women left who can face this darkness alone, as she does. She's a rare soul. But playing dumb only gets you so far. You're about as far from innocent as I've ever known. Must be deadly with this ruse of yours, all pretty and soft-like with a big secret within. Better remember who you are before you find a way back up to the Sky Realm. Wind Weirs are tricky souls and you don't know the trick until the Whispering ends and the deed's already done. They must miss you. Even Reaper clothes can't mask your truth. The Wanderer's way is hard. But the soft life is harder, eh? *Better keep heading east, through the Sinel valley, if you want to find who it is you seek,*" Ībeka winked. "Won't be long before your *friend* here figures out what you're seeking. Easy to lose yourself in Ümfalla, easier to die. Nobody speaks alone through mycelium, Ruthy. Somebody's always listening. Your life's been trying, but all's going to be harder than you can—"

"*You're a Weir, through and through—*"

"**That way's the hardest!**" Ībeka roared, as her eyes went blinding white.

"***RUTHY!***"

Mēna's voice cast a spell of silence in the space. Ruthy fell on top of Mēna and was nose to nose with her, before Mēna could even blink away the lantern light.

"Thank the Goddess!" Ruthy cried, staring down at Mēna, with a toothy smile.

"Tell me I'm not still Hexing," Mēna groaned, shaking her head, while she squinted her eyes. "Do you hear somebody whispering nearby?"

"No."

"Strangest thing...must be the fever passing."

"You *are* alive, right?" Ruthy muttered, wiping away tears. "You're not a Weir trick?"

"The Weirs are dead and gone," Mēna said, looking from side to side. "Where the fuck is my mechanical?"

"You're *back*," Ruthy laughed. "Should you wear your mechanical so soon?"

"Good to see you, too, Ruthy. And yes, I do." She sniffed, "*Lanterns from the Sideons?* Did you call on Screevers?!"

"You're welcome."

"We're lucky we still have teeth in our mouths. Screevers have no code but taking. Now, get the fuck off me, so we can go."

"Absolutely. *Wait*...where's Ībeka?" Ruthy muttered, as she stood up.

"Who?" Mēna asked, while she stretched her good arm.

"I'll tell you later. We have to leave this place. Do you think you can walk?"

"Do you think you can see?"

"That's *funny.*"

After many moments of cursing and aching attempts at reattaching her mechanical, Ruthy managed to relate to Mēna what transpired while she was unconscious. Mēna insisted on finding Ībeka to express her mortal gratitude, but when they emerged and walked through camp, there was no sign of her.

The body of the woman looking for her daughter was gone and the mossy ground absorbed any trace of gore, another soul wiped from existence. Ruthy passed the spot by, without saying a word. At the edge of camp, Dorian was speaking to a handful of warriors in black, from neck to boot.

"We need to leave this place," Mēna said. "There's a voice telling me to go east, through the Sinel valley."

"A voice?"

"Never mind. *Would you look at that,*" Mēna seethed.

"Are those—" Ruthy began.

"Reapers," Mēna said, through gritted teeth. "Let's get the fuck out of here."

"You mean they trade with the same people who steal their children?"

"They're Screevers. Of course, they do. *Look*...Reapers are already heading back up into the Sinels to do their worst. Probably going after someone like you. I wish them the worst."

"So, those same Reapers Dorian was just trading with, might be attacking him a turn from now?"

"Yup. Might use the same weapons they traded him for. Cmon. I wanted to thank the old woman, too. But those Reapers will find out what we did to their own, soon enough. We need to head east. If they knew we slaughtered the others, they'd be on us, already."

"*We* slaughtered? I was useless. Didn't do a thing."

"I remember everything we talked about when we Hexed. You speak through mycelium and you—"

"Just one more thing, Silk!" Dorian shouted, as he walked up to the pair. "I'll let the two of you stay, long as you want, if you give me that sword. I've never seen its like."

"I'd hand you my soul before this sword," Mēna seethed. "Let's go, Ruthy," She took Ruthy by the hand and led her away.

"Just one more thing, Dorian!" Ruthy shouted, pulling free from Mēna's grasp and turning back to Dorian.

"Change your mind?" Dorian grinned, while he stroked his beard.

"Want a quick grope before we go? You gave us quarter and my friend is alive because of it," Ruthy smiled, as she squeezed her breasts through her celium top. "Last chance."

"Ah! The burden of being good," Dorian laughed, rubbing his thick hands together, as he approached.

"Only a moment," Ruthy winked, arching her back.

"The fuck are you doing, Ruthy! NO!" Mēna shouted.

In the midst of Mēna's shout, Dorian was about to lay his hands on Ruthy. Ruthy pulled the knife she pocketed and struck him below his ribcage, dropping him onto one knee, where Ruthy raised the knife overhead and thrust the blade into the nape of Dorian's neck, yanked it out with great effort and struck, once more. Had it not been for the cross-guard, her hand would have slid down the gore and onto the blade.

The preternatural speed of it shocked Mēna into a split moment's hesitation. She watched with wonder, admiring Ruthy's determination, through sloppy thrusts that followed. When Dorian fell over, with blood gushing from his many wounds, bubbling from his mouth, Ruthy leaned over him.

"*The first one was for me,*" she seethed. "I despise your kind. You're lucky I didn't have time to do my worst. The rest are for everyone else, you piece of shit! I'll cut off your face and eat—"

Mēna threw Ruthy over her shoulder and marched out of camp. Screevers acknowledged the incident, but no cries for help or screams for vengeance followed. Dorian was no more, food for an insatiable land.

While Ruthy continued to rage through words invented and mangled, Mēna hoped for ample time to put distance between them and about every soul in the Sinels. Her arm ached but the pain was welcome. She could still hold a raging Ruthy on her back and keep a reasonable pace.

If luck followed, rather than Reapers, they would reach the Seething Falls by the next turn. But if the voice haunting Mēna's dreams carried on—the voice pushing through to the waking world, ever since she woke from her fever dream—she would be lost.

6

INTERTWINED

"**A**RE YOU STILL ANGRY with me?" Ruthy asked, following a few steps behind Mēna, in a rather smooth portion of the Sinels. Mushroom glow from the surrounding landscape provided enough luminescence for her sunborne eyes to navigate. The gored knife from before had been wiped clean, leaving remnants of Dorian on a tuft of moss near the Screever camp, a grim memory over the hills. Now the blade was sheathed on Ruthy's hip. "I thought it was justified. Something else moved me. If you're—"

"No," Mēna said, without looking back. "I was impressed. Horrible timing, but deserved, after what you told me. It was unexpected, but I don't know you, do I?" She glanced at Ruthy, with a look of irony. "Do you feel better?"

"Yes."

"Good. Then stop talking. My head is full of—"

'RAK-AK~RAK-AK-KAK'

Mēna's sword sang an acerbic note to the evening air when she drew it, before the last sound of Reaper calls faded. Even the chirrups of insects diminished as a relative silence fell. Ruthy pulled out the knife from her hip-sheathe, but no amount of guile would serve her now. Her back was pressed against Mēna's and she followed her deliberate steps towards a cluster of greater mushrooms, with overhanging caps, resembling gigantic eagle tails. Ruthy pointed the bloodless knife at the dark-glow of her own mistake, the rash action drawing deadly attention. Rising guilt made her stomach sicken.

'KAK-AK~RAK-AK-KAK'

"They're all around us," Ruthy whispered. "How can they sound like demons? I know they're flesh. Tell me it's going to be okay. Mēna? Are you—"

When Ruthy looked over her shoulder, Mēna's eyes were the brightest lights in Ümfalla, radiant in their power, vital beacons for their pursuers to follow. Her lips were moving in quick succession, but no sound was issuing forth. Every particle in Mēna's being yearned for them to come.

It was the piercing ring from Mēna's sword, Slender, striking down a throwing knife, that spoke to the silence. Slender appeared a natural extension of Mēna's left hand, a sharp attribute, where flesh had no choice but to give way to steel. Accompanied by the mechanical on the warrior's right arm, Mēna was the living manifestation of steel finding its masterpiece. The sword was almost as long as her arm, a deadly match to her deadlier appendage.

Abutting greater mushroom stipes provided cover for their northern side. Without a gesture or word, Ruthy dove headlong into the cover of stipes, making herself small behind them, as a child would appear at play, in a forest of strange trees. She peered around a stipe and into the glimmer of battle.

Mēna was revealing wonders, through dashing steps and leaps—as efficient as they were beautiful—while she forsook steel and used her grace to avoid a succession of throwing knives. Ruthy was bewildered in the glow of the event, the way this powerful warrior was far more fluid than any dancer she ever saw in court. While Mēna's hair danced to the brutal rhythm of Death's song, she appeared like a hawk about to take flight, after feeding on hard-won prey.

Fear swelled back up and Ruthy embraced the stipe with eyes clenched shut. Clumps of mushroom broke into her trembling hands, summoning rich aromas from the stipe, reminiscent of incense burned after a loved one's death, compounding the present with deadly pasts.

Something stirred within her, a need to find *use* in the midst of Mēna's dance of death, strategy, with a touch of cunning. Ruthy thrust her fingers into the black earth between stipes and mycelium reached back.

Deep in the ground, distant transmissions were filtered through hyphae, in a language beyond words, but with a voice sought and familiar. Ruthy *spoke* back through a hidden place in her being, not unlike hidden gifts Mēna possessed, but where the warrior manifested them into action, Ruthy kept this chthonic gift secret. The greater mushrooms, towering above her, remained dark, in conjunction with her subterfuge.

When Ruthy blinked herself out of the deed, Reapers were discernible through the cluster. In spite of their black garb, their moistened celium-wear still reflected a bit of the surrounding glow. They seemed to be watching with more curiosity than malice, as they pressed closer. Ruthy expected another flurry of projectiles to be thrown Mēna's way, but nothing came. She tasted the tannins of her fear, as surely as she saw the encroaching eyes. A deep gurgle came from Mēna, whose back was almost touching an adjacent stipe.

"Ē tráket zu lōthūn ouz essentz!
I'm going to eat your souls!"

From Mēna's mouth, two voices spoke at once. The voices were simultaneous, yet discernible in their union. One was Mēna's voice intertwined with another of a primal tone. It was not a shout but the voices sounded *deeper* than anything Ruthy had ever known. Mēna snapped back her head and stared down Ruthy, through blinding eyes.

"Ouzé zu ou Anderzér!
Yours too, you Seemer!"

Ruthy cowered and stepped back, frantically, deeper into the surrounding stems of the cluster. Mēna continued staring her down, before she flipped Slender in her left hand and turned to face the assault. With another looping motion of her sword, Mēna sliced through a Reaper's stomach and pierced another through the bottom of his jaw and on through the top of his head, in a quick succession of lightning-quick strokes.

Intestines slithered out of the first of the fallen, like dying blood-worms, wriggling along the dank ground. Mēna's sword tore through the second of them and split his head like a rotten fruit. Before Mēna turned back to meet the blade of another Reaper, two more were closing in, one from her blindside. Slender met a pair of swords as another blade was about to strike Mēna from behind.

"NO!" Ruthy screamed.

A glimmer fell from the sky, but in a way far different than Ruthy's plummet. In a sliver of a moment, an iridescent form latched onto the side of the Reaper, about to strike Mēna from behind. Ruthy *felt* the Whisper from the creature, even through the clanging and grunts of battle. The sparkling form unlatched from the Reaper, as quickly as falling, before vanishing. Frozen in mid-stroke, the Reaper lowered his curved blade and walked around Mēna, who was in the thick with three others.

Stumbling behind the other three, the be-Whispered Reaper swung his sword in quick succession, hacking through flesh and bone, through strokes powerful enough to fell a tree. The felled Reapers stared into the black zenith, choking on their own blood, in shock at what had befallen.

Before the be-Whispered Reaper apprehended Mēna, she took his head. It fell will a dull thump, followed by his body, amongst the rest of the fallen, more corpses for the muck. A single pair of glowing eyes blinked in the distance, before vanishing.

Mēna sheathed Slender on her back and bolted around the mushroom cluster. Ruthy stepped around the stipe and followed, where she found Mēna with the creature in her arms. Foam poured from the creature's mouth in continual bursts. Ruthy recalled madness overtaking woodland creatures, where such foaming was indicative of the cureless rage-sickness. This froth resembled sea-foam, accumulating on rocks along the shores of The Churn.

"She needs rich water," Mēna said, stroking the deep-green hair on her head. "I've never seen them this far east. *Fuck*. What are you doing so far from The Mire?" Mēna almost sang, as she stared beyond the moment.

"Do you know each other?" Ruthy asked, standing at a distance.

"No. Phibians were supposed to dead and gone. This one is precious beyond words. And she saved our lives. Cmon," Mēna said, as she strode away.

"Do you really want a 'Seemer' following you?" Ruthy called out.

"That was battle-rage talking! I didn't mean it!" Mēna shouted back, as she carried on with the Phibian in her arms.

"Which voice did?!"

"My own! Cmon!"

7

THE GODDESS AND THE DIRT

THEY WALKED INTO THE thickness of night in search of rich waters. Ruthy marveled at the tenderness unfolding in Mēna. The warrior who scorned the world, in a singular intertwined Voice of pure rage, was whispering soothing words to the Phibian. Once again, Mēna held an unknown soul in her arms and was trying to carry her out of the clutches of doom.

Every step was drawing Ruthy closer to her intent. And yet stumbling in the darkness with Mēna, no matter the direction, felt like an end in itself, a possible destiny. Whatever *voice* was telling Mēna the way, spoke in conjunction with Ruthy's recent mycelial encounters. She could only hope her subterranean transmissions found the other one she sought.

Along the desperate way, Ruthy discerned gills on the Phibian's neck, just below the jawline. They flapped open, revealing a delicate series of crimson under-gills. The finest of films covered her skin, imparting a sheen to her amber tone, a sleek attribute to her body, far more refined than clothes.

Before the Phibian closed her eyes, back at the cluster, Ruthy saw her blink with horizontal eyelids, like curtains being pulled shut. Her limbs were long, sinewed and slender. A patch of hair, not unlike the thickness of the Phibian's head of hair, covered her from her lower waist down between streamlined legs. Her fingers and toes were webbed and longer than a human's.

Every step was drawing them to a water source, or death.

"The Falls feed these hills," Mēna muttered, as she strode on. "But I've never seen this much of the land without a body of water."

"Trees are full of the land's sorrow, but they never weep," Ruthy followed.

"What was that?" Mēna asked, ceasing her strides.

"An old saying from back home. We have to keep mov—"

"*Weeping lands...* Follow me down," Mēna said, striding down into the valley of deeper darkness.

When they reached the bottom of the deepest portion of the Sinels, Mēna gently placed the Phibian on the ground. She drew a pair of her saw-toothed blades from two of the nine sheaths on her waist and drove them into the mossy ground. Within a few strokes, she had torn apart the mossy surface and reached the dark humus in the ground. Mēna grunted when she dug her powerful fingers into the sopping soil. She pulled up heaping handfuls of dirt in a series of rapid motions, leaving a dark mound, interspersed with glowing mycelium behind her.

"Don't gawk at me, get down here and dig," Mēna grunted.

"I—"

"Dig! We owe her our lives."

Ruthy fell to her knees beside Mēna and pulled out the knife from her pocket. In a flash, Mēna closed her hand on Ruthy's and pushed away.

"That's a waste of time," Mēna said. "Use your hands. You could use some scars beyond the sun."

Ruthy held her breath, while Mēna dug out clump after clump of glowing dirt. She considered feigning sickness as she had in the days before Ümfalla, when she wanted to escape duties, or a threat. But secrets she held already filled her spirit to the brim. She found herself digging alongside Mēna, as if watching herself in a dream.

Vibrant warmth greeted her fingers and she relished the experience, the oneness she felt with what was living beneath. But her former *warmths* had always been with the scattered roots of trees, never the overwhelming entanglement of mycelium, this *wonder* she found in Ümfalla. Ruthy closed her eyes, feeling the rush of truth, as Mēna turned to witness what was emerging all around.

Some of the lesser mushrooms burst at their caps while the greater ones pulsed with an array of lights and intensities, turning night to bioluminescent day. Mēna winced and covered her eyes with the back of her hand. She turned back to Ruthy, peering between her fingers, as the valley turned white through intermingling of bioluminescent colors, ranging from white and deep reds, to purples tending towards black.

"You don't need to dig anymore," Ruthy said, through glowing teeth. "I'll show you."

Ruthy's eyes closed, to better receive mycelial transmissions. Her fingers did not move, but remained planted in the soil, like so many saplings. A sly smile fell across her face and she welcomed the conjured light on her skin. The land's confined light beat at a rhythm in accordance to her heartbeat, as Ruthy found the frequency of the messages through mycelium.

She *spoke* back through her fingertips. All Mēna could see were blurred lines of Ruthy's silhouette, leaving her half-blind in her own realm, before the ground began to move.

All around Ruthy's fingers, delicate strands of mycelium receded, twisting and tying themselves into knots of greater thicknesses and strengths. Soil stirred and collapsed, like a buried octopus was tearing apart the land. The chthonic labor rumbled but did not roar like waves did upon the Thunder Cliffs. When water found its way up and made Ruthy's fingers wet, she stood up and the world went dark again. She stood still with dripping fingers and deep breaths.

"Only the Goddess moves the land," Mēna gasped, blinking her eyes, hard.

"You gave me no choice," Ruthy said, with a distant voice. "I am *not* the Goddess. Not even close. She needs rich water, so there it is."

Mēna slid into the deep pool with the Phibian in her embrace. She kicked her way to its center and lowered the Phibian beneath the surface, for half a moment, before pulling her back up. She repeated the process, over and over, while Ruthy waited, without saying a word. Foam no longer poured from the Phibian's mouth, but her skin covered with a film like a dragonfly's wing, was turning sickly gray.

"Tell me you have more magic to fix her," Mēna said, refusing to look at Ruthy.

"That wasn't magic."

"Says the one who tore open the ground. *Look at you*...you're not even winded. Only magic cheats energy," she whispered, clenching her jaw. "Help *me*, help *her*! I won't lose another. Not to them. Not again. I—"

"Maybe the foam is stuck in her throat," Ruthy called out. "I choked on a Bannus Seed once and lost my breath."

"How did you find it??"

"Someone struck me hard on the back. Try!"

"Nothing to lose now." Mēna muttered. "Cmon, now...not too hard!"

Mēna reached her left arm, while the Phibian was embraced by the mechanical, an instrument of torture, turned comfort. When Mēna struck her on the back, the Phibian's eyes opened and she coughed up dark foam into the muddy pool, sparkling with remnants of mycelium. Ruthy was unsure if water streaming down Mēna's cheeks were tears, or signs of toil. They drifted together, in the sparkling pool, while speaking, softly.

Ruthy cursed herself for making the pool large enough for the pair to speak beyond her hearing. Such Whispering gifts on behalf of the Phibian sent a current of panic through Ruthy, the threat of exposing her for surreptitious transmission through mycelium. Had she known how to swim, she would have leaped into the water and joined the communion of strangers caught in each other's embrace. She remained landlocked in uncertainty.

Ruthy was sure the drifting embrace would go on until the end of time. Mēna's face turned to the zenith as the pale light of Sky Tracer showed itself through the spore cloud. The Phibian looked up and pointed her webbed forefinger at the abysmal light, casting malevolence upon the moment.

Ruthy stared at the vessel with a knowing that penetrated its pale red luster and found her mind back in the abominable carriage in the sky, full of screams, empty of hope. Remembrances of the carriage rattling, on tracks made of silk, injected Ruthy with vertiginous sensations. Her stomach turned sour as she looked down from the heights of memory. Ruthy shook away the reverie as the light passed and the Phibian was at her feet, looking up at her from the water.

"I am full of life because you brought this water to me," the Phibian said, in a breathy but resonant voice. "I am Shixee," she said, in what resembled a sneeze. "I see your eyes recognize the light from above."

"My name's—"

"Ruthy. Mēna told me much about you. You fell from the dim light. You bathe in sunlight and you speak to the land. I speak to water. Well, water speaks more to me. The water keeps its secrets. But land chatters throughout. The land is loud, speaking through mycelium, even when the land is quiet on the surface."

Ruthy paled at the Phibian's words, but spoke through the fear, "How did you bewilder the Reaper back there?"

"She's a Foam Weir," Mēna called out, from the center of the pool.

"Yes," Shixee nodded. "Mēna altered the path of my life, long ago, even though she cannot remember. I recognized her eyes, a turn ago. I followed and waited for my chance. I had to return the help. Help is hardest to give to someone, when they have taken almost everything from you. She no longer takes... She has changed. Only her eyes are familiar to me. Time does that."

"So you're a Weir," Ruthy said, crouching down to face Shixee.

"Yes. Who are you?"

"A passenger in Sky Tracer, from the Thunder Cliffs...my only distinctions. Where are the rest of your kin?"

"Most of my people never woke up after the last Hardening."

"The Hardening? I only heard tales, but I grew up hearing many strange things about Ümfalla."

"When the spore cloud lifts and sun shines on this realm: *This* is the Hardening. All falls, but we sleep, until all rises, new again. The spore cloud returns. This marks an Age, maybe a thousand orbits, other times, not so much. I never remember."

"But *you* woke up. What happened to the rest?"

"They were too full of sorrow and took the sorrow with them. The Hardening is trying enough. To take that sorrow into the long sleep is the end. I remember the ways of the realm, but lose memories of the life I lived. I miss those who I lost, the ones who visit me in dreams. I forgot and begin again when things softened and follow the way of things that grow."

"Some legends prove to be true."

"If this one were not true, *I* would be legend. This happens when the land is sick. Mushrooms fall and the Hardening comes. Many orbits pass between. Those who witness, pretend to forget. The ones who come after, never know. Not until the Hardening comes again. Then the ones who knew are long dead. Things keep their secrets."

"How many Hardenings have you been through?"

"I remember I had to exist before the last one, or I would not have forgotten."

"So you could be as old as Ümfalla?"

"Only as old as I remember," Shixee smiled, with an ageless face, bringing calm to Ruthy. "Time is only what we remember. Never forget that, even if you want to forget."

"Did you understand me when I spoke to the ground?"

"Water runs through everything. And mycelium runs through the land."

"You speak in riddles."

"And you speak in half-truths, *Ruthy*, of Sky Realm."

Ruthy's face flushed, "Not so loud. Not just yet. Just tell me if—"

"We have to go!" Mēna shouted, from the far end of the water, as she pushed herself up and onto the embankment. "Reapers will return. You made sure of that, Ruthy. *Twice*. This time was worth the risk. We can find higher ground and more advantage around the Seething Falls."

"You're welcome!" Ruthy shouted back. "And which way are we going?"

"East," Mēna replied, as she wrung out her celium shirt. The water trickled out of her boots with a steady stream.

"East is where you need to go," Shixee said, looking up at Ruthy. "You follow *and* lead, that much I know."

"I go where Mēna goes," Ruthy said.

"There are waterways all along the way," Mēna said. "Water keeps no tracks, so we might lose the Reapers. East is where rarer mushrooms grow. Shixee tells me there are decent people there. Perhaps they can be of help to you, Ruthy."

Ruthy paled at the words.

"East is where the Tree of the Ancients grows," Shixee said. "Very beautiful but terribly kept. The Tree is forever entombed in crystal, cursed. The Tree of the Ancients petrified almost a thousand orbits ago, not long after the last Hardening of the land. Such loss...hurts my heart. I fear the east, but east is where the rarer spores loom. Not the same old ones, taking hold of the rest of Ümfalla. Soon there will be nothing new under the same old blue-empty that haunts the sky beyond the cloud. East is....east is..."

"*East,*" Ruthy whispered.

"Yes," Shixee nodded, before she vanished into the dark pool.

8

OVER AND UNDER

T HE THREE COMPANIONS FOLLOWED a coterminous pathway of creeks and
streams. Dark waterways, enchanted by bioluminescence, delved into subterranean channels along the path through the Sinels. Shixee strode along trickling creeks,
only to swim through sudden streams and vanish into deeper unknowns, for moments
at a time. When she surfaced, it appeared as a dreamer's transition back to the waking
world. Traces of fantasy remained dripping from her streamlined body, glorified by air
and water.

Mēna caught herself smiling, for moments at a time, as Shixee displayed her oneness
with the land, with a grace needing no flourishes, no keen-eyed witnesses to confirm it.
Whispering the timeless tongue of the Weir nearly choked the life out of the Phibian, a
life measured in Ages, rather than the dim passing of orbits. Whatever secrets the Phibian
held about Mēna's past were bound to be explored, but there was no denying a sense of
recognition, as if from a dream.

Then there was the sunborne enigma, without a hope in the Fungal Realm, on her
own. And yet Ruthy moved the earth through hidden workings, magic without a Name.
Mēna believed in magic and mutterings of the Goddess when she was a limp-armed child.
But her rich experiences, throughout the realm of Ümfalla, revealed everything came at a
cost, from the mundane to the magical. Ruthy possessed something beyond the realm of
cause and effect, power, nameless and terrible.

Most of what Mēna gathered about Ruthy's past was under the influence of Hexes
and in the throes of rot, while her sunborne intentions in Ümfalla remained unknown.
Mēna marked Ruthy's self-mutterings, whenever she glanced up at Sky Realm, hidden
above the all-encompassing spore cloud. Whatever life Ruthy once led was beyond Mēna's
imaginings. Something else was inspiring Ruthy to carry on, a need far more critical than

simply following a Wanderer through the Fungal Realm, a necessity beyond survival. Nevertheless, she was bound to Ruthy.

Mēna turned away from her surmises and looked to Shixee, who was striding through a creek with her webbed fingers splayed out at her sides. She turned her bright eyes to Mēna, as the water deepened to her waist.

"I will see you when water reaches back up," Shixee said, before vanishing into the adjacent depths.

"Why are Reapers after you?" Mēna asked, without turning to face Ruthy.

"Who are you muttering to when you think nobody's listening?" Ruthy responded, while she imagined where Shixee would emerge. The glow of lesser mushrooms allowed for her sunborne eyes to fathom what was ahead.

"I could ask you the same thing when you look up towards Sky Realm. Tell me *what* you are."

"Not everything has a Name. You should—"

Shixee surfaced from the limpid spring and laughed, "You should have seen what was beneath."

Quiet followed, while Mēna sensed the linguistic tide turning against her. If Ruthy came from anywhere, it was a place where words were nothing but tools, in service to a game beyond language, or beneath it. Names had little bearing when they were always morphing into something else. Shixee vanished into another hidden waterway.

"I lose control," Mēna began, " What you heard was me, but it was something beyond me, not unlike my dreams, I told you about. I rage and exhale sounds, but the words are not mine."

"Whose are they?" Ruthy asked.

"I don't know. Maybe it was the lost time in the Kronos Mushroom. I kept my memories, but emerged a different person. Shame fills my spirit. You are shifting questions to me. I'm someone trying to fix things."

"So am I."

"And what *are* your intentions? I say *east* and your sunborne eyes twinkle at the prospect. Are you here to bring chaos to Ümfalla? Or will you go about it slowly and find someone else to guide you through the rest of your life? *Nothing*? Then I'll be the one fixing things for you."

"Maybe I'll light this place up for good."

"Sure. Then you can reign over your bright realm, alone. *You* are keeping secrets. Your words were carved, long before, measured for use, or just air. *That* is where you come from, the wind-drunk world of Sky Realm. You keep looking up and imaging whatever is there. You never lived on the Thunder Cliffs. Tell me I'm wrong."

"You're not wrong. But you can't imagine what's up there. *Breathtaking beauty and Hell*. People are proper and they're beasts. I'm powerful and I'm nothing. Here, I'm Ruthy. I'll figure out what my place is here. I swear to you, I—"

"Sky Realm deceit!" Mēna turned away. "No wonder...you speak like the false winds that haunt the heights. You should be more careful with words. I'm wasting my words with a *Seemer*. You plot while you believe I can't sense it, in expectation of *something*. Reapers are not the answer, since they found us from the beginning. I waste words asking you what that *something* is. Our differences are clear. Talking won't solve anything."

"What will? Searching for legends?"

When Shixee emerged, she lacked the excitement to find air again and rejoin her companions. She swam upstream, a little ahead, through a gentle current of sparkling water. The valley was abutted by jagged cliffs, steep and haunted by crisp lichens. The presence of greater mushrooms was diminishing, while multitudes of lesser ones, possessing a rich glow, were scattered across the valley, like clusters of stars, up close. Shixee made sure Mēna and Ruthy were looking into the silver-sheen of her eyes, before she spoke.

"My memories forgotten are not lost. They shape me and my dreams with all the elements that make things real. Just like this water shapes the land. Even if you cannot see, the water is there, all along. I have to remake myself, every time I forget, but those forgotten things are always there, even if I wish them away. I would never wish away someone I cared about, even if they were unsure of themselves. Nothing is sure when everything is always changing."

"*Shit*," Mēna said.

"Yeah, she heard everything," Ruthy muttered.

"I treasure my memories when they surface," Shixee said, as she strode along the trickling water. "They are all we have that make us who we are. I will tell you anything, if I remember. When you forget so many times, memories that remain are what remains of you. No matter how they look or smell. I never understand why humans speak as if they do not know. Or they speak as if they know and do not. We know, what we know. The rest is lost and can never be recovered. Just like death."

Shixee strode ahead and vanished, again, into the mercurial waters of the valley. Cliffs rose steeply on both sides and continued, as far as dark-bright eyes could see. Mēna could *taste* the words of the Phibian, as she walked on, while Ruthy remained a sunborne shadow, behind her.

The slightest scent of brine was on the air from the Seething Falls, out of sight, beyond the cliffs. Mēna considered her words from the past few moments and found herself in the same trap Shixee made so apparent through her inherent honesty.

It was the faintest of sounds, followed by Ruthy's ascending cry, that turned Mēna around to find nobody behind her, until she looked up. Ruthy was hanging from a silk rope, upside down, from a height almost beyond screaming distance. Such ropes were all but invisible, even to the sharp-eyed Mēna.

"*Up here!*" Ruthy shouted.

"Nothing personal!" A man called down, from the heights. "Just a little leverage to keep the people thriving!"

In spite of Mēna's keen eyes, she was unable to make out the man amongst jagged crevices in the cliff. The only detail betraying Ruthy dangling, high above, was the glimmer of her red braid, swaying along with her upturned body.

"We don't have time for this!" Mēna shouted up.

"Oh, I could do this for turns on end," he shouted back. "Best I've done is three. Things turn messy and terribly awkward, when all's said and done. I'm sure we'd all like to avoid that."

Mēna pulled out her throwing knife, honed for such distances, while she marked twinkles from the rope holding Ruthy.

"Wouldn't do that if I were you!" The man shouted. "She either falls, or you lose a good knife," he laughed, as he manipulated the string and pulled Ruthy to a greater height. "I've only lost one doing this. Just up and vanished. *Strangest thing.* But I've learned from my mistakes and my patience is beyond compare."

"What do you want?" Mēna shouted back.

"Your sword would do it!"

"What is it with people wanting my sword?! And how can you even see it?"

"Spotted your blade when you were speaking double-tongue to Reapers, when your friend up here was turning night to day. Hell of a pair you make. Those Reapers have something on you. Never seen such blind resolve on their part. Your dangling friend must be worth a fortune, up there, in Sky Realm. She looks royal to me, but that might just be my greed. Just so you know, my greed is for the benefit of many, honest words on my behalf, I assure you. I take it your Phibian friend is somewhere soaking up lost memories, eh? Can't blame her, she wouldn't get my jokes. Far too dry for her wet wit. Nothing? No laughs? Just give me the sword. You've got weapons and magic enough."

"Nobody touches this sword!"

"Oh, c'mon Mēna!" Ruthy shouted. "You can't be that angry with me!"

"Shut up, Ruthy! You can take my boots," Mēna called up to the thief. "The finest celium cobbler in Ümfalla made them. I—"

"Love your boots, bright eyes. But nobody can go barefoot through this prickly world. I'm cunning but not cruel. Ya' know...it's unbelievable the fascinating things you learn about people doing this. Just three turns ago, I—" He fell silent."Reapers to the west!"

"TIE HER OFF!" Mēna roared.

There was no tell-tale song of Reapers, preceding their approach, but there was a heavy thump of boots, a stone's throw away from Mēna. A man of her height and cloaked in gray glanced at her and winked with eyes that appeared to see into the blue. His hands held no weapons, while his mischievous face bore a wry smile. His gray hood hid most of his silver hair that framed his youthful face and hung just below his sharp chin. Mēna kept her right eye on him, while she backed closer to him, in anticipation of the immanent assault.

"Feel like surviving this?" Mēna said.

"I'm up to that," he followed. "So quickly forgiven?"

"Try anything foolish and I'll cut you in half," Mēna seethed. "You're on *my* ground now."

"We'll put the deal aside and call it even for the turn. Ready to get bloody?"

"And what will you use? Your hands?"

"Sort of," he muttered, as he made a flicking motion with both his arms. A pair of katars appeared from mechanicals, hidden by his sleeves, on the top of his hands. The sleek blades glistened in the shroom light and were as long as his forearms. "I know where you got yours," he nodded, winking at Mēna's mechanical. "Best welder in Ümfalla. Come to think of it, the only one. My name's Briar. Already know yours. Your friend up there can draw a crowd, for something more than her ginger beauty. Guess I got myself into this mess. Here we go!"

"You'd better be good with those blades. Get in my way and I'll kill you."

"They serve my purposes," he winked.

Mēna drew Slender and caught Briar looking at it with relish. She stepped closer to him to keep the steepest of the cliffs at their backs. When she glanced up, Ruthy was so high above the valley, she was obscured by the rocky overhang and all but invisible. Shixee was nowhere in sight, while the stream she delved into, before, flowed on.

A tracer from a lesser mushroom cluster being disturbed caught Mēna's eye. She turned to face the flicker. When she did, Briar pressed his back into hers. Orbits of fighting, alone, revealed grim secrets only experience could uncover. But facing an enemy with another warrior at her back was something altogether new, a danger intensified by Briar's recent actions. Grace was in his subtle movements and control of breath, subtle tells, only rich experience, over many battles, evoked.

"No double-tongue?" Briar whispered. "I hope you're not holding back."

"Stop talking and show," Mēna grunted, before the two of them alternately deflected throwing knives coming at them. Briar's steel sang the same note as Slender, a tell-tale sign of its superior quality.

Needle-like knives fell limp on the sopping moss, before another barrage of blades came at them. Both warriors stepped into swift-footed grace and alternately rolled out of danger, working their way back to each other through elusive maneuvers, keeping Reaper steel from finding flesh. Another blade passed just above the pinnacle of Mēna's hair when she strode into a wider stance. She thrust herself up as three blades gleamed over the ground she had just been standing upon. When she landed, she was back to back with Briar, again.

Mēna spoke, quickly, "Northside is mine. Take the southside."

The pair pushed off each other and ran along opposite sides of the valley, in a sweeping motion, taking them into the thick of Reapers. Mēna thrilled to be fighting alongside another who might be her equal, even if she might have to kill him if things turned. The rush of it drove her eyesight into the white, battle-bright and hyper-keen. Forgotten pride in her own prowess swelled up, as surely as her heart raced to pump ferocity into her entire being.

As they strode along the bottom lip of the cliffside, the Reaper horde divided and subdivided, until the valley floor and rocky ledges were claimed by nine of them. Briar flicked his right wrist and a string—one far more nefarious than the one still holding Ruthy, high above the battle—was thrust out, looping round the nearest Reaper. With a quick tug, he pulled the string tight around the Reaper's neck, where Briar jerked the string and the head was separated from the body.

In simultaneity, Mēna flicked a finger-length obsidian blade, with her right hand, while she held her sword in her left. It struck a nearby Reaper in the throat and penetrated the neck deeply enough to drop the foe.

Mēna leaped off the lip of the cliffside when Briar caught another Reaper in his silk line and whipped them into the proximity of Slender. Before Mēna's feet touched the damp ground, she struck the tangled Reaper with a mighty downward stroke, splitting open his skull. Gray matter oozed out in clumps upon the gray ground.

"YE-ES!" Mēna grunted.

The cliffside steepened along their brutal course, so Briar joined Mēna on the valley floor, where he found himself facing a pair of Reapers. They both fell on him at once and he parried their thrusts with his twin-katars, sending sparks into the half-light. When one of the thrusts struck his cloak and glanced off, Briar swung his left arm and bludgeoned the offender with his hidden mechanical, sending the Reaper tumbling over, where Briar stabbed the foe on the nape of his neck, sending a geyser of blood into the shroom-twilight.

In an act of inexplicable hesitation, on behalf of the other Reaper, who had a moment of advantage, Briar flicked another line around the Reaper's arms. Then he spun the captive in a whirling journey towards Mēna, who marked the approach in the corner of her keen eyes and struck off his head.

"Behind you!" Briar shouted.

When Mēna turned around, a Reaper was disarmed and dragged back into the flowing waters of the valley. There was the slightest glimpse of Shixee's sheen, just before the Reaper vanished, kicking and screaming, underwater. When the screams subsided and the water settled, blood turned the stream red, but nothing surfaced. Only bubbles from subaqueous Phibian breaths followed.

Through battle-bright eyes, Mēna spotted two more Reapers hesitating in the valley ahead. Her mouth watered through a vicious need, temptations from the unknown. Her vision widened, while elements revealed their intentions, both human and inanimate. She held Slender in her left hand and clenched it in a moment of relish, before she bound ahead and leaped higher than anyone Briar ever witnessed:

"Īdra id ouz terminank!

Here is your end!"

Briar gawked, breathless.

Mēna soared, but there was no time for the two Reapers to comprehend the beauty of the feat, before she landed on her left foot, bound towards the Reaper on her right and plunged Slender into the Reaper's chest and toppled onto her fallen foe. She leaned into the blade and cracked the ribcage, before pulling out a saw-toothed knife with her free hand. She yanked Slender out and through manic saws with the knife, she reached into the gaping wound.

When her hand gurgled out, after violently uprooting what she sought to supplant, she was holding the steaming dead heart. She thrust the heart into her victim's mouth and punched under his lifeless chin. The heart burst in his shattered jaw, splattering blood all over Mēna's manic face.

She licked her lips when she turned to the remaining Reaper, who was stumbling along mossy terrain, in a desperate retreat. Mēna bolted after, fell upon the Reaper and tore off the black hood. Bountiful brown hair spilled out. The woman rolled onto her back and faced Mēna, wild-eyed, *desperate*, through a human will to survive.

"Nyctá! *Please!*" The Reaper rasped, shielding her face with her trembling hands. "I didn't know it was you!"

"Finish her off!" Briar shouted.

Intertwined voices in Mēna's head smothered reason, but the Reaper's hyper-presence was disarming, reached into her soul. Trace aromatics on the Reaper from a patch of Lactarius Mushrooms, only found on the western end of the Sideon Cliffs, conjured a wordless conversation from a dream. *Reaper-ness* dissolved as humanity glared back, in horror. Mēna blinked hard, before she sheathed her sword on her back and gestured with her chin for the Reaper to go.

"You're still in there, Nyctá," the Reaper nodded, before stumbling away, westward.

"The fuck was that?!" Briar shouted, as he surveyed the carnage. "Your mercy will come back with dozens more to finish us all."

"She can spread the word of this slaughter," Mēna said, as she ran her fingers through her bloody hair. "Fear needs a witness to do its worst on the rest."

"Tell that to the Reaper at your feet whose heart you just fed to him. That was gorgeous. Do you fly often, or was that some kind of fluke? I've never seen a creature without feathers soar like that. Explains your hawk-hair. You earned that look. Even your Phibian managed to pull off a wild move, herself."

"Save your flattery for those who give a shit. You got what you needed from me."

"We're quite a pair in a pinch, eh?"

"You don't stop, do you? Don't waste your charms with me. I didn't have to kill you. That's enough of a bargain between us. But this is where we part ways. Go back—"

Mēna fell silent when she moved her right arm. She clenched her teeth and was on the brink of screaming. One of the screws for the mechanism on her elbow cracked where it secured the adjoining strip of metal, in the most intricate portion of the mechanical.

While the rest of the mechanical was built from ore sourced from the Sideon Cliffs, making it altogether unbreakable, the intricate screw proved to be from an inferior source. When she bent her arm, the mechanical creaked in its partial ruin. Mēna's eyes turned brighter while she cursed in a language unknown to Briar. When she turned her battle-bloodied face back to him, her raging desperation was clear.

"You don't know who made that mechanical, do you?" Briar said. "I'd tell you the way to him, but directions this far east are about as useful as that dead Reaper's heart in his mouth. Or as useful as that arm without your—"

"Your words are carved. *Enough!* And you'll take me to him," Mēna seethed.

"Sure. Sure, I will. I, *sure as the sky is cloaked,* can't go back west. Reapers everywhere. I've never seen Reapers take such risks. They strike when there's clear advantage. But they're desperate for something one of you keeps and it's not your sword. I was right about your ginger friend. She's a catch for everyone. And if I—"

"*Excuse me*?!" Ruthy shouted.. "I'm still up here!"

"Would you believe," Briar looked up. "Already forgetting my thieving ways. And you forgot your friend. Blood and fury can do that. I suppose that makes me the good guy. Not much profit in that, but I'll manage. On the way up to rescue you, fair lady!" He laughed, heartily.

While Briar deftly climbed the cliffside, on his way to release Ruthy, desperate words from the final Reaper echoed in Mēna's head, the unmasked face, haunting the Sinel Valley. In a moment of absolute vulnerability, where lies and deception were useless, the Reaper *recognized* her. Forgetfulness and lost time were banalities in the face of such uncertainty.

Squeaking from her mechanical ended Mēna's reverie, just before she heard a splash. Shixee pushed herself out of the water and bound over to Mēna, while her deft webbed fingers washed the blood from Mēna's face. She put her dripping lips to Mēna's ear and whispered:

"I remember moments you have forgotten, from the time I first saw you. You had another Name. My words are for you, *alone.*"

9

WAIST DEEP

THERE WERE NO SIGNS of Reapers on their trail, but there was no turning back. For Ruthy, the nightmare of *east* was not coming to her, as her dreams portended. She was walking straight into it. East was ahead and east was behind, as far as the inextricable union of space and thought went.

She listened and watched the enigmatic thief, who was proving to be more than a convenient ally against Reapers. Mēna touched her cracked mechanical, in a series of vain attempts to confirm reality was real. Ruthy shuddered to think a little screw was turning a fearsome warrior into just another soul, fearing the turns to come. Shixee continued her journey of wet and sopping swims and strides, as a being shaped by boundless time and intermittent fears, with the good sense to forget.

Ruthy tried not to look up at the zenith and give Mēna any more reason to bring up Sky Realm. But the more she tried to forget, the more she found herself searching for a way back, even though there was more to be done in Ümfalla. Briar was something far more than a thief turned ally for Ruthy. He held the promise of *east,* within.

The Sinel Valley diminished, as cliffs gave way to rolling hills that tended downwards, until roaring waters ahead screamed the landscape into smooth submission. Sounds entangled with topographical change reminded Ruthy of the legend of the Goddess shaping the world, through a singular Word.

A relative bounty of lesser mushrooms provided meagre glow for her sunborne eyes, but everything sounded like Reapers, even her footsteps. She experienced countless fears back in the world of light, but she always had sunborne eyes to anticipate. The roaring oblivion from the force of nature ahead portended what it was, blind force.

Briar shared stories of a life of solitude, but nothing betrayed his core intentions. Tales of Night Skimmers and rarer mushrooms were interspersed with silences, where loss was too profound to put into words. Mēna listened as one doing her best to glean secrets from him, without having to silence him through violent means. Mechanical-driven torment was shaping Mēna's entire being, even her gait.

Where Briar was prone to laughter, Mēna turned away and clenched her jaw, failing to remember her own past. Their newfound companion's proclivity towards a wink and a smile at the world was met by Mēna's mutterings and indifference. None of Briar's words were directed at Ruthy, only quick-glances in her direction. Nothing betrayed his intentions but the man's consistent outlook on a bleak existence, summed up in his own words: *See what happens (wink).*

Even through sunborne eyes, heavy night spread its wings over darkness, covering the unknown in a further one. Greater mushrooms were all but absent, while lesser ones covered the ground in lights ranging from yellow, to rich orange, tending towards amber. A stream fed into a deep pool where Mēna stopped walking and stretched her arms. She knelt down and pulled a clump of indigo lichen from a rock by the pool, like skin from overripe fruit. She tossed the lichen to Ruthy, who caught the sparkling clump.

"Eat," Mēna said, filling her mouth with another clump. "Lichen keeps your body strong. Shrooms only go so far."

"This looks...delicious," Ruthy frowned, holding the lichen in her fingers, like a dead insect.

Briar grinned, "If you want to keep that regal smile, you better listen to your friend. Don't want your teeth falling out of your head," he laughed, as he put a fistful of lichen into his mouth.

"Down we go," Ruthy said.

Her mouth watered from the sour splendor, her cheeks ached. Lichen plumped through chewing, as her saliva imbued the food with life and it acquired the texture and flavors of the finest fruit she ever tasted, ranging from dark berries to pink citrus.

Her pulse quickened and courage swelled her heart. A feast of flavors was in this fickle food, the dream of citrus come to life. She spotted more grays in the blackness of Ümfalla, a sense of resolution, as if the terrors from before were little more than dreams. When she glanced at Mēna and Briar, they possessed a look of resolve, all their own.

"I had eel a few moments ago," Shixee called out, from the dark pool. "But I love watching all of you relish in Blissel Lichen. It has no effect on Phibians. I wish it did. I could use some joy."

Ruthy closed her eyes and imagined where the sun was setting, alongside the rising moons, a sight into another world, far above the ubiquitous spore cloud. She missed the wind and boundless skies, but envied her companions, who found joy from a bit of life growing on a rock. Eels were fit for queens and mushrooms held more secrets than the most ancient of trees, never mind the power mycelium held.

When the revitalizing effects of Blissel Lichen soon wore off, Ruthy's lips were wet. She licked her lips and found it to be tears.

At the edge of the dark pool, Mēna was already naked and sliding herself in. Shixee floated nearby, while Mēna was submerged, waist deep, as she struggled to take off her faulty mechanical. Briar pretended to be occupied with something in the opposite direction, while Mēna gave into mutterings.

Shixee drifted up to her, wrapping her long webbed fingers around the mechanical, where she performed a series of submerged actions that wrested the device from Mēna's arm. Mēna tossed the mechanical onto the embankment and drifted down, until she was up to her chin in dark water. She closed her bright eyes and appeared to have drifted into unpleasant dreams. Shixee floated beside Mēna, before she closed her Phibian eyes and spoke to Ruthy.

"Water resonates with movement, but only from a humble distance. Mēna needs to refresh herself. We all do. Stay close by. If water trembles with footfall, over the hills, we will have to move."

Shixee drifted along the dark pool and glorified her vital element, gracing the moment, as a living and breathing attribute of water. Ruthy stood on the embankment, a world apart. The enigmatic Mēna was somewhere far away, even though she just a little beyond arm's reach. Briar remained at a distance, leaning against a rock, bearing a wry smile.

"So I was thinking—" Briar began.

"*Fuck off,*" Ruthy seethed, as she walked into the darkness, where a cluster of lesser mushrooms loomed, casting a macabre glow.

"Yup," Briar laughed to himself. "Sounds about right."

While Ruthy walked into the glow of mushrooms, beyond the rocks, Briar considered primal life underground, the actual *reality* of Ümfalla, life that bypassed all. His new-found companions understood this fundamental truth, but in altogether different ways. *Truth* was beneath the surface, secrets Ruthy knew how to access, turning the darkness, bright. There was no time to poeticize, not idly, not when there was more to be done, so he followed her into the dark. Through still waters, Shixee closed her eyes and focused on subaqueous confessions.

In the quiet of Briar's ruminative steps, a ghost was near, always on his periphery. The great love who became that ghost never let Briar get the best of her, in word or deed. On the turn she died, she outdid the greatest feats Briar mustered and saved his life doing them. And yet there was another love who was lost, one who might still be breathing, in the realm where darkness brought stars and Sister Moons. Briar shook away the ghosts and called them what they were, memories.

When he approached a large boulder, a strange light was pulsing beyond. The light was silver-white, contained in its glow, like fire through frosted glass. Its rhythm induced a trance-like state in Briar, who was losing his gift of grace. He stumbled onward to get a closer look, no matter the consequences. Beauty always came at a cost, a cost he was willing to pay, in a world gutted of meaning. He peered around the corner of the boulder and saw.

All of Ruthy was entangled in silver-shining mycelium. Wriggling hyphae reached up to her face and entered her ears, like so many millions of tentacles. Her thick red braid was a trellis for the mycelium, drifting out of the ground, through a single consciousness. Her eyes were open but their outward senses were shut. A bed of glistening mycelium squirmed around her seated body, while lesser mushrooms were pulsing along with Ruthy's heart.

Her lips were parted but unmoving and her teeth sparkled from the light. The thinnest of mycelial threads wound around each other to form a greater whole, as thick as a finger. Hyphae made contact with Ruthy's skin, from her chest, up to her forehead. Only her mouth remained untouched as she breathed methodical breaths. The entrancing union of mycelium and flesh entranced Briar, through power and beauty, intertwining flesh and earth, magic through nature.

What seemed a response to intense cold, was something altogether different. Ruthy's teeth were chattering a cadence, with clear pauses between. She was sending and receiving, with certain moments calling for quicker clicks, while others were filled with methodical *chatters*, grinding and clenching. In the enchanted light of the scene, two thick chords of entangled mycelium were twisting alongside Ruthy's cheeks. They shimmered when she chattered.

Ruthy turned her head like a flower would to the sun. When her distant eyes met Briar's, the chattering stopped and the silver-shine of mycelium dwindled, as the entanglement drifted back into the ground, like snakes seeking shelter. Ruthy stretched her jaw as she stood up. Briar remained transfixed as the darkness returned and Ruthy stood in front of him.

"Is she still with Shixee?" Ruthy asked, in a voice deeper than usual.

"She is."

"Good. I need to show you something. I hope you're not a disappointment."

"I've failed more than I've triumphed. See what happens, eh?"

"You have no idea what I'm looking for."

"And yet I found you."

"You can't imagine the trouble it took to communicate with Sky Realm, in search of you. I was gurgling Reaper blood, digging water holes, stabbing piece of shit mouth-breathers, all while speaking destinies through mycelium."

"You'd never believe the trouble it took to track down the old Weir, over and over again, just to find out what was going on beneath this chatterbox ground. She's a slippery one. I thought I'd lost her for good, around the Screever haunts."

"You mean, *Ībeka*, acted as your intermediary?"

"She's a force of fucking nature, never mind her sanity."

"My desperation in her presence blinded me to her powers. She was supposed to be someone else. So much is lost in those distant transmissions."

"Go on."

"Come closer to me, if you're willing."

Briar stepped closer and realized how quickly his heart was beating. Through Ruthy's sunborne eyes, he witnessed the metaphysical harmony entangling him to her, not unlike the willingness of mycelium to join into something greater, a Singularity beyond words. Many orbits passed since Briar felt this sense of knowing, a hyperawareness of the moment, rather than regret and uncertainty of what was and what was to come.

He wrapped his arms around Ruthy's waist, just as she did his own, as they drifted down to the receiving earth. In the midst of that slow descent—as if they were drifting through water—Ruthy nodded once and he followed, just as their foreheads met and both their worlds became the shared visions of each other's eyes. When they reached their knees, their chests pressed into each other, hearts pounding, while they breathed manic breaths together.

"You miss Sky Realm," Ruthy whispered, just above a bated breath.

"I miss who Sky Realm held. I've lost loves in both realms. Ghosts haunt the air and land."

"The living can't be ghosts."

"I'm too aware of my own survival."

"You need to hear something, Briar. Will you stay close?"

"The world made flesh is holding me. I'm listening, Ruthy."

"There's so much more…"

When mycelium reemerged, the glow hid intricate workings of countless strands, far thinner than a hair, entangling into shimmering tentacles with individual volitions. Ruthy and Briar's bodies were glorified by mycelial emergence, weaving throughout their embrace, uniting earth and flesh.

When Ruthy closed her eyes, Briar matched her, through the harmony intertwining their breaths and heartbeats, while their minds became indistinguishable from the One *thinking* beneath the ground, throughout the Fungal Realm of Ümfalla and up, *up* through mycelium entangled roots, *mighty rhizomes*, feeding the Tree holding up Sky Realm. Ruthy and Briar followed forces that coursed eternal beneath the ground they knelt upon.

By the time they opened their eyes, both of them were looking into a timeless realm, within, a shared consciousness, beyond Naming. Ruthy tilted up her chin with strands of mycelium still clinging to her red braid, swaying in the moment. She smiled from within, urging Briar to do the same. When he tilted his head up, mycelium drifted along his temples and he was thrust into the primal ecstasy of Ruthy and the One, dissolving into something more.

Ruthy *spoke* through mycelium, while their bodies quivered through the ecstatic power coursing through, a world apart from their shared consciousness:

"You perceive her breaths. Allow her voice to find you, Briar. Release guilt and receive. All of us are One in this moment."

"*Orīa.*"

"Feel the truth of her."

"She's near…"

"*Hear her…* Then listen to Yala. She is my proxy in Sky Realm. She knows what must follow."

"Anything. I'll give anything to share Orīa's breaths with my own."

"Leave all the rest to me…"

After Briar wandered off, Mēna drifted down deeper into the water and allowed herself to float. Shixee enlivened the water with her nearness, through enchanting bubbles and gentle currents, helping Mēna settle into a healing bliss. Water took away the weight of the world, while the Phibian poeticized the moment through the grace of a body breathing in two worlds. Shixee's head slowly emerged and her thick strands of deep-green hair floated all around her shimmering face.

Dripping water was the only sound that followed. Shixee took a deep breath as she drifted down onto Mēna's lap and faced her. She blinked a few times before Mēna finally looked back at her with bright eyes. She held onto Shixee's lower back, while the lameness of her other arm left the limb drifting near the surface. Shixee took that arm under her own, pulling gently onto her side. Mēna's fingers rested on her sleek hips, while Shixee struggled to remain silent.

"You move through water like magic," Mēna said, softly.

"There is nothing I must do but eat and breathe. Water is where I can just *be*. I wanted to soothe you. You are a beautiful soul."

"So little of myself is left to give, from here," she pointed to her heart. "You owe me nothing, Shixee. I can't even recall what I did at some time, in some place."

"We are alone, so I can speak above a whisper."

"Are you sure you want to?"

"I believe you are unsure if you want me to. I will tell you anything I can remember."

Mēna looked away and clenched her jaw, "*Tell me.*"

"You know I forget when the Hardening comes. I have to release much of what I experienced, so I can begin anew when things soften?"

"Yes."

"This memory was forgotten because of its violence. A different forgetting. How much do you remember before you became a Wanderer?"

"Far too much."

"Let me try again," Shixee said, drifting down to her shoulders. "Try to remember what you were doing before your great loss. Before your people lost their Name."

"That's simple. I was...well, I was a...I always was a bit of a Wanderer, but I..."

"How many orbits have passed since your great loss?"

"My mind is still drifting. Give me a moment," Mēna said, as her eyes darted, here and there, in search of answers.

"Do you remember this?"

Shixee tilted her head to the side and pulled back her thick green hair, revealing a deep scar, from the right side of her neck, across her upper back. Shixee took Mēna's lame hand and guided the forefinger across the scar, slowly. As she did, Mēna's face underwent a sea-change and her eyes shined to the point of battle-bright. By the time her limp finger reached the terminus point of the scar, along Shixee's shoulder blade, the tale had been told. Shixee gently returned Mēna's hand to the water, bringing her trembling fingers to her warm waist.

Shixee spoke, softly, "You traced the scar, but you *see* the wound that brought you to me, long ago. Much like my own life, yours has been lived more than once. But you are beginning to remember. There is no need to speak at the moment," Shixee closed her eyes. "Let remembrance settle, or it will fly away. Let memory roost in your mind and then speak back. Memory is a fickle, shy bird, that flies too often and lands too late. That winged-truth took me too many Hardenings to remember not to forget."

Shixee remained in Mēna's embrace, as she suffered through the suffering with her. Shixee tracked the fear in Mēna, as a memory begot *memories*, while they divided and subdivided into numerous manifestations, not unlike mycelium, or branches, on the Tree of Avernus. Mēna's paradigm shift was evident through her whole body, from her twitching fingers, to her manic eyes. Shixee promised herself not to let go, even if Mēna suddenly turned on her, like she had, long ago.

"I'm so sorry, Shixee. I'm so fucking sorry," Mēna whispered, as tears streamed from her bright eyes, tears like falling stars.

"I forgave you, a long time ago. Never forget, you saved my life, *Nyctá*. After you wounded me, all those orbits ago, you brought me back to life. You faced your mistake and sought life, creating a gift, a glimmer of who you are still becoming."

Beyond the dark pool and over the rocks, the silver glow of mushrooms crowned distinct moments underway, glorifying breakthroughs through earth and water. Mushrooms pulsed like a thousand and one beating hearts, as if Ümfalla was reminding everyone: It *lived*.

10

AUSPICES AND AUGURIES

WHEN MĒNA REACHED THE source of the glow, Ruthy and Briar were still on their knees, embracing, with their heads thrust back and chests pressed together through the mycelial entanglement. Their eyes were in the back of their heads, while Ruthy's fingers were manipulating the earth at her sides. The entanglement of silver-bright mycelium squirmed throughout the interstices of Ruthy and Briar's embrace, giving them the appearance of a two-headed beast with a common goal.

Mēna was still naked and dripping from her time in the dark pool and her good hand was clenched, while the other dangled at her side, when she strode up to them. Ruthy's teeth were chattering, as her body followed a rhythm of its own. When Mēna pushed Ruthy onto her back, the torn mycelium faded like stars at sunrise.

> *"Ou cōntrashek intz mákren!*
> *You betray us all!*
> *É glāntz zet ou ket!*
> *I see what you are!"*

Mēna glared at Ruthy, with battle-bright eyes, before she strode away and left her to the darkness. Briar was still swaying, bewildered, as if he had forgotten some prayer he dropped to his knees to speak.

Briar muttered, blinking hard, "Your *proxy,* up there, better pull through, for both our sakes. For Orīa's... We've set things in motion that can't be stilled. And now we have a pissed off Simmerian to deal with."

"You *know* this was worth it. All of this," Ruthy said, still seated, with a lapful of dark mycelium in her lap. "You should be thankful my proxy found Orīa. Even Orīa accepted what it would take for me to show you the truth of it all, for you to believe—"

"I've gotta agree with double-tongue back there. Whatever *earthy* magic you possess might be the end of more than us. I trembled through that power."

"And you *loved* it. I relished in you doing so. I showed you entangled wonders only the Goddess wielded, before someone like me."

"Oh, I believe you," he said, standing up. "That's what scares the shit out of me. Power like that comes at a cost, as sure as, *Ūmfalla is asshole of the world...* That didn't roll off the tongue like I imagined. Gotta pull myself together."

"If it means anything, you were great, Briar. I've never tried it with anyone else. You didn't catch fire, like I thought you might."

"You're joking," Briar laughed.

"Am I?" Ruthy glared.

"Well..I don't think double-tongue is waiting for you, this time. And there's probably a fucking horde of Reapers gathering behind us. Truth is, I'd rather fight them, alone, than face your wrath. You've pulled me into this. You'd better not fuck us *all* over," Briar said, as he walked away to join the rest.

By the time Ruthy returned to the dark pool, only Shixee remained, who was seated with her feet drifting in the water. There was no sign of Mēna or Briar and even Shixee appeared to look on Ruthy with eyes of betrayal and disappointment. Then the Phibian blinked and Ruthy saw her face for what it was, rather than her projection. Shixee waited for Ruthy to look her in the eyes and then she spoke.

"Secrets are like the mechanical. They shield us and make us feel stronger, as we try and survive. But hidden parts, the secret parts of the secret underneath, those are what fester and make us sick. By the time we smell it, it is too late. Then we are left to luck, or the help of another. You know that well."

"Sometimes I wish I could forget," Ruthy said, kneeling. "Forget everything and start over. Memories fester, no matter what I do. I want to forget and not even realize I did. Everything would begin again, clear. No secrets."

"Do not wish that. If you truly forgot, you would kill a world within. You would no longer be you. Remember and keep making new memories. Then choose the best ones to cherish. We are all fragile, even this realm. Maybe the new world will outweigh the old. Mine does, or I would be no more. I hear no Reapers. But I worry for Briar's safety."

"That's funny," Ruthy smiled. "Nah. Briar has his own secrets, but he's good. All of you are good. I—"

"You want to be. The water speaks to me and the land speaks to water."

"You mentioned that."

"Water is intertwined with land. If it were not, water would be nothing but a puddle in emptiness. Land without water, would be nothing but rock. A delicate balance keeps the world whole, even if it appears chaotic. Water speaks to the land, just as you speak through mycelium. *I listen.* I am fluent in the language of the One beneath. The One has no bounds but the land and mycelium is its way, its many mouths. It is a scream and a whisper, permeating all. All is One. *You* are screaming with a silent whisper. The ones on the other side are screaming back with fear and rage. Stop listening. Stop chattering. Look around and listen. *Here,* is where the truth is. You look below and try to tell one soul and you tell the whole world. So much is lost in the exchange, when the one who hears, hears what they desire," Shixee said, looking down at the water. "We must go. Reapers will follow, until you are taken back. You must choose. The way you hold back your power is beautiful. I admire such things. So *rare.*"

Shixee vanished beneath the water and was soon standing on the far embankment, visible through her sparkling skin, catching the faintest mushroom glow. Ruthy yearned to be someone else, anyone, but who she was.

Shame followed mycelial transmissions. Communing through entanglement ate away at her spirit, thinning her resolve, when she needed it most. To be a creature who drifted between two worlds, like Shixee, made her imagination swirl, but Ruthy *was* a creature of two worlds, belonging to neither, yet dependent on both: Darkness and light/earth and air.

The infinitude of Sky Realm was bearing down on her, a burden she failed to kill, even through her convoluted fall from Sky Tracer. The more she thought about her jump, the more she believed fate whispered to her and told her life was below, exactly where she fell. But fate was a word the ambitious used to justify their atrocities.

With that in mind, she attached her survival to luck and the courage of a warrior named, Mēna. Briar was the strange luck between. And yet it was *fate* that brought her to him. Across the water, in the glow, Shixee beckoned Ruthy to follow.

When Ruthy caught up with Mēna, their proximity meant nothing, as far as the vast distance that had come between them. Mēna never would have left her behind, that much Ruthy believed, even if the warrior refused to look at her.

The middle portion of Mēna's mechanical was dangling at her elbow, like a broken branch, while she muttered to herself, under the steady roar from the approaching falls. Briar walked a little ahead, as he admired the landscape with a familiarity, bordering on nostalgia. Shixee was walking through swamp-like mosses. abutting a rocky stream, while ankle-high fog drifted in. When Ruthy looked down, she imagined walking over a vast thunderhead, with obscured mushrooms all around, mimicking lightning bolts frozen in time.

A booming cry from above brought the four companions to a halt. In the gloom of the spore cloud, a pair of mighty-winged creatures were flying at a height not far from the hidden tracks of Sky Tracer. Streaks of dark-bright iridescence marked the creatures, articulating the gloom with indigo light, tracing darkness, evoking a sense of nearness to the observers, in spite of their distance.

The pair looped in the sky, at such tremendous speed, the wind from their flight found the four companions and blew fantasy into truth. Their serpent-like tails whipped the air, resulting in a cracking sound, like thunder, to accompany their deafening cries.

As suddenly as they appeared, the creatures flew up into the spore cloud and vanished from sight. Another resounding boom announced their departure. The final rush of wind blew through Mēna's hair, giving her the look of a convert to the deities above.

"Haven't seen one of those since I was a boy," Briar said, staring at the zenith. "Never a pair of them."

"So *those* are Night Skimmers," Ruthy gawked, blinking at the darkness. When she looked to Mēna, her lips moved along with the passing wind. Resonant sounds drifted through them and were carried away with the wind. Mēna's eyes remained closed, while she swayed back and forth. "Are you okay, Mēna?"

"Keep moving!" Mēna shouted, shaking her hawk-hair, like a bird preparing for flight, as she walked on.

Shixee remained transfixed on the zenith, motionless, in the mossy swamp. She shook her head and rubbed her eyes, before she blinked hard, again. Ruthy approached her and looked where Shixee was staring. All she could see were faint undulations of black in the spore cloud. Shixee gurgled, before she spoke.

"When Night Skimmers come in pairs, the Hardening is near... If I remember anything profound from forgetfulness, it is that. I pretended not to see last time. I almost forgot to forget, when it came. I learned this from dreams. I am doing the same this time, too. Almost all the rest forgot to forget and remain in the ground. I miss them. I remember some of their Names. But nothing is certain. Not even the seasons."

Shixee was in the midst of another word, when she splashed and vanished, as she was so keen on doing, in moments of tension. Ruthy ran ahead to catch up to the rest of the group, while the ringing in her ears from the flight of the Night Skimmers remained.

As the ringing subsided, she thought there might be further damage to her ears, when a steady roar took over.

"*Mē-na!*" Ruthy called out.

"Do not call her that," Shixee said, emerging from the edge of the embankment.

"Then what do I call her?"

"Nyctá."

"*Nyctá?* Has she gone mad?"

"No," Shixee said, just above a whisper. "She is trying to remember. Pardon my quick words. The nearness of the falls is making it almost impossible for me to listen for Reapers through water. I would avoid speaking with such pitch, as you just did. As for Nyctá, the bird must be allowed to roost. Do not ask her. Nobody can. She will tell you, when the bird speaks."

"Birds take too long to do anything but fly. Where I come from, Nyctà, is the ancient word for night, indicative of death and evil. *Reapers* called her Nyctá. Names shape us, as much as we become those Names. I know this to be true, as surely as I'm *Ruthy*. And is this really the time for Mēna, or Nyctá, or the Wanderer, or warrior, or double-tongue-r, to go searching her mind for things past? There's too much at stake."

"When is the time? You travel together but your paths are different. You spoke to me about forgetting, just a moment ago. She must remember."

"*Fuck*," Ruthy seethed. "Why do you have to be so precise all the time? And yet you speak in riddles."

"You are falling back into your other self. This is the way you speak through mycelium, to the ones above. I can tell by your words and how you speak them, now."

"I'm trying to figure things out, Shixee. Listening to my hidden transmissions doesn't mean you know my *other* self. This isn't about me. It's *her*," she pointed ahead.

"She needs to discover who she is. Not just memories. *Who*. So call her, Nyctá. It will only help and be kind of you to do. She has been walking in circles, too long. You of all souls should know the importance of Names."

"I guess the ground told the water to tell you that, too? Tell *her* that much and I'll be left in the dark for sure."

"She admires you."

"Does she? *Admires?* I'm almost certain I ruined that. Well, I envy her. Wait! Don't you dare swim away, Shix... RAH!"

As soon as Shixee vanished, in the turbulent stream, the fog was growing thicker and the roar of the falls, greater. Fog was now one with the spore cloud, leaving nothing but bulging darkness. Besides the cadence from Briar's muffled steps and whoever *her* Name was, walking beside him, all was black. Ruthy refused to cry for help, as she took weary steps along the uncertain path. Then Shixee's sopping warm hand found hers and Ruthy followed the gentle pull of the Phibian guide.

'Rak-ak'   'Kak-ak'

'Nyctá-wek'   'Rak-kak-kak'   'Rak-kak'

'Rak-kak——kak-kak——kak——KAK'

Reaper calls were near and far and did their work announcing their arrival, casting fear on the ones they pursued. Ruthy trusted Shixee's hand, blindly, through thick darkness. She caught the glint of Mēna's eyes, glaring back through the fog. It was then Ruthy remembered Mēna's broken mechanical. Not only was Ruthy a further burden with her sunborne eyes, Mēna was left with one functioning arm, making her less than half the warrior she was before.

The profusion of Reaper calls, from various distances, revealed past failures were being remedied through greater numbers. Reapers were flesh and bone, but humans proved to be the worst kind of monster. Whatever deity Reapers followed, never shaped the realm through words, but fed the ground through blood and made the spore cloud dance through screams.

Through the fog, Mēna's eyes looked like two approaching moons, while she waited for Ruthy to reach her. When she did, Mēna turned to Briar, who was looking towards the roar of the Seething Falls, sparkling from an abundance of minerals in the cliffs from which they issued. Across the great body of water at the companion's side, the falls hissed as they struck rocks, from heights unseen.

"Tell me we're close enough!" Mēna shouted, above the tumult of the falls.

"We're not!" Briar shouted back. "We'll never make it to the narrower point of crossing. We're going to have to swim for it! Wish I were a Phibian about now!"

"I can't swim!" Ruthy cried out.

"What?!" Mēna roared.

"I can't swim! It's that simple!" Ruthy shouted.

"I will take her across," Shixee said, in a voice that penetrated the roar of the falls, without shouting.

"See you on the other side," Mēna said. "Go! Now!"

"If you insist!" Briar laughed, before he leaped into the churning water, ecstatic, through its bioluminescence.

Shixee pulled Ruthy, with gentle strength, taking both of them into the swirling waters. Reaper call were indiscernible above the roar, while Shixee's powerful legs flapped together through the water, as she held onto Ruthy's waist with an unbreakable force.

Ruthy swallowed more water than air on her way across and never heard Mēna splash after them. She nearly inhaled seething water when she thought of Mēna trying to cross with one arm. Ruthy kicked her legs wildly, as she had when she was high above the ground in Briar's snare. She tried to imagine she was helping the Phibian on their journey towards somewhere solid.

"Hold your breath," Shixee said.

Before Ruthy could take a full breath, through raging water, she was submerged and a ceiling of rock grazed the top of her head, along the way. Beneath the surface, the pressure of the days leading up to her journey on Sky Tracer and the ones following her to this moment were crushing her skull. She imagined opening her mouth and taking a deep breath. A single breath of water could fix it all. Just a little breath could do more than a fall from the greatest of heights.

"*Just a sliver of a moment,*" Shixee said, in a baritone/subaqueous voice, Ruthy was able to discern.

The darkness was growing darker as panic set in. Her body began to tingle, while her lungs were set ablaze in her mind. She tilted her head up and a drifting glimmer was just ahead. But dark shadows were dancing in her field of vision and nothing was justified in its appearance. Then a mighty kick and tug, on behalf of Shixee, sent the pair swirling upwards, where air rushed down to them and Ruthy's heaving breaths echoed in the cavern.

"How was your first swim, eh?" Briar said, reaching down his hand.

"Where's Mēna?" Ruthy heaved, as she took his hand and was pulled clumsily onto the rocky edge.

"It'll take her twice as long, with a single arm," Briar said. "Where's the Phibian?"

Ruthy stared at the water, without blinking, as she lost her breath again, in anticipation of Mēna surfacing. Her burdensome presence within the group weighed heavier on her. She was sick at the thought of what Mēna was putting herself through for the sake of a sunborne, '*Seemer,*' without a useful asset to help her companions, beyond digging a rather deep hole.

"If she drowns—" Ruthy cried.

"She won't drown," Briar said, wringing out his celium cloak, leaving it refreshed in his hands. "Be patient."

"What if the Reapers follow?"

"Then we'll slaughter them, one by one, as they surface. This place is impregnable."

"*We* got in."

"You're welcome for that," Briar half-smiled.

"What did you do besides jump in first?"

"All for good reason," Briar said. "You'd all be eel food, if I didn't."

"Is that some kind of superstition? This isn't the time—"

Mēna's head emerged from the water and her eyes were battle-bright. While she gasped for air, Shixee held onto her side and looked up to Ruthy, with eyes of despair. The Phibian was holding on so tightly to Mēna, Ruthy recognized the strain on her face and realized the Phibian's hold was to prevent Mēna from going back under. Mēna tried to pull away from Shixee but the Phibian did not let go and had all the advantage, in her watery element, against a warrior with a lame arm.

"Let her go, Shixee," Ruthy pleaded.

"Not yet," Shixee said, as Mēna writhed violently in her grasp.

"What's wrong with her? What happened?" Ruthy cried.

"She tried...to go...back," Shixee said, trying her best not to harm Mēna, in her splashing mania.

"Go back where?!"

"To the Reapers," Shixee said, as she whispered unknown words to Mēna.

"You mean—" Ruthy began.

"She's a Reaper," Briar said. "I fucking knew it."

"Yes," Shixee said, as Mēna continued her struggles, in her grasp. "Their leader."

"Nyctá!" Ruthy called out.

Nyctá looked back at Ruthy, as she drifted in Shixee's embrace, before she roared:

"Anderzér!

Seemer!"

11

THE DIM LIGHT

I T TOOK MANY MOMENTS for Shixee to exhaust Nyctá in her swimming grasp and coax her back to solid ground. By the time she did, Briar was at the other end of the cavern, in jovial conversation with four others, no older than himself, collectively thrilled and infuriated at his arrival. Ruthy was unable to hear anything beyond the tone of the familial conversation, while she stood somewhere between Nyctá and the strangers at the mouth of the mineral-glow in the cavern.

The roar of the falls above the cavern smothered any distinctions of words. While Nyctá sat staring into the water, with Shixee drifting at her boots, Ruthy walked towards Briar and followed him into the darkness. It was nothing more than an arching hole in gray rock.

The passage through the hole was tall enough to walk through standing up and wide enough for two people, shoulder to shoulder, to pass through without struggle. Bioluminescence from mosses speckled the passageway, disorienting Ruthy more than lighting the way. It smelled of mildew and metal, like an armory left to rot and rust. Dark figures moved through a dark space ahead. Echoes from their footsteps and breaths turned a handful of people into many. Voices became the only distinction of persons. Ruthy listened as much as she feared what would follow.

—I can't believe you show up now, Briar. After five orbits.

—Five and a half.

—Close enough, Fálon.

—He shows up when he has no choice. Shows up when it's already too late.

—Aww, c'mon Callisto. You know I always kept you all in my heart of hearts.

—Fuck you, Briar.

—She said it for me. Now that's out of the way, tell me about the ginger walking *sunborne* behind us.

—It's the funniest thing, Elēa...she just fell into our laps.

—Twice! Almost.

—Well played, Ruthy! I happened upon these *Wanderers* back in the Sinels and wouldn't you know it, Reapers show up. So I found myself battling them, side by side, with

—He was robbing us and Reapers changed his mind. *Quickly*. But it took a lot longer for me to see the end of it. Not to mention, the ground.

—Thieving? Is that what it's come to?

—Well, Eléa...it's a hard world out there.

—Torala would be ashamed of you. Not sure about the other one you gave your double-heart to.

—I'll take your snares but leave her out of this, both of them.

—What about the woman with the hawk's tail hair?

—She's here to see Zéffa. Her mechanical's in need of welding. She's just another Wanderer in search of something she believes exists. Same old story. Fierce with a sword, though. And she can almost fly in her leaps, I'll tell you that straight.

—Your words have always been winding.

—And you've always been a rock in my boot, Callisto.

—And the Phibian?

—Just a lucky find along the way.

—Has she any of the gifts of her kind? Can she Whisper?

—Nope. Nothing of the kind. Hell of a swimmer, though. Not much help in battle but good in a wet pinch.

—What are you talking about Briar? Just a turn ago she

—Ah, the Ginger! She's just trying to talk up her Phibian friend. No worries, Ruthy! You don't have to weave stories. You've done enough of that for all of us. My word keeps her safe here, not her deeds.

—And where did you fall from, *Ginger*?

—Sky Tracer. And you'd do better by calling me, Ruthy.

—Sky Tracer?

—She means, *The Dim Light*, Callisto.

Echoing voices ceased, leaving the static sound from the falls, along with drips from the cavern roof, making the relative quiet, palpable. Ruthy searched her mind for what to say when the inevitable interrogation began.

A pair of boots on stone gave away the approach of one of the strangers with a Name, but no face for Ruthy to imagine. A pair of soft-glowing eyes found her own and stared into them. Ruthy only discerned a woman's face with dark hair shaved to a stubble and a battle-scarred cheek. Her fingers were strong but restrained when they clenched Ruthy's shoulders.

—You are going to tell us everything you know about The Dim Light. You are now under the watch of, *The People Who Are Going To Put Out The Light*.

—Never mind the name! It's a work in progress!

—Shut up, Briar!

A blue glow invited them into an adjoining cavern, carved through Time's teeth, beneath the Seething Falls. No more than twenty souls occupied the somber dwelling, with a reflective stone table in the center and a smattering of carved stools. Most possessed a dim glow to their eyes, but various lanterns, filled with blue-glowing minerals, gave away the overall lack of dark-bright eyes, nothing compared to the enigmatic, Mēna/Nyctá.

Ruthy was reminded of Screevers, from what seemed a lifetime before. While there did not appear to be any presences like the stone-dead Dorian, the somber atmosphere and relative silence of the inhabitants evoked a similar mood, as if the world had come to an end and these were the leftovers. She waited for someone to break out into the solemn cry, '*Where's my daughter.*'

Callisto, who confronted her in the corridor, glared at Ruthy. Her shaved head accentuated the symmetry of her powerfully-built form. The deep scar running obliquely across her face, from forehead to chin, was a mark in stark contrast to her wizened eyes, softly glowing, with an inherent sadness to them.

While Callisto continued speaking with Briar, Ruthy marked Briar eyeing her from his periphery, waiting for a subtle sign of her understanding of the situation. Ruthy subtly nodded and Briar winked, while he continued his conversation with Callisto.

Ruthy considered the cavern beneath the Seething Falls as another vanishing-point in space, like so many of places in Ümfalla, good for a moment and gone the next. Souls such as Callisto found a cause to latch onto, an obsession, no different than searching for Resurrection Spores in the murk of the Sinels. Both were fantasy, with one too far reaching to be had, while the other was too legendary to be found. Ruthy swallowed her judgment when she realized her own obsession was both legend and far away. She closed her eyes and tried to think of something fantastical:

Clouds in the wind, articulating the sky,
While a solemn tree smiled at her,
Roots screamed when she listened,
Whispering of fateful choices to come...

When she opened her eyes, there was nothing but the truth of the matter and resolve to seek that truth to the end. She made it this far, making her believe in things like prophecy, since belief was the *realist* thing she possessed, a belief to transcend current limits.

Not only did Briar snare Ruthy into her own plans, he brought them into relative safety, not far from the Tree of Avernus. And yet the miracle who was Mēna transcended prophecy or luck. Mēna was already legend. The legend was doubled when she thought of the *other* life of the warrior, under the abysmal Name, *Nyctá.*

A seeker of truth walked towards Ruthy and her name was, Callisto. Ruthy cringed at the approach, until the resolute woman passed her by. When Ruthy turned, Nyctá was standing in a daze, near the entryway. Callisto was clinching her fists when she began to speak to Nyctá, through gritted teeth.

"How dare you call yourself that," Callisto seethed.

"I call myself nothing. I lost my Names," Nyctá said.

"Briar just referred to you as, *Mēna.* Is that what you call yourself? Speak!"

"I was mistaken. I am not Mēna. I—"

"Get out of my sight! Your double-tongue is an insult to the dead! OUT!" Callisto screamed, pointing to the other end of the cavern, where a dark passage appeared to have been cut out of the stone, just for Nyctá.

Nyctá passed Ruthy without acknowledging her, before she vanished into the darkness. Callisto remained where she was, her hands shaking and eyes clinched shut. When she opened them, she glared at Ruthy, through eyes of torment, rather than rage. Callisto looked to be on the brink of exploding, or crumbling into dust, at the same time. Instead, she walked up to Ruthy and took her by the hand, with a soft touch.

"What you just heard was for me," Callisto whispered. "What I need from you, now, is for everyone. We need you to tell us everything, everything you can, about The Dim Light."

"I'll do everything I can," Ruthy managed.

"Who named it, Sky Tracer?"

"Not Nyctá."

"Well...you should think about joining us. People like her are the reason Ümfalla is falling apart. This realm used to be more than survivors and scavengers. Not long ago, there was culture. I'd kill her now, if I didn't make a promise to Torala."

"Who is Torala?"

"Briar didn't tell you, did he? Of course, he didn't. He's too proud and too much of a little shit. Torala was our leader and she died saving our asses against a Reaper horde, about six orbits ago. Torala was Briar's Partner in life. Both of them left behind meaningless lives and chose to fight against the Reaper oppressors. After Torala died, Briar vanished. Most assumed he ended himself. But I knew he was too arrogant to do that. Others said he found a way up to Sky Realm, in search of decadence. Nobody makes it up there alone. You know that much. I love Briar to the light above the darkness, but I hate to have him back."

"Why? He's incredible in battle."

"He reminds me of Torala. She loved him far beyond his worth. We've never been the same since she fell. And Briar annoys the shit out of me. *There*. I told you secrets. Not too difficult, right? I'm well aware of your evasiveness. And I already know, you are from Sky Realm, sunborne eyes and all. Truths will be told. Now, it's your turn."

"Who was Mēna to you?"

"Now, it's *your* turn."

12

FRICTION, PRESSURE AND LUCK

NYCTÁ LINGERED BETWEEN THE cavern and red glow of the opening ahead. A soul-string was plucked with every syllable of Callisto's diatribe, leaving Nyctá in a state of bewilderment, beyond the one she brought into the cavern. A cacophony of voices from the cavern filled the emptiness of the corridor. Callisto's voice resonated through the stone hollow.

"For many orbits we have suffered together and lost far too many to Name tonight. But fate brought back one of our brothers and he brings news from the Sinels and beyond. Reapers are growing in numbers and continue to take our daughters and our sisters. They continue to steal our children and feed them to The Dim Light. But they have taken to pillaging and destruction of Names across the Sinels and all the way to the Sideon Cliffs. The Reapers are the tip of the spear of the ones in the brightness above us. The kingdom of Avernus, at the top of the Tree, grows stronger as we rot beneath its branches. The Dim Light carries our children over Ümfalla, never to return. This is an inexhaustible beast that feeds without stopping. The newcomer you see was a Passenger on The Dim Light. (Gasps) I know, I know. It is a gift from the Goddess, she survived. She found her way, in spite of her sunborne eyes, to make it to us. Through her words, I believe we can forge a way to cut the tracks of The Dim Light and put an end to this. The Reapers have no code, no honor, but to themselves and to the grim power that made them. Not like us. They follow orders through hate and desperation, a desperation I saw in the face of the woman with eyes that can see into the white, unlike us. She is what waits for us all, if we fail. Solitude, barbarism and shame. I could tell you tales of those.... that...... ....your... ....burst... ....steal.........eth...........Mē"

Words faded when Nyctá walked into flickering red lights, at the end of the corridor. A blast of heat drew instant beads of sweat on her shame-flushed face. In the ochre glow from a chimney, full of crackling minerals, an old man was seated.

Age spots marked his bald head. He wore a tattered gray robe, while his tremendous hands fidgeted at his sides. Hunks of metal, from ruined blades to gleaming gauntlets, were scattered throughout the cavern. From the looks of the old man, he was warming his body in front of the mineral-fire, rather than working on any sort of gleaming instrument of fear.

"If you're cold, you've found the right place," the old man laughed, without turning around.

"It never gets cold in Ümfalla."

"Precisely. Then what are you doing here?"

"Are you Zeffá?"

"Used to be. Now, the youngsters call me something else."

"And what's that?"

"I was hoping you could tell me. I never leave this place and they rarely come to visit me. Hard to keep a Name when everyone around you has their heads in the clouds."

"I heard you were the best welder in Ümfalla."

"That's easy, when you're the only one. Nobody has time for patience to learn, anymore. Nobody has time for anything but dreams and survival. I don't need to look at you to know you need something fixed. Hear it in your voice. Something is not whole and you want me to make it right. You're probably on some perilous quest, in search of something."

"I could—"

"You could do many things, but nothing moves without a little fantasy to keep us going. I used to believe in something. Then I got older and age brings a single thing. Do you know what that thing is, young lady?"

"Wisdom?"

"*Bah*! If age imparted wisdom, this would be a world full of sages. *No*. Age only allows enough time for a person to realize how confused everyone is, including themselves. Fantasy helps us imagine there's some kind of meaning in the world. But fantasy fades and we're left with nothing but less than what we had before. As you can see, I haven't had a chance to have a good chat, not in a long while. But I hope you're listening. Cause if you're listening, you'll realize there's nothing to learn. *Nothing*. We only grow more confused, but there's something interesting in that. Now come up here and let me get a hold of the problem I'm going to fix."

When Nyctá approached, the old man took hold of her mechanical, while his fingers searched for the source of the problem. Throughout deft workings of his warped and scarred fingers, his head remained lowered. Nyctá realized the old man was blind. In the midst of her discovery, the mechanical was already unscrewed, properly loosened and off her arm.

The old man tossed the mechanical near the mineral-fire and ran his fingers up and down Nyctá's limp arm. His forefinger deftly traced the circumference of her shoulder, nearly to the crest of her armpit and then her elbow, while he further traced the shapes of her musculature and ligaments.

"Make a fist," Zeffá mumbled.

"I can't without the mech—"

"*Make a fist.*"

Nyctá clenched her teeth as she glared at her dangling hand in the old man's grasp. It began with her middle finger and soon the rest followed, in what resulted in a fist clenched at such an angle, her fingertips pressed against the underside of her wrist. She looked away and released her warped fist.

"Now, that wasn't so hard," Zeffá said. "You shouldn't be ashamed of it. Not in a world like this, not ever."

"If my mechanical fails, I'll be finished."

"Is that right? So, if I just toss it in the inferno, your life will be over?" Zeffá grinned, as he leaned towards the mechanical by the mineral-fire.

"NO!"

"See there! Easy now," he laughed. "I wouldn't do that. It'd take an Age to melt it down, anyway. Wouldn't go and undo this beauty. Not to one of my finest works from my seeing orbits. The *Goddess*...I was good. You cringe when you face the fire. You see beyond the yellow. Can't say I'm envious. Seeing that deep into the dark comes at a great cost. Anyway, I've babbled enough. Need to keep my mouth shut, if I'm going to fix my past faults. The structure in the mechanical is near perfect, especially, at its nexus point. Subtle strokes of genius, if I say so, myself! But the range of my craft improved, after I lost my vision. Finally figured out how to manipulate Sideon ore into screws, rather than using half-baked shit from the South. Funny how that works, since I look into another kind of darkness. To and fro, story of the world. I see with my hands, *deeper*... Now, out of here. Come back at...I never know the time. Come back when you think it'll be finished.

Your beauty is distracting me," Zeffá winked, with his milky-gray eye, reflecting sparkles from the fiery-blue minerals.

As soon as Nyctá left the chamber of Zeffà, Callisto was waiting for her in the corridor. She stood with her legs apart and her arms at her side. All that was missing was a weapon to give her the appearance of readiness for a duel.

She stared at Nyctá, who was moving unsteadily, without the bracing effect of her mechanical. When she was within arm's reach of Callisto, Nyctá stood still and waited. Callisto broke the silence.

"Mēna called me, *Calli*. I hated it, whenever she did. I felt vulnerable... But I'd give anything to hear, *Calli*, from her living mouth again."

"I'm not—"

"*No!* I speak and you listen," Callisto seethed, stepping in front of Nyctà. "I wasn't sure, when I first saw you. Then I heard you speak. Mēna's voice is *in* you. Her voice is part of yours and I don't think you even know it. I'd ask you, but your words are air. That's what the real Simmerians say: Your words are *air*. Mēna was a Weir. She was a Weir of Simmeria. She was powerful. She was an orphan who grew up to love and nurture, in spite of it all. Powerful and beautiful. Beautiful heart and courageous and she was my one and only love. But she used her power to Heal. She could *Throw* herself with her Whispers, delve deep into another person's mind. She discovered what was wrong and helped them... She was killed by a horde of Reapers. She was always scared to death she would Throw herself into someone and get stuck, imprisoned in their minds and never escape. But it was death that did it. It was death that got her stuck," Callisto said, through tears. She stepped up, face to face, with Nyctá, "Do you hear it? Do you hear, *Mēna*, or do you still believe her voice is yours? Huh? Do you? Answer me! Is she calling for me?! Has she found what's wrong with you?! Is she finished yet? I'm here! Waiting for you! What's even left of you?! Are you in there, Mēna?!! Mēna?!!! **MĒNA!!!!**"

When Briar pulled Callisto from Nyctá, Callisto continued to beg and plead for Mēna, while cursing every particle of Nyctá's being. Nyctá backed away and stumbled back into the heat of Zeffá's chamber, where her shame was open for observation by an old blind man. Nyctá buried *Mēna* in the compost of her mind, full of false memories.

"Back so soon?" Zeffá laughed, while he worked something unseen in his hands. "You don't need to talk. I heard Callisto talking enough for all of Ümfalla back there. She's a good soul but lacks subtlety."

"No shit," Nyctá said, as she sat down on a stone, not far behind Zeffá.

Relative silence followed. The only measure of passing time were deft workings from Zeffá's masterful hands, manipulating the mechanical he made, long ago, like a ghost haunting unfinished deeds. Something about the sounds of mastery, flesh on the hardest of steels, soothed Nyctá. Her reverie was broken when the fixer spoke again.

"There are three things it takes to fix things. Do you know what those things are?"

"No idea," Nyctá's eyes widened at the sudden words. "But I'm sure you're going to tell me."

"Friction, pressure and luck. Those are the essential things. The same goes for welding. It sounds simple when you just say it, but doing it and finding it are the tricky things. What happened out there with Callisto was friction. And what you're feeling now is pressure. Now, you just need a little luck."

"Luck for what?"

"That's for you to uncover. Who is Mēna and who are *you*?"

"You really did hear everything."

"The walls have ears in here. And my oversized ones only got keener as the world grew darker than it already is. If I've learned anything, it's that most things are beyond our control and nothing is unimportant, so you'd best listen, even if there's nothing to be done. There was a woman, once—"

"Oh, the Goddess. Is this another parable?"

"That's up to you. Now, shut up and listen. There was a woman, once, who was looking for something *specific* from me. She was a Simmerian and she had a daughter. This was a long time ago...a *long* time. I'm one of the long-lived, a curse, if you ask me. Anyway, that daughter was gifted in sight and spirit but had a shortcoming, as all of us do. I told the woman the result of my work would come at a great cost."

"And how did she pay you? With Filigrees Mushrooms and a blowjob? That's the way of the world, no matter how long ago this was. My memories are mud, so go ahead and tell your tale."

"The cost was to the child. I made the mechanical for nothing. It was a challenge and my pride was at stake. In spite of my skill, the mechanical could not be made at a fixed size, but had to be able to *grow* with the child, as she matured. Lucky for her, I had the wisdom of the Elves to construct the leather/silk bands to compensate for change. No bowstring, not on the finest of bows, could compare to those on this mechanical, even if bows are unheard of in this Age, after the Elves left us. It's tough going without wood from Sky Realm... The Elven bands on the mechanical are priceless and exceedingly rare, more so now that the Elves are gone from this world. The Goddess knows, you certainly pushed this masterpiece to its limits with your warrior arm. The risk was great, but if it worked, the reward would change the child's life. This was many, many orbits ago...far more than my long-lived nature can count... Never mind that. The mother's name was Thémis and one of her daughters, the child I made the mechanical for, was named, Nyctá. That Name means many things, just as any good one does. This Simmerian believed Nyctá to mean, '*night's merciful dreams*'. I only made one of these mechanicals. What I cannot understand is your age. Simmerians are not gifted with longevity in years, like myself. You should be many, *many* orbits older, Nyctá. Come to think of it, you should be long dead. "

While the old man continued his tinkering and poking sizzling minerals, Nyctá felt like weeping and slicing her wrists. There were plenty of sharp options in the room, full of dull memories, growing hotter and sharper, with every word from the old man. The Name, Thémis, moved something inside her. But she had no recollection of childhood, no fragments to rearrange, no picture of some greater whole. Names were defining but Names were *names*, without context. Her age was meaningless when oblivion drew a curtain on her past. Nyctá surprised herself when she spoke back to the master-welder.

"My clearest memory from my past isn't a memory at all. It is an eater of Time. I fell into a Kronos Mushroom and lost twenty orbits. Everything before and to come stretched out. I'm not sure how long it's been since the Kronos. It could have been an orbit ago, or a hundred... Like a stone falling into the glow on the water, the image is rippled. I only know the shimmer. All that rippled onwards is lost."

"Things are always changing. Even the strongest blade is marked by every encounter. Things give but always take more. The only balance is new things up for the taking. Time always eats its own children. Your sword is the finest weapon I ever forged," Zeffá said, as sweat poured from his bald pate. In his hands, the mechanical was gleaming in its mineral-burnished renewal. "Sideon steel will make any other blade seem soft under its adamant nature, never mind flesh. But you know that, too well."

"You're mistaken. You haven't even touched my sword."

"I did. I touched the pommel when I was measuring your arm. Felt your hair, too. Are you trying to resemble a bird?"

"I..."

"No matter. I made the sword for you, when you came in here as a flaming youth. That blade is unmatched, as I've said. Harder than the clouds are soft. Not a blemish on it.

You're welcome for that. The funny thing is, you're not much older in form, but you are certainly ancient now in spirit, even in your confusion."

"You mean you knew me? Directly? I could strangle and hug you, if I didn't—"

"You have changed. And not just your hawk-hair and voice. The *Weir* is in you. I wish I knew what that will mean for you. You're probably doomed," he laughed, to himself. "And I'd say it was up to you to decide how much of you is *you* and how much of it is Mēna. But there's no way to know where you begin and she ends and so on, in an endless cycle of mind fucks, to the infinite. You were an eager Reaper, long before Reapers turned feral. Lack of clear command keeps them scattered, in spite of their ruthless ways. You held a knife to my throat to make you that sword. You knew nothing but the moment at hand. You were less than a beast, since beasts are still true to themselves. That was before the Weir, Mēna, *wormed* herself into you, before she died. Tell me? Did she Whisper into your ear just before, or after you slit her throat?"

"I have no recollection.. When—"

"Take your mechanical!" Zeffá growled, as his face turned to manic torment. "It's near perfect now! Never shake your sword at me! You already took my daughter! She was a child! Innocent! And you speak with a stolen voice! What else do you want?! Get out! OUT! Torala! Take her someplace else! She smells of Reaper! Torala! Do you hear me, you fool?!"

"Nyctá!" Briar shouted, from the hole to the corridor. "Come! This way!"

"Thank you, Torala!" Zeffá wailed, rocking back and forth, with his massive hands over his face.

Nyctá grabbed her mechanical and strode to Briar, who pulled her into the dark corridor. He took a deep breath and sighed as Nyctá stood with her mechanical shaking in her good hand.

"Zeffá has the Memory Worm," Briar said. "It appeared before I left this place. He's only gotten worse. Such is the nature of it. I'm surprised it took him that long to fall back into the past."

"I don't know," Nyctá whispered. "He knew more about my past than me. It felt true. The end of it was my doing."

"Well..."

"Did I take his daughter?"

"As sure as your name is, Nyctá? But it's not that simple, is it... I was just a child when that happened. Names are as drifting as water. I was a thief just a turn ago and you were still called, Mēna. We do shitty things to survive and try to atone in the stolen life that follows. Let him simmer down, alone. We've got work to do."

"I'm leaving with Shixee, *tonight*."

"Leaving? Just like that? What about Ruthy?"

"We got her this far and she's better off with all of you. I have nothing left for her. Keep eyes on her. Keep her fingers out of the dirt, too. She might open the pits of Hell, next time. I've hardly had time with her, but it's clear she's manipulating more than mycelium. I can't believe I'm telling a thief to watch his back. What the two of you get into is no concern of mine."

"That won't happen again. It was a stolen moment, nothing more. There's nothing between us that furthers that encounter. Both she and I were somewhere far away from the moment. The divine Name, Daphnē, was passing her lips, over and over. She must still believe in the Goddess. I might, too, if I survived a fall from such a height and happened upon luck like you. Well, you and I know better, eh? I don't think I'm betraying her by telling you that. But don't tell her I said anything."

"I have nothing left to say to her that matters. She sees something in me that doesn't exist, an idea, filled with her fantasies. That's dangerous in a soul as powerful as she is. She eyes the sky, so don't imagine she has any intentions of helping your long-winded cause. Let her ambitions take her where they will... Now, let me pass, before I—"

"*Stay*. You could help us pull something off...redeem everything. *Make a real difference*. You should sleep on it before you do anything rash, *Nyctá*. You could use some sleep."

"Dreams only make it worse. There's too much for me to fix."

"There's nothing out there to fix what you have. And there's no Weirs left to help with what lies within. I took the solitary path, after I lost Torala and found nothing, until I happened to fail at robbing you. Maybe I'm being selfish. I'm damned good at that. But we need you. *Ruthy* needs you, no matter her secrets. You are, who you are, now. *Here*. Let your actions to come define your Name. I've done plenty of wretched things in my selfish life and I probably will again. A thousand tomorrows of good deeds won't fix that, but it's better than the alternative."

"The difference is, you remember them. I wish you well, but cutting the tracks of Sky Tracer won't change a thing. Reapers will remain, just like I did. Such *stuff* is as natural as darkness in this Age. My words are my own. Sky Tracer will find its place in the sky, again, before you fall back down. Sky Tracer reigns over this realm for a reason. And I can't imagine how you think you're making it above the clouds. Whoever is up that Tree will fix whatever it is you're risking your life to cut. Cut a shroom down and ten take its place, just like Reapers. Everybody knows that. Sky Tracer is as fixed in the sky as the spore cloud nourishing Ümfalla. You must feel that to be true, as I do. Your people's quest is a dream and nothing more. *Just like mine was.* You can't resurrect or destroy what doesn't exist. Save yourself and the rest and find something else to fight for. You've been honorable to us, Briar. Even if you're still just a fucking thief," Nyctá said, as she walked down the corridor.

"And you're a better person than you think!" Briar laughed, before his face settled and he closed his eyes in torment.

13

CARVED WORDS

WHEN NYCTÁ RETURNED TO the main chamber, everyone fell silent. Not only was she an imposter in the stronghold beneath the Falls, she felt unwelcome in her own skin, but there was no sign of Shixee or Ruthy. Bríar eyed an adjoining corridor, hinting their whereabouts. Nyctà nodded to the hint and headed down the corridor.

In her moment of solitude, Nyctá recognized the masterwork of Zeffá. She felt the skill in not being able to feel much at all. A new set of elegant screws of sleeker and more symmetrical form—as well as Sideon steel—penetrated places in the mechanism of the shoulder, elbow and wrist, with far more precision than the hard-functioning, from before. Adjoining strips on the mechanical were burnished to a renewed gleam, glorifying the streamlined construction. Changes in her arm, through growth and battles, had been accounted for by Zeffá.

In a short period, the old master with the Memory Worm, proved his gnarled hands had forgotten nothing. For the first time in her life, Nyctá was proud to wear the mechanical from the old man willing to share his gift with a forgetful monster.

Near the end of the winding corridor, there was a tell-tale shine from mineral-lanterns, only a soul with sunborne eyes would gather. She winced at the light, upon entering, imparting nothing but blue brightness outside the back of her hand.

"Ruthy?" Nyctá cringed, looking away from the bright glow. "I'm leaving with Shixee. You made it this far... I know you miss the light, but spread it out a bit, so I can see you. Ruthy? I understand. You have a right to avoid me. We saved each other's lives. I owe you parting words. Nothing?"

After carrying the lanterns by their top rings, to the far side of the chamber, Nyctá turned to find a knife was stuck into the table, vertically. Not a soul besides herself was in the room. Nyctá leaned over the table and recognized the knife, hers, until Ruthy took it to stab Dorian enough times to lose count. Letters were carved into the receiving surface of the tree-stone table. Nyctá's eyes regained focus, as she read:

I AM SORRY

HAD TO FIX MY THINGS

MY HEART THANKS YOU

YOU ARE MEENA

ALWAYS

They were the first words Nyctá recalled reading in her scattered existence. Like so many skills she possessed, she read without any recognition *how* she learned to do it. She pulled the knife out of the tree-stone and returned it to her single empty sheathe, amongst the nine on her waist. She rocked back and forth with her fingers clenching the edge of the table. When that portion of the table broke in her grasp, a voice regarded the action.

"Come with me," Briar said, from the entryway.

"Why are you always lurking in places where you're unwanted," Nyctá seethed, through clenched teeth.

"*Shixee* needs you."

Nyctá bolted past Briar and returned to the main chamber where Callisto and three others were holding Shixee against a stone wall. Nyctá drew Slender in stride and struck the main lantern at the center of the room into pieces, leaving scattered minerals, twinkling all around. Nyctá's eyes gleamed in the darkness, as she stood with Slender in her left hand, while her right arm bulged within the mechanical.

"Lōkung ē Phibian!

Release the Phibian!"

"Never cower at her double-tongue!" Callisto shouted, over her shoulder, as she pressed her knee into Shixee's back. "Send her back to the Sinels to rot, Briar!"

It was a quick disturbance of air and nothing more, as far as the sound. When everyone perceived what transpired, the action proved to be of another sort. Slender was *stuck* in the air, mid-stroke, by Nyctá's contrary hands.

The edge of the blade was no more than a hair's breadth from Callisto's neck. Nyctá's right hand, the hand subject to the mechanical, was pulling the stroke away from its target, while her left one struggled to finish the action. By the time Callisto perceived it, she knew someone else kept her head on her shoulders.

"*Mēna*," Callisto whispered, as she ducked the blade and stepped up to Nyctá. "Say something to me, Mēna. I know it's you in there. Say—"

In the midst of Callisto's plea, Shixee slipped through the grasp of Elēa and Fálon. Shixee Whispered into Callisto's ear and bolted, before anyone perceived what was unfolding.

Shixee closed her lips, wiped away a smattering of foam from the quick Whisper and dashed behind Nyctá, who was holding Slender, limply, at her side.

While Shixee attempted to make herself as small as possible, behind a bewildered Nyctá, Callisto was in a reverie of her own, after Weir-words found her ear. A trickle of foam fell from the sides of Shixee's mouth, but the copious foam from times before was absent.

"*She's a Foam Weir*," Elēa gasped, running her fingers through her white hair, splaying across her broad back.

"You told us she lacked the gift of her kind, Briar!" Fálon pointed, as sweat dripped from his boyish brow.

"I've only known the Phibian for a turn or so," Briar held up his long fingers, in supplication.

"Do you know what this means?" Elēa smiled.

"Enough!" Callisto shouted. "That's enough. Focus on the problem at hand, before we plan for the push upwards."

"What did she Whisper to you, Callisto?" Elēa asked.

"That's between us. But it was enough keep me from executing whoever *she* is," Callisto grimaced, eyeing Nyctá. "You don't have to hide behind her, Phibian. You could have Whispered me back to childhood and left me weeping on the floor for the state of the world. But you took a foolish chance. Tell us exactly what you did for Ruthy."

"Oh, the Goddess, Shixee," Nyctá moaned, looking over her shoulder at her. "What did you do? Where's Ruthy?"

"Ruthy is on her way back," Shixee said, still clinging to Nyctá's legs.

"On her way back?!" Nyctá shouted. "She can't even swim."

"But I can. Very well."

"So you just swam her back across and into the belly of the beast? She's groping in the dark with sunborne eyes! Shixee! What have you done?!"

"She asked me to do it," Shixee said, standing up behind Nyctá, while keeping her arms around her. "There is a hole in the rock back there and she needed me to swim her out, without anyone seeing. She has truths to find, beyond anything we can imagine."

"Why? What is she plotting?" Nyctá asked, with her eyes clenched shut and the tip of Slender on the stone floor.

"Please remember, I am only relating to you what she told me," Shixee said, closing her eyes. "She told me...*tell them not to try and follow me. I know how to end this. I will fix what should have been broken, long ago. I thought I could do it all from here. I was wrong. I need to bring what I found back to the source.*"

"Where the fuck did she go?" Nyctá asked.

"She told me not to say," Shixee muttered.

"*I* am telling you to say," Nyctá said.

"My mind feels torn in two," Shixee winced. "When we reached the shore and walked into a mushroom cluster, Ruthy put her hands into the ground to speak through it. There was no running water near enough for me to listen. But in a few moments, a pair of be-Whispered Spiders drifted down from the greater mushrooms, ones that grow up and up, until they reach the trunk of the Tree of the Ancients. Someone already Whispered to them and they were looking for Ruthy. This must have been a very powerful Weir to do so, from such a distance. Ruthy knew their hidden Names and climbed onto their backs, with great skill and resolve. Ruthy possesses a power like I have never seen, a Oneness with the elements. It took great effort for her to hide its reach from all of you. But I believe she did it out of a greater good, not pure deceit. I am drifting like water... She only looked back for a moment, before the Spiders drew themselves upwards with their silver strings and vanished into the thick of the mushroom cluster. That is all I know."

Eléa cursed to herself before she spoke, "We should execute the Phibian for this. The Ginger was our only way of cracking the mystery of The Dim Light."

Callisto smiled, "The Phibian will find a place of honor amongst us, for what she's done."

"What?!" Eléa cried.

"Both for what she did to me and for helping the Ginger escape."

"You've gone mad from the Whispers," Eléa said.

"No. The Whispers cleared me of my selfishness. Cleared away orbits of words, signifying nothing. *Think about it*. We know the Phibian can Whisper and we know the way up is through Whispering to Spiders from Sky Realm."

"I fucking hate spiders," Eléa shuddered.

"Nobody forget," Briar announced, with his hands in the air, "I was the one who brought them here."

"Shut up, Briar!" Callisto shouted, with a grin. She looked back to Shixee, "If I take you to the Spiders at the base of the Tree, you can Whisper to them and tell them to take us up?"

"You don't have to do anything, Shixee," Nyctá said, with her battle-bright eyes on Callisto.

"It is possible," Shixee said, holding onto Nyctá's waist, even tighter. "But not that simple. The Spiders must be drawn to the ground from webs they weave in the heights of the cloud. It must be very enticing. The ones on the ground are rogues, lone Spiders, eaters of rodents and insects, with no gifts for Weaving. The ones who climb are far different, eaters of flesh. I hope you understand what that demands."

"Blood," Callisto said. "Blood will have blood and all of us will offer our own."

"I do not know what waits for you up the Tree of the Ancients," Shixee said. "Some say the spirit of the Goddess haunts the branches. Wind blows, so fiercely, people go mad. The best way is not to go up. Everything we need is here. I—"

"This is where your words stop," Callisto said, while she paced back and forth.

"You do not have eyes to see this through, Nyctá," Shixee said, softly, taking her hand. "Ruthy is finding her own way. Just like you must. Where you choose to go, I go. Everywhere except for up. Up, means never coming down. Up, is no place for me. The waterless wind would finish me."

"Shixee," Nyctá began, "Both of us know Ruthy has power beyond imagining. She holds an elemental magic capable of doing far more than moving earth and making dark shrooms bright. Her rashness could lead to horror for this realm. She carved a few words to me back there and she's intent on *fixing things*. I've only known her for a few turns, but even if she intends to do good, her power could throw everything into chaos. She was willing to jump from Sky Tracer to get here. Just imagine what she'll do now that she's headed back with whatever fucking thing she found down here. Shixee, you of all souls knows about balance in the realms. Never mind these fucking zealots," she glanced to Callisto. "These fools think cutting a thread will set things right. If I know anything about Ruthy, beyond her power, it's that something bigger is at work. She has more than herself in mind. My words are...I don't know what they are anymore."

"Resolve is in your eyes," Shixee said, squeezing Nyctá's waist hard. "I cannot bear to see you leave."

Callisto scoffed, "Plan on *flying* to Sky Realm with your eyes closed? Eyes like yours would go blind in the sun."

"Nyctá!" Briar called out, as he trotted up to her. "I see it in your bright eyes, too. You're resolute. These fuckers are going to get themselves killed. But they've been aching to climb to their deaths for too many orbits to count. It'll be a relief, so the world won't have to hear their banter anymore. Fools, all of them. But I'll go up, if you do."

"I'd be as bewildered as Ruthy was down here, if I go up. Unless you've got a spare pair of eyes," Nyctá said.

"Funny you should mention that. I know a guy," Briar winked.

"Don't you dare say it, or I'll—"

"*See what happens*," Briar said, trotting towards the corridor, with his cloak swaying along the stone floor.

"You don't have to do this for them, Shixee," Nyctá said, squeezing Shixee's hand. "I'll kill anyone who forces you to do anything. Whatever is left of my soul, I open to you and you alone. You, alone, I trust."

"I am a part of this," Shixee said. "I cannot remember doing anything this important and ill-fated before. But I have forgotten many things. I will try. *See what happens*, just like Briar said. You must return, so that we can search together, for what you think you lost. But I have to confess something to you, Nyctá."

"What is it?"

"I am terrified of Spiders."

14

HOLD OF THE HAIRY BACKS

O VER THE COURSE OF a turn, provisions were gathered, along with the souls who would be going up. Shixee believed she could Whisper to one of the Spiders of Avernus, before breathtaking foam from her effort followed.

Weaving Spiders always traveled in threes, the female being head of the three-part arrangement, while males alternated duties of defense and food-gathering. It was the female who made decisions and weaved webs in the moisture of the spore cloud, where eggs thrived and prying eyes would never see. But all of the intelligence was based on scattered memories from the Phibian, who insisted, she might be wrong.

Callisto demanded everyone daring the heights to speak up on their own behalves before any official inclusion. Each one spoke up out of duty, rather than seeking remembrance through words. The six who would be going up included:

- Callisto: '*This is our destiny*'

- Elēa: 'I *hate* Spiders'

- Pippa: 'I'm going because Fálon is'

- Fálon: 'I'm going because Pippa is'

- Briar: 'See what happens'

- Nyctá: ?

They left the stronghold through an obscure passageway, under the falls, beyond the chamber where Zeffá's forge burned and the old man was lost in his present-pasts. When they emerged into open night, the Seething Falls were behind them and tremendous roots ran throughout the landscape.

To the northeast, a monolith blotted out the horizon, in its inky-black monstrousness. Nyctá had no memory of ever seeing the Tree of the Ancients from such proximity. The force of nature was a Singular totem, piercing the spore cloud and pointing to infinity, the primal source of the world's power and mystery. The Tree was *All*.

Around Nyctá's neck, a pair of onyx-glass goggles were hanging by a pliant silk string. Circular black lenses were polished to near perfection and fit snugly to Nyctá's eyes. When she tried them on, in the dim light of the stronghold, she saw almost nothing. She only hoped light above the clouds would brighten the false darkness through black lenses.

There was the possibility that the maker of the goggles, Zeffá, found a way to take his deserved revenge, for his lost daughter. Like everything else concerning the Tree, nothing was certain, while everything else was in the realm of the absurd. All she needed was enough light and luck to rediscover Ruthy and keep her from trying to *fix things*.

Nyctá's leverage to be included amongst the six was her direct connection to Ruthy. Any kind of asset above the clouds was precious and sacrifices had to be made, as far as the outsider's inclusion. Callisto was stern in her resolve when it came to riding with Nyctá. After her near beheading, back in the stronghold, Callisto refused to turn her back on the outsider. But Nyctá recognized Callisto had a deeper reason for keeping her within earshot, the way Callisto looked at her in unguarded moments, while she watched and waited for her lost *Mēna's* reemergence.

In the meantime, Nyctá walked alongside Shixee, who was relying on dew and diminishing springs to remain strong, on her way to Whisper. Every step took them closer to the Tree and those same steps counted down time until the Phibian and warrior parted.

"Are you sure you want to do this?" Shixee asked, grazing Nyctá's leg with her webbed fingers.

"No," Nyctá said. "But there's no choice. This is something more than seeking my shattered past. Ruthy possesses a power beyond Weirs. She's a force of nature. I doubt her as much I feel the need to help her. Even if she refuses it. Perhaps I fear *her* more than anything. This is beyond Wandering through my imagined past."

"Here is your world. Down here, where your eyes were made to see. Here, is where you were meant to be. Up there, is bright and windblown and hard. Polished onyx are all your eyes hope to see through. Look at me. You see me. See me, seeing you."

"I see you, Shixee. And you are the only one I'm coming back to. Do you think you can hold things together while I'm gone?"

"That was pushing away."

"A little."

"I will listen for you in the water. Watch for you in the Sinels. I know who you are. You are you and do not need a Name or memories to *be*. I carry on, even if I forgot all the lives I lived. I have made mistakes forgotten and will make mistakes to come," Shixee halted. "*This is the place.*"

Nothing in Ümfalla was more apparent than the base of the Tree of the Ancients. A translucent shell covered the entirety of the trunk, leaving the bark beneath preserved in crystal. Callisto ran her hand along the surface and her fingertips squeaked along its sleek surface. What came down the Tree would never come back up, not without a line to take them back up and into the unknown, beyond the spore cloud.

"So where do we do this?" Callisto called out.

Shixee squeezed Nyctá's hand, answering, "All of you must offer your blood to the Tree. The Spiders of Avernus must learn your scent and taste it, to carry you. No matter what you do, you must not harm them. That will scare them away and they will not return. They will probably try to eat you on the way up. But that is not their fault."

"Is that a joke to scare the fear out of me?" Elēa moaned.

"No," Shixee said. "This is no time for a joke."

"That's hilarious," Briar chuckled.

"Well, can't stand around here fucking around forever," Elēa said, through a tremulous voice, placing her knife blade to her left palm.

"No!" Nyctá shouted. "Don't cut your palm like a fool. Do you want to be able to use it? Cut here," she placed her knife blade on the outside of her forearm, where the least damage could be done.

Shixee pulled at Nyctá's hand, as she called out to the rest, "Remember to spread the blood across the base of the Tree."

"How long will it take?" Callisto asked.

"They will come, when they come," Shixee said, looking up into the murk of the clouds and the Tree. "I hope they do not," she muttered.

Callisto nicked the side of her wrist, without ceremony, allowing blood to drip on the slick surface. The rest followed and stared up into gloom. Blood ran down the surface of the Tree like quicksilver and quickly commingled. When Nyctá looked back to Shixee, the Phibian was mouthing silent words to herself, as she clenched and unclenched her long fingers.

"I know you're scared," Nyctá said to her. "You're braver than us all, Shixee. Be quick and graceful, as you always are," she said, holding Shixee's cheeks and kissing her softly on the top of her head.

"Yes," Shixee nodded. "I am so nervous."

"I'll watch over you," Nyctá winked.

"Any sign of them?" Elēa whispered. "I don't hear a thing."

"Everyone scatter!" Callisto shouted, with her head on a swivel. "Right behind you, *Elēa!*"

When Elēa turned, eight segmented-legs, issuing from a bulging mass, were closing just above desired prey. Somersaulting free from its grasp, Elēa realized the creature had almost taken her, like any insect.

In the blink of an eye, shimmering strings from silver webs, dropped two more giants from the darkness. The six scattered as the three Spiders tasted the blood offering, while they stared at the group through gleaming black eyes.

"Wish me luck, Nyctá," Shixee cried, before she bolted towards the queen.

Shixee appeared to shrink with her approach to the Spiders bound to a Tree, holding up an entire world, above the clouds. Drawing near the queen, Shixee crawled at a run, beneath eight hairy legs and vanished. Six companions stood, a stone's throw away, while the queen moved her enormous legs, at a frenzy. Shixee's gleaming eyes were visible beneath the abdomen, while the spinneret at the queen's tail was congested with liquid silk, resembling snot.

"She's stuck in there!" Elēa cried.

"If it lies down, she's finished!" Fálon moaned.

"Fuck this!" Nyctá grunted.

Nyctá bolted towards the consort Spider to the left of the queen and held out her bare hands, in front of its many eyes. Hundreds of her distorted reflections glared back from black mirrors in the Spider's convex eyes. The creature's mouth parted and revealed tremendous fangs, as long as Slender and dripping venom. Nyctá flicked trickling blood from her wrist, onto the ground, in front of the creature, drawing it closer to her.

The Spider hissed, like water thrown on embers, at the tantalizing offering. One of the ferocious legs stabbed at Nyctá, but she deflected the assault with the outside of her adamant mechanical. Distracted by the ruse, the queen parted a pair of her eight legs. Shixee pulled her lithe form up one of those legs and onto the hairy segment where head met back.

There were no ears for her to find, but Shixee recognized *hearing* occurred through many inlets in Nature. She took a last glimpse at Nyctá, before taking hold of the queen's tuft of hair on her neck. Shixee parted her lips. The Whisper came from somewhere deeper than the known, a place Shixee always possessed, but never named. Every one of the six companions felt the words but did not hear them. The queen was stilled as words passed into her arachnid mind. Water met web through silken Whispers.

The consorts watched and waited with sixteen anxious legs and a thousand worrisome eyes between them. When Shixee's hands went limp and her body fell from the queen, Nyctá was there to catch her. She carried her, in stride, to the embankment a stone's throw away and set her down on wet moss as foam poured from her mouth.

"Everyone onto their backs! Now!" Callisto shouted. "No time for goodbye's, Reaper! Cmon!"

"I'll miss you more than I can say, Shixee," Nyctá whispered to the Phibian, through heavy breaths.

She struck Shixee on the back and foam poured from the Phibian's mouth. When Shixee opened her eyes, Nyctà was taking Callisto's hand, as she climbed onto the back of the queen. Elēa was screaming when Briar forced her hands onto wiry hair, on the back of the Spider. Just as Pippa secured her feet into a deep segment of the Spider's back, the queen and her consorts jumped in unison and their silken-silver strings, tied to the unknown, above, took them up and up, until the three creatures were nothing but three receding dots in the heights.

Shixee swore she caught Nyctá's bright eyes looking back at her, just before they vanished into the thick of the spore cloud. Sky Tracer appeared like magic from the clouds and its pale red light made Shixee sicker to her stomach than she already was. She cleared her mouth of more foam and bubbles burst, vanishing into the moss. Shixee refused to look back up. She would see Sky Tracer, again and again, in the solitary turns to come.

Part II

'The sun is new again, all day'
Heraclitus

15

THE WAY UP IS THE WAY BACK

"THIS PLAN IS SHIT!" Briar shouted, as the Spider Queen and her two consorts zipped up the tree on their silver threads, not a stone's throw apart from each other.

"Stick out your tongue!" Nyctá laughed, with her tongue dangling. "You can taste the cloud!

"Better pull up those lenses!" Briar grimaced, as the consort Spider he was holding, drifted closer to the queen. "When we make it through, I don't want you falling blind on me!"

"No!" Nyctá yelled. Wind from the sheer speed of the Spider's ascent whipped her hawk-hair back. "I'm not missing this!"

"My ears are crackling like lichen underfoot! " Callisto shouted, pressing her body hard against Nyctá's. "And I can't see anything!"

"I can!" Nyctá laughed, with utter abandon. "If you laugh, it'll help clear your ears!"

Nyctá held fast to thick white hairs on the Spider's back, while keeping the toes of her boots in an adjoining segment. Wonder rushed in, through her journey into the heart of the spore cloud. Gradations of ochres and grays, purples and yellows, swirled throughout. Spores glittered the scene, like a rainbow blown into dust.

A dangling egg cluster, larger than Nyctá, appeared and was gone, as the Spiders continued their ascent. When the queen avoided another cluster of eggs, it was apparent they were her own. Through the medium of air, the Spiders lost any sense of *bigness* and found an ascending grace, soaring and drifting, weaving beauty through the dark ether, only matched through the horror of their fanged visages.

Eléa screamed when the queen took a bite at her dangling leg and missed. Her face remained pale and bore a look of utter horror, riding on the back of her greatest fear, incarnate. Her youthful face was as tangled in fear as her hair, while she cursed the world, above and below. As she did, the Spiders passed a collection of husks in an entanglement of web.

In the gloom, Nyctá and Callisto came face-to-face with a clump of mummified human skulls, complete with petrified screams, there and gone. The churn from the cloud grew turbulent, while an ethereal glow hinted what was above.

Murk turned to mist, as the queen quickened her ascent. Nyctá pulled on her goggles and perceived nothing but flickering grays, before light from the cloudless sky found her onyx lenses. Everyone cringed when they entered the blinding light, all except Nyctá, who was the first to *see* the splendor above the clouds. She whispered a prayer to Zeffá for his gift, the gift of sunlit sight, to *see* magnificence emerging.

Everything was too much, from the blue emptiness, to the brightness of the sun. The Tree they were ascending was more than a force of nature, it was a lofted world upon the world below. The receding spore cloud resembled the ghost of a dark sea. Thousands of birds moved as one, throughout twisting branches of the Tree, reaching up and out of sight. From Nyctá's perspective, she was falling upwards and would continue to do so, until all was blue emptiness.

When the north wind blew across Nyctá's face and sent the queen and her consorts soaring across the sky, her eyes drifted shut. In the darkness of her own being, Nyctá listened to a cacophony of Whispers, all at once. Haunted wind commanded her to listen and filled her with the sense to *hear*. Her lips moved in accordance and nothing existed outside herself.

A single Voice emerged from the multitudes and called her by her genuine Name. She knew the Voice, breathed its truth, as surely as the words resonated through her spirit. That Name took root, like an old memory tucked into fresh soil, hidden, but waiting to emerge into the light of knowing. As soon as the Voice faded, she opened her eyes and was falling.

For the first time in her life, Nyctá experienced herself as a weightless being, free from life's heaviness, in a world where up always came down, in a relatively short amount of time. A silver shimmer in the blue was followed by the Spider's gaping jaws, drifting towards her. She was multiplied in the thousand eyes of the Spider, eyes as black as her own goggles, before Briar's hand found hers. Briar yanked Nyctá underneath him, as the Spider continued to fall, in a windblown drift towards a tremendous branch, rushing up to crush them.

Slowed to a sudden halt through the silken thread, the three companions tumbled off the Spider's backs and into the copious ferns of their new world, before the queen and her consorts deposited the other three around and on top of the fallen. The Spiders hissed collectively, as they plummeted back into the murk on their silver threads and into the spore cloud, many fathoms below.

The six companions remained in a heap, in a collective state of shock and awe. Aromatics from a new world were as bewildering as the blue sky. It was Callisto who made the first move when she climbed over Briar and Pippa and leaned over Nyctá, who was staring at the blueness above.

"*What the fuck was that*?" Callisto seethed, while her eyes watered from naked light. "Never forget you're carrying someone inside of you far more precious than yourself. Pull yourself together, Mēn...*focus.*"

"Oh, I was focusing. Until you blocked my view," Nyctá laughed. Her laughter grew deeper and uncontrollable.

"The fuck is so funny?" Callisto frowned, before a wry smile found her and she broke out into laughter, herself.

Pippa, Elēa, Briar and Fálon all began to laugh, as well, while Callisto fell beside Nyctá and they all shared in the absurdity of it all. Birds of prey and those preyed upon, circled and darted overhead, while tree mice, reptiles, butterflies and woodland creatures of stranger shapes and sizes, scurried through the thick ferns and grasses all around them. Their laughter was carried by the wind, beyond Sky Realm and into a further unknown.

"So...," Briar began, while they all stared at the sky, "how are we getting down?"

Pippa stifled her laughter, "Leave it to you to tell a joke and ruin the laughter."

"The hard part's over," Elēa said. "Now that I'm not holding onto that Spider's ass hair, the rest seems easy enough. Just a little cut and The Dim Light comes crashing down."

"Is anyone else seeing this?" Fálon asked, as the rest sat up.

It was as meaningless to call the ground they were seated upon, a branch, as it was to call, Ümfalla, a speck of dust. The branch-scape was meadow-like, with occasional gaps, giving way to emptiness. Black soil resided in scant spaces between the enormity of ferns, ranging from fiddle heads the size of greater mushrooms, to clusters of ribbed ferns in all the newfound colors of the rainbow. Grasses and woody shrubs were home to caterpillars and iridescent flies, whose wings played games with sunlight. Floral aromatics, ethereal children of the sun, overwhelmed the six companions, struggling to look beyond the bountiful world at their feet.

The main trunk of the Tree rose to heights unseen and shimmered in its crystal tomb. Interlocking layer upon layer of smaller worlds loomed on branches, reaching in twisting directions, throughout the sky. Westward, windmills were spinning secrets. Crystal structures shimmered in the evening light, upon wooded islands in the sky, skirted by balustrades of twisting vines.

Dizzying latticeworks of webs and lichen, hanging mosses and air ferns, amongst the landscapes of branches, imparted the new world with a labyrinthine feel. The Eternal Storm claimed the entirety of the horizons, flickering through lightning strikes, too distant to be heard.

"Where do we begin?" Elēa muttered.

"Not that way," Briar said, looking over his shoulder, to the distant storm.

"That looks like the Goddess is angry with us," Elēa said.

Pippa looked back at the storm and whispered, "It looks like the end of the world."

"Everyone breathe in your wonder and let it go," Callisto said, pulling errant Spider hairs from her celium shirt. "The only way to begin is that way," she pointed ahead. "The rest will follow with a better look at the structure of this place. Looking for your princess up there, Nyctá?"

"The only way is up," Nyctá said, squinting her eyes, as she adjusted to onyx-filtered light. "*Look there*, how this place merges with the next branch. If Ruthy is anywhere, it's up there. Power always seeks the heights."

"We're not concerned with her," Callisto said. "I brought you along for *one* reason. The Ginger made her own choice. If we run into her, along the way, either she helps us, or we pass her by. It might be more reasonable to kill her. If she's not already one of those husks we passed on the way up."

"Did anyone else hear that?" Pippa muttered, looking up and around.

"Be wary," Callisto said. "Everything here is new to us. Especially, the wind. Let's get moving."

While the wind played tricks with Fálon's thick black curls, across his shoulders, he said, "*So vast...* I don't see The Pale Light."

"Yeah, no shit," Briar laughed. "But if we live into the night, we might get a glimpse."

Pippa tensed, "You all must have heard that!"

"It's nothing, Pippa," Callisto said.

"No," Nyctá said. "I hear it, too. It sounds like... Everybody down!"

"AAAAAAAAAAAAAAAHHHHHH!"

16

INTERTWINED MEMORIES IN BLACK

CRYSTAL MELDED SEAMLESSLY WITH wood.

Overarching branches and their exquisite offshoots, shaped by centuries of wind and growth, constituted the chamber overlooking the vast realm of Avernus. The chamber was alive with air ferns, dancing in the wind, while tangled ivy made wooden pillars look like totems to the deity in charge of things that grow. Pollen-rich flowers were haunted by bees and butterflies, while the room itself was carved into the branch, so long ago, the elaborate space of geometric precision appeared a natural attribute of the Tree of Avernus.

She stood in a silk dress. Its sheer fabric played games with light, in a fashion akin to the crystal walls. It was tailored to perfection and reached the woman's shins. The dazzling garment had no predetermined color but the light passing through, revealing its prismatic and reflective quality. Wind made it shimmer, as if the dress were a living thing. A long and thick braid of crimson hair reached to her ankles where her bare feet still bore blisters from days past. Within that braid, a finger-thick strand of raven black hair was intertwined with her own.

Most eyes in the room stared at her in relief she had returned, while admiring her wild beauty. She winced when a beam of light reflected into her weary eyes. Above her was nothing but the cloudless sky. She struggled with an uncanny sensation: If she jumped, she would tumble upwards and fall into blue oblivion. She did not jump, not this time, but glanced up carved stairs of glistening wood, leading to the Seven Seats of the House of the Elders.

One of the seven was leaning forward, in his elaborately carved chair, with depictions of flora and fauna, ranging from the humble bee, to Night Skimmers. His gnarled hands gripped the arms of the chair, while his errant white hair made him look electrified. The rest of the Elders remained with their backs against their chairs, staring into the distance, in deep reflection. The old man leaning forward parted his thin lips and his long teeth resembled an animated Death's Head.

"Arethūsa!"

"Borēan?"

"I see. This is what it has come to. *Stupid* girl. You spend a few turns with the heathens and think you can forsake your position. Never call me by my Name."

"Then remind me, again...what do I call you? My Keeper? Or how about, my creepy old man who gets what he wants and expects me to consider him a father? I hate to remind you, but incest fell out of fashion, before the last Hardening. Even if merely thinking you're my father makes it so."

"You speak like them, too. The Hardening is nothing more than a legend spewed by mud-eaters, who can't even keep time. And they have no history without writing, no culture. Word of mouth is as reliable as the wind."

"Seems to always blow pretty *northerly* here, *Borēan*," Arethūsa grinned. "Oh, c'mon! That was funny. Your Name unimaginatively means—"

"*The North Wind*! And you must come to answer to yours, Arethūsa. Only the Goddess knows why you would have done such a thing as you did. Do you not understand how fortunate you are? In all of my orbits, as one of the Seven Rulers of this realm, I have never seen someone as foolish and *lucky* as you. This is why—"

"Lucky?" Arethūsa laughed. "I'm sick to death of hearing that. I jumped with the expectation of the darkness keeping me. It seemed like a pretty sure bet the fall would kill me. Luck? No! It was a curse. I did find luck, afterwards, but that's a tale unsuitable for your half-deaf ears. The last thing luck could bring me is back to this place."

"And yet you returned, Arethūsa," Borēan said.

"Ruthy."

"What?"

"I prefer to be called, *Ruthy*."

"A heathen name, for heathen fancies. At least you had the sense to contact Yala and get out of that Fungal Realm and back where you belong, where you are needed. But your misinformation, your attempt at cunning with the messages you sent, prior to your cry for help, was borderline treason.

"So if I take one more little step, I'm a traitor?"

"Something like that."

"*Good.*" She took a histrionic step.

"The spores have rattled your brain. You had a little adventure and believe yourself to be liberated from your duties. Children play such games. And what's that filth in your hair?"

"This?" Arethūsa half-smiled, pulling her long braid into her hands. She traced the intertwined black hair as she spoke, "A powerful Weir, who lived in a cursed mushroom, gave this to me. Something to always remember her by. If you touch it, you'll be cursed, too."

"A Weir?" Borēan balked. "Down there, in the darkness? There's not even a breath of wind for them to Whisper."

"Oh, yes. Weirs don't need the wind, down there. We fell instantly in love. She gave me this strand of her hair, just before we made passionate and enduring love to each other. We made love until she Whispered us to sleep. Then we dreamed together and we found each other in the dream and explored a boundless world, without limits. She's coming for me. Soon. You'll see. Don't you believe me? Are your silent Elders blushing, or is it just the light? If wisdom is silence, the Elders are fucking geniuses"

"Your words mean nothing," Borēan grimaced, looking at his fellow Elders, to his sides.

"My words are carved. I've been waiting to speak to you this way, for orbits. Now I just don't give a shit."

"If any of that is true, your actions with the woman were a perversion against the Goddess. Women never share their bodies with each other, not out of love. You are too foolish to love anyone but yourself. Nothing can come from woman love but illusion and a barren world. I will confine your words to exhaustion and spore poisoning."

"If anyone ever craved another woman, it was the Goddess. She made that clear to me, long ago. Good ole' Daphnē knew better than to rest her divine lips on a dusty old cock like yours. I should have spoken this openly to you, from the start. It would have sped things up. I suppose my failed suicide unlocked my mouth from orbits of grinding my teeth in your presence. I'm surprised I have any left," she clicked her teeth.

"You love yourself too much to end it purposely. You are replaceable, Arethūsa! "

"Sure. But then you'd spend all your precious time replacing me with another one, day after day, after—"

"*Anything* but this."

"I have that thing within me that surpasses all. I just don't die. I just keep on giving and replenishing and it's something far beyond luck. You should have seen their faces, down there, when I showed them just a glimmer of my powers. You can replace a face, but not a gift. That's an eternal truth I know you understand. So do the rest of your silent consorts. Remind them to blink a little more often and they'd seem like they were actually living."

"Such a loose tongue after playing in the mud. Were it not for tradition, you'd have been dead, long ago."

"Tradition is the consensus of the dead," she laughed. "Just ask the *wizened* Elders at your side."

"*Yala*!" Borēan shouted to the heavens. "Yala! Make yourself seen!"

From the purlieus of the chamber, where carved wood and crystal was abounded by tangled ivy and flower blossoms, a woman in a thin black cloak emerged. Her eyes shone red, even in crepuscular light of early evening. Long limbs were instruments for her ageless body to seemingly float down the wooden stairs, until she reached Arethūsa. Black hair interspersed with white, flowed from her dark hood, where a serene face looked beyond Arethūsa and towards the labor ahead.

Borēan pointed with a flick of his wrist, "Escort, *Arethūsa,* to Daphnē. Take her out of my sight, Yala. Bring her back to reason."

"Come, Arethūsa," Yala said, in a resonant voice. "Daphnē, is waiting."

"She's always waiting," Arethūsa said, walking alongside Yala and into the boundless world, beyond the chamber.

Borēan groaned at their departure, but found solace when he faced the Elders to his left. Every one of them had seen much and weathered proverbial storms of the present Age. When Borēan looked to his right, the oldest of the Elders had the look of time-weariness, where nothing mattered but regretting mistakes of the past and watching present ones unfold, in silence. For the first time in many days, Borēan took a closer look at his consorts.

At their predestined time, each one of them sat down for the last time, before flowing minerals in the attendant black soil at their feet claimed them. Most of them faced petrification with stoic faces. But the youngest of the six, Līken, had a look of utter horror, a visage petrified in the crystal-clear encasing, an unbreakable shell, no different from the one covering the entirety of the trunk of the Tree of Avernus.

Borēan leaned to his right and looked on the wise face of his brother, Grōl. He was about to say something, on the petrified brink, for countless orbits to come. Borēan shuffled his feet beneath him, pulling up his dark robe in fear, disturbing the ritualistic soil. He spread his toes and stretched his feet in a counter-clockwise direction. Through the tickling breeze on his toes, fate had not caught up with him yet.

Arethūsa relished in the wind through lesser trees, along the winding path. No mushrooms were in sight, nor would there be, but she missed their earthy aromatics, the unpredictable glows and shapes, mystifying eyes like her own. Where the dark earth of Ümfalla screamed of power through her bare feet, the roots in Avernus exuded more of a hum.

Lesser trees remained as they were and showed their splendor through the shining auspices of the same old setting sun. But the sight of mighty Sky Shears, conducting murmurations of starlings at dusk, was a sight she would never call mundane.

The tremendous birds of prey always traveled in pairs and earned their names, every evening, when the dwindling light of the sun confused starlings. Precise murmurations, delving into U-shapes and rising in V's, turned to scattered abstraction when the sharp-winged Sky Shear bifurcated birds, by the dozens, with razor-sharp wings, while its partner caught bitesize halves of prey, below. Arethūsa was thrust back into the memory of Mēna slicing the Reaper in two with her own *shear*, Slender. She paused in her walk and Yala took notice.

"I like the Name you found for yourself," Yala said. "*Ruthy*... It suits you."

"Better than the pretentiousness of, *Arethūsa*. Who came up with that name, anyway? Nobody ever told me the answer to that mystery. They should have just left me as, 'Hey You!' And yet I'm still, *Arethūsa*, to everyone up here but you. Not for long, but I have to live with it, for now. That old bastard thinks he can make me regal with a multi-syllabic name. It's as senseless as calling those statues at his sides, *consorts*."

"You are in a dark place."

"I wish I was in a dark place."

"Yes. You miss it. You succeeded in your aim quickly. And yet you wanted to stay far longer than you did. I cannot blame you."

"What the hell, Yala? Do you read minds now, too? Cmon. Let's get this over with."

"You lied to her."

"Of course, I *lied* to her. Mēna is a force of nature, but she's not up to this. Besides, her eyes weren't made for this realm. What was I going to say to her? *I am the Conductor who keeps this fossil from falling over and wrecking Ümfalla?* Or that *your* sister keeps the cloud dark and perpetual? That if I end myself, countless others will fall in line? The list goes on..."

"No. I mean you lied to her about your intentions with Briar when you spoke to me through mycelium. You never told her the fundamental reason you risked death through your descent. She might have understood and made your ascension a little smoother. You did something you regret."

"The tree-bound Goddess! *Yes*, Yala. I never expected someone like Mēna. I couldn't reveal my deeper intentions. She might have considered me a lunatic and left me behind. Besides, I'll never see her again. But Briar proved himself far more capable than I can express. How he managed to track me down, when I fell so far off my mark, is beyond reason."

"Ībeka is an old friend of mine. The Weir I intended to help you in Ümfalla vanished. Such is the nature of the world. And yet I found Ībeka, the old Weir, so resilient in her ways, beyond Whispering. She went to great lengths to guide Briar. But you falling on a mushroom instead of the dead earth was a miracle. You missed the watery depths of The Mire, terribly. But here you are, whole, with allies growing alongside your purpose. Legend is already being written. Tracking down Orīa to convince Briar to join you was *my* luck. Orīa might prove to be a powerful ally."

"She sure moved Briar during the entanglement."

"Oh, I'm aware. Both Orīa and myself were moved, as well."

"It seemed like the reasonable thing to do at the moment and it actually felt good having someone hold me, someone who didn't want to do me harm or just fuck me. But I just ended up masturbating through mycelium, while someone happened to be holding me and finding a shared ecstasy. Sex is overrated, I swear to the Goddess on that one. It has its moments, but those moments are too few and brief for the effort. The mind is capable of far more wonders, especially, supercharged by mycelium. Then there's the awkwardness that follows and makes me feel like a foolish kid again. Tree roots are bores compared to mycelium. *Pure power*, Yala."

"I have an inkling," Yala smiled. "Remember, I was at the other end of your transmission. Beyond shared ecstasy, you put in motion something realm-changing, Ruthy. What follows from here...I don't know. I know you slept for the past day, but I need to tell you—"

"Your sister is free?"

"That's not funny, Ruthy. She remains bound to that abominable carriage."

"Sky Tracer. That's what she calls it."

"This, *Mēna,* you were just speaking of?"

"That's a damn good question, Yala. She's going by another Name now."

"That's something you know well, *Ruthy*. Perhaps she will decide on one."

"Too late for me to figure that one out. But most people are calling her, Nyctá, these days.."

"*The long night*? That's a bit redundant for the dark realm, don't you think?"

"Right?! But don't tell her that, if we ever go down there. She is *fierce*! You have no idea, Yala. Anyway, I call her Mēna. She *is* Mēna. Even if her stubborn Simmerian mouth won't say it."

"And yet you speak of her as if she were a part of the ends we seek."

"I'm still muddled from the journey. But she showed me a *good* time down there, all the sword mastery, the whole splendor of a real warrior. Wait...what were you going to tell me? Sorry. I just missed you, beyond words, Yala. And Borēan really grinds my wheels."

"And I missed you, Ruthy. I missed your heathen mouth."

"Smart ass."

"Perhaps. Ruthy...Stayx has been pacing his chamber and talking endlessly about you, ever since you returned."

"Are you still—"

"I do what I must, just like you do. Just like *we* must, to live. Enough of that. Stayx wants to speak to you about your time in Ümfalla."

"If he wants to know about his Reapers, tell him Mēna is their worst nightmare. And by the way, Reapers up here are nothing like the horrors in Ümfalla. They've gone feral. If not for Mēna, they would have scooped me up before I had a chance to take a few steps. They might have had orders from above to bring me back on Sky Tracer, but they seek their own grim ends. They really could use a little lesson on being quiet before they attack. Scared the shit out of me, but they really give themselves away. Actually, don't tell him that. That's between us. Let them all *rak-ak-kak* themselves to death, for all our sakes."

"Not that."

"What in the world could that blowhard want with news about the *Muddy Realm,* as *powerful* men like him choose to call it?"

"Who knows? He might be a blowhard, but he chooses his public words, carefully."

"Because he has nothing within that's private. *Great*. We're here."

"Wait," Yala said, stepping in front of Arethūsa and taking her hands. "You speak of passing ecstasies through the entanglement and yet you tell me nothing of how you intend to make this work. Your messages have been so grandiose, I thought you might be losing your mind. I will follow you into the endless dark. *You know this.* Your heart and mind are on fire."

"You speak as if I were about to die. I'm far too busy for that distraction. The only thing in me I'm going to kill is answering to the name, Arethūsa, after this is done. My messages to you before were scattered. There was never enough time. And raw mycelium was overwhelming to speak through, as powerful as it is. Anyway, there's little context when I speak through it. Someone else is always listening. *Always.* How am I supposed to really commune with you from afar, clearly, when we can't see each other's faces? We've related more through this idle banter than we could in a whole turn down there. Now...let's finish."

The last vestiges of light were glimmering over the Eternal Storm, to the west. Sky Shears were wreaking graceful havoc on the starlings and leaves on the gnarled tree in front of Arethūsa were withering. She pulled up her silk gown and knelt on the black soil beneath her, impressing her bare knees in the receiving earth. Elegant vines twisted thickly along the precipice of the branch, providing an exquisite barrier, should the wind pick up and blow anyone close to falling.

The tree before her was growing on the precipice of the great branch at the top of the Tree of Avernus. Its bark possessed deep striations with hairy vines growing within them. When Arethūsa looked upon the tree, twisted limbs, with heart-shaped leaves, were swaying in the wind. Her eyes drifted down and she was face-to-face with the Goddess.

Daphnē was in silent repose within the confines of the tree and secure in her translucent mineral captivity. Her skeletal arms were crossed over her bare chest and her forest green hair flowed over them, until her navel marked the place where the woody trunk of her prison obscured her lower half.

Although her eyes were closed, vestiges of life were in them. Beneath the mineral, within the tree and under her eyelids, the Goddess Daphnē still had power. The soft glow of her skin betrayed it. A yellow leaf blew free in the wind and stuck in Arethūsa's hair.

"I hear you," Arethūsa said, digging her fingers into black soil. "Look at you, Daphnē. I leave you alone for a handful of days and you already go to the yellow leaf. Do you have any idea what this costs? Huh? Silence is not wisdom, Daphnē. In case you were wondering, I took a trip on Sky Tracer. I just got up and left and stowed away on that carriage across the sky. Want to know what it does, Daphnē?"

"Focus, Arethūsa," Yala called out, from behind. "You will only make it worse, if you do not."

"Just getting back into the rhythm," Arethūsa said, digging her fingers in deeper and closing her eyes. "Anyway, Daphnē. Where was I? Oh yeah. All the things I learned.

Figured you'd want to know, since you're stuck here. That carriage is nothing but a convenient way to carry kids from Ümfalla to the Screaming Branch of this abominable Tree. While I play in the dirt with you, some unfortunate soul is getting cooked. I'm the Conductor and they are the fuel. I never *knew,* but I should have. I'm here in my fucking dress, talking to you, while some kid is being turned to cinders, so I can fondle your insides and keep this *fossil* from rotting, throughout. Do you hear children screaming? *I hate you, Daphnë*! I know you hear me. I brought something back with me from the darkness... Wait 'til you see it... Do you *feel* the power rising? This ends with *me.* I'm going to end your—"

After a harrowing journey through the trunk of the Tree of Avernus, mycelium reached Arethūsa's fingers. She fell silent. Arethūsa's eyes rolled back and Yala walked up to her, holding her steady by the shoulders, while her body convulsed. Through the perilous ascent, mycelium grew hardier in nature, carrying bright-yellow specks of slime mold, acquired along the way. Mycelium wrapped around Arethūsa's hands and made its way up her bare arms, until finding her open mouth. Hyphae slithered down her throat, where Yala took firm hold of Arethūsa's thick crimson braid, keeping her head facing up and fixed on the Goddess. Yala avoided touching Arethūsa's face, at all costs.

Arethūsa gagged violently as her mouth was pried open, almost to breaking, by eager mycelium. White tentacles began to glow in the receding light at sunset. Dusk made the mineral surface of the Goddess' confines shine, while Yala suffered through another session, where her instinct to pull the newfound mycelium from Arethūsa's mouth had to be suppressed. Arethūsa's jaw cracked when the ritual was reaching its climax. Her scream was muffled by the mouthful, while Yala rubbed Arethūsa's back, softly, not daring to touch exposed skin, since the silk dress was a natural barrier between air and visceral power.

Never before had mycelium been a part of the renewing ritual, but pain and inner-torment always had. Such magical exchanges with the Goddess always came at a cost. Yala turned away for a moment and saw countless people on Middle Rim of the Tree of Avernus, going about their evening rituals, like so many ants.

Muffled screams did not cease, except for occasional nasal breaths, enough to keep life in the Conductor. It was a quiet horror. Yala understood the fate of a realm was about to be shaped by what a young woman was willing to do, retrieving mycelium from darkness and bringing it to light. Borēan called it playing in the mud, but Yala deemed it heroic, such stuff that toppled tyranny.

Yellow leaves on the tree began to unfurl and turn green again, while stars scattered into sparkling presence across the sky. Tiny leaves budded and grew into maturity, all along the branches. But it would be a long night and only the rising of the Three Sister Moons would mark the end of it. As tears streamed down Arethūsa's flushed face, Yala pressed her hand, hard, to her back, anything to allay the pain. Just as another muffled scream resonated through Yala's hand, another scream echoed from a Rim, far below.

"AAAAAAAAAAAAAAHHHHHH!"

17

HELL IN THE HEAVENS

WHEN FÁLON SCREAMED, EVERYONE marked the black fletching of the arrow fluttering in the middle of his chest. Nyctá tackled Fálon and fell into the thick of ferns and grasses, while the rest followed, dropping to their chests, just before the whizzing of more arrows.

"*It hurts!*" Fálon wailed.

"We have to move!" Nyctá shouted, as Fálon's arms stilled.

"You have to get up, Fálon!" Pippa cried out, from beneath the ferns.

"Can you move?" Nyctá implored, shaking his limp body.

Through arrow-sizzle, Callisto scrambled up to Fálon and began to pull him through thick growth, with the help of Nyctá. Arrows passed over their crouching bodies, while a resounding *click-clacking* rumbled from an adjoining branch. A horrifying chorus of guttural cackling grew louder with the approach of the six companions' predators.

Nyctà threw herself on top of Callisto and Fálon, in the soft fern cover, just as arrows flew past. Another barrage of arrows came, greater in number, but were deflected off course by the thickness of ferns, where those arrows joined the others, in their parabolic descent into the spore cloud, where they would go to rot in the darkness. Abysmal laughter from the encroaching threat was growing clearer in its consonant-cluttered intent. Nyctá glanced at Callisto and shook her head. Callisto kissed Fálon on his sweat-strewn brow and bolted along with Nyctá and the rest of the companions.

"We can't leave him!" Pippa wailed, as Briar grabbed her from the back of her celium pants and tugged her along their scrambling flight.

"There!" Callisto pointed ahead, where a massive burl on a branch, swirled into a black hole.

"Down, my love!" Nyctá roared, in an intertwined voice, falling on top of Callisto, when a cluttered succession of arrows came. The speed and number of them made the wind scream. Nyctá shook her head, violently, in consternation for her words to Callisto, through a voice *doubly* her own.

"I hear him calling! Fálon!" Pippa screamed, just as Briar pulled her into the hole.

Nyctá remained in the ferns with Callisto while hissing arrows impeded their way. Darkness was settling on Sky Realm, so Nyctá pulled off her goggles. When she looked up and ahead, she spotted red faces of their pursuers. Their hirsute legs bent backwards and the click-clacking was from their hooves, carrying them at fierce speed, with barrel-chests of corpse gray, strewn with thick veins, throughout. Their penises dangled between hair-matted legs, like limp totems to some malevolent god.

"Now, Mēna!" Callisto shouted.

With their legs tearing through the ferns, they leaped onto the bottom ridge of the burl. Arrows followed, but failed to find their bodies. Through keen ears, Nyctá flung up her mechanical arm, deflecting an arrow into the ridge of the burl, rather than the back of a descending Callisto. Nyctá was last to leap into the hole, where she rolled down the decline and onto Callisto, who was on top of Briar, in a dark and confined space.

Sickly-sweet wood-decay and things that fed on it, filled the dank air, as the last vestiges of light left the mouth of the hole, above. Everyone breathed heavy breaths, taking in the burl's warm air, sickly-sweet through decomposition, while guttural cackles passed them by and headed towards the wounded, Fálon.

"We left him," Pippa moaned, with her thick curls of black hair between her soiled fingers. "We left him to those monsters. We shouldn't have come. I dreamed about this. I knew it."

"He's not dead yet," Callisto said, looking up at twilight through the hole.

"The arrow tips are poisoned," Nyctá said. "I've seen it before with Reapers. Fálon can't feel a thing right now."

"I take it you've been shot by one," Pippa muttered, through tears.

"No. I've used them. Its acridness invites the memory."

"Here we go," Briar sighed.

"You really were one of them," Pippa muttered.

"Part of her was," Callisto said. "Mēna is emerging," she half-smiled. "This is a waste of words. All of us are here, right now. There's no changing that. Now...what do we do about Fálon?"

"Nothing," Nyctá said.

"*What*?" Pippa seethed. "How could you—"

"She's right," Callisto said. "There's far too many of them and they have all the advantage. The moment we come out of that hole, we're finished."

Pippa ran her fingernails across her chest, "So we should just stay down here and rot while Fálon is...is—"

Nyctá stood up to the starry night through the hole, swallowing her wonder at the sight, "We should wait until they take him wherever it is they're headed. Everything, human and monster, has needs and wants. They kept him alive for a reason. There they go... *Listen*... I smelled the poison on him. It's made to paralyze but keep bleeding minimal. There's still a chance. I'll go."

"Absolutely not," Callisto said.

"I have the advantage here," Nyctá said, looking at the other four, through gleaming eyes. "No sense in the rest of you dying, too. You have a destination. I don't."

"She makes a good point," Briar said.

"Fuck," Callisto cursed to herself, wiping sweat from the top of her stubbled head. "*Go.* But...don't fucking die," she muttered.

"Bring him back to me," Pippa said, squeezing Nyctá's hand, just below her mechanical.

"See what happens, eh Briar?" Nyctá winked, before she crept up to the hole.

"That's my gal," Briar winked to her.

When Nyctá emerged, the sky was pulsing with clusters of stars and two of the Sister Moons were rising as crescents, in the adjoining colors of pink and green. Nyctá remembered beauty had a way of emerging in the grimmest moments, as if beauty required suffering to make itself known.

At a glance, the branchy world above her was a series of tremendous Rims, living platforms, one after the other. Each of those Rims were large enough to hold the greater part of the Sinels, while the top Rim completed the dizzying ascension, with a smaller circumference, in its victorious pinnacle of leafy magnificence.

Something within her brought back the sense of the divine, the mystic moment, when she was thrown from the Spider's back and airborne, subject to a Voice, beyond the moment. The sudden rush of the heights supercharged her being, with a fundamental need to climb higher.

With her chin pointed at the zenith, Nyctá muttered a quick prayer to the Goddess, thanking her for keeping the dazzling moons in regression, as she slipped through ferns and deeper into night.

It was cackling that gave away the place where the creatures were gathered. Nyctá slipped through a thicket of small trees and thick grasses, where an adjoining branch, thicker than the stem of a greater mushroom, reached up and connected to the Rim above.

There were no cries for help, or wails of pain. If Fálon was still alive, he lost the use of language. As she pushed through fresh grasses, swishing rather than crunching, she caught sight of a shadowy ritual underway, in an open portion of the Rim, where hooves had trodden down the life of the place and nothing but woody ground remained.

Their numbers were close to fifty and all of them were profanely male. Many hooves clacked against the wood, in a broken rhythm, obliterating other sounds. Their pale eyes looked like manic captives in red faces, while a pair of swirling horns of various malformations, sat atop their bald heads. Drool poured from their mouths, while clumps of semen dangled from their penises, as they danced in a circle, like intoxicated bees. Nyctá tried to focus through the horror of such a sight, when grim cackling erupted from the dancing creatures.

A glimmer of teeth in the thicket of grasses, just ahead, drew Nyctá's focus. Just before she raced towards it, the creatures bleated, as a pair of dismembered legs were tossed amongst them. A pair of arms followed and eager bites were taken from them all. By the time the limbs made their dizzying rounds amongst the creatures, there was nothing left of them but bones and trailing sinews, without any blood left to drip.

Nyctá fell atop Fálon and his horrified eyes found hers. His lips were stilled, while his torso took halted breaths. Clumps of ferns were on gruesome places where his arms and legs used to be. The horror in his dark eyes spoke for him.

"I'm sorry," she whispered to him. "You sacrificed yourself for all. *You are brave.* This part is between us. My words are my own."

Nyctá pulled out her second-favorite knife and slashed Fálon's throat, so deeply, his head drifted back and hung like a broken branch, held up by its bark. The click-clacking of hooves gave away the creatures' approach and Nyctá scurried through the grasses, down the adjoining branch and back towards the hole in the burl.

The lie she was going to tell Pippa was growing fuller, with every swift-footed step. Just before she scurried into the hole, Nyctá caught a glimpse of something moving beyond the burl.

"*Nyctá*," Briar called out, in a whisper. "Up here."

She climbed over the burl and onto the adjoining branch where Briar was crouched amidst ferns. Nyctá knelt beside him and caught her breath.

"Briar, where are the others? I have to—"

"They've gone ahead."

"Gone ahead? Fálon is dead. Why did they—"

"We were food for worms in that hole. Callisto ordered us to move. She speaks and the rest follow."

"*You* didn't."

"I wasn't going to leave you. We've already been through too much together. Anyway...Ruthy would kill me, if I did."

"Who gives a fuck what Ruthy thinks. We just lost—"

"Fálon will be missed. Nothing more to say. Cmon."

Distant bleating made Nyctá cringe as she followed Briar up the branch and onto the adjoining Rim. With the feast reaching its climax, she hoped the food and macabre dance would send the creatures into the world of sleep.

The next Rim was full of lush trees and marked with gigantic knuckles of the branch constituting the land, with the overwhelming presence of the main trunk of the Tree of Avernus, just ahead. It appeared to be a vertical mountain and everything in the sky reached out from this source. It was the nexus of the heavens and earth.

"They're just ahead," Briar said, walking through wind-warped trees.

"Your words are air," Nyctá said.

"What?"

By the time Briar turned around, Nyctá was standing battle-ready, with Slender in her hand. Her head was on a swivel, as she eyed Briar in-between.

"What do you see?" Briar asked, flicking his wrists to reveal his twin-katars.

"Your *fucking* thieving eyes."

"I'm being serious, Nyctá. What—"

Slender was at Briar's throat and Nyctá hissed from behind him, before she spoke, "What did they promise you? Speak clear, or I'll fucking finish you here."

"Stop fucking around and follow me. They're just over—"

"*Nyctá!*" Pippa screamed, from behind.

When Nyctá turned her head, a blade glimmered, before sliding across Pippa's neck, under a hooded stranger's hand, where streams of blood gushed, before Pippa fell dead on the turf. In the midst of the sight, Briar kicked Nyctá from behind and sent her tumbling forward, where the ground gave way and she plummeted.

Briar stood, heaving, as the stranger in the hood approached and was followed by five Reapers. A pair of them were holding knives to the throats of Callisto and Eléa. When the hooded figure reached the deadfall, he spit into the void.

"Oh, how I missed her," the hooded man said.

"You didn't have to kill her, Stayx," Briar winced, staring at his own katars.

"Briar!" Eléa screamed, with a knife to her throat. "You motherfucker!"

Stayx nodded beneath his hood and the Reaper slid his blade across Eléa's throat, muffling her gurgling screams with his hand. When her body went limp and her head dropped, along with streams of blood, the Reaper released Eléa and she fell in a clump, with her streaming white hair as her funeral shroud.

Before Callisto could respond, she was thrust into the deadfall, where her screams quickly diminished, before there was a dull thump.

"That's the way we do things around here," Stayx smiled. His long blonde hair fell across his weathered face, marked by a liquor-purple nose.

"What are you going to do with them?" Briar asked, through gritted teeth.

Stayx motioned with his hand and the other five Reapers scattered in various directions, "We'll let the Labyrinth decide. Those were orders from above. Boréan still gets a rise out of dropping women in the bowels of this fucking Tree, still believes there are spirits down there. If you ask me, it's just a good hole to starve in. I figure it'll take less than a turn for Nyctá to finish off the other, to save herself. She's a survivor. If it hadn't been for that fucking Mud-Weir in Simmeria, she would still be by my side. If what you say is true, she'll come around. It's been a long time... At least she remembers her Name. That's a start."

"Is she really worth all this?"

"She is. She has no equal. Even if her methods are a bit...*strange*. Weir Whispers will set Nyctá straight back into her old self. The rest of them are Ümfallan trash. What about you? I hope you didn't fall for another cunt, down in the mud, while you were away. Was it worth it?" Stayx laughed, admiring the rising of the Third Sister Moon.

"Boréan was the one who banished me. I found ways to get by."

"Sure, you did. Had it been my call, I'd have killed you for your deception. But it serves me on this night. Well, to the god of greed and self-preservation. I heard a rumor you fucked Arethūsa along the way. Not a bad spoil."

"We had a moment."

"It *was* you! Messages from afar are always a little vague. I see your methods. *Brilliant.* Well, at least you lasted long enough for her to give up her thoughts to Yala. But you've always been one willing to say anything to get what you want, so it couldn't have been too hard. You wouldn't believe the shit I've heard coming from Yala's mouth while she's listening to the roots. I think she gets off on it, too. She moaned right along with Arethūsa. So I guess you fucked them both."

"I don't think it works that way," Briar muttered, looking away.

"Sure it does! Words can fuck as surely as cocks. Even if it comes through the entrails of the world and up this Tree. Don't worry, I like to share my cunts with people I respect. I thought I'd lost you to the darkness, but here you are, Briar. Come! You deserve a drink and a fuck."

"What about the bodies?"

"That's what Satyrs are for," Stayx winked. "I have the best Vescent Wine in Avernus. The bubbles will burst your cares away. But you already knew that. What has it been...three orbits, since you've been here?"

"Three and a half."

"Well, welcome back from that shit-hole below. Wait til' you see Middle Rim, grown since you were last here. Onward and upward we go! That's where the action is. You wily fucker, I still can't believe you made it back with Nyctá. You're the king of thieves. But I've never known you to be so quiet. *Unbelievable.* It only cost me a few dozen Reapers before I realized, Old Forgetful Nyctá, wasn't going down with force. Nyctá is unparalleled, truly. And now the Conductor's back, too. Two pretty birds with one cunning stone. I could go on and on about what you pulled off."

"I know."

"Of course, you do! Hold on...Why should *I* trust you?"

"That's an impossible question to answer."

"Good answer. Otherwise, I'd have to kill you here and that'd certainly ruin the night ahead. Now...let's go before those cock-crazed creatures ruin our appetites," Stayx said, as he put his arm around Briar's shoulders and strolled along the grass, while he sawed the air with his free arm. "I know a shortcut. We really should get around to eradicating those corpse-skinned beasts, even if they've got cocks like gods." He whispered, looking over his shoulder. "*I hate Satyrs.*"

18

THICK-COMING FANCIES

JUST AS ALWAYS, THERE was not a cloud in the sky. Briar tried not to look up at the splendor of constellations pulsing amongst the Three Sister Moons, rising in a tripartite sickle, declaring their rule in the zenith. The first time he experienced the open sky of Avernus, Briar wept alongside Torala, who shared in vacant hopes the sky brought, hopes that would be dashed when they returned to Ümfalla.

Beauty was a consolation for Briar, in a world of pain and death, a gift stolen in quick glances, in the murk beneath the cloud. But the beauty of Avernus came at such rapidity and profusion, the idea of its splendor was smothered in its own too much.

Middle Rim was swarming with people, who appeared to be spirits of the wind, whose sole purpose was to glorify its power. Warm gusts from The Churn blew through the Avernian's thin clothing, enriched with bright colors, while their hair followed in kind. Their drifting style of walking and carousing was an ode to wind, along with strong drinks being consumed. If the wind stopped blowing, it seemed everyone in Avernus would fall dead.

Briar trudged past the Brothels and Vescent Wine Houses, the Fowleries and Arboreal Springs. People shouted offers for their goods and their services, craftsmanship and their bodies. He passed the Temple of Daphnē, grandiose in its towering presence, from afar. When he reached the temple, the exquisite facade, carved with laurel leaves and abstract symbols of the Goddess, was nothing but that. The archway to the temple led nowhere but the trunk of the Tree it leaned upon.

When the tangled balustrades ended, Briar was standing on the Rim's precipice, claimed by the void for the beginning of emptiness. Garrulous chatter had faded, leaving nothing but the wind. He was once an Avernian Reaper and a freedom fighter in the dark, a lover and a thief. Now his senses awakened, after his greatest folly came to pass, a hydra-headed choice, roaring louder and with more confusion, with every passing gust of wind.

In that moment, he remembered another love he lost through his mistakes, a love that began when he was still a child, one binding him to her, so closely, most people assumed she was his sister. Sins of his past rushed back in, as if they just happened, damning regrets, no amount of sardonic laugher would redeem. Briar leaned over the edge, where the spore cloud dissipated and the tumultuous sea appeared. He leaned into the wind and took a deep breath, feeling his weight shift forward. Wind encouraged him to go on, to feel weightless surrender, less than a step away.

"You should jump. It would simplify things."

The woman's voice did not move Briar. But her words failed to send him over, either. He cursed to the wind, staring on, where the storm met the sea. Mist over the water was beautiful and he called it so, before he turned around to face her.

"*Ruthy* is open for business, tonight," she announced.

"Not interested," Briar said, squinting in the wind.

"You never were into such wares. Has the *long night* come to Avernus?"

Briar wiped wind-tears from his eyes and focused on the woman. She wore the costume of her trade, a slip of silk across her waist and nothing more. Glittering jewels on her necklace and a conglomeration of bird feathers, wild in their arrangement, throughout her long black hair, added to the illusion and mysticism of Wind Weirs. The slight tremor of her lower lip betrayed the authenticity of her powers. Like most Wind Weirs in Avernus, she survived through the organ between her legs and fantasies she wove through her Whispering lips.

"*Orīa*...why did it have to be you?" Briar grimaced, walking towards her.

"Has the long night come?" She asked, dutifully.

"You know, she has. Or I wouldn't be here. It cost three lives."

"How many will it take to avenge Torala? Three more? Thirty? All? If I died, would you have done all this for me?"

"You need to Whisper, soon. I see it in your lips, in your eyes. They've grown distant. Orīa, do you remember what it looks like down there?"

"I still dream of it. I wake up before sunrise and think that I'm still in the Sinels, long before that abominable carriage brought me up here. I still see the Seething Falls, smell its vibrance... Then I look up and see nothing."

"The wind up here is enough to scatter any memories of Ümfalla. It's maddening."

"Sometimes."

"*Whisper to me*. Get it out, before you waste it on an Avernian. Tell me your favorite tale."

"Remember the way my father used to take us up to—"

"Not that one. Not that way."

"What do you want from me, Briar? Do you want fantasy, or are you willing to see this through?"

"I want this to end."

"You've always tried to hide your darkness with a wink and a smile. It works on most, but it never did on me. It's bullshit. You fear, as I do, you fear because you still have a soul. But I still love you. Always have. Even if you betrayed me for Torala. You and I have been through too much together, lost more than we've gained. I'm thankful, beyond words or Whispers, you're still alive. Damnit, Briar, we don't have time for this," she said, running her fingertips along Briar's face. She looked over her bare shoulder, speaking, quickly, "Ruthy needs you to find a way to be there when Mēna emerges.."

"*If* she emerges... She's a fucking legend among Reapers, above and below. And I'm the last face she should see when she does. There's no guarantee she'll make it out. You've heard what's down there, in the Labyrinth."

"I have. After you turned your back on me, I went into that kind of darkness. It made me what I am."

"You were never in that place."

"No. I have no time for dead rituals, in a hole, full of false voices. I've been through a far more fickle Labyrinth than the one she's in, the one the Weir's worship. I've lived and breathed my own chaos, for many orbits."

"So your labyrinth showed you how to spread your legs while you tell fairytales to—"

"*Fuck you*," Orīa cursed, so fiercely, she spat on Briar's face. "I'm a survivor, just like you. Unlike you, I had to do this all on my own. Our people, in Ümfalla, raised us for the wrong world. The richness of the spore cloud showed me how to find a little bit of power in a fucked up world. Wind is mighty, but always fleeting, soulless. And yet I'm learning to master it. Whispers cut through eternity, while screams are forgotten. I might have to grin and bear cock-driven Avernians, but at least I have control over them...for a short while. A little more practice and I'll be able to drive a man mad enough to do anything. There are others...others who are like me and want more. My only friend in Sky Realm is a Night Whisperer, like myself. She has a little Elven girl, *Perdita*. As much as she loves the child, she chose to Name her for the very thing this place is, Middle Rim, between heaven and hell. Fuck this perdition. But when I look at that Elven child, I don't see the torture of this in-between, I see joy and hope. I see a little girl who can grow up to be something other than a tool for the ones in power, above us. I choose to look up and so will lost souls like her, so will Perdita. We will find our chance and topple this place. The Night Whisperers will find their time."

"You're listening to your own Whispers, your own fantasies. Just see what happens when—"

"You're still spouting that same line...*see what happens*. Everything happens without you, if you wait. If Ruthy doesn't—"

Briar pulled Orīa into his embrace and kissed her, fiercely, with his eyes wide open. She pulled away, for the briefest of moments, before realizing his intent. She sensed the duality of the moment, the heartfelt need for them to touch each other and the mechanics of what needed to *seem*.

Briar grimaced when he reached behind her and squeezed her cheeks and closed his eyes, as Stayx approached. Briar struggled not to get lost in the moment, through the disarming presence of Orīa, as he waited for Stayx's restless mouth to set things in motion. But Stayx remained at a distance, watching them, with eager and expectant eyes.

"Does he know?" Briar whispered into her ear.

"He thinks I'm from here. I'm just a Weir-whore, remember?" Orīa whispered back. "Do what you have to. Pretend you still love me and just—"

"I don't have to pretend. I just have to imagine you love me still."

Stayx nodded, with a smile, as Briar picked up Orīa. She straddled his waist and moaned softly, while Stayx remained where he was, watching and nodding.

"Pretend to enjoy it like a customer," Orīa whispered. "All of this is nothing, if he thinks we know each other."

"This is going to get you killed," Briar whispered back, as he began to let go. "Walk away and live. For me, Orīa. I can't lose you, too. You know I love you beyond—"

"Whispers are the shape of silence, my love. Silence holds power. Know this to be true. Listen to my story..."

The moment Orīa began Whispering into Briar's ear, he squeezed her back twice, with his fingers, an age-old sign of his willingness to let go for her, to hear. She knew her powers were growing stronger, but Briar was no customer. She Whispered through love's lips, intertwined with ineffable power.

She told him a tale, taking him to another realm in space and time, an imagined place, never having the chance to exist, filled with people the way they should have been. She *Whispered* a tale to give him a moment of joy, while she suffered through another session of doing what she must, to stay alive. In this case, her suffering was holding the man she always loved and pretending not to melt.

When Stayx drew nearer, in the midst of Orīa's Whispering, she kept to her story, until the end. It was a story of their lives if they remained together and found a different way to survive. There were hardships but their love only grew stronger, the kind of love intertwining two souls, an unbreakable union, an enduring Oneness.

In the midst of pretending, she began to believe and was thrust into another life, for a split moment. When her Whispering fell silent, warm wind was cold on her trembling lips, soft attributes of a mouth holding magic through the wind. Briar's eyes returned to the present, changed.

"You are one sentimental son of a bitch," Stayx said, standing over Briar, with his arms crossed. "Your tastes have changed. I always took you for the cocksure warrior. But this one's a pretty bird, a very pretty bird," he said, running his fingers through the feathers in Orīa's wind-strewn hair. "What's your name, pretty bird?"

"Magda, your grace," Orīa said, curtseying, with a half-smile.

"Such a typical name for an exquisite creature. Your tits are even more divine than your face," he grinned, running his fingers between her breasts. "The goddess, Briar, pull yourself together."

Briar's lips were still moving, but no words were issuing forth. When he blinked hard at the swirling pseudo-reality, settling into the present, he was swaying back and forth, in conjunction with gusts of wind, while staring up at Stayx and Orīa. Stayx ran his fingers through his own blonde locks and his grin marred Briar's momentary bliss.

"Since when were you one to blush after a little handsy embrace, Briar?" Stayx guffawed, patting Briar on the shoulder, with force.

Briar grinned, "She took me to a place I've never been before. Showed me parts of me I never knew existed."

"Really? She *is* that moving, eh? Cunt Weirs always disappoint. As soon as it's over, everything goes back to what it was. Same as it ever was."

"You have no idea, with this one. She changed my whole perspective on things."

"Cunts can do that. But it always passes. *Always*. Even if she's a Night Whisperer. Tricks of the wind and nothing more. You've been down in the Muddy Realm too long."

Orīa stepped between Briar and Stayx, "Do you want to show him, Briar? Show him how life changing my cunt is? I'm always open for business."

"What do you think, Briar?" Stayx winked, putting his arms around them both. "I know you're not afraid of getting a little messy."

"I've been down in Ümfalla long enough to know messes," Briar said. "What do you think, *Magda*? Is he up for it?"

"He sure is," Orīa said, as she Whispered into Stayx's ear.

"Not yet," Stayx said, turning his ear from her.

"Right now?" Orīa asked, licking Stayx's ears.

"Right now," Briar said, just as Orīa winked.

When Briar flicked his wrist, the katar's point peeked out the other side of Stayx's back and he was on his way to the edge, in both their arms. Orīa made the last push, separating Stayx from Briar's blade.

The last thing Stayx saw, before he was in a free fall, towards The Churn, was the resolute stare from Orīa, as she watched the power of her words at work. When she turned back to Briar, he was heaving from the labor, with his bloody katar still exposed.

"Well," Orīa smiled, "what do you think?"

"About what?" Briar smiled back. "Went just as planned."

"I missed you, Briar. We have a love beyond reckoning."

"You tell me that every night. I think it's your Weir superstition coming out," he said, rubbing his eyes. "Where's Torala? She still throwing them back at the Vescent House, while we do all the work?"

"Of course, she is. *You know, Torala*," Orīa smiled, kissing Briar on the cheek. "She'll be excited to hear what we did. She has her eye on you. But my days of jealousy are long past. We have far greater things to worry about."

"Just another day in paradise. Everything feels new, again. The Goddess, I've always loved the wind here."

"*Me too*."

"We should return, before Torala thinks we fucked up the whole thing."

"You always fuck things up a little."

"Fair enough. Let's go, before we look any more suspicious."

"You're right," Orīa said, swallowing hard. "But turn your head for me, you've got some blood on your neck...right around...*there*."

Orīa pulled back Briar's silver hair from over his ear: *She Whispered*.

She interspersed portions of the tale she told before, with old news of Torala's death. Rather than telling the truth of Torala's betrayal by her own people—the people she had traded life as a Reaper for, just as Briar had—Orīa weaved a tale of a hero's death, at the hands of those freedom fighters. She untold tales of deceit...

What remained was the fantasy of their unbroken time together, above the clouds, the reality of what they just shared, when *nobody* was watching. Ümfalla became more of a dream, enchantment from their shared childhood, one Briar returned to, long enough to trick Nyctá and retrieve Ruthy. Their love was the only thing left unscathed by Whispers, love, that critical element holding this particular magic together. Early orbits and their tale of love she passed along with her Whispers, memories too precious to touch. The rest she left to magic and promising days to come.

19

UNDER THE NIGHT AND INTO THE SHADOWS

WHEN CALLISTO CAME TO, she was altogether whole, but Nyctá was nowhere in sight. The ground's soft decay broke her fall, but the confined darkness of her circumstance was beyond the spore cloud: *It was an eater of light.* Only bioluminescent speckles from decay, all around her, provided a glimmer. In the vastness of the grim-dark place, she was just as disoriented as the Ginger was in Ümfalla.

Faint sounds, reminiscent of a reed pipe, haunted the air, while gusts of errant wind blew through the unknown, but never found Callisto. She tried not think of Briar's betrayal, but a streak of blood from Elēa trickled down her chest. When she touched the blood, her fingers verified reality, while the need for revenge grappled with instinct for survival.

There was no way back up from where she fell, no direction to go when she was nowhere. In the gloom, she sensed the terrible vastness. It was evident there were impediments, by the wind's failure to find her form.

She had to walk somewhere, other than in a circle. She feared calling out for Nyctá, *or Mēna*, in a place where uncertainty reigned. Callisto listened to the sound of reedy wind and headed towards it, through groping hands as guides and her despair in tow.

Interlocking walls possessed a smoothness akin to the most polished of onyx surfaces, altogether unclimbable. Wind-sound remained at the pitch from when she first heard it, while time passed, indeterminate. Callisto took a bite of Blissel Lichen from the satchel on her waist. When she finished chewing, with a bit of vigor from the ration, she turned around. A pair of dark-bright eyes glared back.

"You could have said something," Callisto gasped, swallowing, hard. "How long have you been standing there?"

"I thought I'd lost you."

Callisto almost fell over when Nyctá embraced her, with such tenderness, it brought tears to her eyes. Deep breaths in her ear carried the ghost of Mēna's voice. Trembling tenderness, imbued with a hidden strength, were in those breaths, a hope tending towards a lost voice.

"Is it you?" Callisto asked, through tears.

"What's left of me," she said. "This way. I have to show you something."

Callisto followed sure steps from the bright-eyed soul who was leading her through darkness. Through twists and turns her hands failed to find, along hidden passages her eyes would never see, she followed. Deeper into the Labyrinth, through Callisto's keen-eyed guide, faint sounds became a deafening song of broken voices singing in a singular harmony of the dead.

Throughout the journey, Callisto wanted to reach out and talk to the voice of Mēna. But something about the voice sounded so fragile, it would break, if forced to come forth. Instead, Callisto kept her eyes on glimmering forms, scurrying along the walls of the wooden Labyrinth.

They had no defined shapes, only strange presences, through streaming glimmers emitted when they moved in rapid bursts, like lizards. The undefined creatures followed them, without making a sound, while the wind and broken voices grew louder.

"How do you know this is the way?" Callisto called out, in the midst of chattering wind. "Mēna?"

"Don't you hear them?"

"I hear noise in the wind."

"Listen closer. The voices point to a secret law. And if you call me Mēna again, I'll leave your dull eyes behind."

"*What*? Then who am I talking to?"

"Not Mēna."

"Do *you* have a Name?"

"Names are fleeting here. Only truth matters. Yes, yes...*I* hear you," she said to the wind.

The Nameless one, leading the way, walked with resolution and never stumbled along tangled roots and shallow pitfalls plaguing Callisto. They were heading into the heart of the Labyrinth, the source of wind and voices. All was an echo chamber for Callisto, a cataclysm of competing sounds, but she trudged on, through the headwind. Had it been the breath of some god, they were headed down for its voice box.

"This doesn't feel like the right way!" Callisto shouted. "We should be going up! Mēna!"

The blade of Slender was at Callisto's throat, while battle-bright eyes stared into her own, "Why are you following me?"

"You're leading the way," Callisto gulped, with the blade at her throat. "Tell me what to call you and I will. Nyctá?"

> *"Nyctá id lōz hin. Ouz Mēna id dreckèn luz ēn gemerbel.*
> *Nyctá is not here. Your Mēna is food for the dirt.*
> *É stinék īdra!*
> *I reign here!"*

"Listen to me, Mēna. Cut my throat if you're not somewhere in there. But if you are, show her. Whisper to her and show her. The winds are strong and so are you! Show her! Show her! SHOW!"

****1*********0*******11*****

****1********00***1**0***

000**1*****

110*

**1*

0

Interlude

WHISPERED TALES OF DISCORD

HER BRIGHT EYES HAUNTED the Ümfallen night, with quick glances, portending nothing but the death and decay to follow. Twenty-one followers, dressed from head to foot in black, waited for the signal from their commander, while Slender gleamed in the light of mushroom clusters, all around.

Undulating gills from a Titan Mushroom loomed overhead, breathing in the gloom. Nyctá ran her fingers through the sides of her profusion of raven black hair, tied in a knot on the middle of her armored back.

"The Simmerians have a Weir with them," a Reaper said.

"She'll be easy enough to spot," Nyctá said. "I'll find her quivering lip. Leave the Weir bitch to me."

"Orders from Avernus are to take five daughters."

"Better than last time. Odd numbers always make it more interesting."

"You always were superstitious. Sometimes I forget you're from over The Churn. Maybe the Goddess—"

"To hell with the Goddess. We make our own luck."

"Now?"

"*Now.*"

With a nod from Nyctá, Reapers swarmed the Simmerian village, like bees to the first blossoms of spring. Nyctá followed with Slender in hand, through swift-footed steps, carrying her to the dark-heart of the matter. Expected screams and moans filled the night, while Reapers tore apart flesh with their swords and ransacked niches within the Sideon Cliffs, where Simmerian people carved their exquisite homes, countless orbits before.

Nyctá kept her head on a swivel, while her Reapers performed the grunt work. Marking the fluttering lower lip of the Weir woman from afar, she sprinted towards her, leaping, with Slender pointed obliquely downwards.

Her Reapers called her, Nighthawk, for her gift of flight in her jumps. along with her ill-boding eyes, beacons of death, always finding their prey. As she descended on the dark-haired Weir, wearing a tattered cloak of crimson, the Weir made eye-contact with Nyctá. Her eyes looked through the descending threat and the Weir watched Slender enter her chest, showing its bloody tip, through her back.

Nyctá held the Weir up with Slender and was transfixed by the bright eyes dimming in front of her own. Nyctá saw herself through eyes seeing themselves back. It was then the Weir leaned her head onto Nyctá's shoulder, turned up her bloody lips to Nyctá's ear and began to Whisper.

I am you and you become me,
From you I came and to you I become.
Mēna is Nyctá and the child in the womb,
One is born and both will scream.
To come into this world again entangled,
When the knot is undone a Name is left.
Hear my History and know yourself again,
I will eat your soul on your way to me.
You were the Seemer who lost her own self,
In orbits of Time you forgot.......

Words in the Whisper became a whirlwind of the Weir's self, through her dying confessions. The world of her short life was *loaded* into Nyctá's mind, in the instant. When the Whispering lips went cold and the corpse who was Mēna slid free from Slender, the woman who held the sword witnessed herself falling dead, onto the dark ground.

In that instant, the intertwined spirits within her lifted up the Name of Mēna and confined Nyctá to the darkness of her selves. She held Slender with her left hand, the hand free from the mechanical's grim workings, unbound and untainted by what came before.

"Nighthawk!" A Reaper called out, from an approaching trot. "You finished off the Weir before we ever had a chance to fear her. We have the five—"

Slender separated the Reaper's head from his body, while the words were still being spoken. Bodiless eyes stared up at Mēna from the bloody ground, with confusion, before they went dark. Mēna faced the unaware Reaper horde and turned the cognitive dance of the Weir into a dance of her sword, a grim succession of swift masterstrokes, slaughtering one Reaper after another, in a singular act of violence.

One of the Simmerian witnesses—through the eye he had left—called the slaughter, '*beautiful*', within earshot of Mēna. By the time Mēna reached the gleaming Sideon Cliffs, the five captured *daughters* were cowering at her approach.

"*Nyctá!*" One of the three Reapers watching over the five girls, shouted. "I always knew you were a Seemer! Time never clears away the histories of your ways!"

While the Reaper spoke, the other two closed in on her, from both sides. Mēna turned her boots inwards, dropping to one knee and nearly kissed the earth, in swift defense from the assault. The sword-strokes glanced her scalp on both sides, sending clumps of her raven hair onto the ground.

Before the hair settled, she pulled a pair of her knives from her hip sheaves and plunged them into the Reapers' hearts, where she twisted for deathly measure and returned the knives to their proper places on her hips. She stood up, drew Slender and tilted towards the girls.

Fierce trickles of blood fell from the sides of Mēna's head, at her approach towards the final Reaper, who was cowering more than the young girls he was beside. Mēna acknowledged the girls, in stride, when she sheathed Slender on her back.

With a seamless action of her right hand, Mēna pulled out a knife and slashed the Reaper's throat, reached in and pulled out his larynx, stuffed it down his throat and stomped his head on the ground with her black boot, giving it the appearance of a rotten melon. Mēna did not look behind her. All the Reapers were accounted dead.

"Mēna?" One of the girls cried out, while her lower lip trembled. "You look different."

"Hello, sweet girl" Mēna said, with blood pouring down her face and neck. "I'm sorry this happened to you. My words are my own. How do you know my Name? You must be new in Simmeria."

"It *is* you. Can I tell you something, before you go?"

"What is it?" Mēna asked, crouching down.

"Just *this*."

The girl Whispered into Mēna's ear, while survivors moaned and wailed, throughout Simmeria. While the mellifluous words were Whispered, the other four girls stared into the darkness, with quivering lower lips, where no words would follow, no Whispers or screams to accompany the atrocity. When the Whispering girl went silent, Mēna slowly rose to her feet and looked towards the dark horizon, eastward.

She believed...if the Resurrection Spores were anywhere, it would be east. East was where the Night Skimmers flew and the Tree of Avernus reached up to the heavens, up to a sunlit place where the Goddess kept watch. The way would be winding, but she would find what she was searching for, no matter how long it took. East was her destiny... Mēna felt this truth in her bones.

20

THE FATHOMLESS DEPTHS

CALLISTO EMBRACED THE NAMELESS one, throughout the ordeal, where violent convulsions and turbulent syllables turned her body into a living torture chamber. When the turmoil passed and the body in her grasp took steady breaths, on her way back to the conscious world, Callisto released her and stepped back. Gleaming eyes, like dark stars, found Callisto and stared at her without blinking, while the wind roared all around.

"Who are you?!" Callisto cried out.

"*Nyctámēna.*"

"Which one?!"

"This one."

"Then where does one begin and the other end?"

"I am who I was and who I have become. Mēna Whispered herself into Nyctá and this is who I am. I emerge from forgetfulness, into myself. Do you see, Calli?"

"What did you call me? Say it again!"

"*Calli.*"

Callisto fell into Nyctámēna's arms and felt her embrace *her*, in that specific place, where back met buttocks and knew it to be Mēna, or, *enough* of her. Her arms were far stronger, her body denser than Mēna's, before she died, but Callisto sensed the Weir's spirit, in the *way* she was holding her.

She wept while wind screamed all around and neither of them said a word. The shimmering creatures watched from the wooden roof, celebrating the strange reunion with flickers through iridescent bodies, while they scuttled about to get a better view. After many moments passed, Callisto raised her head from Nyctámēna's shoulder and looked into her gleaming eyes.

"What now?" Callisto asked, with a hoarse voice.

"I know the way out."

"How?"

"The Creepers told me," Nyctámēna half-smiled.

"Those creatures?" Callisto asked, looking up. "Did the wind tell you their Name?"

"I made it up, Calli. We have to call them *something*. I mean, look at them...they *creep*. But they know the way, not their Name."

"Sounds like someone I know," Callisto muttered.

"It's a long way up, Calli. And there's no telling what's waiting for us."

"Just give me Briar."

"*Yes.*"

"Tell me something."

"What is it? We need to keep moving."

"Do you know the Creepers' thoughts? Are they *speaking* to you?"

"I can *hear* they know the way. The rest is foolish chatter. They're like us, just without a reason to leave this place. This isn't their Labyrinth, but their home."

"That'll do. For now... Lead the way."

"Onwards and upwards, Creepers!" Nyctámēna shouted, with a laugh.

Callisto lingered while Nyctámēna strode into fierce winds, deeper into the dark. The creatures followed her, crawling over and under each other, while they stared down, with shimmering curiosity.

Callisto imagined them seeing Nyctámēna for who she was becoming. Lifetimes of memories melded into an indistinguishable whole, becoming the singular: **Nyctámēna**. Names fell together, like raindrops in the sea, rejoining the whole.

It was what loomed in the darkest depths of that sea, in Nyctámēna's self, that gave Callisto pause. Every memory was mixed to the point of there being no mixture any longer. The heterogenous contents were the authentic thing in herself. But the Callisto of five orbits ago, was not the Callisto of this turn. Nothing came out alive, not even the ones fighting with every particle of their being to do so.

21

PETRIFIED HOPES AND DREAMS

AFTER HEARING NEWS OF Briar and Orīa's success, Arethūsa proceeded as planned. With well-chosen words, Whispers in dark corners and glances from afar, promising allegiance, Arethūsa and Yala felt as secure as they could, in such a volatile circumstance. With Stayx gone, the balance of power amongst Reapers was uncertain and their mercurial natures were anything but reliable, without strict regard. But Reapers in Avernus were still capable of taking fundamental orders from a recognized leader.

Beneath the spore cloud, in the otherworldly air of Ümfalla, Reapers were horrific enigmas, subject to their own grim ways, worlds apart from the ones above. Their ruthless efforts to gather living fodder for the Screaming Branch were means to their own ends. Sky Tracer signified the grim course of such ways, primal and severe.

Orbits of fantasy regarding the plan about to unfold seemed a dream, now the *long night* had come. The only other thing Arethūsa hoped for, beyond present hopes bearing fruit, was for the emergence of Mēna. She prayed for that very thing to the Goddess, who was petrified in the gnarled tree in front of her. Yala stood, in reverent silence, from behind.

"This damned tree blossoms all the time," Arethūsa began, staring at the face of Daphnē. "But every time I think there's going to be fruit, the blossoms shrivel and die. No matter how often I give to this tree, no matter how much, fruit never comes. The blossoms are beautiful and they smell of honey. But you can't eat them. You can't pick them and take them with you to look upon at the next sunrise. *They are illusions.* Your power remains behind that mineral veil, Daphnē. *It must.* I feel it every time I touch the soil that keeps you. Tonight, give me one fruit, just a single berry, in your orbits of keeping them from me. Avernus needs you. I brought raw mycelium to you. Show the people your power and I promise to find another way for you. I promise, even if it takes a lifetime."

"Orīa is approaching," Yala said, beneath her dark hood.

Far from the Middle Rim and the hand of silk once covering her waist, Orīa approached, with eager steps, wearing the crimson-hooded cloak of the Weir, with her head lowered. She bore a wry smile beneath the hood. The rest of her face remained in shadow, in the light of the Three Sister Moons. Her bare feet crunched along dead leaves beneath the tree, holding the Goddess. When Orīa reached Arethūsa and Yala, she bowed with pride and rose to reveal a sly visage, not unlike the one Briar so often bore.

"I was told to refer to you as Arethūsa," Orīa said.

"Briar told you true," Ruthy nodded. "But the Name, Arethūsa, dies tonight. Only after our success may you call me, Ruthy. Names must be earned."

"Such a pity," Orīa said, "Arethūsa is such a beautiful Name."

"And *false*," Arethūsa seethed, causing Orīa to flinch. "Where's Briar?"

Orīa spoke softly, "He is doing as the dead Stayx commanded, waiting for the Reaper, Nyctá, to emerge."

"She is *Mēna*, the Name of the one who guided me through darkness."

"Briar misinformed me. His mind has been known to drift."

"Things change quickly, in times like these," Arethūsa said. "It's foolish for Briar to be the face Mēna sees when she emerges. And certainly not if Callisto survived. Things would go badly."

"*If,* she emerges," Yala said, solemnly.

"She will," Arethūsa said. "She's far too strong for an old wooden Labyrinth to keep her. It's nothing but a relic. Yala?"

"Yes?"

"Go to Briar and take his place. Tell Mēna everything, when she emerges. She'll see the sincerity in your eyes. Orīa wouldn't fair so well in the face of Mēna's gaze. She reeks of Briar. If it takes her longer to emerge, I'll be there to greet her myself, after this is finished. You know the place."

"I, too, emerged from there," Yala said, glaring at Orīa.

"Well, enlightenment comes through many kinds of Labyrinths," Orīa said. "Some of us had to pay for it with a lifetime of suffering."

"Forget about where any of us came from," Arethūsa said, "or *who* any of us have been. The forgotten shall rise, renewed. Tonight is the *long night*, the night we truly change Avernus."

Yala closed her eyes and nodded to the Goddess in the tree, "Soon my sister will finally be free of her bondage to that abominable carriage."

"We can't be too hasty, Yala," Arethūsa said. "Without Sky Tracer, this place will topple over in a handful of turns. The spore cloud would vanish and a false Hardening would come. Things must remain, that must remain. But only long enough to find another way. I *am* breaking ground with the Goddess, in a way far deeper than before. You'll see, tonight. I just want to be honest from the beginning, so you'll trust my words to come. Don't worry, Yala, before we grow tired of celebrating, Sky Tracer will be a thing of the past, a bad dream forgotten. Your sister will be by our sides, soon. She is a hero of Avernus *and* Ümfalla."

"Of course. A bit of patience is nothing, after all these orbits of suffering," Yala bowed. "I wish both of you the grace of the Goddess tonight. Daphnē be with you."

"And you," Orīa winked.

"See you on the other side, Yala," Arethūsa said.

"She is so fucking pious, I could vomit," Orīa said, as Yala receded into the night. "Do you trust her?"

"More than I'll ever trust you," Arethūsa said, turning to face the Goddess. She kneeled and closed her eyes.

Orīa began to Whisper behind her, using the wind to carry her words, while she kept her eyes on the kneeling Arethūsa. Orīa needed to reinforce the Name capable of toppling a realm, one she held power over. She knew, *Arethūsa,* was the Name the woman kneeling before her needed to keep if Sky Realm was to flourish into a new Age.

Ruthy was the Name Orīa sensed she held no power over, a defiant Name, no Whisper could influence. If the Name, Ruthy, remained, there would be no chance for Orīa to find leverage for herself in the days and nights to come. In the depths of Orīa's being, she evoked the Name of Arethūsa and let it fill her mind, while her lips enchanted it. When Orīa's upper lip stilled, she was smiling, while her lower lip continued to flutter. Orīa closed her eyes and absorbed the power of wind.

Magic filled her being.

The second of the Sister Moons reached its zenith and Arethūsa knew the time had come. She said nothing when Orīa departed for the chamber of The Seven Seats of the Elders. Everything had already been said and a certain sense of inevitability was taking hold of her. She remained on her knees, in the dirt, facing Daphnē.

The Goddess remained, silent and still, while Arethūsa waited, with fidgeting fingers, for the third Sister Moon to find her place at the top of the heavens and shine back down on her, with everyone in their proper places. When the Moons' pale light found her, the future would be in the instant. The wind shifted and was blowing northerly. Arethūsa opened her mouth to taste it.

When Orīa passed the Reaper sentinels, guarding the entrance to the chamber, suspicion was in their eyes. Her passage was arranged by Arethūsa, earlier in the day, through a journey to Borēan's seat Arethūsa was forced to make, from the time she showed her first signs of womanhood.

Orīa marveled at the splendor of the chamber, carved with exquisite figures, embraced by exotic flora of Avernus, the likes of which she never knew existed. Twisting vines adorning the ebony pillars were of a species beyond her reckoning, naturally adorned with glowing air-roots, flickering in the wind. Borēan appeared as petrified as the rest of his fellow Elders, as he admired her approach from his seat. Seven Reapers stood behind seven chairs.

"Nobody told me it was a *Weir* coming tonight!" Borēan shouted, with a tremulous voice. "Have you been through the Labyrinth without my knowing?"

"I emerged, only last orbit, your grace," Orīa said, pulling down her hood, revealing her hair, undulating in the wind, like waves in a black ocean. "I have been *deep* in the studies of my Order, ever since."

"Well, you *look* like one. Is that not what matters in the end?"

"Your grace?"

"Looking the part! That's all that matters. Make everyone believe and the rest comes with it. You are young. You will learn the truth of that, in time."

"I thank your grace."

"Come closer, so my old eyes can get a better look at you. And take off that ridiculous Weir wear. I'm too old to be fooled into thinking your *Order* is anything more but tricks up those crimson sleeves. Fantasy for the brothels, below, that's what Whispers are good for. Magic leaked out of this realm an Age ago. Come along, get over here. My time is short."

"I am sure it is, your grace."

Orīa pulled her robe from her shoulders and let it drop to the chamber floor, glistening in the light of the Sister Moons. Borēan flicked his fingers and the seven Reapers departed, where they would stand guard at the entryway. Orīa approached the Ruler of Avernus, emboldened in her nakedness. A lifetime of men's eyes on her naked body allowed Orīa to seize advantage and arouse her *customer* for the night, without appearing to be biding her time. Through her bare skin, wind found every pore, energizing her entire being.

Power rushed in.

She gloried in the truth of her magic, her entanglement with the wind, a sense of purpose. Orīa glanced up at the Third Sister reaching the zenith. When she looked down at Borēan, the old man was masturbating in his elaborate chair, with his thick tongue hanging from the side of his pursed lips. His bare feet were planted in the rich soil, a ceremonial plot, running the length of the Seven Seats.

"I inspire you," Orīa smiled, cupping her full breasts in her hands and shaking them, as she walked with long and deliberate strides.

"Some things never age," Borēan said, with a flushed face and fluttering strokes of his hand on his half-erect penis.

"I want to taste power."

"Power comes only for those who bow."

"Yes, your grace," Orīa said, kneeling, when she reached him.

"Worship your Ruler," Borēan moaned, as Orīa slowly pulled away his hand.

"*Yes*, your grace," Orīa winked, lowering her head.

Borēan closed his eyes, in conjunction with the Third Moon reaching the zenith. Experience taught Orīa not to be too eager, or passive, through her actions. Such deeds used to make her sick, but the promise of what was to come turned the present one into a noble deed. But this was no service paid in meagre earnings.

Through a deep breath, invigorating Orīa's elemental gift, she blew a Whispering current up and along Borēan's chest, from cock to chin, never allowing her liberated lips to touch him. Along his face and into his ears the magic went, as soothing to the Ruler of Avernus as it was devastating.

When he opened his eyes, Orīa smiled at her own gift looking back down at her, through be-Whispered eyes. She reached down her right hand to touch his bare feet on the pliant earth, black, in its richness. His feet were harder than the stair she was kneeling on. Arethūsa's actions through mycelium, from afar, was finding the chamber.

Orīa reveled in her magic, letting it course through her, while she joyed in Borēan staring down his own decline. The old man tilted his wizened head back. When his thighs hardened, Oria lifted her head, looking Borēan in the eye, with a sly smile. She leaned towards Borēan's flushed face, to the point where her lips were almost touching his own. She released his penis just as an eternal hardness found it.

"This is no fantasy from a whore," Orīa smiled, as she licked Borēan's lips. "Your pathetic cock is preserved for everyone to see, for all time. Your pleasures end with me.

I do this for all the ones who couldn't. Suffer your end through *my* magic, you fossilized piece of shit. Look down and see. See what this *whore* has done to you. See what I, the Wind Weir, Orīa, have done. I will take my place above you...*above them all.*"

Borēan's neck already hardened, but he was able to tilt his chin down to see his petrified form. He looked back up to a smiling Orīa, who stared at him, as the ecstasy in the old man's face became silent horror, with a scream never to be sounded, as minerals found his voice-box, before his eyes were fixed in an eternal look of horror.

When Orīa tapped the top of Borēan's head and it clinked, she turned around. Seven Reapers were standing at attention, outside the threshold of the chamber. All of them were facing Orīa, swords drawn.

"Arethūsa will reward you for your loyalty," Orīa announced, through a fierce smile.

"Hail, to your grace," one of the seven Reapers said, who was echoed by the rest. He fell to a knee and the other six followed.

"Yes," Orīa nodded, looking down on the kneeling Reapers. She arched her back in pride.

Orīa was standing in front of the seat where Borēan joined his fellow Elders, in a posture he never would have imagined. Orīa looked up to the Three Sister Moons and raised her arms overhead to feel the power of the wind on her naked body. She closed her eyes and imagined the days to come and yearned for the man she always loved, for Briar to see what she had done. By the time she opened her eyes, Arethūsa was standing on Orīa's cloak and staring at her, with expectant eyes.

"Hail, Your High Grace, Ruthy!" Orīa shouted.

"It's Your High Grace, *Arethūsa*!" Arethūsa commanded, as she clenched and un-clenched her dirty fingers. "Lowliness has passed for me. And you would do better, *down here*, where you belong."

"I beg your pardon, Your High Grace...*Arethūsa*," Orīa smiled, flushed with vitality. "Things change quickly, in times like these," she said, descending the stairs. "Such a powerful Name for *our* Ruler of Avernus."

22

THE HOLE OF BABEL

Y ALA'S JOURNEY TO THE thicket of twisted trees, where the exit to the Labyrinth loomed, took longer than she anticipated. Cognitive pitfalls gave her pause, along an otherwise gentle slope, leading to the northwestern edge of Upper Rim. Her approach evoked memories of her sister and the day she was confined to the mast of Sky Tracer, to Whisper the worries of Avernus away like dark lullabies, for turns without end.

Recent words from Arethūsa haunted her steps, over the uncertainty of days to come. When she saw a man pacing back and forth, through the thicket of leaves, she blamed her feet for bringing her to the place. She blamed her heart for making the journey a hell unto itself.

Yala looked back towards the chamber, over the hills, where The Seats of the Seven Elders resided. The rare sight of flames licking the sky cast a red halo on the night. Yala's initial fears were allayed, while others burned anew, through the fiery sign of success for Arethūsa and doubts concerning Sky Tracer. The ferocity of the flames signified the many Reaper corpses it took to ensure the transfer of power.

Over the orbits, Reapers and Rulers rose and fell, like so many trees. Replacements would be plucked from Middle Rim, as always, if things were to remain balanced in Avernus. Yala pulled apart the leafy branches and made herself known.

"I've come to bring news," Yala said, pulling down her hood.

"Tell me they've done it," Briar said, with vigor, pulling down his hood, with nervous hands.

"Go to Orīa. She needs you."

"Has something gone wrong?"

"Everything has gone right. Look at the fire in the sky. Everything appears to have gone the way of natural events. The Seventh Elder has found eternal stillness. Reapers have given themselves to fire, showing the way to the future. Old, has given way to new. This is the Long Night."

"The first glimmers of day are coming," Briar said, looking to the east.

"You cannot be here when she emerges."

"So, Ruthy really pulled it off," Briar said. "Orīa will be—"

"Ruthy has emerged. She vowed to bury the old Name of Arethūsa."

"Sure, sure," Briar laughed. "I leave this drudgery to you. Oh! Put it in some good words for me to Nyctá. The killing of our companions was never a part of the plan. Stayx payed dearly for it. *Tell her*...what happened before was for something far greater. For *this*," he said, staring at the distant fire, through the leaves. "The others died in service to it. Their plan to cut the chord of Sky Tracer was a child's dream. Nothing is that simple. Ruthy made it known to me of Sky Tracer's mechanics. I understand its importance for places above and below. I haven't forgotten good ole' Ümfalla. But now everything changes."

"Of course," Yala said. "I have seen many changes, over the long orbits of my life. Go. Your old love, made new, is waiting."

When Briar departed and the branches he disturbed on his way out fell subject to wind again, Yala crouched over the hole. Errant roots and clumps of grass were growing over the precipice to the void, no larger than a pair of humans could fit through, at once. She remembered when she emerged from that very place, all those orbits ago...

Three women entered the Labyrinth and one Weir emerged. The others' bones remained behind, after the echo-chamber drove them mad. What proved to be a chorus of enlightening voices for Yala, was a grinding cacophony of chaos for the others. They tore off their own ears, before crushing their skulls against the Labyrinth.

It was on that turn Yala realized, all the horrors of Hell could be experienced in a single day, that was plenty of time. And the Hell one person could suffer, was no greater than if a thousand others were suffering all around. One person's Hell proved to be another's triumph.

Somewhere, in the nowhere of the Labyrinth, Callisto was babbling to herself, while Nyctámēna held her by the hand. The embrace was more to keep Callisto from leaping off the narrow pathway and into the abyss, rather than a hand guiding her out. What were guiding voices, unlocking forgotten chambers within Nyctámēna's mind, were swirling consonants bereft of merciful vowels for Callisto, gutting her sanity, one windy syllable at a time. Blood trickled from the top of Callisto's head, from her fingernails tearing into her scalp, on the maddening journey up.

No amount of physical effort—no matter how strong the person—kept another mind from destroying itself, a brutal truth, eternal. Creepers loomed, while two souls pulled in opposite directions. In spite of Nyctámēna's superior strength, Callisto was too resistant and in the grips of mania, to be carried the rest of the way. Nyctámēna closed her eyes, gazed on a renewed darkness, in search of places unknown, through her present collision of Names.

"*Put them out!*" Callisto screamed, while roaring wind swallowed her words. "Put out the noise! Take my ears! Throw *me*! Throw me! THROW!"

While Callisto raged against the Labyrinth, Nyctámēna let her own lips go slack and felt her lower one tremble, through something other than wind. She put her lips to Callisto's ear and the world went silent, within. If an infant recognized the moment babbling sounds were deemed a *word* by others, such awareness was akin to Nyctámēna's first Whisper.

Wind empowered her subtle words, sounds of a different nature than the roaring words of her double-tongue. They flowed like wind over the sunless sea, articulating dark waters, Whispered and received. By the time the Weir closed her lips and opened her bright eyes, the work was already underway.

If a rainbow fell asleep, Creepers were its dream. Somewhere within their swirling actions of prismatic radiance, Callisto was standing. Creepers swirled in fluid motions, far too brisk for eyes to determine where one ended and the other began. Their glowing bodies swarmed Callisto and took on her shape, performing radiant antics, round and round her body.

Nyctámēna stepped back from what she conjured, marveled at effects beyond her control. When the fantastical performance concluded, all the Creepers faded and returned to their wooden roof, where they appeared like ethereal lizards again.

Callisto stood, statuesque, with her eyes fixed on some point in her imagination. Nyctámēna took Callisto's slack hand and her feet followed. When they reached a steep incline, Callisto followed, climbing along the knobs and holes in the wall, on her way up, *up*, towards a place of lesser darkness. As Nyctámēna continued to climb, she felt her lower lip trembling. She sensed the past yearning to say something more.

Yala was humming a song over the hole, while memories of orbits past swirled in her mind, in conjunction with the wind. Words to the song were long forgotten, but the harmony remained, like the memory of a face without a Name.

Her sister sang it, whenever Yala was frightened as a child, a child who became the woman who lived through hundreds of orbits, through the same old song of the world, with assigned voices, rising and falling in their mortal tunes.

She tried to hold onto the melody, but such harmony demanded the presence of another. The words were too painful and cried out for her sister, who remained tied to the rack of Avernian ambition. Yala yearned to bask on the sunny slopes of home, far over The Churn, where trees grew with reason and clouds passed, as surely as seasons.

A pair of living stars rose from the black hole at Yala's feet. When the figure's hawk-hair pointed out of the darkness and her weathered hands took hold of earthbound roots, Yala stood up and backed away, slowly. She was taller than Yala expected, even after Arethūsa's vivid descriptions.

A look of calm resolve was in the warrior's face, when she reached down and pulled up another soul. Bewilderment was in the other's face, signifying only one of them heard the chorus below. One emerged, *Changed*.

"You, alone, heard the hidden chorus, below," Yala said.

"And you heard it long before me," Nyctámēna responded, squinting at the east, where the first glimmers of day were turning the sky red.

"Both of you have suffered much and lost companions along the way. But just as a new day begins, so Arethūsa sheds that Name like a snake its skin.

"Who?"

"I forget. You don't know that Name," Yala said. "*Arethūsa,* is no more. She was and is again, Ruthy. The Seventh Elder has—"

"Wait a moment," Nyctámēna said. "Ruthy went by the Name, Arethūsa, but goes by Ruthy, again?"

"Yes."

"She never told me. No surprise, there."

"I know it's strange."

"No. Not really."

"Is your companion, alright?"

Callisto stood, as she had, after her experience with the Creepers, dumbfounded and muttering to herself.

"*Yeah*," Nyctámēna sighed. "She had a *long* turn. She'll come around."

"The madness found her and you found a way to lead her out. I failed when it came to that. The signs exude from you. You have emerged a Weir. Everyone's experience is their own, in the Labyrinth. Yours is something far different than I have seen in any other. *Interesting*. I envy the feeling you must have, a sense of ecstatic renewal. I knew it, a long time ago. Your lips move with a fresh vigor. Time will tell what they invite."

"There's need in your eyes your words are concealing. Where is Ruthy?"

"She is now the High Grace of Avernus and Ruler of Sky Realm. The Seventh Elder has stilled and the long night has come and gone."

"Speaking of that," Nyctámēna mumbled, pulling on her goggles, as daybreak brightened the world above the distant storm.

"What a fickle contraption that is," Yala half-smiled, staring at the goggles, while Nyctámēna adjusted them.

"Nothing vast without a curse, ya' know? Now, give up the truth. You're stalling, but there's no malice in your eyes. Wait a moment...what's your Name?"

"I am Yala. And I believe your Name to be Mēna and that must be Callisto."

"You're half-informed. I am, Nyctámēna. And that's all, Callisto, over there. *Oh, no...* Pull it together, Calli!"

"This will be a problem."

"Calli? Nah, she'll be fine. Just a little wind-drunk."

"Your name. Ruthy is expecting Mēna. She is quite insistent about that. It might seem a trifle, but Ruthy changed, since she returned. The woman who was, Nyctá, she spoke of with wrath. She fears her. She spoke of her double-tongue and her unpredictable wrath. Ruthy—"

"Ruthy fell from Sky Tracer, a mystery and remains one. Only her deeds to come will define her. But we went through the grinder together. She can call me, Mēna, if she desires. She can call me Skimmer Shit if it blows up her silk. I just need to speak with her and try to discover her intent. You *are* stalling. But I see honest intent in your eyes, *feel it*, through whatever it was I found in the Labyrinth. This is not my first transfer of power. It's messy. Especially, when the ones who take it, try to make it neat."

"I will speak to you, as I would my sister. Your emergence has brought with it more than marvel for me. I hope to find an ally in you. Even if it costs me my life. To be honest, I have nobody else to tell and Ruthy will be here, soon."

"Speak."

"Ruthy intends to have a Weir named Orīa and myself at her side. Briar is the intended replacement for commander of the Reapers, Stayx. Briar and Orīa killed Stayx last night. That was a deed I cannot condemn. Stayx was monstrous and caused more than myself orbits of torment. But Orīa and Briar are a force with a bond beyond love. I do not trust them and neither should Ruthy."

"Yeah, no shit. When Calli comes around, Briar will face her wrath."

"Considering his actions, your companion is justified. Those orders never came from Ruthy. But I don't trust Ruthy, either. She is full of good, but I believe her ambitions are blinding her. She speaks of *change* but intends to carry on with the mechanics of that abysmal carriage you call, Sky Tracer, for the sake of the Goddess and the Tree. It is all she knows, her obsession, never mind her seeming change through a different Name. My sister has been the Whispering engine and conjurer of the spore cloud, for orbits. Another Wind Weir did the same before her, another before her... My heart is bound to my sister's and it is stretched to breaking, every time I see that abominable carriage set forth. I hear the screams of children arriving for their doom. Even if the child sacrifices come to an end through Ruthy's power, as she promises, my sister continues her course through hell. I did everything I could from up here, while *Ruthy* conjured mycelium from your Ümfalla. She suffers from its power and dismisses it, in the name of the common good. She risked everything to bring raw mycelium up here."

"*That* was her intent in Ümfalla... What follows? How does she intend to use that kind of power to—"

"Her intent is to bring balance to the realms. Arethūsa speaks of change but only promises some kind of miracle, some time in the future. I have lived long enough to know such a future is a never-ending tomorrow. She speaks of awakening the Goddess, in the heart of the Tree of Avernus. She believes a fundamental change would destroy Ümfalla, as well. I cannot stand by her side and watch the same thing carry on. I will kill my sister and myself before the sun sets, if the mechanics remain the same. I swear to the Goddess, I will. I know this world is foreign to you. I speak of things strange and unnatural."

"Part of me knows this place. That probably sounds strange and unnatural, too. But I have something within that escapes words."

"You heard much in the Labyrinth. I see dueling spirits through your eyes that look like dark stars, through onyx. My words are my own."

"Say that again."

"The whole story? There's no time, Nyctámēna."

"No. What you just said: *My words are my own*. Where did you find that phrase?"

"From my home, far across The Churn. A realm called, Forlindea."

"We have turns of talking ahead, Yala. I hope we live to see them. Something *regal* is heading towards us from the east. It must be, Ruthy."

"Promise me you will keep my words to yourself, alone."

"Your words are carved in me."

"*Words are carved*...," Yala chanted, in wonder. "I have not heard that phrase in a hundred orbits."

"Well, take me to her. We might appear cunning, if we stay here," Nyctámēna said, before turning to Callisto. "Calli?"

"*Yup*?" Callisto said, with her head drifting, up and down.

"You said a word," Nyctámēna smiled. "That's good. I'm so proud of you. You'll be talking everyone's ear off by nightfall."

23

COUNTERVAIL

THREE SOULS WALKED OUT of the thicket and into the open air at sunrise, where ferns and grasses danced in the wind. Sunlight peered over the eternal storm, casting rays in Nyctámēna's eyes. Goggles gave her the gift of veiled sight, but everything had its limits. As she approached Ruthy and her vast array of Reapers and consorts, she discerned little, but what her imagination was able to piece together, through bright impressions.

Back down in Ümfalla, the spore cloud played games with the darkness, an endless array of shadows in the half-light, grim beauty, a world suited for dark-seeing eyes. In the cloudless world of Avernus the sky played no tricks when there was no curtain for mystery and illusion.

Sky Realm was a pure medium for light. If the sun was, indeed, new again all day, its changes in Sky Realm were as predictable as its own risings and settings. Nyctámēna's eyes watered at her first sunrise, but she refused to look away from the sparkling approach of Ruthy.

Fifty Reapers walked in tight formations, flanking the ruler they knew as, Arethūsa, who was shimmering in her silk gown, in the rising sun. Orīa walked directly behind her in her streaming Weir robe of deep crimson, giving it the appearance of bloodstained cloths stolen from the sky of an Ümfallan morning. Briar stood at the head of the Reaper cadre, to the right of Arethūsa, dressed in a cloak of stark black.

In spite of the newness in the transfer of power, Nyctámēna sensed something old and rehearsed in the approach, a hidden script, every player was following, line by faded line. When they were within speaking distance, Nyctámēna laughed at the stark contrast of her own ragged appearance, in the face of regal splendor of the woman she considered, Ruthy.

"You've made some changes since you've been back!" Nyctámēna called out. "I hope you intend to do what's best for both realms. Change is a delicate thing."

Nyctámēna shielded her eyes, while she took long strides, closer to the irradiant Arethūsa. After she blinked away tears from the sun, the world in front of her turned black. Reapers stood as sentinels, shoulder to shoulder, in hooded formation, guarding their new Ruler.

A sparkling tiara, atop Arethūsa's head, was visible behind the cadre of Reapers. Then a pair of freckled hands parted the Reapers and Arethūsa stepped through, facing Nyctámēna. Wind blew her long red braid to the side and Nyctámēna saw the thick strand of her own hair, intertwined with Arethūsa's.

"It feels like a lifetime ago I gave you that while we Hexed," Nyctámēna said, running her fingers through her own hawk-hair.

"It *was* a lifetime ago," Arethūsa said, distantly. "It was a powerful gift for you to give me. I felt stronger because of it, even when you fell sick with rot. Then a Weir saved you, the same one who intervened through mycelium, on my behalf. And now, you've become a Weir, too. I see it in your lip. Your power keeps growing."

"And you look...*clean*."

"The lies I told you down there were necessary. I hope you understand that. This is a complicated structure," Arethūsa said, holding out her arms, to the horizons. "Make one change without regard and everything topples to the ground. The Goddess must be tended, for the sake of everyone, above and below."

"Tended? No Goddess would need such actions reserved for mortal things."

"You're in Sky Realm, now. Look around...this realm is as mysterious for you as Ümfalla was for me," Arethūsa half-smiled.

"*All is entangled*. Ruthy, you—"

"Ruthy is dead!" Arethūsa shouted, as her face went flush. She swallowed hard, "She served her purpose. I am *Arethūsa*, Ruler of Avernus."

Orīa smiled at the distant look on Yala's face, after the pronouncement of the chosen Name, on behalf of Arethūsa. Orīa nodded when Yala made eye-contact with her.

Arethūsa composed herself and continued, "Perhaps it's the sun and the fresh air confusing you. Or it might have been your passage through the Labyrinth. Time will unfold what *I* descended into the darkness to bring back to the Goddess. Without question, I owe you my life. I saved yours, too."

"And you owe Callisto more than one life," Nyctámēna said, through clenched teeth. "Through Briar's deceit, we lost—"

"The deaths of of those who followed you up were avenged," Arethūsa said. "Briar is guiltless and already avenged those who sacrificed themselves for this day."

"Praise Daphnē!" Orīa chanted, holding Briar's hand, firmly.

Nyctámēna glared at Briar, "Let Briar decide if he's guiltless." She looked back to Arethūsa, "Drop the act and speak plainly to me. There's nothing to hide, now. I know you want to. I came a long way just to be right here, with you, to see that you used your powers justly, for the sake of two realms."

"Mēna?"

"Yes?"

"Good. Just checking," Arethūsa sighed. "I truly love what you're wearing to shield your eyes. So clever. But I feel like I'm missing something that was always so clear down there, in the darkness. You're hiding something."

"We both have secrets, but I choose to seek answers to my own, not embrace illusion. Whatever you choose to call yourself, you possess an undeniable power, *Arethūsa*. But I'm all me, right here. If you find more of me, let me know."

"I was someone else, before I jumped from Sky Tracer. Who you found was a ghost and you gave that ghost a chance to find raw power and bring it back, reinvigorating my spirit, as much as it will the Goddess. But there was a whole world of me you never knew. Few ever did. I am not who I was. Not before you met me, or after. But the woman I am, *now*, Ruler of Avernus, is a potent mixture of all those selves. You know that mixture through yourself. Now, I am One in myself. *Pure as Wind*. Do you see me?"

"You speak of yourself as if you're somehow One with this Goddess. I don't know of her and your ambition is turning you into—"

"My *ambition* will save us all."

"Your words are more jagged than the Sideon Cliffs. Your words are not your own."

"That's Ümfallan talk. You need to leave that down there. *Carved words* for a dark world."

"Was everything, *down there,* an act? Because Ümfalla is below us, just as vital as Sky Realm." Nyctámēna pointed, with thrusting gestures. "You can't see it, but it's as much a part of this place as this Tree. Mycelium you risked everything for is proof of that. That's why I'm up here, half-blinded by the sun. I fear for Ümfalla, for countless souls who call it home, as grim as it might be. Why can't you just let things be and fix the mechanics of your people?"

Arethūsa looked beyond Nyctámēna and in the direction of a distant Yala, who remained beside Callisto. Callisto's eyes were regaining focus and were fixed on Briar.

Arethūsa shouted, "Yala! Why do you linger in a place that is not your own? Your place is by my side! Get over here and join Orīa!"

"*Ruthy!*" Nyctámēna scowled.

"*That girl is dead!*" Arethūsa seethed. "Say it again and you will be, too! She was a moment, a dream," she said, with composure. "Ruthy tried to live up here, but the air choked her to death. Never speak that Name to me again. You of all people understand the importance of Names."

"Remember Hexing and laughing at the world?"

"Stop it."

"Remember falling the sky like a fucking Goddess? I thought you were the Goddess, until I saw your fear, a fear that became resilience. Or when you dealt justice on that piece of shit, Dorian. Remember saving my life? Remember this?!" She shouted, pulling out the knife Ruthy used to carve her goodbye.

A succession of blades were drawn by the Reaper Guard, when they surrounded Nyctámēna.

"Hold!" Briar shouted, with his twin-katars shining above his hands.

"I remember," Arethūsa said. "I remember, like I remember my nightmares. Even the worst of them have shining moments, in the darkness. It might have been a handful of *days* ago, but it passed and now I'm awake. I treasure those moments for what they engendered, but here is where all of us belong. I have chosen a Name of power, one I will—"

"*Briar!*" Callisto roared, from the distance.

"Don't say another *fucking* word, Calli!" Nyctámēna shouted, over her shoulder, where Reapers were close enough to feel her breath. She turned back and glared at Orīa, "*Your lips are aflutter.* I might be green in Whispering, but I sense the deceit you're spouting into Arethūsa's ear. That Weir is controlling you, Arethūsa!"

"I'm beyond such Weir tricks," Arethūsa said. "Such contrivances are nothing but wind to me."

"You really are be-Whispered. You're lost."

"Don't speak to me of being lost. Tell me, have you found those Resurrection Spores? You found some passing fancy to latch onto, to keep you from killing yourself in the mud.

That's self-deceit. If you weren't so powerful, such an ally, you would no longer have a head on your shoulders. I *know* what I seek. The Goddess speaks through me and I am her vessel. All will be revealed."

"When? Tomorrow? I know nothing of this Goddess *you* speak of, never heard her voice, never seen her. But *you* have the power of the people, right now. Here and now. Above and below."

"You must choose where to stand in the unfolding future I bring."

"The future never comes!" Yala called out, from afar. "How dare you wear the tiara of the Goddess! How dare you pretend to bring change when my sister is still bound to that carriage! I should be holding her, in my arms, as we speak! You cannot cheat the course of Nature forever! You are betraying everything we talked about, your whole life! How dare you!"

"*You* are—" Arethūsa began.

"BRIAR!" Callisto screamed, at Yala's side. "I'm going to gut you and leave you to the slugs, you sister-fucker!"

Reapers turned to Briar, who swallowed hard at Callisto's vitriol. Near forgotten mockeries from an Ümfallan childhood, regarding his love for Orīa, rushed back in through Callisto's words, the assumption Orīa was his sister. Such childish trifles still stung the Captain of Reapers.

Orīa laughed away the false epithet, while Arethūsa turned towards what was transpiring. When she did, Nyctámēna snatched the tiara from Arethūsa's head and burst through the Reapers, on her way back to the hill where Yala and Callisto were standing. A look of shock was on Yala's face, while Callisto bore a wry smile, turning her face into a caricature of joy at Nyctámēna's surprising act of mischief.

"She takes a piece of me, I"ll take a piece of her!" Nyctámēna shouted, as she approached. "*Run!*"

"Where?!" Callisto shouted back.

"Away!"

"I know a place!" Yala cried, eyeing the cobalt sky, to the west.

"Then run!" Nyctámēna shouted, grabbing Yala by the crook of her cloaked elbow and pulling her along.

"Wait," Yala said, in a voice deeper than her own.

Yala planted her feet and tilted her lips up to Whisper to the wind. Meanwhile, Reapers were listening to conflicting orders from Arethūsa and Briar. Through faint sounds upon the wind, Nyctámēna surmised where Yala's Whispers were going.

A pair of Sky Shears were circling, high above, after a night decimating murmurations of starlings. The streamlined birds let out a shrill cry and Nyctámēna recognized cadences from a lost language, but could not translate the words. She marveled at the stillness of the Wind Weir at work. Only Yala's dark cloak moved along with her lips. When she lowered her head, the Sky Shears were descending, at such speed, the wind whistled.

"Go!" Yala shouted. Her stillness turned into a run. Her skeletal frame moved with grace, but paled in comparison to the pair of warriors. "Head west!"

While the three companions fled, Reapers obeyed the final word from Arethūsa, through Briar's mouth, as they set forth in pursuit. Orīa reveled in the event and joined a stoic Briar, taking him by the hand. She swelled with pride through the power of Briar and herself at work. Arethūsa glared at the united pair, with rage in her eyes, before returning her gaze to the field.

"If they kill her, I'll have your head, Briar," Arethūsa said.

"Their orders are clear," Briar said, staring ahead. "If they kill her, I'll go ahead and kill myself."

"That's a foolish thing to say," Orīa scoffed, glaring at him.

"I've always been a fool," Briar said, pulling his hand free of hers.

The way became tangled with twisted trees and clinging vines, while the two warriors kept a steady pace, in compensation for the third. At least twenty Reapers were closing in on them, but their intent was to capture their quarry, not kill them. The pursued realized the Reapers intent, since arrows would have felled them before they had a chance to turn their backs. When five Reapers were within arm's reach of Yala, a deafening whistle caused everyone to glance back.

Two Reapers were in stride but no longer had heads. Their bodies ran themselves into the ground, when another whistle was accompanied by the black blur of another Sky Shear. The bird of prey looped back up into the blue emptiness, while the work of its wings spilled onto the ground.

Three Reapers were squirming along the ground, trying to put their stomachs and intestines back into their wing-cut midsections. Reapers, trailing behind, headed for the thickest portion of trees, while the three women carried on, in the ebb and flow of their flight.

Whistles from Sky Shears became fainter as the sun cast its full splendor on Avernus. The three companions found themselves within a dark forest of gnarled trees, warped through centuries of wind. Yala stopped running and fell into a crouch, where she heaved over bundles of roots. Entangled trees casted long shadows.

"We have to keep moving," Nyctámēna said, with her head on a swivel.

"No," Yala managed, between breaths.

"I'll carry you, if I have to," Callisto said.

"No need," Yala heaved, slowly rising to a stand. "They cannot follow us in here. Only a Weir who knows the *Names* can walk through these woods."

"Orīa is a Weir," Nyctámēna said.

"Brother-fucker," Callisto spit.

"Orīa has the gift but not the way. She looks like a full-fledged Weir, but fails to hear. That is dangerous for everyone, especially herself. I was a fool for leaving her alone with Arethūsa. Orīa is more of an enigma than I thought, but we needed her. Her powers are volatile and cannot speak in here. Power pales at hard-won wisdom. She knows she cannot enter this place, not without help," Yala smiled. "You are far more of a Weir than she is, Nyctámēna. You hear but do not understand. Not yet. Keep listening. And what you are listening for will reveal itself, when it is time. You will hear."

"So what now?" Callisto asked, eyeing the conglomeration of ancient trees. The air was so thick, it obliterated any sense of time and place. Every syllable was followed by a foggy accompaniment.

"Now?....," Yala smiled. "Now, we walk. Sky Tracer, as you have Named it, is through these woods, to the west. My sister is there, waiting for me. Always waiting. To hell with tomorrows."

24

THE NAMING OF THINGS

THE OPEN SKY OF Avernus seemed like a fever dream, through the fog and twisted trees. It was not a walk through the woods: They were becoming attributes of the woods, as much as the dead leaves on the ground and haunting voices, echoing through the mist. Whenever Yala Whispered another Name to a looming spirit, the presence of hidden things became pronounced. When the spectral voice faded, Yala turned to Nyctámēna and simply spoke.

"If you only knew how much I want to run, until my heart bursts, to reach my sister," Yala said, with a trembling lower lip. "But things cannot be rushed in here."

"Story of my life," Callisto said. "The long wait, while the truth is just ahead. Speaking of truths, what are you planning on doing with that?" She asked, tapping the tiara on Nyctámēna's hip. "Planning on wearing it?"

"Nah," Nyctámēna grinned. "Not my style. I figured I'd give it back to the Goddess, someday."

"She sleeps in the Tree, always," Yala said, listening to the wind. "It is said the tiara was taken from Daphnē, the night she was entombed in crystal. But it could be another pretty lie."

"Well, I'll just hold onto the tiara, until she wakes up."

"You'd look pretty great wearing it," Callisto smirked, with a wink.

"Oh yeah? There's enough going on with my hair, as it is. Perhaps there's a sparkly tiara waiting for me in another life. But who knows, I might try it on sometime, for the hell of it."

"You're already a world of surprises, Mēna," Callisto said, rolling her eyes.

"Mēna?" She half-smiled. "You're halfway there, Calli."

"Am I missing something here?" Yala asked, looking at the warriors, on either side of her.

Callisto laughed, "You're the one keeping the pissed off spirits of Ages past from doing terrible things to us. So you just keep on focusing. I can't manage to get a single Name right, when she's standing right next to me. You two would be fucked, if I was leading."

"I'm sorry, Yala," Nyctámēna said. "We shouldn't be joking. Not in times like these."

"No," Yala smiled. "This is refreshing. And it always seems to be, *times like these*. Wait for another time and you realize you are already dead."

"Well said," Callisto laughed.

"It has been quite a while, since I laughed," Yala said.

"How old *are* you?" Callisto asked.

"*Calli,*" Nyctāmēna groaned.

"I mean, you look great," Callisto said. "But it's pretty fucking clear you've seen the better part of an Age. Because you're so wise and powerful and communing with the dead."

Yala squinted her eyes, before she spoke, "I am seven-hundred and sixty-four orbits old."

"Holy shit!"

"How is that possible?" Nyctámēna asked. "Only the divine live through the Ages. Well, so do Phibians. But things forgotten on their parts are like deaths," she said, clenching her jaw.

"I am from a realm far to the east, where The Churn is called Oceána and things grow according to the gifts of Nature, rather than the Goddess. I lived on the Rolling Hills, in the sylvan realm of Forlindea. In the heart of the forest, the trees are so entangled, light hardly passes. Ancient Forlindeans were said to have inherited the stars and see into dark secrets. They were already diminishing, by the time I departed for Sky Realm. They spoke a language I heard you mumbling, Nyctámēna. I do not know the words, but I recognize the music..."

"Wait a moment," Callisto interjected. "Are you saying she's a Forlindean?"

"I've been many things," Nyctámēna said, dismissively. "I'm not up for another walk through the Labyrinth, just yet. And dark-bright eyes aren't that rare in Ümfalla."

"You're the only one I've met," Callisto said. "Nobody else sees into the white."

"Well, you've had your head down, obsessing about Sky Tracer, for most of your life."

"I've got dreams. Things you could never imagine. Stick with me and you might see. But I'm with Yala, the all-knowing. Your mysteries reach across oceans."

"What is important to understand," Yala began, "is not the fact you know the words, Nyctámēna, but the *way* in which you speak them, even in your mumblings. Anyone can say words. That has been shown, throughout the Ages. Only the initiated can say them in a way that gives them meaning, in the stream of life. Pardon me for a moment—"

Yala closed her eyes, *catching* the voice through her lips. She tasted and swallowed, before she Whispered a Name and the incorporeal voice dwindled, like thunder on a mountain. Nothing changed, as far as the essence of the foggy woods, but a presence receded and the hidden path was further revealed to the ageless Wind Weir.

"I hope you are paying attention," Yala said. "I am only doing this for you, once."

"Your words are being carved in me," Nyctámēna said.

"You are like walking alongside a ghost," Yala said.

"Tell me, Yala, how were you able to Whisper to the birds of prey from such a distance?"

"Ah, the Sky Shears," Yala smiled. "I've known that pair since they were fledglings. They are quite receptive, unlike the larger creatures who haunt the skies. They were already listening."

"The creatures in the Labyrinth were listening. Callisto wouldn't be here, otherwise. But that was luck and they were within my voice's reach. I've seen a Foam Weir pull off feats on the scale of what you did and it almost killed her. You were unscathed. It reminds me of Ruthy speaking through the ground. It's magic."

"No. Everything comes at a cost," Yala said. "The creatures were listening, the Shears were listening and so was the mycelium for your version of, *Ruthy*. She pays for it, dearly... I imagine your Foam Weir's Whispers were to unwilling ears."

"Reapers and Spiders. So, yes."

"My Whispers to the Shears were reciprocal. They were willing and they trust me. My days of forcing Whispers upon the unwilling are long gone, for my own and everyone else's sake. I Whisper to those who want to hear. Therefore, I was subject to that balance. It is imbalance that takes. Always remember that."

"While we're confessing our deepest secrets—" Callisto began.

"You mean, Yala's," Nyctámēna interjected.

"Sure," Callisto said. "Which Goddess is Ruthy, or whatever her name is now, speaking to?"

"Daphnē, the Goddess in the Tree," Yala said.

"And how did, *Daphnē,* get there?"

"She was tricked, long before I reached Avernus, with my sister. Some say her daughter tricked her. But it was probably some ambitious mortal with divine help, or unfathomable magic. My sister and I were seeking help from Avernus for a terrible war. Daphnē was not even a thought to me back then. We worshipped another, One beyond Naming. The Avernians were always our allies, in times of need. The reasons for the war no longer matter. It never did, like most wars. When the Seven Elders of the time saw our power through the wind, in the heights of Sky Realm, they took us as ransom, tools for their own ends. Over a short amount of orbits, many Weirs in Forlindea were lured to Avernus, on a oneway trip, by sea and sky, to feed the mechanisms of power. Power is power. It never dies, simply moves on. Daphnē's power is still contained, but her spirit is gone. She is nothing but a vessel and I fear Arethūsa is becoming the same. I was deceived by hope for balance in the realms. Arethūsa is a living copy of the petrified Daphnē. Something else moves her. I have known Arethūsa from the time she was taken from her family as a child. I know her heart and what you saw back there is not her. Orīa Whispers her own ambition through her. Something else is stir—"

Yala spread her arms and opened her mouth wide when the voices turned silent fog into a rumbling portent of doom. She Whispered many Names and never wavered, as she continued to walk and give back, just as much as she received. The two warriors, at her sides, knew not to walk beyond the limits of Yala's outspread arms. When the voices diminished, Yala let her arms fall and she opened her eyes.

"Where was I?" Yala asked, swallowing hard.

"What happens if you fail to name them?" Callisto asked.

"Silence follows. For all of us," Yala said.

"*Now*, you tell us. Is she serious?" Callisto glanced at Nyctámēna.

"Yup," Nyctámēna said. "Spirits of these woods don't approve of the living"

"You *are* listening," Yala smiled.

"Are those a pair of spirits ahead," Callisto pointed, as two pale red lights appeared through the fog. "Look there."

"No," Yala said. "That is my sister."

"The Dim Light."

"*Sky Tracer.*"

Sky Tracer's beauty from the darkness of Ümfalla had always taken Nyctámēna's breath away. But sickness accompanying that beauty reminded her that good and evil had nothing to do with the beautiful. Beauty was like power, beyond good and evil, without regard to anything else. When she approached Sky Tracer through the fog, beauty fled and the dark carriage remained, the horror of its grim workings. Yala ran to the dim red lights, through the fog, as the three women passed the haunted threshold of the woods and reached the dizzying heights of the End.

"Give her a moment," Nyctámēna said, grabbing Callisto by her shoulder.

Through the fog, the red glow from the Weir's eyes waited. They dared to walk closer where Yala weeped at her sister's side, while she held her skeletal hands in her own. The Weir was bound by silk ropes to an oblique mast, at the head of the dark carriage, large enough to hold a handful of young souls, within. On the underside of the carriage, a trap door hung wide open, fluttering in the wind.

Over the precipice, in the crook of a branch, there was a pool of dark water. It was apparent the carriage was fixed to open and drop its load upon arrival. The silk tracks were nearly invisible from a distance and the carriage itself swayed with the wind.

The Weir's head hung limply on her thin neck, where every vertebrae was visible, just as the rest of her bones, throughout her naked body. Her black hair obscured her skeletal form, windblown, beyond the Weir's bony feet. The Weir's red eyes were unblinking, bulging from their dark sockets. All her body was atrophied to stillness, besides her fluttering lower lip. Yala kept her forehead pressed to her sister's, as she spoke words only a sister would understand.

"Shouldn't we get her off that abominable thing?" Callisto muttered.

"I don't think we can," Nyctámēna said. "Her existence is bound to Sky Tracer. Look at her. She's eating the air and nothing more."

"How can you know that?"

"Yala would have freed her already, if she could. Her love delves deeper than her age."

"We have to go," Yala said, without turning away from her sister. "*Now*, is the time."

"May I know your sister's Name first?" Nyctámēna asked, approaching slowly.

"Ask her yourself," Yala said, looking up with radiant red eyes, from weeping.

Nyctámēna approached the Weir and knelt before her, to look her in the eyes, the source of the red glow crowning so many Ümfallan turns. In spite of their shine, Nyctámēna could see the torment, intertwined with joy, from the Weir seeing her sister. The Weir's top lip moved, along with her lower, at the sight of Nyctámēna. Bright eyes of opposing natures met each other at the edge of the end of the world. For a fleeting moment, the Weir lifted her head, to speak faint words.

"It has been so long...*remember*...I am Ákonitē. Saw you...so many times..."

"We must leave this place," Yala said. "Another Weir is leading them through the woods. I hear the Names being called."

"We need to fly!" Callisto shouted. "Some creepy Weir is a stone's throw away!"

"It's Seerinx," Yala said. "She's even worse than I am."

"Didn't realize you were bad," Nyctámēna said.

"The terror of the world," Yala said, with a wink, as she leaned over her sister. "This is the last time, my dear," she Whispered into her sister's ear. "I promise you. One more time," Yala concluded, kissing Ákonitē on her sunken cheek. "Climb on," she said, to the other two.

"On top?" Callisto shouted, running up to them.

"Nobody is riding inside this hell," Yala said, as she climbed on top of the carriage.

"I came here to cut this thing and now I'm about to take a ride," Callisto cringed, while she climbed up, behind Yala. "*Not* my hidden dream."

Nyctámēna followed and the three situated themselves on top of the carriage. Without warning, the carriage creaked into motion, when Ákonitē began to Whisper, deeply. A hidden mechanism within Sky Tracer propelled them onward and downward, in grim quietude. Ákonitē's eyes turned bright red, casting a pair of macabre beacons through the fog. The fog gave way to empty blue sky and the setting sun found Nyctámēna's goggled eyes.

When she turned away, she saw the glittering form of Arethūsa, standing next to a hooded Weir, with eyes like liquid onyx. Nyctámēna almost waved at the sight of Ruthy, but remembered the soul she wanted to see was no more.

Arethūsa stood as still as the Goddess Daphnē, while she watched Sky Tracer vanish into the blueness beyond.

When Nyctámēna turned away, the spore cloud was churning against the overlying emptiness, where blue met black. Fierce winds whipped Ákonitē's streaming black hair, beyond the dark carriage. For a moment, the four women were in a placeless place, drifting through abstraction. Behind them, the Tree of Avernus' branches spread darkly throughout the sky. Below them, the murk of the spore cloud was approaching.

The wind died before the gloom found them and Nyctámēna pulled off her goggles and breathed in Ümfallan air, once again, as she looked into the half-light with naked eyes. Callisto sat and gazed in wonder, Yala wept and Nyctámēna listened to Ákonitē, as the familiar voice Whispered them across the sky, while her red eyes stared down the darkness.

25

THE WIND IN THE LEAVES

A RARE SHIFT OF wind blew from the north, as Briar and Orīa walked along trodden ferns, on their way to the Eighth Seat. A touch of chill was in the air from the rogue wind, bringing with it tinges from colder regions of the unknown.

They were both hooded and silent in their slow progression to the first of what was destined to be many Gatherings of influential peoples of Avernus. The way was flat, but the final push towards the chamber, where the Seven Elders were fixed in time, loomed high in the distance. The sun vanished behind the Storm and the last glimmers of day turned the land to long shadows.

"You should have killed them when you had the chance." Orīa said.

"You've been telling me that, all week. Saying it more than once, doesn't change what happened. I was following orders," Briar said, keeping his eyes ahead.

"Yala is pious *and* powerful which makes her dangerous enough. But with her sister, she is a force. There was a reason the Elders confined her to that contraption."

"Nothing is that simple. Nyctá was with her and she's not our enemy. She might be the best of all of us. As for Callisto...I already betrayed her, once. It would have been like killing my own kin."

"But you would never betray me. And I am something far different and deeper than kin. We made our own world together. We have that which transcends Naming."

"Everything finds a Name, in the end. You need to remember your place in all of this mess."

"*I am right here*, right where I was destined to be."

"And yet you haven't seen Arethūsa all week. Nobody has. That worries me."

"Someone has. Arethūsa has been seeking counsel from that old hag, Seerinx. It wounds me to the heart to think what that crone has undone. Arethūsa is powerful beyond reason and it takes all of me to Whisper her into our intent. Too much of her old self persists. But I did find a time to see Arethūsa for a moment, two nights ago."

"What did she say?"

"Nothing. I only had a chance to wish her well, in a way only I can."

"I know you, too well, Orīa. *Stop it*! If I didn't know how much you loved me, I'd think you'd already Whispered me into your will. A little more than a week ago, you were still a Night Whisperer."

"And you were nothing but a fucking thief in the darkness."

"You're not the first woman to remind me of that, even if those memories are scattered. It's as if my time back in Ümfalla was all a dream.."

"Good," Orīa smiled. "*Look at us*, Briar."

"I only see you, reaching for things beyond anyone's grasp. Yala might be pious, but you're just as devout to something else. Stop being cunning and just *be*. This is enough. All of this," he said, with outspread arms. "Stop all this fucking intrigue and *be*."

"Start being a little smarter and give a shit. I know what you're capable of and it's far more than you've been willing to show."

"I'll do what I must and you do the same," Briar said, as they approached the entrance to the chamber. A group of thirty hooded Weirs were lingering at the threshold and chattering to each other, in their girlish voices. "I never knew there were this many Weirs in Avernus."

"The brothels are emptying," Orīa smiled. "I have been busy, while you have been brooding."

"They look far too young for this."

"They were old enough to suck cocks and be fucked, while they Whispered to pathetic old men that everything was going to be okay. Everything is far better than, *okay*, for them now. It's about to get much worse for those who cling to dead traditions. Such tradition rots from its core and *I* am the *Wind* come to blow it all to pieces. The present Age thrusts responsibility on the strong, no matter their age. Older ones with the gift went mad, or became food for the darkness of Ümfalla. I am ancient in my twenty-five orbits of existence. Let youth inherit the world."

"We're walking on thin air."

"Then the sky will be ours," Orīa said, taking Briar's arm in hers, as she raised her chin and glared at the young Weirs she passed.

When the Wind Weirs pointed in wonder at Orīa, she pulled Briar tightly to her and smiled at the moment. Briar took his place amongst the Reapers, at the threshold to the bustling chamber, after Orīa kissed him on his forehead, before she entered. She vanished into the thick of the crowd, on her way to her place atop the stairs of The Eighth Seat.

The Seven Elders glistened in torchlight, but were diminished by the multitudes within the chamber. Borēan's petrified form was shrouded up to his neck, concealing the truth of what Orīa had done. She relished in what was lying beneath the regal cloak.

The chosen, from the Middle and Upper Rims, filled the chamber floor, while Orīa stood to the right of the Eighth Seat, with her thirty eager Wind Weirs occupying the stairs, below. All of them wore identical crimson Weir cloaks of a lighter hue than Orīa's. Young Weirs fidgeted in their newfound garments, while they peered down at a crowd that purchased their bodies at will, only a handful of turns before.

On the opposing side, Seerinx loomed darkly, with her onyx-hued eyes fixed on some indistinct point. Her gray hair, streaming from her black hood, imparted a look of wizened years on her wrinkled visage. Seerinx stood at the head of her twenty Moon Weirs, all standing in silence and far older than the bright-eyed Wind Weirs on the other side. All of them were dressed in weathered black robes, worn with a stillness, indicative of experience.

In the center of it all, Arethūsa was standing in front of her exquisite wooden seat, freshly carved with images of the world, above and below, from mushrooms to the Morning Star. The Ruler of Avernus was wearing a silk gown, shimmering in the light of the rising Sister Moons, giving her the appearance of wearing reflective moonlight, nothing more. Arethūsa sat down with ceremony and the chamber fell silent.

When she opened her mouth to speak, Seerinx's lower lip began to flutter, in conjunction with Arethūsa's cadence that followed. Silver light from the Three Sister Moons made the Weir's black cloak shimmer. The old Moon Weir's eyes were as dark and distant as the spore cloud.

Arethūsa focused on something beyond the chamber, as if she were speaking from a dream:

"*Change has found Sky Realm,*" Arethūsa chanted, evoking nods and restlessness from the masses. "*We have gathered on this night to proclaim the natural progression of power...to show all of you...order will...*" Arethūsa clenched her teeth, as she closed her eyes. Wind whistled through the chamber. Orīa looked at Arethūsa, but marked a nearby Seerinx deep in Whispers, clenching her teeth, like an old copy of Arethūsa. Orīa shut her eyes and delved into her magic, within, as her Whispers joined the updraft of wind, finding her Ruler's face.

Arethūsa raised her head, refreshed. She carried on, speaking in warm tones, "For over an Age, the Seven Seats were awarded through blood and gender, rather than justice and Avernian will. As you can see, I am no man," she half-smiled and winked, to warm laughter. "I share no blood with those preceding me, bore no title at birth. I descended into darkness to bring rejuvenation to this realm, fell into darkness to return to the light of a new Avernus. Nothing is done alone, no matter what tradition tells us. Many of you are looking to my sides and wondering who these *imposters* must be. They are the future. Power leaks out of everything. over time...from trees, to the people of this realm. But power finds fresh life to inhabit. These Weirs you see are vessels of power, precious souls, hidden in plain sight. Weirs will be feared and oppressed, no longer. Their words will no longer be wasted on the coward's ear, but in service to Avernus. We will embrace them, not only as our own, but as our destiny. But it's the will of each and every one of you that will guide Sky Realm into a bountiful future. From the infants, to the elders, all of you are like the branches of the Tree of Avernus, wonderfully distinct and part of the whole. Your will shall bear the fruit of what's to come. The future of Sky Realm is the zenith. Nothing collapses, not when we are united by a common ideal, rather than rigid decrees."

Arethūsa took a deep breath, while applause and joyful shouts filled the wind-swept chamber. On both sides of her, Seerinx and Orīa were trembling through agonizing labor. The old Moon Weir continued to Whisper through the power of the Sister Moons, while the young Wind Weir's lips fluttered manically through the wind.

Before the crowd settled, Orīa gasped and her lips went still, in conjunction with the wind settling in the chamber. Seerinx opened her onyx-eyes and grinned at the looming Sister Moons. Arethūsa spoke in the chant-like cadence, from before.

"Through the power of the Goddess, I will make this Tree grow higher and the sun shall shine brighter on all of us. The Tree will grow broader and The Churn will give way to the calm waters of Oceāna. Everything must be earned. Nobody is beyond reproach. On this night, on the first Gathering of the Eighth Seat, under the glory of the Three Sister Moons, I will show you the truth of my words. Words are nothing, unless matched with deeds."

Arethūsa looked over the vast array of people from Avernus' Rims. Wind-inspired garments, lavish and formal, hung limply on the many bodies in the windless chamber. The vibrant hues of the people stood in stark contrast to Reapers and Moon Weirs. When

Arethūsa's eyes fell upon the Captain of Reapers, she frowned and pointed at Briar. All eyes in the chamber fell upon him and Briar smiled, dutifully.

"*Nothing comes without sacrifice,*" Arethūsa chanted on. "*The Captain of our Guard, Briar, will show you the verity of my words. He is newly appointed and I am well aware there are doubts. But this man has inherited an Order that lost its way, under the rule of our last Elder. The former Captain, Stayx, fell into shame and despair, casting his body down into the darkness.*" A gentle breeze blew into the chamber and Orīa's lips found their flutter. Arethūsa blinked hard and continued, "In that same darkness, I saw a *single* woman slaughter the once dreaded Reapers by the dozens. They have lost their way and must reclaim the ferocity of the Name they bear. Under my rule, Reapers will thrive, just as Weirs are rising. Therefore, if anyone sees why this man is not fit to lead the Reapers, let her, or him, approach the stairs." The breeze settled and so did Orīa's Whisper. Seerinx flourished in the moonlight, while her young Ruler continued, "*Blood has always been the truth of this Order and blood will have blood, on this night. In the approach to these venerable stairs, know that this gesture will be followed by a fight to the death in this very chamber.*"

Orīa's stifled scream was smothered by the clarion-voice of another in the chamber. Another voice followed and three more, as five Reapers approached the stairs and kneeled, in unison. Seerinx nodded at the Reaper approach, while Orīa watched her do it, before turning her gaze to Briar. A brief look of consternation fell on Arethūsa's face, as she took another deep breath and nodded.

"*Five of you,*" Arethūsa said, as if she had just awoken. "Clearly, there is discord in your ranks."

Arethūsa stood and made a parting motion with her arms. Ushered by Moon Weirs, the crowd stepped back to open a makeshift arena, in the center of the chamber. Arethūsa glanced at Orīa, who was unblinking in her horror.

Five Reapers were dressed in the black cloaks of their Order and had their hands on the hilts of their swords, still in their sheaths. They all drew, at once, when they stood and waited for Arethūsa's command. Briar remained near the threshold of the chamber, with his cloaked arms crossed and a wry smile on his weathered, but youthful face.

"When the five of you turn to face your opponent, the trial begins," Arethūsa said, with gravity. "If you prevail, I will ask you your Names. Until then, you are the Nameless, facing your future, in the instant."

While Arethūsa was speaking, Briar approached the arena, through mutterings from the multitudes masking his steps. He glanced up at Orīa and she nodded when he flicked his wrists, in his subtle ways, donning his twin-katars. The moment the first Reaper turned his head, his open mouth of determination was filled with Briar's katar. While Briar was holding up the dying man with his blade, the Reaper beside him turned, losing his head, before realizing the sudden shift, from chamber to battle arena.

The other three Reapers backed away, with their swords in hand, moving as one, against Briar. While the combatants circled the arena, Orīa observed Seerinx, who bore grim determination on her face, while muttering to herself. Arethūsa's face remained inscrutable, until her eyes betrayed deep suffering at the event.

For Orīa, the cause for Arethūsa's suffering was as hidden as the Third Moon at dusk. She turned her gaze back to the arena, where Briar held both of their futures in his blades. She found courage through cool determination on his face, while he stared down terrible odds.

Cries and screams at Briar's actions turned to grunts and guffaws, whistles and shouts of encouragement, for someone to make another lethal move. Wind Weirs watched the head of their Order for any sign of what would happen next, while Moon Weirs remained stoic, under Seerinx's gaze. Briar moved with subtle grace, keen-eyed and fluid, while three Reapers closed their distance on him, one strategic step at a time. Had it been a battle in the grim darkness of Ümfalla, Briar's lethal silk lines would have evened the odds, but in the civilized arena of Avernus, he remained unfavored.

A flurry of blades fell on Briar and he met them with lightning-quick actions from his twin-katars. His footwork exceeded the three opponents, but their advantage was clear, when one of the dizzying assaults struck Briar on his right thigh and sent blood streaming onto the time-worn floor of the chamber.

Briar did not flinch at the wound, but used it to his advantage, deftly flicking blood into his opponent's eyes, when the offending Reaper glanced at his own work, for a sliver of a moment. The Reaper's blood, from his slashed throat, joined Briar's on the ground, before the Reaper fell, gurgling his last breaths.

A pair of Reapers remained, moving shoulder to shoulder, grazing eager onlookers with their cloaked backsides. Briar recognized them, two brothers, who swore their undying allegiance to him, when he saved them from an aerial assault by Sky Shears, just a week before. One of them reached into the crowd and threw a young boy at Briar's feet, while the Reaper's brother came at Briar, from the side.

Briar met his blade when the other struck at him from overhead. When Briar's left katar parried the other's, the offender's weapon was destined to fall directly on the terrified boy's head. Briar turned up his boot and heel-shoved the boy forward, with such force, he rolled into the crowd.

With both brothers at his side and in the midst of counterattack, Briar took a single step forward and the sibling's overeager blades found each other's bodies. The brothers stood, face to face, with both their blades sticking through the other's back. Briar stared at the deadlock for a split moment, before dropping to his knee and finishing what the brothers started. His blades were plunged into their sternums.

When Briar rose to his feet, the weight of the siblings' own bodies, along with the sharpness of Briar's Sideon steel blades, slowly split them open, from their chests, to their neck, where Briar performed a brutal final thrust and up-work with his katars, bifurcating their faces and splitting the tops of their heads.

Briar raised his bloody blades to the night sky and held them there, in triumph. At his feet, the dark places where the dead hearts of the slain resided were visible to all, while gray matter from their brains clumped onto the chamber floor, no longer a fighting arena.

A general hush fell, as Briar withdrew his twin-katars, into hidden places of his mechanical, beneath the sleeves of his cloak. He turned to Arethūsa, who bore a face of smiling resolve, in what transpired. Orīa never blinked while she stared at Briar with pride and a desire for something beyond the flesh. She held her hands firmly to her stomach, where their future was growing with every one of her quick breaths.

Seerinx stared into the distance, through her onyx-eyes, just as she had prior to the event, as her weary body diminished in posture. Wind returned to the chamber, blowing the smell of death away, while Orīa's lips fluttered in exquisite harmony.

Arethūsa raised her right hand to chest level and Briar fell to his knee. Her lips parted and trembled in the silence, before she spoke.

"Not only has Briar shown his legitimacy as Captain of the Guard, he risked his own life to save another from a treacherous act. A boy is alive and a Captain has risen. Stand up, Briar, stand up and see your deeds preserved in everyone's eyes. Let it be known what transpired here, in front of hundreds of witnesses: *Honor and selflessness in the face of death*. Words fall short where deeds such as this have taken place. Therefore, I conclude this first Gathering of the Eighth Seat. Remember what you have seen and spread the word, throughout the Rims of Avernus. A kind good night to you all, as our Third Sister

Moon has risen to look down on this place of honor and the wind reminds us of its inexhaustible power."

Briar remained standing in the center of the chamber, while passersby congratulated him and patted him on his weary back. Blood trickled from his wounded leg, but the cut found no mortal places. Wind Weirs giggled all around him, while Seerinx departed in silence, hobbling down the stairs, followed by the rest of her Moon Weirs. When Orīa passed Briar, alongside Arethūsa, she leaned close to him and Whispered, as she always did, when they parted.

A sudden urge to pull Orīa into his arms and never let go, overtook Briar's thoughts. But he remained where he was, struggling to keep the wry smile of indifference on his face, a face witness to countless acts of violence in his life, hands that ended so many lives, the same ones that failed to save others. Orīa walked behind the radiant Arethūsa, a careful march on her part, on the brink of walking ahead of an ever-watchful Ruler of Avernus.

On the winding path to the Goddess, Arethūsa's steps were growing natural, along with her thoughts, as the crowd's eyes became the eyes of Orīa, alone. Violence stoked excitement amongst the Avernians and the night would be one of festivity, throughout the Upper and Middle Rims of Avernus. Cantankerous Satyrs on Lower Rim would dance and rage, as always. But the Goddess was waiting and Arethūsa was almost thankful for the suffering to come.

"Did I sound like a fool to the people back there?" Arethūsa muttered.

"A fool?" Orīa gasped. "You spoke from your heart and soul. The people were enamored with you, as much as they showed reverence."

"It's strange...it felt as if I were speaking in a dream. I was nervous."

"It didn't show."

"Well, I hardly remember what I said. Just trying to get through it. I felt the absence of the tiara, as if I were wearing a fruitless crown, nothing but hair and dreams. I can't imagine what Mēna did with the tiara," Arethūsa said, with a half-smile.

"She's not wearing it. That much I am sure of," Orīa laughed, softly.

"Thank you."

"For what?"

"Doing this with me. I couldn't bear Seerinx standing over me, while I gag on the entrails of the world. Her counsel is wise and informed, but her presence lies heavy on my spirit. You lift me, Orīa. I do miss, Yala, though. She saved my life, more than once. Comforted me, until the End."

"I will never leave your side, Arethūsa."

"What happened, tonight...with Briar—"

"You don't have to say anything."

"I knew he would prevail. Otherwise, I never would have demanded a trial. It took me all week to come up with that speech. I hate speaking formally. *Words become air...* Sometimes the people need more than pretty words, they need blood and ritual to remember the truth of it all, especially, in times of great change. It was best I left you in the dark, to keep you from worrying. I've seen Briar in action, when I was in Ümfalla. His only equal in the realm is, Mēna. Seerinx agreed with me. I just didn't expect five Reapers to challenge him. Everything unfolded before I had a chance to... It almost seemed planned."

"I was under the same impression," Orīa said, furrowing her brow.

"Such a bloody ritual won't happen again. That's how old ways worm their way into the new. Such stuff rots the tree from the core. *Never again*," Arethūsa said, looking away. She blinked hard and looked back to Orīa, "Nights such as this make me miss the woman I was...the woman I became, down there, if only for a moment."

"Ruthy will always be a part of you."

"Ruthy will haunt my days and scream in my ears at night. I can't be rid of her. Something else moves me. Perhaps it lies in the nature of seeking the greater good."

"*You are the Ruler of Avernus,* a near impossible task. But you are superior to the ones before you. You have a heart. Otherwise, you never would have approved of my starting my own Order, with these forgotten souls, with so much wasted power. Turning tricks in brothels is now weaving power through wind, for the greater good you seek. You will surpass all the ones who came before you. *I see it.* I am honored to be by you and be able to call you, *Arethūsa.*"

"I feel like I've always known you, Orīa. I admit, I doubted you, at first.

"Understandable," she nodded.

"And we'll see about my greatness. But what vexes me...what drives me to madness, is I can't understand *why* Mēna didn't cut Sky Tracer. I certainly thought of cutting it, when I watched her riding off into the spore cloud. I almost waved to her when she left. *It's ridiculous.* And yet, days pass and Sky Tracer remains. I've tried to find some kind of reason behind it, but nothing fits."

"Perhaps she understands how complicated this structure is. She's clearly far more than a Weir and warrior. From what you've told me, she is as wise as she is strong. But wisdom only goes so far. *You see beyond.* She must fear what would happen in Ümfalla, if she cut the chord. Down there is her world. This place must feel like one of the Sister Moons to her. That's what it felt like to me, when I first ascended, so many orbits ago."

"When I fell into the Fungal Realm, I was sure I was dead. It *is* another world, even if it's just beneath us. My survival only revealed stranger things, *beautiful* things..."

"Did you really want to kill yourself, Arethūsa? I'm sorry...that was rash—"

"That's a fair question, for such a night as this, especially, after what I put you through with Briar. At the moment, I did want to kill myself. I finally learned what Sky Tracer really was and I looked into Yala's sister's eyes and..."

"What did you see?"

"Rage and emptiness. It was red oblivion in Ákonitē's eyes. She didn't see into me, see saw *through* me. She showed me how meaningless everything was and the only truth was pain, until death. I leaped from Sky Tracer out of fear and emptiness. I was willing to risk death to bring back mycelial life. Otherwise, I was worse off alive, for everyone. Then Mēna brought me back to life through more than her actions. Even then, I kept looking up at the darkness, imagining this place. Through Yala's guile from up here, I was able to fortify a plan with Briar. And she brought you into all this. *Brilliant.* I speak of it all as if it had happened an Age ago. I suppose that's the feel of Time when great things unfold. I couldn't be rid of Sky Realm," she trailed off, looking up. "I'm waiting for some cataclysmic event to finish this place. I imagine it as the simplest of things. A Sky Shear is blown off course and cuts my throat. Briar gets the itch to rob someone and takes the first Spider back to Ümfalla. You do realize, being a prostitute is far more stable than following me around."

"I'm so sorry, I'm laughing."

"Laugh away. I need a little encouragement beyond fucking pleasantries from everyone else. Then it's back to reality. Sky Tracer is literally hanging by a thread and Yala has been re-united with her sister. If Ákonitē survives, I fear for the whole world. I dream of who I was every night, in the spare moments I'm not dreaming of Mēna's haunting eyes, seeing into my soul, or Nyctá or, Nyctá-fucking-Mēna. Can't she just pick a Name?! *I* did. But, as for Yala... You don't know what she and her sister did, before we were born."

"I've heard stories."

"Stories are words and little more than dim reckonings, in the light of the actual. The Weir Sisters' powers combined were unstoppable. Only dumb luck and a change of the wind stopped them."

"The wind is blowing northerly. tonight. The cold lifts my spirits. I believe Yala and her sister will retreat to their home in Forlindea."

"Perhaps. Something grim is on the horizon. I only wish Mēna was on our side. Nobody can stand up to her, not even herself. It's a foolish thought, but that's *Ruthy* emerging. I miss the power Mēna exuded, the certainty of it. I suppose that equals nothing. I have so much to say to Yala and Mēna, so much that could never be spoken, before. It was never the right time and now the time has passed. I can only imagine how many people have said that, over the Ages: *Never the right time, until...fucking tomorrows...*"

"Perhaps you will say it to them both, some day to come," Orīa said, whimsically. "I waited for Briar through orbits of hell and he returned to me. But we *are* love. Nothing stops that, not even death.

"You fought hard for Briar. You deserve all you have...far more, now that I think about it... Anyway, here I am, reflecting on power and loss and Sky Tracer is running through my mind like a nightmare."

"Speaking of Sky Tracer, who is to be chosen as the replacement for Ákonitē?"

"I leave that to you. I cannot bring myself to do it. And you know the fledgling Weirs in your Order in a way I never will. Only a Wind Weir with a kinship with the elements can do what Áknoitē did. You must choose amongst them. *Soon.* I trust your judgment. But make it known, their confinement to Sky Tracer will be short-lived. No more children will burn, not under my reign. The few amongst the Weirs will suffer for all, but not for long. It's all for the greater good. I'm on the brink of something world-changing with Daphnē."

"So we are are going to keep on calling it, Sky Tracer? It sounds so permanent."

"That *is* its Name. I've seen it from below and agree with it. It will remain, Sky Tracer, until its chord is severed, for good."

"There she is."

"Same as She ever was, though, I have Changed."

Arethūsa's hands trembled at the sight of Daphnē and the dark soil at the base of the tree. She dutifully pulled down her long braid and it fell at her feet, as she pulled up her gown and kneeled. When Orīa took hold of her braid, in preparation for the ritual, she saw the long black strand of Nyctámēna's hair was still intertwined with Arethūsa's own.

When the braid went taut in Orīa's hand, as thick strands of mycelium entered Arethūsa's mouth, Orīa leaned over and put her lips to Arethūsa's left ear, but made sure not to make visceral contact. The one time she had, the silent scream of the Goddess almost finished her.

She Whispered words she intended for the past week and those influencing Arethūsa's intentions, in the days to come. Orīa Whispered away the ghost of Ruthy and reinforced the presence of Arethūsa. Orīa knew not to push too far with Whispers, such extremes would destroy them both.

She felt the presence of moonlight, but the wind and her Whispers governed the moment, rather than the elemental conflict from before. When tears began to stream from a squirming Arethūsa's eyes, Orīa wept along with her, while she stared at the fluttering eyelids of the Goddess in the Tree. Leaves sprouted and replaced the dead, while withered ones found soft greenness again. When Orīa finished Whispering, the place was silent, silent, except for the wind in the leaves.

26

A Few for the Sake of All

THE JOURNEY ON SKY TRACER began as a reflective one. The spore cloud evoked a sense of familiarity for Nyctámēna and Callisto, while the presence of Ákonitē brought with it fathomless memories for Yala, far beyond words or tears. But the slow and gradual descent of the dark carriage quickly became a raucous ride on a Weir-powered vessel, hellbent on reaching its final destination.

As the Wind Weir's eyes grew brighter, at the sight of The Churn, the three ad hoc passengers held onto whatever screw or edge they could, grappling to remain onboard and not become an unlucky version of Ruthy. When they passed above the shoreline of Ümfalla, a vast encampment of Reapers scurried along the coast, like disturbed ants, where crimson dots betrayed the presence of Wind Weirs.

Had the carriage been a little closer, projectiles and Whispers would have be in range. Rather than comment on the bellicose *gathering* on the shore, the three souls braced themselves for the final push of Sky Tracer, over The Churn and into its port of the unknown.

Whispers from Ákonitē on the mast suddenly became shouts as fierce winds, over The Churn, inspired her to do her worst. She was a Weir possessed, as winds whipped the carriage and sent it reeling. Rain pelted them and wonder at the atmospheric event in the two Ümfallan's faces was quickly supplanted by fear. Blinded by wind and rain, the passengers on Sky Tracer were weightless, in the final stretch.

All three passengers floated in their free fall, just above the carriage, while they held fast to hope, in the form of each other and the sheer strength of Nyctámēna's hand on a large screw. Had it not been for the adamant strength and masterful design of Nyctámēna's mechanical, the force of her desperate hold would have warped most metals into ruin.

In the moment, Nyctámēna resembled a three-headed bird, with her hawk-hair streaming in the wind the rest of the journey down. Just as jagged rocks by the sea appeared to fly up and crush them, the carriage settled along the silk tracks and drifted into port.

Rain, rocks and The Churn, were all that was seen by Nyctámēna, when she drew Slender and leaped off the carriage, before it came to a halt. Callisto followed, while Yala tended to her sister, whose eyes were so red-bright, it turned the storm-tossed shore, pink.

The spore cloud was replaced by grim fringes of the Eternal Storm, but Nyctámēna's eyes still suffered from storm-light and fierce rain made it impossible to wear her goggles. She scanned the rocky shore for anything beyond waves crashing, on all sides, while the sea roared along with the primal chorus of thunder.

When her squinting eyes glanced at Yala and her sister, she saw Callisto with her sword overhead and directed at the thick line of Sky Tracer. Nyctámēna bound towards Callisto and grabbed her by her wrists and twisted, until the upraised sword clattered onto the rocks. Callisto pulled out of the hold and faced Nyctámēna, with rage in her eyes.

"*What the fuck was that*?!" Callisto seethed, while pelting rain gave her the appearance of a Phibian.

"Leave it alone!" Nyctámēna shouted, over the thunder. Sky Tracer brought us here, but it holds together far more than any of us can know."

"Are you fucking mad?! It's right there! There!" She pointed, with arms so tense, veins throughout, looked to be on the brink of bursting.

The scar across Callisto's face appeared to be on the verge of tearing open. She reached for her sword, but the moment she did, a wave crashed onto the rocky shore and washed over everyone. Callisto rolled on the rocks, while Nyctámēna kept herself upright, holding onto Sky Tracer's line. She retrieved Callisto's sword and gripped it at her side. Yala was holding onto her sister, sheltered from the waves behind the grim carriage.

"Cut that line and everything we know will be gone!" Nyctámēna shouted. "The spore cloud will give way to the shine! *Everything is connected*!"

"I'll chew through this fucking line, if I have to," Callisto roared, baring her teeth, as she grabbed hold of Sky Tracer's silk line, further down from Nyctámēna.

Before Callisto bit down, her bloodshot eyes grew wide. Nyctámēna looked over her shoulder and followed Callisto's line of sight. Reapers were making their way down the silk tracks, from the distant Ümfallan shore, through indiscernible mechanicals powered by hand. Their progression was slowed by storm winds, but they were drawing ostensibly closer. Another wave crashed upon the rocky coast, blindsiding Nyctámēna and Callisto, knocking them both onto their knees. When they looked up, through salt-blurred eyes, Yala was upon them.

"There's no time, follow me!" Yala shouted. "Callisto, I need you to hold onto my sister. She has no strength left. Keep her close, no matter what happens. *Clear*?!"

Callisto eyed the silk tracks. Through manic breaths, she nodded and bolted to Ákonitē, while Nyctámēna took Yala by the arm and they trudged beyond the carriage, through the tumult of wind and waves.

Shielded from the waves by the carriage, Callisto curled up next to Ákonitē, holding her tight, but the warrior's eyes remained fixed on the silk line, while the rocks sizzled from sea foam. The Weir's hair looked like black seaweed on the wet rocks, splayed across her skeletal body, like a funereal gown.

Her gleaming red eyes dimmed to a pale glow, while her lower lip fluttered, along with the raging wind. Yala held onto Nyctámēna, in the full onslaught of wind, beyond the carriage. Tears in Yala's eyes were evident, even in the storm, but Nyctámēna could feel the Weir's power growing through the fierce wind.

"Follow my lead and don't move," Yala said. "This is our one chance. I hope your nearness allows me to pull it off. You've only just discovered your gift. Take my hand and shut your eyes. What's coming will distract you. Focus on the *feeling*. Leave all the rest to me. *Oh*...and try to keep up," Yala winked, with a sly smile, before Nyctámēna closed her eyes and dug her boots into the rocks.

In her storm-tossed Weir cloak, Yala pulled down her hood and her silvered-black hair tumbled out, as she raised her right arm to the storm. Her eyes grew brighter through the wind, her face, stoic, while her lower lip fluttered through Whispers.

On her periphery, Reapers were drawing closer, a little more than a stone's throw away, fighting against a headwind, but gaining momentum along the silk line, hanging just above the crests of passing waves. Yala held fast to Nyctámēna's hand, with preternatural force. Ákonitē's eyes became red beacons in the growing darkness, in conjunction with her sister's altering state of being.

The flicker of lightning strikes evoked flashes of red behind Nyctámēna's eyelids, before a *hum* began to pass from Yala's hand to her own, evoking pitch-blackness in the warrior's perception. Callisto's shouts were challenging the thunder in pitch, but those shouts sounded drawn out, as if Time was being stretched. When another fierce wave pummeled the shore, Nyctámēna stood as a bulwark for Yala, while her eyes remained shut, delving deeper into the moment.

In that instant, Nyctámēna felt something stir within and her lower lip began to flutter. A deep cry rumbled from the sky, the call of Night Skimmers, but far closer than Nyctámēna experienced in Ümfalla. Her bones resonated through their approach, as the nascent magic swirled in her core.

Behind closed eyes, Nyctámēna sensed the colossal approach of the creature, just as Yala's hand grew ice-cold through their embrace. An ancient Name emerged within Nyctámēna, the primal signifier for the creature drawing near. She listened from within, through an inner-realm of entangled voices, beyond Time:

'I hear the Voice in the darkness. I hear it as one does a drop of water, in the infinite stillness of the sea of Time. In that Voice, I hear her own, the Intertwined truth, the truth that can never be unraveled because we are One. That Oneness finds the One beside me, the One approaching, in this placeless place. I let my lips fall subject to the forces moving hidden things in the world. I Whisper myself into Being. Another One's Voice is faint with weakness, but sings the song in the distance, the song she sang to the spore cloud, Whispers allowing our Voices to meld into One. We are One and we are Beautiful. We are Power beyond words.'

When Nyctámēna opened her eyes, the dragon was staring back at her...

Part III

'Already have I once been a boy and a girl, a bush and a bird and a silent
fish in the sea'
Empedocles

27

Diverse Paces of Time

I F TIME MOVED AT a snail's pace in Ümfalla, the course of time in Forlindea moved at the geologic pace of mountains. Time never remained still. There would be no time and no space. If the river of Time came to a halt, it would drown itself in its own confined Space. But Time always played games with the elasticity of the universe and some places were far more pliable than others.

Forlindea was a place removed, organically stretched out from the grinding nature of Avernus. Nevertheless, the world made its orbits round the sun seven times. Deciduous leaves of the great forests sprouted and fell seven times, seven cold winters passed and seven springs reminded the peoples of Forlindea, things changed, even when they appeared as they did, seven orbits before.

The four women's arrival on the dragon's back, in the dead of night, established a sense of wonder in the people of Forlindea. Legend preceded truth and stories of the women's origins grew as profound as the fetus in the egg of the dragon who delivered them. The ubiquitous forests of Forlindea had only grown denser and claimed more of the land, since Yala and her sister's departure, centuries before.

People remained and people departed, over the course of generations, along with migratory urges, sweeping others away. Ships took people to distant shores and brought others in and those remaining forgot they came from anywhere other than Forlindea.

The Rolling Hills of their ancestral home proved an impossible return for the sisters. After so many orbits staring down the abyss on Sky Tracer, Ákonitē's eyes were more averse to sunlight than Nyctámēna's. Her dependence on wind made the greater portions of Forlindea unviable to her needs. Only the half-light of the wind-whipped Northern Woods were suitable for the Weir. It was there the four companions established themselves as newcomers, in an old land, interlopers, who had forgotten they were meant to be there. The scattered Weirs of Forlindea began to appear, shortly thereafter.

If Ákonitē's fragile state did anything, it made pilgriming Weirs see her as a suffering prophet, one who held up an entire world, through her singular Voice. Her skeletal frame accentuated her profound red eyes that hardly blinked, her full lips, always on the flutter.

It took an entire orbit for Ákonitē to find her feet and take her first steps, again. When she did, almost a hundred Weirs were at the threshold of the old temple to the Goddess of the Woods, Proserpīne. Those first steps were guided by Yala, who stood with her sister, in triumph. All the Weirs fell to their knees, in reverence.

In that time, Nyctámēna and Callisto took long sojourns to the Southern Woods, where calmer air reminded them of Ümfalla. Countless species of trees, creating an interlocking canopy, throughout, were a reasonable substitute for the spore cloud, especially, when leaves gloried those branches. But where pliant mushrooms, ever-changing and diverse, never ceased to astound back in Ümfalla, the hard trees of Forlindea remained the same, despite beauty through autumnal leaves. Winter left a skeletal canopy, haunted by lichen and mosses, like an endless shrine to Death.

In that time, Nyctámēna dreamed of Sky Tracer and saw it as she had from the murk of Ümfalla. Shixee was always nearby in the dream, but already forgot the fleeting moments they shared. The first time Nyctámēna awoke from such a dream, she headed to shore where the calm waters of Oceána lapped on roots of the Forlindean coast. On that night she saw a lone dragon circling, high above, just as the creatures she once called, Night Skimmers, did in Ümfalla.

She knew the dragon was set apart from the rest: *She faced the empty skies, alone, without the urgency of the endless cycle of mating and nesting.*

The dragon was as much a Wanderer as Nyctámēna. The dragon was thinking of her, as surely as she was thinking of the dragon.

Callisto shared the soft ground of the woods with Nyctámēna and they shared each other's bodies, as well. But Callisto soon realized the presence of Mēna was not an ebb and flow in Nyctámēna's spirit. The Weir Callisto had known and loved, who was killed by the same body she now possessed, was no longer a distinct entity. She was an indistinguishable part of the whole of the being who became, Nyctámēna. Whenever Nyctámēna headed to the shore, in deep night, Callisto remained in the woods, where she tried to convince herself she came to Forlindea by choice, a realm so far away from home, the Sister Moons felt nearer.

Around the time Ákonitē took her first steps, Nyctámēna was on the dark shore, Whispering through the breeze, when a fell cry from above found her. What began as coincidence, turned into contact, between the warrior and lone dragon. Bright-eye met bright-eye, in a union of spirits, one drawing the dragon closer. Neither was willing to beg for the other's presence, leading to a presence they both wished for. When the dragon landed on the twisted roots of the Forlindean shore, Nyctámēna reached out her hand and the dragon watched. Contact was made between soft flesh and adamant dragon scales:

Hand to beak, fingers tracing scales, soft and adamant, bare feet to ridged-back, woman and dragon, breeze turning to wind, entangling two spirits, into a flight of Oneness over Oce ána...

There were no pilgriming Weirs to see the paradigm shift of Weir/Dragon taking place. Only the Three Sister Moons and stars, sparkling throughout the sky, witnessed. Their flight from the hard earth was so swift, the lapping waters of Oceána turned to crashing waves, even the Thunder Cliffs would envy, if rocks and water possessed consciousness. The pair were One, flying into all the nights to come, in relative secrecy.

While the scattered Weirs of Forlindea gathered to the new Order of Yala and Ákonitē, nobody fell to their knees in reverence of what was *becoming* on the Southern Shore of Forlindea. All the ships and fishing boats in Forlindea were set apart, on the Eastern and Western Shores, while the woods remained largely uninhabited.

Seafaring folk were subject to superstition and ancient trees were gifted with casting shadows of mystery and fear. Over the course of seven orbits, the Northern and Southern Woods of Forlindea became places of magic.

Callisto stumbled into the role of de facto diplomat between the burgeoning Weir Order to the North and the Dragon Weir to the South. The ad hoc post imbued Callisto with a sense of importance, but it also gave her a glimpse of the fertile soil between shores and the seeds of discord being sown. Some were beginning to sprout.

Relative equanimity of power in Forlindea was finding its opposite, in a quiet race for power. Words sowed the seeds of discord, whispered and spoken, but inspiring deeds to come, shifting the course of events.

Through the seasons, Nyctámēna drew the attention of rogue Weirs, who were drawn to the alluring presence of dragons. What began as one Weir, no older than Ruthy when she fell from Sky Tracer, became five, with a gift for Whispering to creatures and a knack for keeping discoveries to themselves. They listened to Nyctámēna's words, like every syllable was carved, following her lead in everything but her nocturnal flights.

The young Weirs failed to establish the vital connection to dragons necessary for flight. In spite of their inherent gifts for Whispering, gifts capable of summoning birds of prey and woodland creatures, the dragons were unmoved. A critical element was missing. Within a few seasons, the young Weirs began to move on, often without warning, in search of purpose, in the sylvan realm of Forlindea. None of them flew above the clouds with Nyctámēna, not until the night the stars failed to shine and a young Weir appeared with eyes as dark-bright as Nyctámēna's.

Her Name was Scylla and her lanky limbs, on her tall frame, made her look like a sapling who had overgrown her own spring. Scylla's bright eyes were matched with hair as red as Forlindean ochre, on a face the color of tree sap, in autumnal light. She was clever in word and fierce in deed. Her life in Forlindea was one of orphanhood and struggle, a life not unlike most who lived in a declining realm, wild and near-forgotten.

The eastern and western ports were little more than gloried docks, on a vast island, acting as a rural nexus in the heart of Oceána. What was once a realm of united Weirs and magic, was now rocky coastlines with scattered fishermen, while the woods remained sovereign to itself.

Forgotten souls—victims of the ravages of seafaring and human nature—haunted the woods and the coastline, where their only luck in the world were edible bounties from the trees and sea. Ships came and went, but only for the essentials of freshwater and repairs, while the trees of Forlindea continued to entangle what was once a realm of dazzling wooden structures and temples to forgotten deities. Nature was reclaiming all it once shared, even if the trees no longer grew tall and mighty, but twisted and tangled.

Where some lost souls banded together to fish rich waters, or found passage on ships to realms unknown, Scylla's life was one of relative solitude, crowned by mystery. Her understanding of the natural world was exhibited in the way she moved through it, much like a squirrel reveals her dynamics through leaping from branch to branch. Scylla's life *seeing* the night and half-light in the vast woods of Forlindea—through dark-bright eyes—engendered a cohesive understanding of living things most only dreamt of. This kind of 'seeing' was not overlooked by Nyctámēna, who shared in that dark-bright vision, even if her former life was one of fungi-engendered darkness.

Scylla never knew her mother, never encountered another soul with eyes like her own, not until a dragon delivered Nyctámēna to Forlindea. It was through Nyctámēna's nocturnal flights Scylla's eyes spotted the Dragon Weir, soaring high above the tallest of trees, on no particular night. Scylla followed her eyes and found the source. Her training began as naturally as the sun rose the next morning.

The first time Nyctámēna watched Scylla spar with Callisto, in order to establish an understanding of where the Weir stood in experience, the flame-haired youth was as cunning as the fox, but lacked any experience with a sword or martial arts. While Scylla could be as clumsy as she was graceful—in such a novel situation—she possessed a strength and speed akin to the Phibian, Shixee. Where Nyctámēna found ways of turning the brutal mechanics of battle into beauty, Scylla moved through the air as if water, fluid, contorting her wiry body into seeming knots, before dashing clear of a blow, even if she failed to land any herself.

Hers had been a life of perpetual motion, through the hyper-complexity of the forest and into the embrace of Oceána. She loved to swim, unlike most Forlindeans, who feared Oceána's currents. But the gift lifting Scylla as high in the heavens as her mentor, the gift no mentor could teach, was her Whispering ways with dragons.

Where Nyctámēna established a kinship with the solitary dragon she came to call, Īō—an ineffable bond, making one incomplete without the other—Scylla summoned a different dragon, every night. The Forlindean skies were spotted with the looming presence of dragons, whether the creatures were seeking a mighty tree to nest upon, or searching for a mate. Curiosity and a restless spirit filled the young Weir with a need to experience the ways of dragons she had yet to encounter.

If speed was her intent, a streamlined dragon of lesser bulk would be sought out. Her dark-bright eyes searched the night sky, while her inherent gift for Whispering grew stronger, through the guidance of Nyctámēna. If power and the occasional destruction of inanimate objects was desired, Scylla Whispered her way onto the dragon of greatest bulk. In spite of Scylla's restlessness, Nyctámēna recognized the patience and reverence the fledgling Weir held for dragons, a *way* that could never be taught, only exhibited from within, a gift far more precious than strength or speed.

As the seasons passed and Scylla's talents grew, Nyctámēna insisted Scylla find a kinship, just as she had, to establish a deeper connection, beyond the passing Whisper, a connection bringing a dragon *back* to her, without a Whispered breath in the breeze. But Scylla's curiosity and need to explore skies on a different dragon's back, every night, inspired Nyctámēna to learn from the virtuosic Scylla, as much as she taught her.

What she learned was to maintain her bond with Īō and make it as fathomless and adamantine as the dragon, herself. Truth revealed itself through the strength of binding opposites, just as the bow drew resistance, releasing its own truth.

The two Dragon Weirs shared the sky as opposites, in their own kinships, Scylla's nameless dragons flying alongside Nyctámēna's beloved and trusted, Īō. Nevertheless, Nyctámēna and Scylla established themselves as the sole Dragon Weirs of Forlindea and ruled the skies, bereft of any threats. All that threatened their reign of the sky was the dragon's instinctual need to return to Forlindea, every turn, at dawn.

It was on a gray morning the two Weirs were resting on the shore, where Īō lingered on her haunches and showed her trust by exposing the vast network of shimmering black scales on her underbelly. No mortal instrument matched the exquisite harmony of her scales, such adamant precision, not even in dreams. Scylla smiled at the dragon's presence.

"I've known good-hearted hounds less trusting," Scylla said, squinting her bright-eyes in the morning light.

"Someday you'll know this shared trust," Nyctámēna said, running her long fingers along the length of Īō's mighty front talon. "It wasn't long ago, I thought the rest of my life would be one faced alone."

"You're telling me," Scylla said, turning away her bright eyes from the dragon. "At least your eyes made sense where you came from. I can't tell you how many fisherman I horrified when they saw me in the dead of night. If they didn't run, they called me a demon. But the ones my age were worse. I thought there was something wrong with me, that I might really be some kind of demon. You're not, so maybe I'm not, after all," she laughed. "Either way, here I am."

"You hardly speak of the past, Scylla. I never wanted to press you."

"Well, my heart thanks you. When I was little, I was *so* sure I'd find others with eyes like my own. Just imagine falling asleep on the shore, only to wake up to a blinding dawn. Night has always been my companion, but the forest embraced me with its half-light, even if winter's bare branches forced me into the heart of Forlindea. If it weren't for the lichen and mosses haunting the leafless branches of the old trees, I guess I'd have gone blind, many winters ago... Then you come along and make me these onyx goggles," she patted the satchel at her side.

"Onyx is plentiful enough, along the shore. Just needs good shaping and polishing. You can thank an old blind man for that craft. And you know I never faced the light, not until—"

"That changed everything, *the goggles,* I mean. But I'll never not be connected to the trees. I love them all... This realm belongs to the forest, not the ones who supposedly used to live in Forlindea. But the trees here are failing. Even in my short time in this world, I've yet to see a sapling survive a winter, while the trees along the coast are yellowing in the green season."

Nyctámēna looked to the east, squinting at the horizon, holding her past, "Everything is connected. That much I know. Ümfalla is held together by a thread. Change is in the wind, but I can't pretend understanding. Perhaps everything must fall for another Age to rise."

Scylla looked over her shoulder, towards the gray woods, at dawn, "Maybe it was supposed to be this way, an island of trees and lost souls, slowly fading into dust. Ships just drift on by... I don't know...then you show up, like a goddess on a dragon's back."

"I thought the same about someone, *once*. As sure as she wasn't a goddess, I'm even farther from it."

"You mean Arethūsa!" Scylla almost shouted, leaning into Nyctámēna.

"Who told you that Name?"

"I meant Ruthy," Scylla muttered, biting her lower lip, as she did, whenever she felt her eagerness overcoming the moment.

"Calli's been telling drunken stories to you, eh?"

Scylla nodded, before exhaling a deep breath she realized she was holding.

"I only heard the Name once," Scylla said. "Not the kind of Name to be forgotten."

"Sure isn't."

"It's strange," Scylla said, "I just realized you and Calli are the only souls I've ever been able to look at straight in the eye. Even the old fisherwoman who took care of me, from time to time, never really met my gaze. Who knows what she *really* thought of me. At least she took care of me, long enough for me to run after her, when she left on one of those ships from the North."

"You're not being left behind again, Scylla. *Know that.* You've found your home on the Southern Shore. But you need to start focusing on finding a dragon to Name."

"Do we have to talk about this every time we return to the same old shore? There's so much waiting to be seen beyond these waters, far beyond Forlindea."

"Sometimes you really do show your age, but that's not your fault. Forlindea is a refuge, as well as home, Scylla. Dragons have shown us that much. All that lies over that horizon is soulless ambition."

"The stories I've heard about Avernus tell me otherwise."

"So you've been spending your days in the North?"

Scylla crossed her long arms and her stomach tensed, giving her torso the look of a sentient creature, trying to squirm out of its Forlindean top, wrapped around her apple-sized breasts. Her knobby knees and protruding hips gave her earthy wood-cotton pants a topography screaming of restlessness. After Scylla found a moment of stillness, she answered.

"You know, I *have* been going up there. Not everyone is content to while away the days down here. while the dragons go wherever it is they go. Yala is probably older than the oldest trees here and she tells a good tale. She's actually pretty funny, too, unlike her sister, who scares the shit out of me. And the Wind Weirs don't fear me like they did before Yala established some kind of *path* for them. I still feel strange around them, though. They're so elegant looking and I'm...*not*." Scylla fidgeted with the tangles in her hair, for a moment, then looked back to Nyctámēna, with vigor. "You should *see* what the Sisters are doing. How long has it been since you've seen the change up there?"

"Down there, up there...your words remind me of Avernus."

"So can we go there?!" She smiled. "To Avernus and see the Goddess in the Tree?"

"Dragons have enough sense to fly beneath that abomination. *Down* is where the good things lie, at least when it comes to such things you speak of. Roots descend for trees to rise."

"You sound like the mother I never had," Scylla said, looking away. "You used to talk of Ümfalla and Avernus, all the time. Well, mostly Ümfalla... Now, you change the subject anytime I bring them up. I'm left to Calli and the rare chances I get to speak to Yala. And Ákonitē is so caught up in being a goddess herself, I'm actually scared to even look at her. Her red eyes could stare through a mountain, even if I've never really seen one up close. And that's coming from me, the kid-demon everybody feared."

"Ákonitē faced a hell nobody could fathom, for orbits on end. I'm thankful she survived the transition back to Forlindea. Avernus sounds like it's some kind of monument to mortal greatness. From a distance, it appears that way. But that place is Hell in the heavens, a realm fueled by screams and suffering, horrors I hear, every time I dream."

"Calli was talking in her sleep last night."

"She always talks in her sleep. And it's mostly about fucking or food."

"She said the most peculiar thing. Something about a *Sky Tracer.*"

"Fuck."

"Why did you leave that part out of your stories? Is Sky Tracer what Ákonitē was bound to?"

"I don't even know why you're asking me. Nothing is what it seems, for better and worse. Even dragon wings push down on the sky to stay aloft. *Be patient*, Scylla. But I'm sure Calli already talked your ear off about the nightmare that was Sky Tracer."

"*Is*, Sky Tracer."

"You cut to the bone sometimes, Scylla."

"Only because I want to see everything."

"*Smart ass...* Some things are hidden for a reason. Sky Tracer is the mechanism haunting my turns, whether I'm sleeping or awake. Before I knew its horrors, I used to trace its course like the Sister Moons do the heavens and I always called it beautiful, *every* time. But I should have payed attention to the nauseous knot in my stomach, accompanying that foolish ritual of mine."

"I did the same thing with dragons passing overhead, before I learned how to Whisper to them. But I always felt this strange kind of excited sadness...always called them beautiful."

"The difference is, you were right to feel that way about dragons, the reverence. Beauty means nothing when it comes to what something is, something like Sky Tracer. That mechanism is what shaped Ákonitē and carries the innocent from Ümfalla, into the Hell of that abominable Tree, that abysmal relic you want to see. Trees in Forlindea are far more *alive*, in their own rights. *Believe me.* Sky Tracer is the mechanism ensuring the very existence of Ümfalla. What is *down,* keeps the *up* of Avernus alive, too. It seems contrary in simplicity, but the more you try to fix Sky Tracer, the more complicated it becomes. *Everything* is connected. Nothing will stop that. Not a sword, or a Whisper, or a Dragon Weir. And you can't look at it as good or bad, that's madness. Sky Tracer, *is. Never* speak of it, again," Nyctámēna said, an octave lower.

"I didn't mean to—"

"As many gifts as you have, remember you're still green...*very* green."

"And how do I fix that without seeing anything but this island and surrounding skies?" Scylla stumbled, taking a step back. "Doesn't the world make us stronger? I mean, we're the only Dragon Weirs around and we don't go anywhere exciting. Aren't we both just *wandering,* like you were back in...." Syclla's face flushed at what was already said.

"And what's your cause? Do you want pretty yourself up like the Weirs to the North? Or is it power you seek?"

"We already have power. So do the Wind Weirs of the North."

"What are you saying, Scylla? Because this is the kind of language that leads to more of the same. I've seen what power-lust does to a person. I don't know what led to this...*entanglement*. It's as if merely the Name, *Sky Tracer,* cursed our words. You are too good for this."

"So says the one who just told me not to think in terms of good, or bad. Maybe I just, *am.* I'm just saying we have the kind of power to topple whole realms, if we choose to. We could change the world. For the better! *Good,* right?!"

"Who has been Whispering in your ear? I know a woman who reminds me of you. She had a strong heart and unbelievable power, just like you do. *The Goddess*...she even had hair of the same redness as you. She wanted to topple a realm and she did. Before she could even sit her pretty little ass on that throne, Whispers already turned her into something else. I wish I had a word for it... *Arethūsa'd!* I know of pretty Weirs who have done far more damage than a dragon, with a few flutters of their soft lips. You have *no* idea, Scylla."

"We can be different. Whispers only go so far. We have dragons and no Weir can reach the heights we can."

"Dragons are *not* tools for destruction. Every moment with them is a gift."

"Dragons love to shake things up and you know that. I've spent my whole life watching ships come and go, to places I can only imagine. I almost got on one of those ships...I don't know how many times. Now, we're both gifted with dragons, the same dragons that passed me by, until you showed me the way. When you feel the dragon's scream fill your heart, when they destroy something, you get that truth in your bones. Just two turns ago, I—"

"You really are a child. *Stay out of the North.*"

"You are *not* my mother."

"I am your..."

"What was that?" Scylla smiled, tapping her boot on the roots. "What exactly are you to me? Because I've been waiting to hear it. Nobody called me anything before you. Am I just Scylla?"

"You're far more than that to me and you know it in your heart. You might be powerful, but you're still *young.* I've known Sponge Mushrooms less impressionable than you."

"I don't even know what a Sponge Mushroom is."

"It's really *fucking* impressionable!"

"*Got it!*" Scylla screamed back, with a flare of her arms.

"Your greatest weakness is your belief you only think for yourself, that you have it figured out. Plenty of Weir-tongues are waiting to do that for you. And not all Whispers are Weir-words. Some are more cunning. Stay out of the North, or I'll banish you from the skies. None of your nameless dragons can prevent that."

Nyctámēna thrust herself up and her mechanical gleamed in the light of Dawn, before she strode off, into the shadows of the woods, while Scylla cringed at the gray light, over a silver-watered Oceána. She looked to the bulging clouds, obscuring the rising sun and tried to imagine what the Tree of Avernus looked like, from a distance.

Tales of Vescent Wine and court-intrigue filled her imagination, with fleeting shapes of people she never met. Fragments of stories concerning Sky Realm bulged like thunder-heads in her mind.

Just as the spore cloud settled on her Avernian thoughts and obliterated her bright fancies, Īō groaned and blew a hot breath onto Scylla, from the dragon's restless mouth, looming higher than the trees.

"You said it, Īō. But your breath smells of death. That's alright, I still love you. Love your Weir, too. Don't you dare tell her I said that! She'll brood for a whole orbit. She *is* a brooder these turns, isn't she? I bet she's homesick. Wish I could feel homesick. *Truly.* You have to love and lose to feel that kind of sickness. But you can't do that, unless you're in a place where things actually happen. Did anyone ever tell you, Īo, you're a really good listener? Well, you are. Even if you don't have much to say. Other dragons never stick around, but I tell your Weir I prefer it that way. How did you pick your Weir, Īo? How did she convince you to stick around? I don't want to mess this up... I have nightmares the dragons forget me, just fly over, like they did before, until *your* Weir came around. Got any friends, Īo? I could really use one. No? Don't you want to fly to a Tree you can actually perch in, without fear of it breaking? I want to look up at one that makes my insides churn. Not around here. Not in this fucking forgotten realm. I heard of such a Tree. I heard of a *Sky Tracer* and a woman named, *Arethūsa.* Just saying her name sounds powerful, right? Stick around and I'll tell you a tale of a place called, *Avernus.*"

28

THE ORDER OF THE WIND

THE JOURNEY TO THE Northern Shore was a flight of fancy for Scylla. Whenever she felt the urge to visit the Wind Weirs, she summoned a dragon and was transported there, in a handful of moments. Just as the action was brief, so was Scylla's interaction with the random dragon who took her there. As soon as she landed on the Northern Shore, the dragon departed, often, without looking back at Scylla.

For Callisto, the journey to the same shore was a trudge taking an entire turn, where she camped in the heart of the woods—Scylla's old haunts, places the flame-haired youth showed her—before finishing her trek around mid-afternoon, the following turn. Distance was relative, a fundamental truth Callisto relearned, whenever she saw a dragon pass overhead.

The woods were plentiful in game and fresh springs and the idle warrior enjoyed the benign uncertainties of the sylvan realm. Callisto still wore her celium wear from her home, just as Nyctámēna did. Wood-cotton of Forlindea never agreed with either's skin. Whenever Callisto reached a certain place in the forest, somewhere near its imagined center, the trees became something more.

Time was spun into stillness within the trees, through hidden rings in trunks, keeping an Age's secrets, often longer. Drought, fire, bounty and floods shaped the towering trees, entangling their trunks with others, as if mycelium dreamed of living in thin air and it came to pass in Forlindea.

It was here Callisto felt a semblance of home, an arboreal realm, distantly kin to the fungal one, an environment that allowed Scylla to survive through its merciful darkness and bounty of nuts and berries, even if the forest could be as brutal as the Fungal Realm. Brutalities held true for the sea and air, Callisto knew that much, but she avoided both, at all costs.

To the east and west, the ports were little more than ancient docks, with a smattering of humbly constructed wooden shacks, the likes of which would never last a season in Ümfalla, but made it through a storm or two on the Forlindean coast. Perhaps the only thing linking the scattered peoples of Forlindea was a common language, the same tongue holding true, throughout the hemisphere, as far as Callisto experienced, through random encounters with mercantile sailors, from distant lands.

Beyond the ports, Forlindea was little more than a ghost realm. The heart of the woods brought Callisto moments of joy, before the torment of Ümfalla came rushing back, as surely as the Seething Falls seethed.

A season passed since Callisto last visited the North and her approach to the Temple of the Wind brought with it shock at the sight of change. The ruined temple to the Goddess of the Woods, Proserpīne, was now a fresh construct built upon the old. A narrow steeple made of midnight wood stretched taller than any tree in the vicinity. The rectangular temple was made of cedar-oak and the aromatic smell loomed in the air, from a good distance. Tripartite eclipsing full moons were carved above the vaulting entrance. Atop the steeple, the four-part, obliquely-set of wavy lines, signifying the Winds of the World, were the crowning symbol of the Temple.

Youthful Wind Weirs moved as the nature of their Order implied, in a will o' the wisp manner, where gestures rustled, just like wind through the trees. All of them were cloaked in dark crimson and appeared to be focused on fleeting abstractions, beyond their grasp.

Yala was a stone's throw away from the temple, swaying in a hammock, hung between a pair of ancient pines, while she drifted in the wind, singing to herself. When Callisto saw her, she stepped around a few Wind Weirs and stared down at Yala, whose eyes were closed, as she sang softly. Callisto said nothing while she waited for her presence to open Yala's eyes. But the ancient Weir, with an ageless face, only moved her lips.

"Hello, Callisto. Will you do me a favor?"

"What is it, Yala?"

"Step a little to the side...you are blocking the sun."

Callisto took a step to her right and beams of light, through a break in the canopy of trees, fell on Yala's skeletal form. In spite of her regal cloak, the Weir looked like a wiry tree, elegantly warped into grace, through centuries of wind. A smile fell across her face and Yala opened her eyes to the light.

"I only miss two things from Avernus," Yala said, staring into the shine. "The naked sunlight and Ruthy."

"I miss more than two things from Ümfalla," Callisto said. "If I started Naming them, we'd be here til' sunset."

"We all make sacrifices in our lives. We all live and die, more than once. But here, we have found a place to grow, beyond mere survival. Here, we have peace to spread the Word of the Wind."

"Here, I have peace to wile away the time, watching everyone else grow, while I decide whether I want squirrel, or sparrow for dinner. I grew sick of fish, ever since that eel incident."

"The world you knew back in Ümfalla no longer exists."

"I have to disagree with you on that one, Yala. Nyctámēna made sure everything remained the same, before we flew into the sunset, on the dragon. Never thought I'd say that in any of my lives," she muttered to herself. "You know she dreams of Sky Tracer every night."

"Ghosts follow us, *always*."

"Ya' know, Yala, I always appreciate your wise words. But you sure know how to be vague in that wisdom, when you want to be."

"And I always appreciate your words, Callisto. They are always your own."

"Speaking of words," Callisto said, looking at the Weirs, throughout the woods, "When do you plan on spreading that *Word of the Weirs*, or the Wind, or whatever it is, these days?"

"Oh, that!" Yala laughed, as the hammock swayed in accord. "The first Weir left the western port, three orbits ago."

"You're joking," Callisto half-smiled.

"I have been known to. But my words are my own and have been carved."

"Time is a fickle fucker in this place. What have you been doing...sending Weirs on ships, in the dead of night?"

"No. That is the way of the Dragon Weir. Stealth and secrecy. We operate in open silence. And there are more than enough ships trading with surrounding realms for our Weirs to find passage. You would have noticed, had you stayed with us. And I would have told you, had you asked. Just as I am telling you, now."

"What the fuck was I supposed to do here? Cook supper? I'm not a Weir, I'm a warrior. Well, I used to be, but now it seems I'm just a shitty messenger. Give me another season and I'll be scooping dragon shit. I've got dreams, too."

"You always manage to make me laugh, Callisto. I miss that. If the Weirs of the Order lack anything, it is a good sense of humor."

"Well, it sure looks like you've all been far too busy sailing to the four corner of the world and building that...what is that? It used to be a temple to Proserpīne but now it's something else, with very sharp angles and it's... I prefer *softer* structures."

"Of course, you do. You are from the Fungal Realm. *My sister*," Yala sighed, "she is certainly making up for lost time. That is the Temple of the Wind. What was scattered has Gathered and that is the sign of the times. As for the ships, we will not stop until the Word spreads throughout the realms of Oceána. Weirs here are strong, like the many trees. Forlindea has always been the womb of the Whisperers. Now the Order has come back together, after centuries of forgetfulness. When we create a common cause, throughout Oceána, Avernus will be next."

"You're not going to sail to Avernus and then Whisper enough Weirs up that fucking Tree to do anything meaningful. I've seen dragons and magic, over the past seven orbits, but that's a hammock dream."

"There is always a way. Gales might move a world of water, but the soft breeze of a Whisper can move mountains."

"I—" Calliso broke off, when she spotted a familiar face, amongst the Weirs. "Hold that thought, Yala. I've got to see about something."

"I will be here waiting, *just for you*, Callisto," Yala smiled, closing her eyes and resuming her swaying song, in dappled sunlight.

In a wooded enclosure, between Yala and the temple, seven Weirs formed a make-shift circle around someone, whose glistening red hair betrayed her identity, in spite of the surrounding crimson cloaks.

Laughter and idle words were in the air, when Callisto pushed her way through and escorted Scylla, by the crook of her elbow, out of the conversation and into the shadows of a tremendous oak nearby. Scylla was flushed with embarrassment, but still bore a toothy smile on her face, from her encounter with the Weirs.

"What the fuck are you doing?" Callisto almost grunted.

"Just chatting," Scylla said. "You know, making friends my own age."

"You can't trust anyone here."

"You sound like an old curmudgeon, Calli. What happened to the woman who swore to the world, she didn't give a fuck? What happed to, *see what happens*?"

"Those were drunken words, on a rare night. You should see what happened to the man who always said: *See what happens.* Sister-fucker," she spit. "At least, that's what I was told. It still feels good to say it. Never mind that—"

"I spent most of my life hiding from Weirs my own age. Now, I can almost look them in the eye, without running off. And most of them lived near the ports, so I never got a chance to meet them. There are a *whole lot* more Weirs in Forlindea than I imagined," Scylla smiled, catching her breath. "I'm trying to catch up for lost time, Calli. I mean...who am I supposed to trust beyond you and Nyctámēna?"

"You can't even trust Yala," Callisto whispered, with a glance over her shoulder.

"So it's down to us and them, already? You *came here* with the Weir Sisters. They're friends, right?"

"More like allies in a pinch."

"That's too bad... I thought I'd all have a little more time for idle chat with them."

"Who do you think these Weirs want on their side?"

"More of themselves, I suppose."

"That's easy. Look around. I swear to the Goddess, these girls multiply every time I come back and countless Weirs are already sailing to the four corner of the world. They pop up like weeds and hit Oceána green and eager."

"Sounds exciting."

"Believe me, that kind of excitement doesn't last long. The yellow leaf comes quickly. These girls in women's clothes don't want your pretty fucking face and your clever words. *They want a Dragon Weir.*"

"You can't expect me to be like you and Nyctámēna, *hermits* of the Southern Shore. And nobody can tell me what to do with the dragons. I told somebody that much, earlier today."

"I bet that went well."

"It went...*somewhere*," Scylla bit her fluttering lower lip. "Anyway, it's easy to say the world is shit when you've already seen it."

"I'm not saying the world is shit, I'm just talking about the company. You need to see that for yourself, before you really fuck up," Callisto said, poking Scylla in the chest.

"Did you just poke me in the chest?" Scylla laughed.

"I'll drag you out of here, if I have to, because I care. I forget you're just skin and bones because you're still a fucking kid. Those Weirs," she pointed, "over there, don't give a shit. Nyctámēna and I do. Just be you. You're a force of nature, Scylla. Don't let these blabbering leeches bleed you dumb and dry. I never thought I'd say this, but I'm sick of being around this many females. Maybe I'll just say *fuck all* and become a fisherman. Wile away the days drinking and pretending to work hard, while I can see time passing underfoot."

"I have dreams, Calli. Dreams that I'll make real, no matter—"

"*Avernian* dreams! I never should have said a word about Sky Realm. I can only imagine what the Weirs, up here, have told you."

"Yala talks about the better days in Avernus, when she and Arethū..*Ruthy* were trying to do something good for the realms. She even told me about the Goddess in the Tree and how close they came to waking her up, if only—"

Callisto clenched her jaw, while she spoke in a guttural whisper, "If we were back there, you'd be fodder for that fucking Tree I never should have told you about. It's easy to dream about a nightmare, after it passes. Never mind Yala's tales... If I were a giant with a big fucking axe, I'd hack that Tree down, first thing. Well...I'd probably get the people out first, but that's just details. Even talking about Sky Realm makes my insides churn. Don't let somebody else's stories dazzle you into fantasy. Fantasy is the kind of stuff that delivers you into real trouble. Trust me, I was the leader of a fantastical group of young idiots who went up that fucking Tree. Scylla, you're a good soul and you're sharp as Slender. Trust me about Sky Realm and all that nonsense. You're just the right age for that hell-machine. You're right where you need to be, right here. Well, maybe a little more to the South, but you get my point. I need to stop drinking Forlindean beer, it makes me too honest."

"I appreciate your honesty, Calli. Truly."

"With a fleet, these Weirs just might conquer Oceána. With a dragon, they—"

"I get it! I'm green, but not deaf. I'll stick to my *flights of fancy*, in circles, round and round this place. But I know you miss it back in Ümfalla. At least, admit that."

"Of course, I miss my old home. But home is not just a place, it's a people and those people are gone."

"So we're stuck here? *Great.* I'm getting a better view of the same place I've been since I can remember. At least you know where you were born. For all I know, I washed up on driftwood from the Antipodes."

"Did somebody tell you that?"

"*No.* I made it up, just like I made up the mother I never knew. All I know is, the Antipodes are to the south and that's where some dragons fly in winter. But who really knows...Nyctámēna won't let me fly out of sight of Forlindea."

"Give her time and be patient. The world's going to be there."

"It doesn't feel like it... When *can* I visit, Yala? Only under adult supervision?"

"Not right now. That's all I've got for you, until I speak with Nyctámēna. The Goddess! She's been such a buzzkill lately. No amount of beer can drown my depression around her."

"I know. But it's no wonder. She has at least two spirits within, constantly trying to overthrow each other."

"That's more true than you'll ever know. Anyway, we'll figure it out. Now let's get the fuck out of here, before they start chanting or some shit. If I hear about the importance of my breathing again, I'll draw blood and it won't be my own. Make me vomit up my lunch. It took me all morning to catch that squirrel and I'd rather keep it down. What an exciting life I lead. At least you have your dragons."

"Yup. I have those."

When Callisto walked away with Scylla, Callisto looked over her shoulder and into the darkness of the temple's entrance. Birds nested on the fresh wood of the overhang and were chirping in crepuscular light. The late afternoon sun imparted the silhouettes of kneeling Weirs with the look of dark statues.

A pair of red eyes shined, deep inside the Temple, unblinking, staring down the slow retreat of Callisto and Scylla. Callisto put her arm around Scylla, to keep her from looking back, but found herself unable to turn away from the macabre eyes staring *through* her. By the time she reached the thick of the woods and those eyes were no longer visible, a lone dragon darkened the sky and Scylla was heavy in Whisper.

29

FLIGHTS OF FANCY

WHEN THE DRAGON LANDED on the wind-whipped Northern Shore, Callisto already departed for her long walk back south. Nothing was out of the ordinary, as far as the sudden departure of the forlorn warrior. Callisto accepted the dragon's back was a place she did not belong and her fear of heights made the reason all the more ironclad. But the moment Scylla made eye-contact with the inquisitive dragon, the creature's hawkish eyes *looked* back. Scylla hesitated and stared, in silent wonder. Tears streamed down her cheeks, for the first time in orbits.

She scanned the sky for others, but this dragon was as much a loner as, Īō. Unlike Īō, this she-dragon was built for speed *and* strength, with her streamlined body of tremendous proportions, yet balanced in form. She was the Realm Crusher Nyctámēna warned her about, the dragon Scylla dreamed.

The proportions of the dragon seemed impossible, in the union of grace and size. Her wing talons were larger than any Scylla encountered, with a restless tail carrying rare mutation of spikes, along with tail-fangs. Sharp attributes adorned the dragon's sides, on a body of iridescent blackness, doubling the size of Īo. Her ridged neck was proud and bore scars from battles with other dragons, her crown of horns, a testament to the beauty of such instruments of fear.

But the jaw-dropper for Scylla was the dragon's visage. Her sharp eyes burned like indigo-minerals and her mouth, with fangs betraying her youth, appeared to bear a wry smile, one of endless mischief. This dragon looked *into* Scylla, rather than at her. No dragon shared a full gaze with her, not even Īo. The brain resting beneath that impenetrable skull was reeling at the encounter, while Weir and dragon were finding a way to say the very thing they already agreed upon.

Scylla bit her fluttering lower lip to make sure she was awake. When blood flowed, the dragon put her nostrils near Scylla's lip and the Weir put her forehead to the dragon's beak, nearing the size of her entire body. The dragon beckoned Scylla on, through a wordless language, one she never felt before, but one as clear as Oceána was salty.

She leaped onto the dragon's weaponized neck and climbed up, until she reached the niche on the dragon's back, a possible destiny, an adamant nexus, where balance existed and nothing could dismount the Dragon Weir.

The dragon was already tilting towards the zenith, with a few strokes from her streamlined wings, breathtaking appendages, equivalent to the largest ships sailing Oceána. The back of a dragon was always a cold and hard place for Scylla. But this dragon's back exuded warmth and was shaped, in such a way, implying a necessity for the pair to establish their union. She said nothing as they broke through the clouds and the first stars appeared in the evening sky.

Ice clouds, at the limits of the sky, played games with light from the rising Sister Moons. Scylla's lower lip fluttered and she wanted her first words to the dragon to be as specific as anything could be, in a chaotic world. She wanted it to be what it became, the dragon's Name:

"Nīya"

Tears streamed from Scylla's eyes, after she screamed the Name to the dragon, but the sheer speed of Nīya blew the tears away before they ever found the Dragon Weir's cheeks. Such words were heard *within* the Dragon and Weir.

Clouds beneath them passed, in a frenzy, as the open sea of Oceána appeared, far below. Ships looked like bits of wood floating in a dark lake, full of stars. Scylla and Nīya seamlessly alternated the role of navigator, as the dragon showed her strength in the sudden turns and unexpected descents, taking them so close to Oceána, Scylla was soaked in sea-spray.

Wind whistled when it passed over the streamlined body of Nīya, whenever she flew up, towards the zenith. Unlike most dragons, Nīya found cunning ways to use the wind to her advantage. Rather than seeking its current at her back, she maneuvered through turbulent winds of the North and performed aerial feats, escaping belief.

In moments such of those, all the young Dragon Weir could do, was hold on and see what happened. But speed failed to keep Scylla from seeing the dragon for what she was, without question: *Beautiful*. In those moments, Scylla felt beautiful, too.

The Sister Moons rose and set, but storm clouds at Dawn did not affect either Weir or dragon. Scylla was somewhere far beyond the limits of her former nocturnal rides. But even the threat of the clouds breaking and the naked sun finding her dark-bright eyes failed to move her anywhere, but the place they were headed. Besides, she had two pairs of onyx goggles at her hip, for such an event, means to face the shine at dawn. She felt no thirst or hunger, just the need to carry on, in the flight of fantasy, something far more *real* than anything she experienced.

The eastern horizon beckoned the pair on, as if their swift course were as predestined as the rising sun. When Nīya glanced back at Scylla, with her burning eyes of indigo, Scylla winked. Power was reclaiming its seat in the heavens.

30

CHANGE ON THE HORIZON

SEVEN ORBITS PASSED LIKE the wind in Avernus, where the Tree reached its timeless branches into the icy heights and spread near the edges of the Eternal Storm. The chamber of the Seats of the Seven Elders was sealed. Fresh Tree-growth, above, became Sky Throne, where the Ruler of Avernus was shielded from cold winds by a chamber of crystalline perfection.

It resembled a gigantic teardrop, allowing endless winds to blow along its sleek shape. Vacant blue skies of day brought splendor from the pure light of the sun, while nocturnal star clusters adorned the majestical roof, along with the Three Sister Moons, whose light made Sky Throne look enchanted through the crystal.

Fresh growth of the Tree invigorated the growth of industry, as more windmills of greater size and propulsion, shot up, throughout Sky Realm. More wind brought more power to windmills and Weirs. The Name of the Goddess began as a prayer to the heavens for prosperity. Prayers were answered and the Name began to signify more.

Under the spore cloud, in the murk of Ümfalla, change had also come. Sprawling roots from the Tree of Avernus grew in bulk, in accordance with the branches, claiming the greater portion of the eastern Sinels. What was the mineral encasement of the Tree, shattered, soon after Arethūsa wielded her mycelium-charged power.

Abundant varieties of rarer mushrooms were supplanted, while the noxious fungal forest of the Vernox overtook the entire southern portion of Ümfalla. Greater Mushrooms fell, never to rise again, as signs of the seasons vanished into spore-thick air, while a nebulous form of Time took hold in the Fungal Realm.

Under the authority of Briar, Reapers of Avernus became a unified force of disciplined warriors, re-establishing their reign in the Fungal Realm, in little more than an orbit. Spiders became vessels for elite Weirs and warriors to ascend and descend, whenever needed. Gone were the clannish ways of Reapers, haunting the Ümfallan darkness, before.

Seerinx oversaw the return of Moon Weirs in Ümfalla, where their Order took absolute hold of most minds. But Seerinx's hold was only on the Ümfallans who remained, after many of the people's bodies became food for the earth, or vanished into darker places, through the ruthlessness of Reapers. What gathered, over an Age in Ümfalla, scattered in a few orbits, but there remained glimmers of hope in the darkness.

Scavenging Screevers fell under the leadership of the old Weir, Ībeka. The ancient Weir, who vanished in the night—after saving the Wanderer who became, Nyctámēna and acted as intermediary between Briar and Ruthy— turned Screevers into a group of assassins, who struck with their knives and Whispers in the darkness, before vanishing.

Ībeka assembled mothers who cried to the spore cloud, for orbits on end, lamenting their '*daughters*' and used their skill and knowledge of the land to the Screever's advantage. Beyond that, there was little to lose, when everything but their lives had been taken. If Seerinx faced any kind of threat to her onyx-eyed authority, it was Ībeka and her band of vengeful mothers.

Satyrs remained Satyrs, while the exponential growth of the Tree of Avernus signified crowning proof, above and below, Arethūsa was sovereign and merely a breath away from *being* the Goddess. Daphnē remained, as she had for centuries, cross-armed and tight-lipped, her eyes remaining shut, inside the tree.

Sky Tracer ate its own Whispering Weirs, taking Ákonitē's place, orbit after orbit, as unfortunate Wind Weirs confined to the mast either went mad, or wasted away to nothing, on their journeys over the darkness, where their Whispers sustained the spore cloud. Twenty-seven Weirs suffered this fate, over the course of seven orbits. All fell to their deaths, after despair wasted away what was left of their bodies and spirits. Yet another Weir was tied to the mast and was assured: *Arethūsa was on the brink of fixing what was half-broken, for centuries.*

Throughout the many tiers of Middle Rim, thousands of Avernians prospered, through the influx of rich waters, pouring from springs in the Tree. What were countless brothels, in every portion of the densely populated Rim, were flipped into markets, carrying bounties of rare fruits and nuts, once reserved for the elite. Sparkling mineral waters abounded, unique to their sources, drawn from the core of newly sprouted branches, growing as quickly as mushrooms in the darkness, below.

Just as the Tree of Avernus was growing taller, over the past seven orbits, so Middle Rim was expanding, allowing for the many thousands to claim more of the sky for themselves. Even the birth-rate rose, in accordance, leaving the largest of former brothels a nursery, since women were now as entangled in Avernian culture and politics as men. Plans for construction, in the coming seasons, were based on thin air, since exponential growth promised more to come. What transpired, high above, in Sky Throne, was deemed inherently good, considering the rich bounties and newfound freedoms. The spore cloud, far below, was nothing but a dark reminder of the glory reigning above: **Sky Realm**.

A profound change took place, a victory, hidden in plain sight. The fact it was forgotten was proof of its miraculous quality. Following the departure of Yala, Arethūsa was spending more and more time at the foot of the Tree of Daphnē. With her hands in the dirt and her eyes fixed on powers within, Arethūsa found a way to feed the hidden parts of the Tree, through murmurings with the Goddess. Mycelium Arethūsa brought back up with her, seven orbits before, was powerful enough to compensate for what was an integral part of the renewal ritual.

Gone were the screams of the children on Sky Tracer, unfortunate souls, who were carried to their doom, into the infernal heart of the Tree. Gone were the days where innocents were nothing but food for sustaining the greatness of Avernus. But everything came at a cost, just as it had from the first division of cells in primordial creatures, squirming in the depths of the darkest waters in Oceána, before bubbling into complexity, along forgotten shores.

Arethūsa sat in Sky Throne, in her resplendent silk gown, hanging loosely on her concave chest. Her eyes protruded, dazzling any onlookers, through dark sockets on sunken cheeks, acting as ciphers for a body moving like a puppet made of finely-carved sticks. The defining feature of Arethūsa was her crimson braid, grown beyond her feet and trailing many hands-length behind her. In the top of the braid, a distinguishing lock of raven-black hair remained, a testament to times almost forgotten, but always at her back.

In the fleeting moments when Arethūsa slept, most often at midday, when the light was too much, she always dreamt herself as, Ruthy. Her dreams were haunted by the dark-bright eyes of Mēna, who never said a word, in any tongue. When she awoke, there was a fleeting moment where she forgot who she was. It was only after her nightly communion with the Goddess, through the soothing words of Orīa, while the Weir held back her head by the braid, Arethūsa felt like *Arethūsa.*

Orīa rose, as far as Seerinx descended, in both their greatnesses. Wind Weirs ruled the sky, while Moon Weirs wielded absolute control of those below. Arethūsa knew the Weir schism was not coming, it already began, before the Orders were formally re-stablished. If anything was unpredictable, it was the Wind and Sister Moons. At the moment, in the glorified light of Sky Throne, the most unpredictable thing in the world was the child of Orīa and Briar, the seven-orbit-old, Īris.

She had the fair face and dark hair of her mother and sardonic mouth of her father, the mouth turned to stoic bitterness, over the course of his seven orbits. The only time Briar appeared like the roguish thief he was in Ümfalla, was in the presence of his daughter. Otherwise, grim experiences as, Captain of the Reapers, turned his face to stone. When he broke out into laughter, in the chamber of Sky Throne, Arethūsa was pulled out of her reverie and smiled upon the scene.

"What are you doing now, Īris? Flying?" Briar managed to say, through laughter, as he traversed the crystal chamber with the child in his hands, high above his silver head of hair.

"I'm a dragon!" Īris shouted, making the most fearsome face she could manage.

"Where did you learn that word?" Orīa asked, watching the love of her life, carrying her even greater love, across the room.

"I dreamt it!" Īris laughed, as Briar swooped her down to the chamber floor. For a moment, his swooping black cloak completely covered the child. Īris peered out, before she ran to the center of the chamber.

Arethūsa was already staring at Orīa when the Head of the Order of Wind Weirs looked up at her Ruler. Briar and the child continued to play, while the silence between the two women made Orīa's lower lip flutter, as it would, whenever she was Whispering, or worrying. She waited for Arethūsa's constant weariness to break the stare, before she dared look away. Arethūsa's protruding eyes were the only part of her withering body that remained vibrant, even more so, since the retreat of the rest of her form.

"Tell me, Īris," Arethūsa began, still staring at the child's mother. "What do dragons look like in your dreams?"

Īris spoke with relish, "Well, they're *really big*, bigger than Avernus. They make the sky dark. They breathe fire and burn anything that tries to stop them. And their brains are on their backs!"

"Brains on their backs?" Arethūsa laughed, looking away from Orīa. "Tell me more."

"*Well*," Īris said, trying to catch her breath and rearrange her dark silk pants and shirt. "The dragon is *so big*, she needs two brains. So one is in her head. Just like us. And the other," she said, reaching behind herself and pointing, "*is on her back*. The brain glows because it watches. So a dragon can never be caught by surprise. Not like my Daddy, when he isn't looking and I do *this*!"

Īris somersaulted into the back of her father's legs and Briar played along with a dramatic tumble to his knees and tragic fall, flat on his face. Īris stepped onto his back, in her bare feet, holding her proud arms outward, flapping them like wings, in triumph.

"*I am the Dragon Weir!*" Īris shouted, in a conquering voice.

Arethūsa's eyes darted back to Orīa, who refused to meet the stare.

"Why don't you go see what the starlings are up to, Īris," Orīa said, in a tremulous voice. "They make the best shapes in the sky, this time of light."

"Sky Shears kind of look like dragons," Īris said, stepping off her father's back. "I'll go see."

"Put on your cloak, before you go out," Orīa said. "You know how cold it is up here."

"And your boots!" Briar shouted, in a Captain's voice.

"K!" Īris shouted, bursting out of the chamber, with a black cloak and boots in tow.

"I don't know what to say, Arethūsa," Orīa muttered.

"There's nothing *to* say," Arethūsa said. "Your daughter already said it."

"It's just dreams," Briar said, as he stood up and reassumed his stone visage.

"Īris has shown her gift of prophecy, even before she could speak," Arethūsa said. "The wind is just wind, for most. But Wind for Weirs is something else. Dirt is just that, for everyone but me. The same goes for dreams, with Īris. I dream of the eyes of the Weir, in the darkness. My dreams are the past that's always there. Your daughter dreams of tomorrows. To deny those dreams, is to betray your child's gifts."

"She is *seven*-orbits-old, Arethūsa," Briar said. "If I listened to every one of her dreams like the word of the Goddess, I'd have mushrooms for arms and fairies flying in and out of my ears. Leave it alone."

"You know, Ümfallans always called them Night Skimmers," Arethūsa said. "You of all people know that, Briar, along with Orīa. From the murky depths of that place, dragons looked like large birds. Don't be mistaken, I saw them down there and that's exactly what they appeared to be. From here, I know just how enormous those creatures are. Their absence on the western horizon of Avernus makes them loom larger, in my mind's eye. And all of us know, it wasn't a large bird that carried Yala and the rest away. It was a *fucking* dragon."

"I believe Yala would have shown herself already, if her intentions were to return," Orīa said.

"*Yala*, is over seven centuries old," Arethūsa said. "Seven orbits are like seven days, for her. And I know her sister is only growing stronger. The Weir Sisters are probably goddesses to the sea-faring people of Oceána. I see this Tree growing taller and broader and can't help but think of all *this*, as more fodder for dragons."

"Dragon's don't breathe fire. That's the stuff of Īris' daydreams," Briar said. "And I doubt they have much of a taste for old wood."

"And how would you know that?" Ruthy asked, as she squirmed in her exquisite wooden throne. "If I were that colossal and powerful, I'd love to break apart this Tree, just to hear the noise it made, when it splashed into The Churn. Then I'd set this land on fire to smell the fungal smoke."

"I've seen plenty of Skimmer...*dragons*, in my life," Briar said. "It might have been from a great distance, but any fool would notice flames in the sky. Especially, in the darkness below."

"I'd never seen a woman, who could best any man in this realm, weapons or not, until I did. We can argue in circles forever on this," Arethūsa said. "I suppose my point in all this, *is*, I've come so near and so far with Daphnē. We are just as vulnerable as before. Perhaps, more so."

"It is incredible what you accomplished," Orīa said. "The Screaming Branch has gone silent. No more, are there child sacrifices."

"Just more sacrifices of the Weirs on Sky Tracer," Arethūsa retorted. "Growth has its limits. Power never remains, just because the vessel is large. I cannot lose focus on waking up Daphnē."

"Her eyes are fluttering," Orīa began. "I saw—"

"You saw the same thing you've seen for the past seven orbits," Arethūsa said. "It's maddening. I've established a murmuring with her, but she still won't speak to me. *Open your eyes, you lazy hag in the tree!*" Arethūsa roared, sinking into her dark throne.

Arethūsa's emaciated body, crumpled in the throne, made her appear as a child. Her long braid wound down the crystal stairs and the sky, below, made it look like some kind of Cosmic Serpent, at rest. Orīa felt a sudden sense of vertigo, as she traced the braid along the translucent floor with her eyes.

She turned to Briar and he was watching Īris, who was pointing at fluttering murmurations outside, with an attendant Wind Weir by her side. A Sky Shear darted through countless starlings and the headless body of a starling struck the crystal wall, snapping everyone out of their reverie, while it left a meagre trail of blood and guts.

"There's a *fucking* augury for you," Briar said.

Arethūsa laughed first. It began as a refined chuckle, but morphed into unadulterated laughter, turning her pale pallor, red. Orīa's look of astonishment became laughter at the laughter and Briar followed with his laughter, at the laughter of the laughter, from his own joke. The room became an echo chamber from a brief time in the past, when the three had freshly united and everything seemed possible and good. The paradox of Time reared its horrifying and laughing head, before it snapped back and revealed itself for what it was: **Now**.

"Īris points to her own dreams."

Arethūsa's words turned everyone's eyes in the direction of the western sky. A smudge of black on the horizon was quickly becoming a distinct point of an ever-growing truth. When the wings were discernible, the joyous screams of Īris penetrated the crystal chamber of Sky Throne, but nobody within said a word.

The dragon flew, up and up, into the orange glow of sunrise and everyone's eyes followed. The Eternal Storm churned in the distance and appeared to give birth to the fated vision, captivating the witnesses in the crystal chamber. When the dragon screamed through the emptiness, Īris screamed to the sky, along with her.

31

A Tale of Two Fisherman

CALLISTO'S CLUNKING STEPS PRECEDED her appearance, by two or three moments, while Nyctámēna fumed on the Southern Shore of Forlindea. Iō was dancing in the wind, high in the sky, after another night fell without a sign of Scylla. The dragon's scales blended into the night sky, making her almost invisible, except for stripes of indigo iridescence, running the length of a body born for speed. Such iridescence bewildered the observer, rather than revealing the size and precise location of the dragon, while the dragon enchanted the sky through indigo tracers.

In spite of Nyctámēna's anger, bested only by her worry, she did not fail to marvel at the beauty of a creature she was so fortunate to bond with, a dragon-soul she loved beyond words. When another love stumbled onto the shore and nearly fell, when her boot found a nook in the tangled roots, Nyctámēna turned her head from the sky and looked down on Callisto.

"Where the fuck have you been?!"

"Funniest thing," Callisto slurred, as she stood up, with a sway, "I was asking Scylla the same thing, earlier this turn."

"You've both been gone for four!"

"Four? Oh!" Callisto laughed. "Time flies, even if you're walking, alone, through the woods. I'm left to my own two feet, so the world moves a lot slower for me. But funniest thing...I ran into these two fisherman, along the way...and they got to talking and I got to listening and we got to drinking beer...*really good beer*...really strong—"

"Wait a moment. Where is Scylla?!"

"She flew away on a dragon, like always. *Whoosh*!" Callisto laughed, with a flight of her hand.

"I thought she was with you! She hasn't returned?!"

"*Oh*. Well, shit. That's not good. I thought my stern talk to her set her straight."

"Stop talking."

"But I—"

"Shut your mouth and let me think," Nyctámēna said, through clenched teeth. She paced the shore for a moment, before she turned back to Callisto, "What did you say to her up North?" Callisto locked her lips with her thumb and forefinger. "Sometimes I wonder who the child is. Those fisherman are going to be the end of you, someday. You can talk again, Calli."

"I was talking to Yala about all the changes they've made to the place. You should see it. They—"

"I know about the Temple. And I know about Weirs boarding ships to surrounding realms. I can see secrets you're dying to tell me in your eyes. *I know you*, Calli. And I know more about the North than you can imagine. I've got a great view from up there," she pointed, towards the dragon in the sky. "And yet I failed to see Scylla take to the skies."

"So much for my messenger service. I really have grown useless."

"We'll figure that out, later. Focus, you sot. *Scylla*."

"Right...*her*. I was talking to Yala, when I saw Scylla, surrounded by those girl-Weirs. So I pulled her bony-ass away and told her to stay away from them. Just like you and I talked about. Told her they wanted her for her power, not her company."

"Aw, fuck. Calli! You don't tell a young woman that. *Ever!*"

"I was a young woman once and I wouldn't have cared. Neither would you."

"Well, we're...*different* than most. How did Scylla take it?"

"She took it fine. She's well...*Scylla*. Brightest spirit I've ever known, even if she knows just how to piss me off and make me love her, at the same time. Maybe *that's* what those mothers were talking about. Anyway, she hugged me goodbye, before she summoned a dragon."

"*A* dragon?"

"Yeah."

"Not a pair, or four, or—"

"Just one. All by her lonesome."

"*Fuck!*"

"That's your word for today, eh? I thought I had reign over that one."

"Did she say anything, *anything* out of the ordinary, before she left?"

"She was less talkative than usual, which is strange, because she never shuts up. But she kept bringing up Avernus, when we were still at the Temple. That's my fault. I shouldn't have told her stories. Most of them were about Ümfalla, but she loved to hear about Sky Realm, couldn't get enough of it. And I know Yala's been telling her tales of orbits past, giving her details of Arethūsa and the Goddess and—"

"*Enough*!" Nyctámēna shouted so loud, Īō took notice from the heavens. She took a deep breath and ran her fingers through her hawk-hair, "It's not your fault, Calli. You *do* drink too much these days, but I don't blame you. I brought you to this place without your heart's consent. You stood by my side, while I searched for the people Yala convinced me I came from, in these woods. And you know what we found?"

"Fucking fishermen."

"*Fucking fishermen*. But you remained by my side and never wavered in your love. Then Scylla burst out of nowhere and now we're like a pair of defective parents."

"There's more than you and Scylla's eyes that speaks of a shared people between you two. *Dragons*."

"That past is lost to both of us. Calli, you're just as heart-bound to her as me. I've neglected you of late and I'm sorry. I've been solely focused on Īō and Scylla with her dragons, I... And you've been more than a friend, throughout. I love your spirit, Calli, your *heart*."

"Shit," Callisto cried, wiping her tears, with the back of her hand, "Fucking Forlindean beer makes me cry. I love you too, Nyctámēna."

"You actually said my Name, for once. That's magic."

"Magic is for kids."

"Yeah, no shit," Nyctámēna half-smiled. Then she looked to the east, "I don't have to tell you where Scylla is probably headed."

"No."

"I spoke words to Scylla, before, I regret. Failed to say what I should have. I push too hard... But that kid has no idea what that Tree stands for. What it holds."

"She's a Dragon Weir. Don't forget that. She *is* a fucking kid, but I'm pretty sure there's only two Dragon Weirs in the whole world and one is standing in front of me. The other one is in deep shit, when we catch up to her. Can't say I blame her for being a little curious. But she has no way of knowing what's out there. We're wasting time and I don't want to lose my courage."

"How do you feel about getting back on the dragon?"

"I'll probably puke again, but what's a gal to do?"

"Īō is *really* fast."

"Aware of that."

"And she won't hold back when she sees what we need."

"Yup. Clear, too."

"Wanna go ahead and take some courageous breaths right here?"

"*Yup!*"

Callisto fell to her knees and breathed heavily onto the tangled roots, before she kissed the Southern Shore. Brine greeted her lips and tasted just like her tears. At that moment, Callisto wished for the mossy softness in the land of Ümfalla. When the ritual passed, she could almost smell the spore cloud. Her fears of the heights to come were supplanted by vibrant heartbeats brought on by impending adventure.

For the first time in seven orbits, Callisto felt a little like the warrior she was. By the time she looked back up, Īō was overhead, flapping water into waves, breaking along the shore, where they washed away foamy sins of turns past.

32

SWEEPING COURSE

SCYLLA HEARD TALES OF the Eternal Storm circling Ümfalla and the crowning Sky Realm of Avernus. But she never expected the view of the storm from above to bring with it such beauty. Lightning revealed hidden parts of the clouds, while tumultuous winds within, spun the storm into whirling designs, with infinite gradations of gray, far beyond the world of mortal perception, limited by Time.

When the Tree appeared on the horizon, she believed the mere sight of it would be enough. Proof of its existence, from afar, was all she needed, before she turned back with the Tree of Avernus tucked into her brain, like a pretty pebble from the Forlindean shore.

Through swift-wings, the Tree began rising in perception, straight into legend. All the fragments she gathered, through tales from Callisto and Yala, even the silence of Nyctámēna, were galvanizing into a living whole. Words Scylla received and later enchanted were manifesting into the magic she was approaching with Nīya. Scylla wondered if anyone ever witnessed the approach to Avernus, in such a way.

"*Only the Goddess,*" she said.

Beyond the storm, tremendous branches of the Tree's new-growth were beneath, articulating ubiquitous sea-foam of The Churn, bubbling and re-bubbling into being. Leaves became distinguishable and Scylla yearned to be able to touch them.

She wanted to *smell* the mysteries of Middle Rim and *see* the people, *seeing her*, in return. A lifetime avoiding the gaze of others was becoming a need to be seen, to feel as real as the dragon who dared to look into her soul and not turn away.

Ümfalla was a beautiful nightmare, below, disenchanted by the spore cloud, in absolute contrast to the glory of the Tree, above. Contrasting darkness and light evoked a sense of beauty Scylla never experienced before, as if the world was becoming as real as the Dragon Weir. Scylla imagined her approach on the back of Nīya and the Avernian's reactions, to be perceived as a Dragon Weir, a sense of belonging in the sky. Scylla glanced behind her and saw nothing but the storm on the horizon. Then she tilted, onwards and upwards, into the heights of Sky Realm.

A new world was rushing into her lungs, as the air grew drier and clearer. Nīya's excitement was evident, through her sweeping course, aerial performances, meant to dazzle witnessing Avernians, since the dragon and her Weir were feeding from their entangled excitement.

Scylla's heart raced through the dragon's spirit and she found herself unable to distinguish between her own choices and Nīya's, while their heartbeats were identical in rhythm. It was a seamless harmony, an absolute sympathy of Weir and dragon, one carrying them far beyond Upper Rim and into thin air, overlooking the branch embracing the crystal chamber of Sky Throne.

The view from above made the Tree of Avernus appear as a spiraling infinitude of arboreal magnificence, where windmills and crystalline constructs of the realm were natural emanations from the Tree, the many people scurrying about, like so many ants. Throughout Middle Rim, rolling hills and meadows, markets and temples, crowned colossal branches supporting them, Rims reaching out to the horizons in all directions. The Tree stretched to infinity.

This was the heart of Sky Realm, a world aloft, holding multitudes, thousands of Avernians, who only knew this view. For the young Weir, she was an airborne witness to more people than she imagined lived in the whole hemisphere. Windmills spun secrets through the power of the wind, while springs shot up from every tier of Middle Rim, creating shattered rainbows through cloudless light. These dazzling games of water and light directed Scylla's gaze up. The crystal structure, at the top of the Tree, glimmered in the morning light. Whether it was Nīya or Scylla who spotted it first, was of no consequence. The unified pair, who were One, continued their ascent.

Sky Throne played games with light, bewildering the curious dragon and her Weir, through rainbow splendor. When Nīya flew over the crystal chamber, the fierce downdraft from her wings made the spiraling top of the structure tremble, blowing up debris from hidden places in the Tree, until the teardrop-shaped chamber shattered.

Shards were mostly blown away and fell in shimmering pieces, down into Ümfallan depths. Scylla watched the pieces fall, with horror, as Nīya tilted up and away from the scene of their folly. As far as the Dragon Weir perceived, nobody was within the shattered chamber. The essential ingredient of guilt forced Scylla to head down towards a suitable spot on Upper Rim. It was a grassy place, enchanted by ferns, an enormous niche that appeared to be groomed for the dragon's landing.

At their approach, many figures dressed in black gathered, while a single figure shimmered apart from the rest, in the morning light. When those faces became distinct, a young girl was pointing up and flapping her arms like wings. What followed was an event unfolding in slow-motion for the Dragon Weir, but happening in the blink of everyone else's eyes. The girl's fluttering excitement took her to the edge, where the protective balustrade was weakened enough to break. She toppled into emptiness of what constituted the greater part of Sky Realm: Emptiness.

Scylla's fear fed the dragon's intent, when they shifted their course down, bolting into a whistling flight, mimicking an assault on the Tree, itself. Through the Tree's lesser branches, snapping like twigs in the dragon's dive, Scylla expected to hear the girl screaming. But the plummeting child was still flapping her arms in the air when she spotted them and looked at the Dragon Weir, through eager-eyed wonder, rather than fear.

The union of the dragon and her Weir took them under the child, with such synchronicity, the girl landed in Scylla's outstretched arms, as if falling from a low-hanging branch. The girl laughed, holding out her arms when Scylla plopped her in front of her, while Nīya soared back up to the heights of Upper Rim.

"I knew you'd come!" The girl shouted, through laughter. "Just like my dreams, but *better*!"

"What's your name?" Scylla asked, through anxious breaths.

"Īris!"

"Hello, Īris. I'm Scylla."

"I know!"

"Next time, tell me about your dreams. Don't show me."

"Then they wouldn't be true! And you weren't here yet for me to tell you."

"Well, put in a good word for me, up there. Okay?"

"K! *Whoooooooooooo! Fa-ster!*"

Scylla's heart was beating so quickly while the girl was in her arms, the landing was a reality detached from her own sense of fantasy. Nīya's talons dug into ferns and grasses of Upper Rim, while Scylla adjusted her onyx goggles.

Nīya's wings settled and Scylla kicked her leg up and over the helm-spike on the dragon's back, slid down the edge of her wing, with the girl in tow, before her boots landed, impressing upon the verdant ground of Avernus.

Īris shouted, "I told you! I saw a little deeper into days to come this time!" She leaped with joy from Scylla's grasp and ran to her mother's embrace. "*The Dragon Weir!*"

The awkwardness of being, *Other*, was thrust upon Scylla, while she stood in the cooling winds of Sky Realm, with countless warriors standing at the ready. A woman was approaching, whose shimmer hurt Scylla's eyes, even through the goggles. Īris was speaking in triple-pace to Orīa, while Briar followed Arethūsa.

The skeletal Ruler of Avernus, who wore the light more than the silk reflecting and refracting it, drew nearer to the Dragon Weir. Arethūsa's exquisite gown and trailing red braid evoked insecurity in Scylla, who wore a meagre wood-cotton top and earth-toned pants, tailored for action, rather than ritual. Nīya loomed, darkly, on the edge of the Rim, in all of her disproportionate beauty and power. Her wings remained outstretched and cast a long shadow on the scene. The shadow cast by the dragon's wings was a gift to her Weir's dark-bright eyes, obscured by onyx goggles.

"*Sorry about the damage!*" Scylla shouted, articulating every syllable. "Wish I could fix it, but I lack the skills! Not a good way to start!"

"You don't have to shout," Arethūsa said, as her bare feet settled in the ferns, within speaking distance.

"Holy shit!" Scylla cried, pointing in a way betraying her youth, with her other hand over her open mouth. "You're Arethūsa! I can't believe I'm standing *here* with *you! Arethūsa!*"

"So says the Weir with a dragon. Knowing my Name tells me *who* you know. But who are you?"

"She's Scylla!" Īris shouted, from her crouching mother's arms. Orīa stood up and nodded at Scylla.

"Well, the kid got it. I'm Scylla. Scylla, all here. Fully Scylla," she turned her head and cursed to herself, in nervous excitement.

Orīa bit her fluttering lower lip, before she called out, "Thank you for saving my daughter! I don't know if I should should hug you, or kill you."

"Dragon diplomacy," Arethūsa half-smiled. "I would expect no less from a Scylla, who comes from a *Mēna*, across Oceána."

A moment of silence fell and Scylla squirmed, while trying to stand still. She sensed every eye upon the dragon and herself and it felt nothing like she imagined. Even though Nīya was just behind her, Scylla was vulnerable, making her skin go cold. She waited for Arethūsa to say something, but was met with prying eyes from a wan face, picking her apart, bit by bit. The fledgling Dragon Weir crossed her arms, uncrossed them, adjusted her top and put her hands on her hips, all to no avail. Nyctámēna's voice rang through her head: '*Stop fidgeting and focus!*'

Scylla searched for something to say, in a situation she fantasized about, over and over again, full of hugs and warm regards, to friends long separated by time and misfortune. It was *her* fantasy, one created through fragmented tales, drops in the ocean compared to the hyper-realism of the moment. The wind shifted, before Scylla opened her mouth to speak.

"I have come...to bring you word from the most *fished* realm in all of Oceána... *Forlindea*," she said an octave lower than usual, with her wiry arms held out wide. Muffled laughter, throughout the Weir and Reaper ranks, followed. "Nyctámēna has sent *me*...her..."

"Her what?" Arethūsa asked, with a wry smile.

"Her daughter. I am her long, lost daughter."

"Her long, lost daughter?" Briar guffawed, beside Arethūsa. "You look like the offspring of Nyctá and Arethūsa, if such things were possible. Nyctá was raiding villages back at your conception, not spreading her legs for any cock, in Forlindea. And you possess the look of someone beyond her element. I've been there. I pity the feeling, Dragon Weir." Briar looked away from Scylla, betraying his torment to the wind, alone.

Scylla's arms fell to her sides and she spoke plainly, in spite of the manic fluttering of her lower lip, "Family is re-forged every day. It doesn't flow freely, like a lazy brook, but through the streams of ourselves," she concluded, with a look of surprise for her words. "More than blood makes kin."

"You speak beyond your years," Arethūsa said.

"I have two good teachers. And the woods of Forlindea speak through me...*sometimes*."

"Sounds like the *Mēna* I knew, a crowning achievement of the Fungal Realm. I'll be clear with you, *child of the woods*... Already, you shattered Sky Throne, lured a child over the edge and saved her, through winged-luck, before you even landed here on your dragon. Your words are your own, as one of your teachers likes to say. But your actions seem carved. Īris spoke of a Dragon Weir and here you are."

"Yup. Here I am. *Pull it together Scylla*," she muttered to herself. She cleared her throat, "It sure is cold up here," she grinned, crossing her arms, over her chest.

"What do you mean?" Arethūsa glared.

"Just saying it gets cold up here, when the wind shifts, right? It was warm, a moment ago."

"You had no intention of landing. Īris' fall forced you. I see mischief in your eyes, as sure as I see your naivety. I was you, once," Arethūsa said, taking a step closer, pointing at Scylla. "You were spying on us. Yala probably Whispered her intentions into your overeager ears. Īris forced you to land, not your poor attempt at a message. If you really knew the history between your *teacher* and myself, the betrayal, you would never have come here, not alone. If Mēna wanted to speak with me, she would have come here, herself. She's probably wandering, just like she did in Ümfalla. You know it's true…I can see the look in your eyes, beneath the same goggles she wore to deceive me, while you were probably still running feral in the Forlindean woods. Mēna is a waste of life, a waste of power."

"What is that word, *spying*."

"Looking without permission."

"The sky is free."

"Not the skies of Avernus."

"Nobody controls the skies, nobody but the Goddess and she loves to be looked upon."

"The Goddess lives, *here*," Arethūsa said.

"I thought she was everywhere," Scylla said, spreading her arms wide.

"Her essence is here. Her *soul*."

"I thought time would have smoothed over any wrongs between you and Nyctámēna. But I don't really know this shared history. You call her, *Mēna*. It's funny, that's what Calli calls her, sometimes. Calli is kind of like my older sister. She lets me get away with tons of shit, but kicks my ass when she has to. I'm saying too much. But I hate keeping it in. Yala only speaks highly of you. She misses you… *So nervous, I'm losing my breath*… I admit I dreamed of being here. That was foolish of me to say… It feels like magic to say, *Arethūsa*, to *you*. I dreamed of fixing things, for everyone. But everything feels wrong…strange. Nobody else cold? If I could ever get to know you and tell you how—"

"You will. You are already beginning to know me and I look forward to getting to know you better, Scylla. Take a deep breath. No need to be nervous. *Now*…tell me about *Nyctá*mēna."

"She's basically my mother. Even if she won't say it. Taught me just about everything I know. But she's a private kind of gal."

"Secretive, is what she is," Arethūsa said.

"She's honest," Scylla said, through quick breaths. "My words are carved in truth."

"Secrets are secrets. They have nothing to do with honesty. Secrets can topple entire realms, cause more destruction than any dragon.."

"Don't tell Nīya that," Scylla pointed over her shoulder, at the ever-watchful dragon. "She's already shattered your Sky Throne. *By accident!*"

All the Reapers, Weirs and the Ruler of Avernus turned their attention to the dragon, who was eyeing them, through her burning indigo eyes. Nīya's size made everything in Sky Realm seem small, everything but the Tree, itself.

"Do you really talk to the Goddess?" Scylla asked, trying to turn attention away from the dragon.

"*Directly*," Arethūsa said, with fierce eyes. "Soon, she will awaken."

"What then?"

"You are endless in your prying questions."

"Can't help it. I've seen little and want to know it all. I just got here and I'm already amazed. Even the wind blows differently here... So what happens when the Goddess awakens? What then?"

"You'll see."

Scylla began swaying in the wind, while her legs shook, "Ya' know...you're telling me all kinds of secrets. You should have done that with your Mēna. Would have saved a lot of trouble. But then I wouldn't have found her. Funny how bad and good can't get enough of each other. By bad, I mean the trouble between you two. But without Nyctámēna, I would have been one of those Weirs of Forlindea, talking to the wind. The littlest things can change everything. And then there's dragons, but that's different. You're being a fine host. Is that what it's called? *Host*? I heard that word in a story... I guess a Ruler isn't a host, if it means, what I think it means...right? *Whoa...* Why do I feel drunk?"

"It's the wind up here," Arethūsa half-smiled. "It can bewilder."

"Sure does," Scylla slurred, as her head drifted down and snapped back up. "Feels kind of like..."

The Dragon Weir's knees buckled and she fell into a heap on the ferns. Before her body settled into stillness, Nīya cleared the surrounding area with the force of her flapping wings and thunderous cry to the heavens. The dragon flew up and glared down, upon her fallen Weir, while the ones who toppled over through her flight, ran to the far end of Upper Rim.

Below, Scylla remained motionless in the ferns, with her red hair blowing in the dragon wind. Arethūsa stood fast in the fierce winds, in spite of her lithe form. Thick chords of mycelium entangled her bare feet to the ground, fortifying themselves through roots. Orīa held Arethūsa by the arm, while shouting, through dragon wind.

"Do you know how long it took to Whisper her down?!"

"*Scylla is strong,*" Arethūsa shouted back, squirming her bare toes in mycelial-ferns. "I feel her strength through my feet. The ground shimmers at her presence. Stay close to Scylla. This dragon might be a realm-crusher, but she can't pluck her Weir from us, not without risking harm to her. Power always has a weakness," Arethūsa smiled, staring at the looming magnificence of the dragon. "*Such power.*"

"I could have dropped a hundred Reapers with the Whispering that required. I threw seven Whispers through the wind and none of them moved her. Not until she looked back at her dragon. Were she not so naive and wide-eyed, I never would have succeeded. It will take me many turns before I can do it again."

"No need."

"You can't believe there won't be more Weirs to follow."

"Oh, I'm counting on it. There's another Dragon Weir on the horizon. And when the next one comes, *I will not be, as I am.*"

"What do you mean?" Orīa asked, with a noticeable twitch to her lower lip.

"You'll see."

"That scares me. You sound like Briar when he's about to do something foolhardy. Perhaps we should speak of this in a place more removed. Talk softly over these heavy matters before—"

"Nobody asked you. You've Whispered enough. Go be a responsible mother and make sure Īris doesn't fall headlong into her own prophecy again. You're no good to me like you are. And I don't need your counsel. Everything is clear," she said, squinting her watery eyes in the dragon wind. "Briar!"

"Your Highness?" Briar called out, as he trotted up to Arethūsa, his gaze fixed on the dragon.

"Gag the Dragon Weir and make her bindings double-sure. She can Whisper to more than dragons. You can see it in her lips. Take her down to my other sanctuary."

"Don't you think—"

"Don't think! Do!" Arethūsa seethed. "You and Orīa's words are like acid in my ears. And make sure that dragon isn't provoked. That's a Realm Crusher with wings, who wants her Weir back."

"Well," Briar began, while Arethūsa walked out of the shadow of the dragon. Mycelium receded back into the ground, at her departure. "Are you satisfied?"

"I accomplished what I intended," Orīa said, glancing back at Īris, who was in the arms of an attendant Weir. "Took a little longer than I expected."

"Seven orbits is a long time to Whisper her into your design. Surprised she knows anything beyond her Name. You need to pull back on your cunnings."

"Oh, that. I thought you were speaking of yourself. Don't you know I make myself perfect in your mind, every time I Whisper you to my designs?"

"You would never," Briar said. "Not to *me*!"

"You always react like this, whenever I tell you I've been Whispering to you...ever since that night on Middle Rim, the fateful night we reunited. *Feel* me Whispering you back into the mind I want you to be, at this very moment. It's a beautiful thing when I find your resonance, because I love you, the harmony allowing me to Whisper, while I speak. You love me, beyond any devices. You love me, more than you love yourself. I love you, Briar, father of our child and core of my heart."

A half-smile found Briar's face, "I love you, too, Orīa, mother of my child and queen of my soul," he said, before he looked down and shook his head. When he looked back up, he had a look of resolve, "I understand what you're doing with Arethūsa. But her resilience never quite falters... In the end, you'll rise... Then you'll be satisfied."

"I'm never satisfied. But Arethūsa has finally forgotten who she was. She lives the Whispers, now. Don't you see?"

"As clear as the Avernian sky. But she still dreams of Ruthy."

"They are nothing but dreams. Ruthy was a ruse, never real. Keep an eye on her. We don't want my masterwork to overdo it. Not just yet."

"You've always walked the edge, in your own too much, Orīa. Perhaps that's why I love you."

"You know why you love me. And look who we made together," she said, smiling at a distant Īris, who had a look of consternation at the Dragon Weir being dragged away, unconscious.

"You have two children to tend, Īris and Arethūsa," Briar said. "And both of them are far too eager for their own good. One is enough for me. I'll see you tonight, at the tree. I need a drink. My head's killing me."

"And I need to sleep," Orīa said, kissing Briar on his grizzled cheek, with her fluttering lips. "Our new beginning is near."

"Sure," he said, looking back up at the dragon's rage.

Nīya was flying high enough above Sky Realm to resemble the dragon's other Name, in the murk of Ümfalla, the Night Skimmer. She tore the atmosphere with every scream for her Weir, who was as much a part of her, as the dragon was to Scylla. Centuries of existence provided no shelter for Nīya's tormented thoughts. In her power and size, she could never pluck Scylla from her captors, not without destroying the same soul she was trying to save.

All that remained was the sky, growing heavy, for the first time in the dragon's existence. That niche on her back, the helm destined for Scylla, felt like a chasm in the universe of Nīya, a black hole consuming her. When the sun set behind the Eternal Storm, Nīya remained a fixture in the sky, a sky bereft of clouds, but full of the dragon, the dragon waiting for the moment to do something other than scream and wait for her Weir's return.

33

HEARTWOOD

WHEN SCYLLA OPENED HER eyes, her head was pounding, in synchronicity with the beating light in the room, exuding warmth. Her forehead, wrists and ankles were bound to a pole, on a rectangular platform with wheels. If a tree dreamed of itself, visited its own core, then Scylla was the dreamer, gazing on a wooden chamber shaped by arboreal heartbeats, over the Ages.

She was inside a giant's heart, with gill-like ridges, exuding an ochre-glow like red clouds at dawn, portending storms to come. It smelled of blood and soil. Scylla tried to turn, but the bindings were too tight and the gag on her mouth kept her head in place. She knew someone was behind her, but Scylla remained silent, while she tried to wriggle free from her confinement.

"No use trying to pull free," Arethūsa's voice resonated in the chamber. "Silk ropes are stronger than steel. It's funny...you can cut silk with a knife, as easily as a young branch. But try and pull silk apart and the strongest hands would fail. I hate to keep you silent, Scylla. You're a good soul. Time hasn't twisted you into many knots. It's clear you're loved. But I know you Whisper to more than dragons. I know what it feels like to want to see the hidden parts of the world. Here you are. Well done. But it's all the same...I hate to tell you that truth. The only difference is the view. I'm sure your *family* told you about Sky Tracer. Well, this is the place where children were delivered into the heart of the Goddess. It was called the Screaming Branch. It's a terrible name, for a far worse place. *But it's beautiful*. For over one hundred orbits, young women, not unlike yourself, fed this burning heart. Women have suffered for other's ambition, for countless orbits. Men inherit the bounty of the suffering, while they reward each other for it. But I found a way to change that. Screams no longer Name this branch. It's astounding how the most beautiful things are the most deadly: The Vernox Forest in Ümfalla, Sky Tracer from below, Mēna's wrath, Daphnē, this place...you and your dragon..."

Arethūsa stepped in front of Scylla and knelt at her feet, looking up, through weary eyes. Scylla glared down, through her onyx goggles, instinctively chewing on the gag. Arethūsa stood, slowly, staring at Scylla, before she pulled down Scylla's goggles and waited for her to meet her gaze.

"It's incredible how much your eyes remind me of Mēna's. It's not just the dark-bright quality. There is a wellspring of lives within them, a whole world of others, in One. There's no denying you two must have sprung from the same kind, whoever they were. Unparalleled, both of you. I have been many things, but what I have become, is just another version of incompleteness. It all leads to *this*," she said, looking back at the heartwood, pulsing into deep crimsons, imparting the air with a blood-like quality. "It takes the strength of binding opposites to do more than feed the Goddess. Opposites create the harmony I seek. The only woman I've ever encountered with the strength it requires is, Mēna. I admire that as much as I envy it. In a handful of turns, Mēna made it clear just how powerful one soul could be, even if she chose to waste it. And then you arrive on the back of a dragon. I never believed in fate, or destiny. But I know opportunity and how to *will* it into something more. You know what power feels like. You're a Dragon Weir. You know the feeling, the *knowing*. Few people in the world know that. Fucking and loving and the thrill of battle, none of that will ever compare. Together, we can wake up the Goddess. I've been mumbling to Daphnē, from a distance, for far too long. I can feel her voice in my ear like a faint Whisper, whenever I play in the dirt like a child, in front of the Goddess. She mocks me and twists my being a little more, every time. Look at me. I can't keep this up," she half-smiled, looking down at herself. "Even my womanly qualities are gone. I used to have breasts and my body was strong. Only my spirit remains potent. I'm nothing but bones with a tired heart and weary eyes. And I refuse to turn back to barbarisms of the past, back to child sacrifices. You and I are going to shake Daphnē awake, from her insides. She's been taking advantage of me, of all her victims, for too many orbits. I thought mycelium would be enough, but I needed another spirit as powerful as me. Now it's my turn to take control of this Tree. You flew here on a breathtaking dragon, from the backwaters of Forlindea. Yala told me enough about that place to know. People fish away their lives and Whisper to the dull breeze. You're an orphan from nowhere, about to commune with the Goddess. You and I were born for this. You are the One and I am Nothing. But our powers united will be so much more."

Arethūsa pulled down the gag enough for Scylla to open her mouth, but made sure her lower lip was covered, tightening the gag to make double-sure. The strain left Scylla's upper teeth gleaming, in the blood-light of the cell. Her tongue licked saliva from her bottom teeth, while her eyes shined, battle-bright.

"I feel the power you speak about, Arethūsa. But I didn't take it. The dragon found me and chose to allow me to share that power with her. Nīya...I didn't even know her, until a turn ago. Now I can't imagine life without her."

"Of course, a girl your age is only worried about her dragon. Only a day with your Nīya? That's not surprising to me. *Young love*... Time means nothing. I only spent a handful of turns in Ümfalla and I was never the same."

"You can't force your Daphnē to share herself with you. Power is not a thing to be taken. It only crushes and remains as it was. Neither is love, if you've ever had it. It just *is*. I never had love, not until Nyctámēna and Calli, now Nīya. If I know anything, that's something of it. My words are my own. I haven't seen much, but what you seek is impossible. You'd have more luck forcing yourself onto an unwilling dragon's back. Nothing in the world could do that. It takes a sort of agreement already, for an agreement to be made."

"Mēna keeps your head in the clouds. *Force* is the critical element of power. Otherwise, it's meaningless, just like Mēna. Your dragon would never have *consented* to you climbing on her back, not unless she felt your power. Both of you share in the gains. *That* is a fundamental truth. It's a selfish-giving. Love comes later, if it ever does."

"I may not know your ways. But you could have asked me and I would have stuck around."

"Not for this. And words have run their course. Whispers make me want to vomit. I know Wind Weirs have Whispered me into something beyond my reckonings. I'd have to be an idiot to think I could escape a breath of wind from a Weir's mouth, throughout my time in Avernus. I know the seeds of my truth, even if the fruit is rotten. I *know* how powerful I am, that I have prevailed, as myself. But I've reached my limits. I'm wearing thin, Scylla. Then you come from the sky, through a much more graceful fall than my own, in Ümfalla. But neither of us will be the same, not after this fall. You'll see."

"What about Ruthy?"

"What?"

"*Ruthy.*"

"That was a dream and nothing more. Ruthy is meaningless, a Name to get what I needed. Now—"

"*Ruthy!*"

"*Ruthy* is dead!" Arethūsa screamed into Scylla's face, in a voice far different than her own. "*I killed the bitch while she was playing in the dirt.*"

"Something else moves you. I can hear it!"

"Now," she said, back in the voice of Arethūsa, while she shook off the rage, "don't scream. It just makes it worse, *believe me*...I'll be right next to you, when it happens. See you on the other side."

Arethūsa pressed her forehead to Scylla's, before she pulled up the gag and walked behind her. Scylla flailed beneath her bindings, but the pole was secure in its platform and wide enough to resist toppling over. Scylla had no choice but to stare into the heartwood, pulsing in front of her. It resembled a giant's heart, cut vertically, with profane inner-workings, rumbling into wakefulness. There was a distinct dividing line of dark wood between the two sides. The left-half she was staring into, was brighter than the soft red-glow of the other.

When the wheels squeaked and she drew closer to wooden gills of the bifurcated *heart*, ivory rhizomes appeared from hidden places in the ceiling. They writhed and wriggled, sentient, on their twisting route towards Scylla.

Where root and mycelium began and ended in the entanglement was of no importance, since they were One. Hyphae tips caressed Scylla's face before slithering along her head, around her neck and down her body, until nothing of Scylla was visible but her shining eyes, full of utter horror.

Arethūsa methodically untied Scylla's bindings, from behind, as the tension of rhizomes began to pull her closer to the heartwood. When the last knot was untied from her ankles, Scylla's body was lifted from the platform and drifted through the strength of the entanglement, on the way to her destination. The gilled left-side opened like a mouth and Scylla was consumed before the void closed on itself.

It was a silent action. Not even a breath was to be heard on her delivery into the void of the heart of the Goddess. Arethūsa walked to the right side of the heartwood, where another set of rhizomes were eager for her arrival. She, too, was wrapped in their eager embrace and was devoured, without a scream or a whisper, to mark the moment.

34

BLOOD~FRUIT

ORĪA TRIED TO RECALL the last time she visited the Goddess without Arethūsa leading the way. She was aware of the rumors surrounding the place, rumors that had come and gone in Middle Rim, only to surface again, as rumors did. Some told of Arethūsa speaking directly with the Goddess, that the illusion of silence was an instrument of fear, keeping the people in Avernus under her yoke.

Others were convinced the Goddess died long ago and her body, entombed in the tree, was nothing but what it appeared to be, a dead reckoning of what once was, just like the Seven Elders. Orīa knew the truth and ignored the rumors, just as she ignored talk of her own past, as a Night Whisperer of the brothels, who had a child with her brother. Barbed rumors from her childhood were such stuff inspiring her to hone her Whispers over the orbits, turning words into weapons, a power she carried with pride.

She rose to Upper Rim through her own power, became a loving mother to a prophetically gifted child, all while sharing her life with the man she loved from childhood. Even Arethūsa, the all-powerful Ruler of Avernus, was under her Whispering will.

Orīa tried to imagine what was transpiring, down in the Screaming Branch, but only felt winds of uncertainty on her face. The dragon remained, circling the night sky, high above Sky Throne. Orīa believed the beast was supposed to be there, that something so powerful was summoned to Avernus, as a witness.

Her bare feet tread with purpose, upon the receiving earth, leading up to the dark plot where Arethūsa kneeled to the Goddess, countless times. Lunar light from the Three Sisters made the mineral encasement of Daphnē shine. She pulled down her crimson hood and her hair flowed as freely as her thoughts.

For the first time in her life, Time was an ally, a palpable thing she was able to see, right in front of her. When she pulled up the hem of her Weir Robe and rested her bare knees upon the dark earth, she looked up at the face of Daphnē. The soil was warm and her knees sank a little, before she settled in, to witness the undoing of what some dark cunning had done, an Age before.

Orīa looked upon the face of Daphnē and saw her as Arethūsa would. Rather than closing her eyes, she blinked and imagined what the Goddess' eyes would look like, were they to open. Daphnē's hair was an earthen green, while her face was gaunt and jaundiced yellow. Her lips were pursed in a fixed gesture of pain and surprise. Her crossed arms, over her bare breasts, were straining against what took place, binding-magic, from so long before, orbits no longer mattered.

Just below her navel, the hidden parts of her were tucked into the trunk of the gnarled tree. Heart-shaped leaves fluttered in the breeze and blossoms from the night before remained a soft cream color, with bright yellow stamens, no bigger than an eyelash. Orīa's tired lips fluttered, as always, before she spoke:

"I always prayed to you, from a distance, Daphnē. You answered me, only in my dreams. You gave my child the gift you promised. Through my dreams, you showed me the truth of your power. My Whispers have been in your service, Daphnē. Arethūsa is your vessel and I am your Voice. I am here to witness your Awakening. I am your suppliant and commit myself to do your bidding. Nothing will be the same when you open your eyes, to see the world again. You have slept for far too long, Daphnē. I give this offering to you, a gesture of my fealty. I, alone, know your desires. I give you my blood, so you may prosper and bring me into something more, a truer form."

Orīa pulled a dagger from her cloak and placed the blade on her left wrist. She did not hesitate when she slid the blade up her wrist, cutting deep into her forearm. Blood spurted from the wound and onto the black earth. She squeezed her arm, encouraging the blood to flow, streaming through her effort. She cringed with joyful-anguish, as the dark soil drank it. Her body went cold. Her eyes drifted closed, while dark blood continued to pour from her wrist. Just as she began to fall forward, a pair of hands pulled her up.

Briar cursed as he tore fabric from Orīa's cloak and tied it tightly around her upper forearm. The blood-flow began to slow, until it fell at a trickle, down her hand and into his lap. He shook her cold face, but only Orīa's lips responded, in a Whispering chant, beyond his understanding.

"Wake up!" Briar shouted, while he shook her by the chin. "Wake up, you crazy fucking cunt! Wake up and see what you've done to yourself! It's just blood on the dirt! Blood on the fucking *dirt*!"

While Briar rocked, back and forth, cursing Orīa and the Goddess, he failed to notice the tree blossoms folding, in and upon themselves. In the light of the Three Sister Moons, clumps of blossoms metamorphosed into green berries, expanding at a rate beyond reason. By the time he looked away from the deathly pallor of Orīa's face, the green fruit was already blood-red and the size of his clenched fist. When he looked back down, he saw Orīa's dead eyes, staring at the night sky.

"No! No, no, no, no, no!" Briar wailed. "Not like this! Not for that fucking bitch in the tree! NO! Think!" Briar roared, heaving over the dead body. "Show me. Show me what to do, Daphnē. You speak to her, now speak to *me*. Prove you exist, you fucking bitch!"

Briar's manic eyes fell on the ripening fruit dangling from the twisted branches. He watched them plump before his eyes. He rested Orīa in the dirt and strode over to one of the branches and pulled off the fattest fruit he could find. When he plucked it, another blossom immediately showed itself through the stem and began to undergo the same metamorphosis as the rest. Briar's hands strained through the heft of the fruit, a burden heavier than a stone of equal size.

He kneeled over Orīa, whose mouth was wide open, with motionless lips, for the first time in her life. Briar squeezed the fruit with both hands and it burst, with such violence, the red juices covered them both. It smelled of death but tasted sweetly-sour on his lips.

An intense vigor, beyond anything he ever felt, made his entire being radiate with unbound energy. He continued to squeeze the fruit over her open mouth, until there was nothing left but wrinkled skin. Orīa looked like she bathed in blood from the juices. Briar put his lips to hers and blew into her mouth, until the fluid rushed down her dead throat.

"BWUUUUUUUUUUH!"

Orīa sat bolt upright and heaved at the world. Her lips were moving, so quickly, they appeared like insect wings aflutter. She looked at Briar, with eyes of a brighter hue, eyes unmatched, in the infinitude of colors they possessed. Through preternatural strength, she pulled free from Briar's embrace and stood, tilting her head, from one side to the other, in a methodical fashion. After she swallowed hard, she turned back to Briar and smiled.

"*It worked*," Orīa said, in a voice that sounded like many Orīas, speaking at once.

"Damn right it did," Briar said, through tears. "It's *you*. It brought you back. It fucking worked."

"Not me. *Her*."

Orīa turned to face the tree and Briar did the same. Beneath the crystal encasement, Daphnē was watching. The Goddess' eyes darted in many directions, but never wavered in their focus. When her arms parted from her chest, her breasts heaved, beneath deep breaths. One of those breaths cracked the crystal encasement. The two mortal witnesses heard Daphnē's breaths, through the cracks. Then her lips parted and the Goddess smiled. Deep within the Tree of Avernus, a rumble began to shake the ground.

Over Sky Throne, Nīya screamed with a ferocity matched by the hidden source of rumbling in the Tree. Had Briar and Orīa any reason to look away from the Goddess' eyes and towards the western sky, they would have seen another dragon approaching, at a speed beyond belief.

When Orīa's skin went cold in his embrace, Briar looked down at her. The eyes returning his look were no longer hers. Before Briar could say a word, Orīa's bones began to crack and shift, warping her form, as if every joint were under siege, or trying to resemble the twisted branches bearing the fruit. It was then her skin repelled Briar's horrified embrace, through a burst of negative energy, thrusting him onto his back. When Briar managed to lift his head, Orīa was perched atop the curving branch nearest the emerging Goddess.

What were once eyes looking upon Briar with love, through a lifetime, turned to gleaming yellow and devoid of humanity. Below the perched creature who was once, Orīa, Daphnē made eye-contact with Briar and winked, just before the cracked crystal encasement shattered. The Goddess emerged...

35

THE GLIMMER

Īo never wavered, through the winds over the Eternal Storm. After almost a turn battling turbulent air, in pursuit of Avernus, catching sight of the Tree was invigorating. Not until Īo spotted another dragon, circling the zenith, did the dragon alter her course and head upwards, with caution and curiosity.

The spore cloud loomed like an old dream, drifting back into reality. Callisto held onto Nyctámēna's waist, as she did throughout the flight, while her boots dug into interlocking scales on the dragon's back. The rod on the back of Nyctámēna's mechanical proved an ideal place for Callisto to find an adamant hold and anticipate sudden moves from the Dragon Weir.

"She's looking for her Weir!" Nyctámēna shouted, as the wind subsided, through the dragon's oblique flight, upwards.

"How can you tell?!" Callisto shouted back, as they soared higher into the night sky.

"Ever seen a dragon fly in circles?"

"Only with a Weir nearby."

"Exactly. Cmon, Īo!"

When Nyctámēna leaned her head forward, Īo did the same and the three of them flew towards Sky Throne, in a sweeping course, taking them to the precipice of Middle Rim. Screams and tell-tale signs of panic were evident before Īo ever had the chance to cause the fear. When they flew closer to younger branches of the Tree, leaves and branches trembled from something other than wind.

Just before they reached Upper Rim, a pillar of white light issued forth, from the western edge. The two women and the dragon looked away from the brightness, shifting their winged course north, towards a place removed from the grim magic's shine.

"What the fuck is that?" Callisto moaned.

"*Arethūsa*," Nyctámēna seethed.

"You don't think she's—"

"I'm going to rip her heart out and feed it to her."

"What about Scylla's dragon?"

"She's fixed on finding her Weir. You can see where she landed before. Look there!"

"What's the next move? We're on a fucking dragon. We can't just swoop down and figure out what's going on. All I see are screaming faces and a light from Hell. Īo's too big and fast to pluck Scylla out from the masses."

"If Scylla's anywhere down there, she'll find us. We're landing close to where that light is coming from. Scylla's a damned magnet for the heart of trouble."

When Īo flew by the circling Nīya, the dragons acknowledged each other, through a resounding cry. In spite of the dragon's rage, Nīya recognized an affinity through their Weirs. Īo circled downwards, until her gleaming black talons found the disturbed ground, where Scylla and Nīya landed before.

Nyctámēna and Callisto raised their legs and slid down the dragon's back and off the battle-spiked wing of Īo. When boots struck ground, Callisto stumbled to find solid earth and drew her sword, in spite of her flight-sickness. Nyctámēna drew Slender in her left hand, but stood firm, with legs long accustomed to flight. Where they stood, the ground rumbled and the crystal structures all around them shattered, from a force far different than a dragon's passing wing. Īo made eye-contact with her Weir before she took to the air and joined Nīya, in her circling flight, soaring upon uncertainty.

The two warriors scanned Upper Rim for any sign of Scylla, or Arethūsa. It was clear the shattered Sky Throne was the seat of the Ruler, but recent destruction was changing everything into screaming ruin. Weirs and warriors, alike, were scattering to the edges of the Rim. Twisting branches, carved with exquisite stairs, uniting Upper and Middle Rim, were proving too narrow for the onslaught of fleeing Avernians. Protective balustrades of twisting vines, along the limits of the Rim, were mangled into ruin.

Tell-tale screams from people falling to their deaths marked the general uproar, with high-pitched interludes. Reapers blended into the darkness but most of them removed their dark hoods, exposing their faces to impending doom, through wide-eyed fear and confusion. While the dragons, circling overhead, were dark portents of their own, the horror was coming from the Tree, itself.

"Nyctá!" A man called out, from the fleeing masses.

Nyctámēna and Callisto turned to face the voice, swords in hand, side-stepping Avernians running by. A hooded figure approached them, at a trot, with a young girl in his arms. When he drew near, his face was stained with blood-red juices from the fruit of the Goddess. Callisto pointed her boots inward, assuming a position to strike, but the sight of the child in Briar's arms stayed her sword.

"Kill me, if you'd like," Briar said, in a voice stripped of its sardonic quality. "I don't care, but this one must live," he said, kissing Īris on her dark hair.

"Where's Arethūsa?!' Nyctámēna growled.

"The Goddess is awake," Briar said.

"Yeah, no shit," Callisto said. "I see you made an abomination with your sister," she spit. "Now you're a motherfucker, too."

Īris turned her head from her father's chest and was smiling at Callisto, "That's funny, even though it's untrue. My mother is *not* his sister. But I like to laugh when I'm scared."

"Aww, fuck," Callisto winced. "You're fucking *adorable*. Sorry about that one, little gal."

"There's no time!" Briar shouted, as his hood blew back, in the dragon wind. "Arethūsa took Scylla to the heart of the Tree."

"*Where is it*?!" Nyctámēna shouted.

"Only Arethūsa can open it. If they're still alive, they're somewhere in between. Where that light is coming from," he pointed. "Down the chasm, in the tree," he pointed, as the pillar of light drifted into motion.

"Ruthy used Scylla to wake up the Goddess?!"

"Yes. Arethūsa was always ambitious, but Whispers turned her into a fucking monster. Orīa made sure of that, made sure of me, too. We're all fucking guilty. Īris is all that matters to me, now. I wish you all the luck in the heavens and hell. You two are good souls, the best of them. But there's no navigating something like this," he said, looking over his shoulder.

Īris turned her head to Nyctámēna, "*When the darkness screams, the night will burn black.*"

"The fuck is that supposed to mean?" Callisto grimaced.

"Īris dreams the future," Briar said. "She's beginning to see deeper into days to come, but it's too late. Her words are carved by now, if you know what I mean."

"I'm sorry I can't tell you more," Īris said. "I only the dreamed the words, this time. They were written in light."

"Thank you, Īris," Nyctámēna nodded.

"If you see Orīa," Briar said with anguish, "*run.*"

"Take the little one down," Nyctámēna said. "The tops of trees go first, you know that. You could have been better in this life, Briar."

"See what happens," Briar winked, before he vanished into the masses, with Īris.

"Put them in," Nyctámēna said, reaching into the satchel on her hip.

"Now?" Callisto asked.

"*Now.* Keep your head on a swivel."

"Going into battle with the Goddess, deaf and standing on a falling fucking tree."

Both warriors pushed clumps of beeswax into their ears and popped their jaws in accordance with the change of internal pressure. Callisto struggled with the wax in her left ear, before she tilted her head to the side and pressed the clump in with the force of her thumb. She shook her head with vigor.

When Nyctámēna shouted Callisto's name, the battle-hardened warrior took no notice. Ringing in Nyctámēna's ear sounded like a Siren Song to the Dragon Weir, a song with a single note, drawing her to the edge, where ground gave way to emptiness and absolute uncertainty. Whispers capable of upending everything, in the briefest of moments, were nothing but a clump of wax away from the warrior's mind. Only Scylla mattered, a categorial imperative, no different than the one Briar declared for his child.

Nobody remained on the purlieus near the Tree of the Goddess, leaving an eerily spacious plenty for the two wax-deaf warriors to navigate. Screams from the northern portion of Upper Rim corresponded with the drifting light, casting a spotlight on the circling dragons. When Nyctámēna turned her head back to mark the presence of Callisto, she spotted a figure crawling at a preternatural rate across the ferns and smattering of wind-warped trees.

Nyctámēna signaled with her chin and Callisto turned. When she did, a head of black hair was twitching amidst the ferns, while the figure's hands and bare feet clung to the ground. The body twisted in mind-bending ways, breaking into alternate positions. When the head twisted round, Orīa's deathly face stared down the warriors.

She shed her cloak, leaving her body clothed only in the juices of the fruit and her own blood. In spider-like fashion, Orīa raced across the ground at a pace beyond mortal perception. When the pair spotted her in the branches of a tree, her lips moving, with such vigor, the Wind Weir's mouth appeared to be haunted by the fluttering ghost of her own lips.

The moment Nyctámēna took a step towards the Weir, Orīa vanished and re-appeared, perched in a tree on her periphery. When Callisto attempted the same approach,

Nyctámēna realized the strategy of the mad Wind Weir, an instant too late. As Callisto followed the preternatural movements of the Weir, quick-motions of the warrior's head, moving this way and that, pried loose the clump of wax from her left ear. Before Nyctámēna reached her, Callisto was already swooning, from Whispers in the Wind.

Blade met blade on a battlefield of Whispered confusion. When Callisto spun her sword in a vicious action and struck a cautious Nyctámēna across the shoulder, Orīa vanished and left the two companions battling from opposing worlds of intent. The wound was deep but Nyctámēna retained the use of her bloody arm. When Callisto thrust towards her Whispered foe's chest, Nyctámēna side-stepped and struck Callisto across the face, with her mechanical elbow. Blood poured from Callisto's mouth, while the warrior's bloodshot eyes glared at an indistinct point, beyond Nyctámēna.

"Pull it together, Calli!" Nyctámēna seethed, through gritted teeth.

"You killed her, you fucking cunt!" Callisto roared, to deaf ears. "You killed my Mēna!"

In the corner of her eye, while she held off violent thrusts from Callisto, Nyctámēna spotted the pale face of Orīa, in a nearby tree. The Wind Weir was Whispering at the same rapid pace, while her position was situated upwind, so her Voice would be carried to Callisto's ear, all the truer. Nyctámēna did not dare betray her cognizance of the Weir's position. Her right hand drifted down towards her hip, while she deflected Callisto's overhead stroke, with a spark of swords colliding. When the spark lit up the air, for a faint instant, the Dragon Weir flicked her wrist and sent her favorite throwing-knife flying.

The onyx blade found its mark and was followed by a bone-chilling scream, from something other than human. A dull thump followed and Nyctámēna pulled out the wax from her right ear and watched Callisto breathing deeply, as the bewildered warrior stared at the ground, rumbling beneath her boots.

"Well," Callisto heaved, rotating her jaw. She spit a bloody stream, "that's over. Sorry about that. I didn't mean—"

"I know. I couldn't hear a thing you said, anyway," Nyctámēna half-smiled. "Now, put the beeswax back in your ear."

"What about the Demon Weir?"

"She's gone."

"Dead?"

"Gone. No sense in looking for her. Her Whispers have passed. *Cmon.*"

When they reached the tree where the Goddess emerged, the crystal encasement where she was confined for an Age, was nothing but a gaping hole, fringed with tattered wood.

The greater portion of the tree still remained, with its overripe fruit hanging heavy on gnarled branches. Scorched earth marked the path of the Goddess, on her way north, where she was treading along, in her enlightened way, towards some destination, unknown.

Nyctámēna pulled out the beeswax from her ears and Callisto followed. They peered down the pitch black chasm within the tree. Hot wind whistled from its hidden depths and smelled of sulfur, through a hole too narrow for either of them to crawl inside. Their wordless realization at the direness of the situation found articulation through Nyctámēna's lips Whispering to her sword. She closed her eyes.

When she did, the ridge of Slender touched her lips, while Callisto listened to words resembling Nyctámēna's double-tongue. The difference in those words was in the singularity of the voice, turning brutal consonants into a mellifluous series of drifting Whispers. After half a moment of Whispers, Slender's blade glimmered blue, before it turned to a white-shine, forcing Callisto to look away. Īo swooped down from her circling heights, on her way towards them.

"You'd better duck," Nyctámēna said, as she took a knee and pointed the shining blade at the tree. When she did, she made sure the bright blade glanced her wound and cauterized the cut. Searing pain brought deeper resolve in the Dragon Weir.

Callisto fell to her knees, just as the swift-winged Īo soared a hair's breadth above the warriors and obliterated the Tree of the Goddess with her passing wing, studded with battle-spikes across its front.

The tree shattered at its top and its lower portion was uprooted from the aerial assault and toppled over the ledge, on its way down to the Fungal Realm of Ümfalla. By the time Callisto looked up, Slender was dimming, until it dulled and Nyctámēna sheathed it on her back.

"Since when could you Whisper your sword bright?" Callisto winked.

"Īo showed me how, while you were drinking beer with fishermen."

"Fair enough."

"No sense in us both going down," Nyctámēna said, staring alternately at the gaping hole and Īo, rejoining Nīya above the ruins of Sky Throne.

"Not a fucking chance you're going down that hell hole, not without me."

"Remember the Labyrinth?"

"Shit. You make a good point. Confined places aren't my thing. Neither are heights, but here I am. You really think that light over there is the Goddess?"

"Probably one of them. Fuck 'em all."

"Yeah, fuck 'em all."

"If that light comes this way—"

"I'm running."

"*Yup.* Calli?"

"Don't die."

"I'll do my best. When you see me, I'll be yelling Scylla deaf and dumb."

"Punch her in her pretty fucking face for me, as soon as you find her."

"Yup. We're stalling. C'mere."

They embraced, squeezing each other in such a way that spoke deeper than words. Nyctámēna kissed Callisto on her forehead, above her right brow, where the oblique scar on her face began. They pressed their damp foreheads together and met eyes, before Nyctámēna took a long pair of steps and vanished into the hole in the ground. Callisto listened for any sign of turmoil within, but was left with the faint screams from Avernians, in the distance. She looked to the drifting light from the Goddess, but refused to linger on the sight. She turned to the circling dragons and imagined a sunrise journey, on Īo's back, while she held tightly to the woman she loved.

In the periphery of her imagination, Scylla was leading the way, on the back of the other dragon, the creature dwarfing Īo, in her sky-filling magnificence. Fancy faded when Callisto put beeswax back in her ears and listened to the rapid thumping of her own heartbeat.

36

BLINDED HAND

THERE WAS NOTHING TO see. There were only the sounds of her own breaths and the rumbling of the Tree, marking any sense of Time. Nyctámēna squirmed through the dark ruin of slime and ash, like a worm navigating the bowels of Hell.

She coughed violently on her convoluted journey, while her muffled breaths only exacerbated the torment of having nowhere to go but deeper, down into the hot mud of roasted innards, towards the heart of the Goddess. Sulfurous air was giving way to the unadulterated stench of death. Rotting corpses in Ümfalla never putrified the air as much as the miasmic *arboreal-artery* the Dragon Weir was pushing through.

Fortune found her, even in pitch-blackness, when rumbling from the Tree of Avernus shook free muddy detritus blocking her way. Clumps of ruin fell and settled into spaces below, merciful cracks and gaps, allowing Nyctámēna to push through, along with merciful drafts of air. But ancient roots and splinters beneath the muck tore at her hands and stomach, as the growing heat slow-roasted her lungs, one tarried breath at a time. There was no down or up, left or right, only a little bit farther, in her journey to find anything resembling life.

When she opened her eyes and remembered the darkness, she realized she passed out for an indeterminate amount of time. Nyctámēna always sought darkness, relatively lightless places, only her eyes could fathom. Now the darkness of death was finding its full embrace of her being and there was nothingness, even through eyes capable of seeing into the white.

Fear of passing back out and never waking up drove her on, with bloody fingers pulling her along, while her legs followed, like a frog kicking at slime in a dried-up pond. Through the unbreakable nature of her mechanical, Nyctámēna broke through petrified roots and carbonized wood, allowing her to push on, deeper.

She thought she would see life in some kind of conciliatory light when death was near. Nothingness was ahead, while nebulous regrets followed through the grime. Her journey only grew hotter and more meaningless, with every scraping squirm of the way. Handfuls of mud and mouthfuls of ash greeted her efforts.

Muffled quakes sounded like screams, but it was the expansion of wood, through heat and tremors. A desperate reach with her left hand found a chunk of cinders and she squeezed it in despair. The effort was met with a faint cry, like water escaping a fresh log when it reached a boiling point in the flames.

Her fingers settled and the warmth on her fingertips seemed cool in the heat. Her blinded hand possessed visceral *eyes*, discovering another hand in the grime. When she squeezed the hand, detritus fell away, bringing familiar flesh near. She held the hand before and would never forget, after she first took it, soft and resolute, still humming with elemental power. Nyctámēna thrust herself over the body and pulled away the mud and soot from Arethūsa's face. In the pitch blackness, a faint voice spoke in broken words.

"*Ruthy*," she heaved, wheezing a whisper. "Mēna...Sorry...So...sorry...Scylla is...down...Scylla made of...*fire*...saved me."

"Ruthy!" Nyctámēna said, in what was a scream, in the confined space. "Scylla's alive? Down there?!"

"*Down...*" Ruthy huffed, before she crumpled into a violent bout of coughing.

Nyctámēna was propelled by tears and hopeful breaths, raging through what was lying ahead, tearing apart scorched impediments with her mechanical, in what was becoming its prime reason for existing. The smell of death morphed into the unmistakable odor of charred wood and the thick air felt like acid in her lungs. Only salamanders born in fire would have known the way, eyeless and wriggling in the char.

Mud turned to compounded earth, cooked to rock-hardness. When her bloody hands could no longer scrape through the impediments, she contorted her body. until her boots were leading the way, through violent kicks, leaving her upturned body covered in ash and hardened dirt. Her body rattled along with the Tree, while she kicked at the cooked mud with her boot heels.

At some indistinct point, her bone-rattling kicks cracked the rock and a pile of sludge and ash poured over her, settling through interstices beneath. She fought instinct and reached into the scalding rubble, squeezing embers, living wood reduced to its burnt essence.

She felt a clump of hair in her hands. She pulled at it and a head followed. She wailed in the confined space and her ears suffered, to the point of bursting. Nyctámēna reached down and found the body's armpits, felt the soft hair in them. The reality of something so delicate enduring the oven, in the heart of the Goddess, made Nyctámēna believe she was hallucinating. But a heart was still beating in Scylla's chest, a heart pounding against uncertainty. The Dragon Weir pulled her child in life out of the scalding debris and headed up, up to that realm where stars still sparkled, in spite of another Hell waiting.

When Nyctámēna emerged, with Scylla and Ruthy in her arms, only one of the retrieved was breathing. Callisto carried a heaving Ruthy to a place removed, in the ferns, while Nyctámēna fought through her violent coughs, as she shook Scylla's head by the chin. She put her ear to the mouth of the fledgling Dragon Weir, but heard no breath.

Scylla's cotton-wood clothes were incinerated in the dark inferno, leaving her body covered in ash, but altogether whole. Fire failed to consume her. Nyctámēna's hands were shaking from shock and confusion as she searched her mind for anything to do. Then the memory of Ruthy's advice, down in Ümfalla, how to bring back breath to a foam-choked Shixee, rushed up in desperate remembrance.

She raised her arms over her head, clenched her hands together and struck Scylla on her sternum, with such force, her body bounced off the soft ground.

"OPEN YOUR EYES!" Nyctámēna roared. "BREATHE!"

She raised her arms again, as tears fell onto the ashen body of Scylla. Wailing from Callisto woefully crowned the course of heaving cries of Nyctámēna. In the midst of another collision of her clenched hands and the chest beneath them, Scylla's eyes shot open and she heaved. The force of Nyctámēna's action resulted in her striking the girl in the chest, with the same force as before. Scylla groaned through staccato laughter, when she turned her head and coughed up black sludge from the Inferno.

"*FU-UCK!*" Scylla heaved, with streams of black bile, hanging from her lips. "You didn't have to hit me that hard," she groaned, spitting and turning her head to look back at the Dragon Weir, above her.

Nyctámēna tried to speak, but emotion overwhelmed words, so she fell on top of Scylla and held her hard. Scylla's skin smelled of earth and ash, as if the young Weir spent a long night in The Mire of Ümfalla, where Puffball Mushrooms darkened the air with spores and she rose to Sky Realm as aromatic proof of life. There were no signs of burns, or the unmistakable stench of burnt hair. Her hardy cotton-wood clothes were reduced to ashes, leaving the fire's fleshed-out essence. Only cuts and bruises on the fledgling Weir gave Nyctámēna the impression the Inferno gave birth to a Scylla.

"She is fire," Ruthy's faint voice intruded. "She embraced me in the Inferno and faced the flames."

"How did you—" Nyctámēna began.

"I don't know," Scylla said, as she pushed herself up, into a seated position. "I saw the black flames, so I grabbed Ruthy and held her tight. Everything went dark. Now, I'm here. I'm *freezing*."

"You should be!" Callisto shouted, throwing Scylla a crimson Weir Cloak. "Here's a goddess damned cloak for you. You *fucking*...I can't...I just can't, with you."

"Love you, too, Calli," Scylla laughed through coughs, as she pulled on the Weir Cloak. "This robe smells like death. How is your gown still whole, Ruthy?"

"You faced the fire and held me. I was like a silk-worm tucked into you," Ruthy said. "So long to this," she said, holding the scorched end of her braid. The strand of black hair remained intertwined in the tangled ruins of her own. "Good riddens."

"You good to move?" Nyctámēna muttered, between coughs.

"Yeah," Scylla said, pulling up the hood of the cloak. "I'm better than you sound. You need Forlindean air. I actually miss the place. Crazy right? You two were right about this place. Only the beauty was real. All the rest is a fucking nightmare. Don't get me started with her," she glanced at Ruthy. "And I can't burn. *That's strange*."

"Well, she's back," Callisto muttered to herself, while Scylla rambled on.

Scylla continued, "How many turns have passed? Time is crazy. Oh, look! Our dragons are flying together! I was scared they wouldn't get along! Victory! By the way, her name is Nīya and it's spelled with a, 'y'. Oh, shit! *What the fuck is that*?!" She moaned, pointing at the pillar of light, in the distance.

"Ask Arethūsa," Callisto seethed.

"That Name is gone," Ruthy said.

"You can't just speak it away," Callisto said. "I should toss you off the edge."

"We'll deal with her later," Nyctámēna said, finding her full breaths.

"That's Orīa's cloak," Ruthy pointed at Scylla. "Is she dead?"

"She's no longer, Orīa," Nyctámēna helped Scylla up and checked her eyes. "What remains is what she sought."

"Then it wasn't the Inferno," Ruthy said to herself. "It was Orīa's fall that brought me back. Whispers fade with a passing Weir."

"So who the fuck are you, now?" Callisto asked. "Whatever fits the moment?! You'd do better to stop talking. Fucking seemer. *Pick* a Ruthy!"

"Leave it alone, Calli," Nyctámēna said, arming Scylla with a hilted knife. "If anyone can understand the mire of identity, it's you and me. But Ruthy has to live with what she's done, just as I do for my past. None of that changes what's here, now."

"I'll spend the rest of my life reclaiming my Name," Ruthy coughed, violently. Tears streamed down her face, "*Look at what I've done.*"

Callisto pointed at Ruthy, "You spent seven orbits bringing this to pass."

"Enough of that. Are you ready to fly?" Nyctámēna asked Scylla.

"Hell yes. You wriggled your way through Hell to find me. Don't know how you did it, but—"

"I love you, Scylla," Nyctámēna said, kissing her on her forehead.

"Love you, too," Scylla smiled.

"We have a problem," Callisto said.

"What is it?" Nyctámēna asked, looking in the same direction as the others.

"I think the Goddess is following the course of the dragons," Callisto said, pointing at the dragons, circling over the fallen Sky Throne. "Watch her drift, when they do. Like a fucking moth to a lantern shroom. Her brain must be worm-wood eaten by now."

"She's drawn to their power," Ruthy said. "If I know anything about her, that's it. That's not Daphnē. That's a fucking Demon. I see why the Avernians of old, whoever they were, confined her to that tree."

"Wisdom arrives late, *again*," Callisto said.

"We'll brood and surmise about that later," Nyctámēna said. "If we summon the dragons, the Demon will follow."

"*Fucking* Demons," Callisto spit.

"How fast is the Demon?" Scylla asked.

"As fast as she needs to be," Ruthy said. "I still feel her, here," she said, tapping her filthy chest.

"The dragons land and we're fucked," Callisto said. "And this Rim isn't full of places to land. Can we jump off the edge and onto their backs?"

"No," Nyctámēna said. "Their wings would strike the Rim. If we jump, the fall is too much, if they flew below."

"And the edge is far too brittle," Scylla said, eyeing the precipice of the Rim. "Trees are tricky."

"What if we summon only one of them?" Callisto said. "If that Demon keeps her eye on the other one in the sky, we can climb on and get the fuck out of here."

"We have to do something," Ruthy said. "This Rim is about to give way. The core of it is—"

The ground beneath their feet began to give way. Centuries of earth, compacted dirt and roots, filling the interstices in the branch of the Tree of Avernus, was suddenly giving way to primal forces threatening to bring everything down, even the world itself, through the course of enough Ages.

In the midst of the crumbling state of affairs, Nyctámēna and Scylla Whispered to their blades and both weapons turned bright. Through the Whispered shine, the dragons screamed and shifted their courses. The four women ran, in the only direction they could, towards the center of Upper Rim. When Ruthy stumbled, Callisto pulled her up, just before the ground gave way and there was nothing but air and skeletal framework of the branch behind them.

As they headed to the only place the dragon's could land, the swift-winged Īo and Nīya were followed by the light, now a distinct figure. The Demon drifted across the rumbling landscape like a bright nightmare.

Drawing closer, a scream was issuing from the Demon's mouth, a shrill howl, the source of the pillar of light. The Demon's head was tilted towards the zenith, while the scream resonated at a frequency that was neither high nor low. It was a scream howling from the inside of the four, while they sprinted and stumbled along a falling Sky Realm. Their approach turned them deaf to the world.

In the screaming silence, the Demon vanished behind Īo and Nīya, when the dragons landed, wing to wing. The four companions leaped over gaping holes and crumbling earth, as they ran towards the wings of the dragons. Nyctámēna and Ruthy climbed onto the wing of Īo, while Scylla and Callisto did the same on Nīya. Just as the four companions' feet touched the wings, the Demon appeared between the dragons.

The Demon's head drifted down, while she conjured a ball of blinding light, between her illuminated fingers. Her scream faded when her focus fell on the ball of light, at her pale chest, in a bone-bright body with translucent skin.

The rumbling of the Tree supplanted the deafening scream. Before anyone else had a chance to see the Demon's swift approach, Callisto already leaped from Nīya's wing and stood in front of the Demon, with nothing but her bare hands held in front of her.

"C'mon, you *tree-bitch*!" Callisto shouted, waving the dragons off with her hands. "THIS WAY!" She roared, spitting in the Demon's bright face.

Her saliva sizzled when it struck the Demon's gaunt face. Callisto drew her sword and struck the Demon with a masterstroke, from chin to crown, but the tip of the blade passed through the abysmal face, as if it were supercharged jelly. The Demon smiled to herself, as her head drifted up and her green hair squirmed on the ground at her feet.

"*Run, Callisto!*" Nyctámēna screamed. "Back on the dragon!"

"I'll catch up to you!" Callisto laughed, just as she slashed the Demon across the neck. The sheer power exuding from the Demon sent the sword flinging out of Callisto's hands.

"*Calli!*" Nyctámēna cried.

Callisto clapped her hands and taunted the Demon, just as she would a beast she wanted to lure closer, in the darkness of Ümfalla. The ball of light between the Demon's hands condensed to the size of an acorn. The Demon's black eyes rolled up white, staring through Callisto. When Callisto looked down at the tickle in her chest, the acorn-sized hole was smoking.

She only had a split moment, when she looked up to Nyctámēna on the back of the dragon, before her body charred to cinders, from the inside. Her eyes were the last to go and the final thing they received was the horror in Nyctámēna's eyes. A gust of north wind blew her pitch black corpse into ashes, scattering, on their whirling journey back down to the Fungal Realm of Ümfalla.

"*CALEEEE!*" Nyctámēna screamed from Īo, who already took flight, along with Nīya, in a twisting course, up and out of range from the Demon's wrath.

37

AND THE SKY WEPT

WHILE RUTHY HELD ONTO Nyctámēna's heaving chest, on their near vertical flight towards the Second Sister Moon, the Dragon Weir not only looked like a natural attribute of the dragon—with her battle-blown hawk-hair and intertwined movements with the creature—her flesh and bones felt like one, too.

Nyctámēna's back arched, on their twisting course upwards, while Ruthy sensed the visceral power in the rage of the Dragon's Weir's entire being. Her skin was electric and her manic heartbeat was palpable, even across her bare stomach. Nothing would dismount the Weir from the dragon.

Īo and Nīya flew in a double-helix pattern, up and up, on a desperate journey to the icy heights, where nothing lived but the light of the heavens. Scylla's tears turned to ice as they fell, while she wept through emptiness. Ruthy turned her head, but unmooring vertigo was nothing compared to the horror of the Rim-grounded Demon Goddess, malevolent in all aspects, even from dizzying heights. Ruthy turned back to face the zenith and her breath was thick, while her lungs burned, in a subzero Inferno in the sky.

When the light of the Three Sister Moons made the dragons gleam, dark-bright, their ascent ended and they hovered, so high above Avernus, the Demon was a speck of light. Nyctámēna's chest fluttered under Ruthy's hands and the former Ruler of Avernus could only hold on tight, out of necessity and grinding regret. Dragon wings beat down emptiness, while their Weirs haunted the air through sobbing breaths.

If the icy heights did anything to Ruthy, beyond numbing her face and fingers, it cleared her mind from seven orbits of dreaming. The nightmare of her Whispered transformation into, Arethūsa, overwhelmed her mind, stifling her breaths more than thin air. She had no answers, only the rush of thinking for herself, the *Ruthy* she hoped was real. It was then she spoke into Nyctámēna's ear:

"I speak through regret and shame. But I speak as myself, *Ruthy*. Your journey is entangled with more than one soul, but you possess the courage to live as One. Look at your daughter on her dragon. She's suffering beautifully and fully, for love and loss. She's waiting for you to show her the way. Your presence kept me alive, in the darkness of days past. But I lacked the courage to face it alone. My failure is the Demon, below. The dragon waits for her Weir to let go. Don't you feel it? Let go and be all the things you are and she will, too. Yours turns of suppression are over. Embrace all your selves, Nyctámēna. You've held back, too long. That Demon, down there, is returning to her hellish consciousness, as I speak. Open your selves up, all of *You*. *Rage*, Nyctámēna. Rage and rain down your own Hell. Unleash your power. Do it for Calli. Do it for Scylla. *RAGE!*"

In the midst of Ruthy's confession, the Dragon Weir never stirred, while she hung her head and stared at the adamantine dragon spike at the helm. Breaths became less forceful and broken, while tears continued to fall. Nyctámēna's course of breaths deepened, her back straightened, while Ruthy ran her verbal course. When she reached the word sourcing from the depths of her being, *Rage*, she felt a sudden change in temperature of Nyctámēna's skin.

Sinews of her midsection went as hard as the dragon's back and her chest expanded, in a breath going on and on, to the point of bursting her ribcage. Nyctámēna's skin turned cold and her billowing breaths iced, when her eyes went battle-bright. The Dragon Weir dropped her jaw and Īo did the same:

The Scream tore through the sky.

The dragon and her Weir screamed as One, in an event beyond words such as *loud*. It was a scream to quiet thunder, a brutal harmony of pure rage. Emptiness received an eruption of silver-blue flame from the dragon's mouth, filling the sky with an ever-expanding force, beyond Nature: *It was magic*. When Scylla marked her mother's metamorphosis, the young Dragon Weir Screamed as One with Nīya. From the dragon's mouth, a blinding white flame was articulated with blood-red tinges, searing the sky.

Ruthy turned her gaunt face away from the superheated flame, in spite of its great distance. When the flames from opposing poles subsided with the Screams, the Dragon Weirs made eye-contact. Ruthy interlocked her hands across Nyctámēna's stomach, as they plummeted down, in a direct course towards the speck of light. Through their meteoric speed, the speck was becoming a blotch, irradiated with macabre energy.

The wind whistled at their approach and Ruthy's eyes burned, through the harrowing descent. Through the union of Weir and dragon, there was no distinction between Nyctámēna's skin and the dragon scales beneath. Both were cold and adamant, living proof of the Eternal. To think of where the dragon ended and the Weir began was meaningless.

Their Oneness was beyond the synchronicity of their movements and thoughts, it was a harmony singing deeper than anything known. The living elements of Fire and Ice were plummeting towards the Tree of Avernus, in the strength of their binding opposites, the entanglement of their beings.

When the Demon Goddess marked the blurred approach of the swift-winged dragons, she spun her intent into a knot of white light between her hands, released through her growing consciousness. The ball of light expanded, tumbling upwards, at ever-increasing speeds. Nīya and Īo lowered their outer wings and the dragons diverged—in divine opposites—at such a pitch, Ruthy was nearly thrown off in the action.

The ball of light obscured the Three Sister Moons in its course and lingered high above them, at the zenith. The Dragon Weirs marked its place in the heavens and flew in a criss-crossing descent, *down*, closer to the Demon.

There was no sensation of heat with the near miss of the Demon's false moon, only the unmistakable sense of its supercharged power. It had a consciousness linked to the Demon, as surely as the dragons and their Weirs. When the Demon opened her mouth, the preternatural effect of it sent the dragons reeling off course. Tormented cries turned the night to a deafening world of bewilderment. While the dragons pitched and roared from the silent workings of the Demon, Ruthy closed her eyes and let go Nyctámēna's chest.

Time, for Ruthy, slowed down, to a near halt. She grew aware of stray molecules from the Demon in the turbulent air, now stilled. Had she opened her eyes and seen the world as it was, she would have seen Īo flapping her bewildered wings, while Nyctámēna eyed Scylla, in fear. She would have seen the false moon of the Demon in its stilled-descent, towards the unaware dragons, along with the smile on the Demon's face.

But Ruthy was somewhere deep inside the near-forgotten world of herself, a point outside Time, where she once communed with the Goddess, for orbits, suffering through the gagging half-truth of it all.

In that remembered darkness, under shadows of forgetfulness, Ruthy *found* the Demon Goddess:

'From a Singular seed, I raised the Tree. Through Ages, I tended roots, breathing life into darkness. Emptiness was spoken into branching life when the sky descended to greet my power. Wind worshipped my face and I spoke the Word, giving Names to the world, shaped mud

into Being. I dreamt away the false Age, waking into Truth, Now, remaking the land in my image. Roots will stretch across oceans and spore clouds will vivify skies beyond. I am the Beginning through the End, beyond mortal knowledge, the bringer of—'

Entangled with the Demon's thoughts, Ruthy was no longer herself. She was neither a witness, nor a vessel, she *was* the Demon, riding on the back of the dragon.

Just as the Demon made the sky come down to her, through the rise of the Tree, over the course of countless orbits, in what seemed a few turns for her, so the course of the Demon's confession took the blink of an eye. In this blinking instant, the slightest of movements changed everything.

Before Ruthy's solipsistic timelessness, Nyctámēna felt her let go her waist and spread her arms. Despite the Dragon Weir's focus on the fight, she instinctively reached behind, to pull Ruthy's arms back onto her waist. Nyctámēna's middle finger of her mechanical hand was a hair's breadth from the crook of Ruthy's elbow, during the fickle course of the demonic confession. As the Demon's words further possessed Ruthy, the Dragon Weir's finger made contact with Ruthy, where she was *touched* back into herself. In that instant, Ruthy tore away from the possession. The sudden schism sent the Demon reeling.

The dragons and their Weirs found their bearings and ended their idiosyncratic flights of bewilderment. From a distance, where the Demon Goddess' face was discernible, in her bone-bright rage at the schism, Nyctámēna and Scylla looked down on her, tilting their heads back, along with their dragons. In a split moment, the dragons and their Weirs were staring straight up at the Three Sisters, with mouths agape.

The Demon's sphere of light was on its sizzling descent of heatless force, at such a rate, it was no longer a sphere, but a beam of light. The four beings, The Dragon Weirs, acting as One, let out a deep gurgle, before their heads dropped down to face the Demon.

All was entangled flame, but Ruthy *felt* the Demon move when the swirling duality of Ice and Fire struck her. The Scream of the Dragon Weirs intensified, tearing apart the atmosphere, crackling darkly through its magic, as the blue and red flames intertwined. Hissing steam and fire burst from the ground beneath the Demon's feet.

The Demon emerged from the onslaught and was facing the full force of Ice Flames from Īo's mouth. Ruthy suffered the cold the Demon suffered, through subzero Hell, but the flame was failing to allay the Demon's movements. Ruthy turned and the sphere sputtered, high above, but sensed it reconstituting itself, at a tremendous rate.

When she looked back down, the Demon was ice, but she was moving in shattering steps through the blue flame following her. Just as the looming sphere tumbled down, at a rate and magnitude meant to break the world, Scylla tilted with Nīya, in a flight beyond mortal perception, bringing the dragon's mouth to a vantage point, just behind the Demon.

Scylla dropped her Scream an octave and Fire from the dragon's mouth purified into black, exuding such magnificence of power, air took fire, embracing the Dragon Weir in a world of flames. The very instant the black flame struck the Demon, who was still facing the onslaught of Ice Flames from Īo, darkness erupted, in an explosion through entangled opposites, the negating power of Fire and Ice, blowing everyone out of sight, or hearing. Only the Three Sister Moons saw what remained.

38

STILL REMAINS

THE OLD WEIR, ĪBEKA, saw the rise and fall of many things in her life. People had come and gone, Reapers gathered and scattered, countless mushroom withered and prospered, but magical things in Ümfalla faded, along with her youth. In spite of this disenchantment, there was a touch of magic in the metamorphosis of the Screevers.

Necessity and a bit of foolish luck turned a band of scavengers—a smattering of individuals, bound by the code of equal trade and nothing more—into a formidable group of assassins, striking silently in the fungal night. Grief turned to anger, fueling the nameless things necessary for Ümfallan women to do more than grieve, alone, in the darkness. They embraced that darkness and turned Horror's head back to its source.

Whether there were twenty of them, or a hundred, was never clear to anyone, not even the Screevers, themselves. Over the course of seven orbits, under the guidance and earthy wisdom of the old Weir, Ībeka, the numberless group sowed the spores of discord, from the western shore of The Churn, to the ever-growing roots of the Tree of Avernus, far to the east. Poison from the Vernox Forest was used on Reapers and Moon Weirs, as surely as snares and pitfalls.

An outright battle was never an option. Lack of numbers and weapons made the arrival of such a state of affairs, a sure sign of the End. For many turns, Screevers caught glimpses of that End on the dark horizon, but pushed it away, for another turn.

The powerful Moon Weir, Seerinx, had seen more orbits than Ībeka, in a life of tragedy and pain, little love and much loss. Most of that suffering was through events beyond her control. A tumultuous existence of oppression, under the same old Three Sister Moons, brought power, along with anger and bitterness. Orbits spent lingering in the shadows, through bright Avernian days, under the iron fists of the Seven Elders, sowed vengeful seeds of discord in the onyx-eyed Weir.

She witnessed fellow Weirs go mad in the winds of Avernus, when there were no mentors to show them the way. Those who remained became Whispering toys for the elite in Sky Realm to fondle, fuck and weep upon.

Patience and luck—a kind of luck she associated with the stars and Moons—brought Seerinx and what remained of her Order, back into the light of the Three Sisters, even if moonlight was hidden by the spore cloud. Over the course of seven orbits, she all but solidified her place as absolute Ruler in the Fungal Realm of Ümfalla.

The Old Weirs saw each other, from afar, when Seerinx first appeared in Ümfalla, on the back of a Spider, seven orbits before. Ībeka was just another lost soul, amongst the rest, in the scavenging Screevers. When the old Weirs met eyes, under the heavy night, something stirred in them both.

Seerinx remembered those eyes, glaring from a younger face, a face just as beautiful and eager to learn. But the repression of Weirs in Avernus pushed many over the edge, or into the brothels. In spite of Seerinx's pleas for Ībeka to remain, the latter vanished into the spore cloud, never to be seen again, not until that fateful turn when one leader looked on the other, through ancient eyes.

Both suffered and waited a lifetime for their moment to rise again, in a coterminous journey of light and dark. One of them sought control of it all, a reign to ensure the Order of the Moons would find its foothold and never fall.

The other merely hoped scattered offensives would cause enough disarray in the ranks to eventually break them and leave Ümfalla to itself, for better or worse. But on this thick-aired night, in the Fungal Realm, the Screevers found themselves pinned between the Sideon Cliffs and the uncrossable mud of The Mire. Reapers and Moon Weirs were gathered, in what was becoming the battle to wipe Screevers from the face of the dark realm, forever.

Seerinx spotted the glimmer in Ībeka's eyes and knew she finally pinned her old acquaintance down. Remorse for the coming End, came and went, as quickly as Seerinx saw those eyes. With a cadre of Moon Weirs by her side, she Whispered the Reapers into action, as easily as a child manipulated a puppet. As the many Reapers crossed the sodden land, marking the beginning of The Mire, with single-minded speed, Seerinx walked in the direction of the assault. The hem of her black Weir Cloak soaked up pooled water, as she did. Twenty Moon Weirs of her Order followed.

The End was near, but Ībeka faced it with the same bold-faced resolve she had the countless days *and* turns of her life, through light and darkness. A band of mothers and daughters, who had been in a place of despair—a solipsistic Hell, far worse than death—were now facing death with firm resolve. None of them fled when Reapers began their fresh assault and not a single one of them cursed the fate that should have come, long before. Ībeka spotted the hubris of Seerinx, as the onyx-eyed Weir followed the course of the battle, in deliberate strides of satisfaction. When the first Screevers fell, Ībeka prepared herself for a deliberate End.

Ībeka Whispered away Reapers, who came within a breath's length of her, but suffered the many assaults, with gashes and glancing wounds, drawing blood, from her neck down to her weary feet. She crowned the night with a fresh assortment of Whispers, novel magic on-the-fly, a nod to the endlessness of what was possible in the world.

Three Reapers, who suffered those Whispers, turned on each other and began to consume one another, with ruthless jaws of sudden cannibalism.

With a burst of energy from her verbal resourcefulness, Ībeka drew closer to Seerinx, on the Whispered harmony of her final song, through a lifetime of improvisation. The old Weir would never close the distance between herself and Seerinx, but she needed that proud Moon Weir to see the look on her face when she fell, the look of ironic victory, a gaze no words or Whispers could describe.

When a cluster of Reapers spotted her, while Screevers were falling dead in the muck of the Mire, muck began to bubble, all around. Ībeka smiled to herself and stood still on a mossy embankment to watch what was already underway, beneath the surface.

"Still a little magic left in this place," Ībeka laughed.

Bubbles became disturbed water that turned into glistening forms, emerging from the mud and latching onto any Reaper or Moon Weir within reach. The Phibians burst forth into their sudden assault on the common enemy, through their numbers and concise movements, through their fluid element they poeticized into deadly beauty. Foaming Whispers turned Reapers into their own enemies, as The Mire became a battlefield of sparks, from blade finding blade. Moon Weirs Whispered themselves to death, as their faulty lips spelled their own demise.

In the strategic confusion, Ībeka trudged on, within a stone's throw of Seerinx, who was side-stepping two Phibians' emerging attacks, landing them on a pair of young Moon Weirs, instead. Foam fell at Seerinx's feet, along with the dead Weirs. The pair of Phibians vanished into the waters of The Mire, only to emerge at some undisclosed place, where foam-induced suffering from their own Whispers would pass.

One Phibian seamlessly attended the other, after the Foam Whispers, with a quick slap on the back, since Phibians were never meant to Whisper alone. Ībeka was armed, with nothing but her lips and ire, when she drew closer to a distracted Seerinx, who was cognizant of everything but the threat at hand.

Ībeka was so close to Seerinx she could smell her, when a Reaper emerged from the shadows in the darkness and swung his sword at an unaware Ībeka. In mid-stroke, a Phibian burst forth from the muddy water and latched onto the Reaper's side.

By the time Ībeka reacted, the Phibian already Whispered the Reaper into a quick suicide. The Phibian fell to the mossy turf, foaming at the mouth, without a breath more to give. In stride, Ībeka kicked the Phibian in the back and foam poured from her choking savior's mouth. When Ībeka's Whispers found Seerinx, time stretched into stillness, for both the old Weirs.

'I am the Voice silencing yours,
I put out the light to save darkness
Time is a game played by Nature,
But Time is Hell for all us others,
I speak for those who fell before.

Free are those who see into Others
Bound are they who see only 'I',
Worms are eating what's left of you,
Whispering lips crackle to Death,
Swallow truth and choke on your art,
I'll end with a rhyme and so depart'

In the split of a moment, the leader of the Order of Moon Weirs chewed off her own tongue and was choking on it. Her onyx-eyes stared at the quiet darkness, since all the Phibian's but one vanished, along with any threat from the defeated Weirs and Reapers.

Foam commingled with blood, on a battlefield already being swallowed by its own nature. The Mire fall still and silent. When the last vestiges of life left Seerinx, Ībeka turned back to the Phibian who saved her, who was waist-deep in the muddy waters and watching the dark sky, to the east.

"You should work on your delivery," Ībeka said. "You choke on your own too much."

"I always forget, whenever I begin," the Phibian said. "Too much is better than nothing at all."

"What do you see?"

"Only expectation of what will emerge. But I have waited for a long time to see it. A very long time."

"Leave it to a Phibian to forget her own heroics and look towards what's yet to come. Maybe a little longer and you'll see. But look at anything long enough and something's bound to happen. Would you look at me... I'm bleeding all over you. Pardon an old woman, while she gathers an old remedy."

Ībeka gathered moss and applied it to her wounds, while the Phibian stared on, in silence. The Phibian sensed the nearness of Nyctá, in spite of the tremendous gulf between them. Shixee knew nobody in the world could make her feel that kind of beautiful disturbance within herself, nobody but the woman who had been called by many Names. Their time together had been short, but all the time in the world meant nothing, when no one like Nyctá ever came before. She missed her heart, the truest part of her being.

When the first burst of light in the spore cloud cast dim light on Ümfalla, Shixee fidgeted in the water and knew the old Weir was watching from behind. She knew every living soul in Ümfalla was watching what was transpiring, above the spore cloud. There was no choice. She knew many things were to come, but said nothing of them, since they were already about to happen.

"I remember this," Shixee said.

"No, you don't. You knew, *before*," Ībeka said, as she watched the lights through battle-bright eyes. "But you'll forget it soon. And then the same will return, again. *Eternally*."

When the sky went bright in Ümfalla, for the first time in an Age, neither Shixee nor Ībeka were startled. The rumble from the explosion followed and the entirety of the land shook, in accord. Mammoth mushrooms fell, while the Sideon Cliffs remained unmoved. Waters of The Mire spilled into the Vernox and the dead were further swallowed by an already ravenous field of battle. Buried mycelium was thrust up, glowing in its disturbance.

Burning ruins from Upper Rim came toppling down. For every soul in Ümfalla, it was the first *fire* they had ever seen. Even Phibians, who survived the Ages, failed to remember even a glimmer of such a phenomenon.

"The top always falls," Shixee said.

"It's the ones in the middle who are left to face tomorrow," Ībeka muttered. "There's a whole world of souls, up there in Middle Rim, about to find themselves back at the top, in moments. Funny how that works. Maybe next time the whole Tree'll come down. Then, Phibian, you can see it again, for the first time."

"Chaos leaves beauty in its wake, too," Shixee said, through closed eyes.

While the east burned, Shixee remained in the thick waters of The Mire, with an unflappable Ībeka, standing behind her. Two souls watched as the fire spread along the roots at the base of the Tree of Avernus. Even though they were more than a turn's walk or swim from the place, they could already smell the smoke from the conflagration.

Both of them knew the Tree would stay rooted, even if the crown ambitiously *thrust* upon it was gone. Just as their eyes began to adjust to distant firelight, something descended through the spore cloud and turned the world blinding white.

Behind closed eyes, Shixee and Ībeka heard the unmistakable scream from Night Skimmers, flying over the Fungal Realm. When the blinding light diminished, what resembled one of the Sister Moons, faded into the West, along with the pair of Skimmers. Shixee looked away and spotted the pale red light, above. Sky Tracer was running its course, just as it had, for so many orbits. But as the Phibian's eyes re-adjusted to the fickle light, the pale red light was falling. Shixee did not blink, until the light was extinguished by the darkness, below.

"The dark bird of wisdom flies at dusk," Ībeka laughed

"*Nyctá*," Shixee said.

"Nyctá? Well, I suppose that's a good Name for such a time as this. *The long night*."

"Yes," Shixee said, closing her eyes. "That, too."

39

WORLDS APART

THE SUN WAS CASTING spangles on her chest when she opened her eyes to the waking world. A steady wind made the changing leaves above her swish, along with the faint sound of waves crashing on the Northern Shore of Forlindea. Nyctámēna was swaying in the wind, on a hammock between two pines, just beyond arm's reach of another hammock where her daughter slept. Scylla was still wearing the crimson Weir Cloak from before, imparting the idyllic moment with regret. The hands that tossed her that cloak were no more, nothing but ashes in the receiving earth of Ümfalla.

Through the trees, Nyctámēna spotted Īo and Nīya flying, in drifting patterns indicative of weariness. The dragons' courses were further articulated by ice clouds, higher up, in the mineral-blue sky, a series of prismatic streaks, relating the beauty of the world and nothing more.

Nyctámēna's body ached, from her head to her bare feet, but she was altogether whole. Her mechanical was still sound and on her arm, but it was clear someone took the care to loosen it enough to wipe clean the filth from battle. The internal wound that still bled was the superimposed presence of Callisto, a ghost without a voice, a Name without a life.

Nyctámēna's last memory, before the present moment, was the bold flight of Scylla behind the Demon Goddess and the glimmer of black fire. Nothingness followed, devoid of duration. Now she was swaying in the breeze, in the woodland splendor of Forlindea, an effect without any causes for justification.

She was not dead, the pain and strangeness of reality was far too present. But something other than luck navigated the falling Sky Realm and directed them back to Forlindea. Īo was more than capable of navigating convoluted places of the world, but the magnitude of what transpired through Ice meeting Fire shook Īo to the core, a truth Nyctámēna sensed from the dragon. Something else moved them.

"*Calli*" Scylla whispered, as she turned her face to Nyctámēna, with tears streaming from dark-bright eyes.

Nyctámēna met Scylla's gaze, receiving the young Weir's pain, sharing in it. Moments passed, with no need for blinking, not when both of them were shedding enough tears to turn the dark earth beneath them to mud.

Scylla began breathing manically, before her breaths turned to cries, just as her eyes went battle-bright. Before another breath passed through Scylla's mouth, Nyctámēna already rolled from her hammock and was kneeling at Scylla's side, where they held each other in a heaving embrace, while they swayed through their torment, rather than the wind.

"*Look up*," Nyctámēna whispered, as Scylla went limp in the hammock. "Nīya and Īo are mourning with us. You're not alone in this, Scylla. The heavens and the woods weep for her, too."

Scylla's eyes were bright with tears, "Calli loved the dragons, even if she was scared of heights. She came for me, in spite of it all. *She...*"

"She loved you beyond reckoning, Scylla."

"And it's because of me she's gone."

"It's because of you she found love again, Scylla, a love beyond anything she could have imagined. She told me so, many times. Nobody in Ümfalla could have brought her that."

"All I remember is her face, just before she turned to ash. *She was smiling at us.* Calli is..."

"Calli's deeds were legend before she even fell. Her courage and love are eternal, an epic song in herself. Only the dragons and ourselves will know the truth of that. She died more than a warrior's death. She died for something far greater."

"I can't remember what happened after the dragon's entangled their fire."

"Neither can I. What followed is oblivion, before I woke up here and—"

"You're awake!" Ruthy shouted, from the grounds of the Temple of the Wind.

When Ruthy approached, she was wearing a fresh set of wood-cotton clothes, not unlike Scylla's usual garb. Ruthy's hair was a bob of wild red hair, blowing freely in the wind. She remained skeletal, fragile in her posture, but her eyes lost their manic glare and a bit of color returned to her face. She moved as one would, if that person never experienced the splendor and constraints at court. Ruthy stood as she had, in the darkness of Ümfalla, with her arms akimbo and a look of restless uncertainty on her face.

Ruthy broke the short silence, "Do either of you know how in the hell we made it back here."

"*No,*" Nyctámēna said, without looking back at her, while she continued kneeling by Scylla in the hammock.

Ruthy continued, "Apparently, Yala saw the dragons circling the sky and found us on the shore. She said all three of us were unconscious, but we were *arranged,* as if we curled up together to watch the sunset and had fallen asleep. She also said we smelled like dragon fire, so I told her—"

"What do you remember about the black fire?" Nyctámēna almost shouted.

"I know that I saw it. Then there was nothing. Not a thing, until I woke up here, yesterday. I've been talking to Áknoitē, while you were still sleeping. That was awkward at first, considering the whole Sky Tracer history. But she's full of wisdom. I suppose she had a long time to reflect, but—."

"How are you so fucking *sprightly*?" Nyctámēna said, standing up, slowly. She clenched her jaw and faced Ruthy.

"Because I've been sleeping for seven orbits, *be-Whispered,*" Ruthy said, taking a step back.

"*Arethūsa!*"

Only Scylla's lips moved when she screamed the declaration, a scream followed by the deafening cries of the dragons, Nīya and Īo, still circling, high above the trees. Even roosting birds went silent at the screams.

"That Name is no longer mine," Ruthy said, warily looking up at the dragons through the trees, her face as pale as Scylla's eyes were bright.

Scylla turned her head in the hammock and glared at Ruthy, with her lower lip fluttering, "*Arethūsa* is who I found and Arethūsa is who I see, standing here." Scylla's entire body was shaking. She rolled over and stared at the dragons through the leaves.

Nyctámēna remained standing before Ruthy, as still as the surrounding tree trunks, glaring down at the former Ruler of Avernus. Ruthy turned away and her tears made the colorful leaves at her feet stir like the first drops of rain, after a drought. The Dragon Weir watched those tears fall.

Nyctámēna returned to Scylla and kneeled beside her trembling form, while she held her in an embrace requiring no words. Through that embrace, Nyctámēna's mechanical glistened through an unbreakable bond, uniting the suffering Weirs, symbolizing the kind of resilience that made a broken world work. They swayed on through their embrace, in a wind of their own, a wind blowing from the dark caverns of memory, filled with voices that could no longer speak, but would always be present. When Nyctámēna let go her embrace, Ruthy was gone.

****

Over the course of the turn, Scylla remained where she was, in deep sleep, while Ruthy reacquainted herself with the world. Gone was the mycelium of Ümfalla, but the roots of the trees nurtured her inherent need to commune with the earth through every step, just as much as breath was life.

Ruthy walked around the temple grounds, as if in a dream, her barefoot steps, slowly corresponding to the aerial course of the dragons.

Nyctámēna spoke with Yala and related what transpired in Sky Realm. The revelation of Scylla and Nyctámēna's emergent power, in accordance with the dragons, interested Yala far less than the story of the Demon Goddess, who was falsely worshipped as Daphnē. In spite of Yala's patience and wise words, through a soothing voice, Nyctámēna failed to remember anything after the entanglement of dark fire. Another forgetfulness found Nyctámēna, in an existence shaped by it.

Ruthy spent much of her time in the Temple with Ákonitē and the fledgling Weirs, but Nyctámēna noticed something peculiar in her own right. Youthful Weirs who flocked to the young Dragon Weir—on the turn Callisto made her final visit—did not go near Scylla, never looked in her direction, as she swayed through her torment in the hammock, in a most fast sleep.

It was something other than simply allowing Scylla to sleep in peace, it was as if a sleeping dragon was in their midst, rather than a young woman who was beyond exhaustion, whose heart was broken. Wind Weirs turned their faces from Nyctámēna, whenever she drew near and said nothing to her, not even, '*Hello*'. Nyctámēna dreaded the onslaught of Weirs eager to please and learn of the outside world, but that dread was supplanted through palpable silence, the loudest of fears. Only Yala treated the Dragon Weir as she always had, different, but equal.

Night fell and invited the dark-bright eyes of Scylla to show themselves. When she finally stood up and saw Nyctámēna watching the dragons through the trees, Scylla gave her a moment. The Temple loomed darkly and crickets articulated the wind, rather than Weirs. Even the waves on the shore diminished into little more than a lapping sea of calm. In the moment, Scylla wanted nothing more than to remain exactly where she was, neither here nor there, without a past or future. But the past rushed back up to seize her, as surely as her next breath.

Scylla approached Nyctámēna, but neither of them spoke. Scylla joined her, watching the dragons trace the star-filled sky with their splendor. Scylla imagined the overhanging leaves as a reef in the blackest of oceans. The stars were mysterious creatures of the deep and the Three Sisters were their ambassadors. Shooting stars were playful eels, while drifting clouds were food for the bottomless ocean of night. Breeze became Wind and blew Scylla's thoughts back to the hard world beneath her bare feet.

"This is no place for us," Nyctámēna said, softly.

"Nothing will be what it was."

"Losing someone doesn't make the next time any easier. I'm sorry to tell you that, Scylla."

"Calli is everywhere."

"She wouldn't have it, otherwise. Her love lives beyond her life."

"Should have told her how much I loved her, more often."

"You showed it, Scylla, always."

"If I had just listened to you and stayed away from that Tree and—"

"Don't fall into blame. You couldn't have known the horror waiting, a Demon awakening and... That way leads nowhere but ruin. Calli died for love, for you to live, along with countless others. She died to allow us to blow that fucking Demon into oblivion. She would have loved it."

"Definitely."

"So...you know I love you with all my heart, right?"

"Yes. And I love you with all mine. *Always*. Every time I try to think of what happened, I hit this...*void*. It's not even the forgetfulness of sleep. It's like a thing I can touch that's more nothing than nothing. So much more...it has form in its nothingness. I'm rambling."

"That's good," Nyctámēna half-smiled. "It means you're coming back to yourself."

"Is it okay if we don't talk about Avernus for a little while, after this moment?"

"Of course."

"It's not because I want to forget. I can never un-see Calli's bravery, her heart bigger than this world. Fuck, I *miss* her. I want to remember more, but I want to let it happen. I refuse to pretend I can make it come back. What do you think happened to all the Avernians in the Tree...after it..."

"It would take the world's end to uproot that Tree. I saw Middle Rim while everything up top was breaking. I believe it held strong…" Nyctámēna struggled for words, while she watched the dragons in the starlight, "Time will unfold what became of Sky Realm, what's left of Ümfalla. All of us need to heal, before we consider anything more."

"I just want to be with you and just…*be*."

"Wanna go for a ride?"

"Hell yes," Scylla half-smiled, through tears. She closed her eyes, "What about the…*former Ruler of Avernus*?"

"She's going to stay here with Yala. She needs to sort through who she really is and only Yala can guide her, since they have a shared past. She'll keep eyes on Ruthy. Trust is hard-won in the best of times. As for Ruthy… Her life is more tangled than your hair."

"Too true," Scylla said, tugging at a knot in her thick crimson hair. "What if she proves to be a threat?"

"Then I'll kill her myself. In the meantime, I'd rather have Ruthy on the same island than somewhere else. She has powers that need to be watched. But those powers could prove to do good for the world. I've seen glimmers of that goodness, as much it pains me to say that. I had more than one chance in my tangled life. Ruthy has *one* more, or her heartbeats will end through Slender."

Scylla let go a held breath, "I've lost my fascination with this place."

"With Forlindea?"

"*No*. The Goddess, no. With the Order and all that. Avernus changed the way I see. I want to go home."

"*Home*," Nyctámēna half-smiled. "Let's go home."

As the Dragon Weirs departed, Nyctámēna walked a little ahead, while Scylla lingered, taking in the place she believed she was leaving forever. She remembered Wind Weirs surrounding her, in the same spot place she was standing, only a handful of turns ago.

Scylla's eyes refilled with tears, as she recalled the strong and loving hand of Callisto, pulling her away from the young Weirs to speak Ümfallan wisdom to her, in plain words. It felt like a lifetime ago and Scylla realized it was. Nothing would be the same. Scylla, from before, was as much a ghost as Callisto.

Through the grim entrance to the Temple, a pair of red eyes were staring at her. Just above those eyes, glorified by darkness, a tiara was sparkling, giving off glints of crimson and silver, like hundreds of sentient stars watching the Dragon Weirs depart. Scylla's heart palpitated and she lost her breath. She felt her jaw dropping and wanted nothing more than to scream, but she had no breath to do so. Nyctámēna's hand touched her shoulder and the horror passed. When she shook her head and looked back into the Temple, it was pitch black.

"You okay?" Nyctámēna asked.

"Yeah. Just tired. Need to sleep where the air is quiet."

"We know a couple of dragons who can take us there."

"We do. The Goddess...I *love* them."

"Good. Cause we're stuck with them. Now, c'mon, let's go."

"*Home.*"

Epilogue

Turns passed and Fall became Winter and slowly turned to Spring, on the island of Forlindea. The Dragon Weirs remained in the South, where the cold winds of the North failed to reach them, in anything other than a Whisper-less breeze. Nyctámēna and Scylla donned their onyx goggles on their daily flights to the outer reaches of Oceána, while the nights were left to the dragons and their own flights of fancy.

Īo and Nīya were bound by far more than the love of their Weirs, theirs was a bond forged in Fire and Ice, a metaphysical entanglement, distinguishing them from other dragons of Oceána, with a certain absoluteness.

Time failed to heal torments of turns past, but Scylla accepted passing time, without regard to tomorrow. Neither of the Dragon Weirs spoke of their emergent powers, erupting in the Battle of Avernus. There was nothing to be said, since the resultant void demanded silence.

Their understanding of their respective dragons grew, turn after turn, in ways far different than magic. Īo and Nyctamēna found Singularity when they took flight, while the same intertwining occurred in Nīya and Scylla. For the dragons and their Weirs to consider life before their entanglement was impossible, leaving Sky Realm as a cipher, haunted by magic and regret.

Ships continued to sail, full of ambitious Wind Weirs, on their journeys to the four corners of Oceána. Fishermen made the trek to the Southern Shore to pay their respects to a fallen Callisto, someone they considered far more than a drinking companion. Through those tributes, fishermen detailed reports from the eastern waters of Oceána.

The Eternal Storm diminished and ships were able to sail close enough to Ümfalla to see the Tree of Avernus, standing strong, after the crown fell into the darkness of the spore cloud. Beyond such distant reckonings, the fate of both realms was unknown. Beer-bathed rumors also passed those fisherman's cracked lips, from time to time, long after their respects were paid to the growing legend of Callisto, a warrior and friend, strong, both in heart and deed, even if she never learned to fish. Nyctámēna listed a handful of these rumors to Scylla one night and Scylla matched them with her own, while the dragons soared to places unknown. Through the laughter at the list, Calli's presence was almost palpable:

- "So...Calli's old drinking buddies said Ruthy is communing with the forgotten Goddess, Proserpīne, whose spirit is living in the trees...

- Yala is older than dirt, literally...

- Ákonitē could break the world with her words...

- Fish are most likely to bite when dragons are near...

- Wind Weirs are actually devout gossipers...

- The cause of wind is a thousand and one dragon's wings, flapping from the North...

- The cause of the seasons is the restless world....

- Dragon Weirs eat light and nothing more...

- Sudden growth in the forest is a sign of prosperous days to come..."

While the verity of the rumors was contained in the nature of rumors—a little of everything was partly true—the rumor concerning the sudden growth of the trees was veritable. When growing things were supposed to be in a living state of death, in deep winter, the ancient trees of Forlindea found a strange spring.

Unflappable branchlets and leaves sprouted in the dead cold, on the shortest days of the year. The strongest north winds failed to blow them back to sleep. Saplings that failed to survive winters past were flourishing along the coast, while lichen and mosses began to spread beyond the heart of the woods, a sign of sylvan prosperity, bringing Scylla traces of joy, after tremendous loss.

Now that it was Spring, the entirety of the woods in Forlindea thickened and had grown demonstrably taller, with no end in sight. Wildlife flourished, while migratory dragons found more nesting places in stronger trees, through an elemental magic that failed to upset the overall balance of creatures and growing things.

Rather than pushing the Dragon Weirs to visit the North, the sudden fecundity, indicative of another land, far to the East, kept them to the South. Both Dragon Weirs already faced too much, in the not too distant past, to invite it back in again. Nyctámēna had a strange hope in an awakened Ruthy, revealing itself in the harmony of it all, so the seeming miracle of the trees was nothing out of the ordinary, not for the restless fingers of the former Ruler of Avernus.

Just as merciful rains poured down after a drought, so the elemental magic Ruthy possessed was revitalizing a realm in decline, bringing vibrance back into the forest. Power was power, in spite of the good or bad the one possessing it chose to do. At the heart of it, Nyctámēna was relieved Ruthy's hands were not idle. She was finding a way to express herself and spend a bit of her own magic, every turn, even if a lifetime of regrowth could never undo what Ruthy had done, no matter her chosen Name. More than anyone in Forlindea, the Dragon Weirs understood the fundamental need for *expression*.

Needs came and went, just as the sun and Sister Moons ran their courses, across the inviting sky. Nyctámēna dreamed of Ümfalla and of the Phibian, *Shixee*, who remained a living cipher of the Fungal Realm. The prospect of Shixee having already forgotten her frightened Nyctámēna, more than the thought of her death.

For Nyctámēna, the fate of the Phibian was inextricably tied to Ümfalla's, as well as Sky Realm. Shixee's forgetfulness would mark the end of an Age. Both Dragon Weirs faced forgetfulness, following the Battle of Avernus and nothing changed that oblivion. Nyctámēna said nothing to Scylla about it, but was no longer able to hide her need to go back, to return and see for herself, what was becoming of the Fungal Realm.

It was a night not unlike all the others, on the Southern Shore of Forlindea. Ïo and Nīya were somewhere, far to the West, doing ineffable things dragons did, beyond mortal witnesses. Scylla was sitting on the shore, where root gave way to rock, on an unusually warm night for Spring, with the water lapping on her bare feet. Nyctámēna was standing next to her, with her eyes fixed on the dark waters, eastward.

"You should go," Scylla said, with no particular gravity.

"Do you want some time alone? I can go back and get—"

"No. I mean you should go and see Ümfalla. Go and see if you can find Shixee."

"Shixee is fine. She's lived through more Ages than she can remember."

"Exactly. Don't you want to see her before she forgets? I might be young, but I'm learning there are few souls we ever really know. I have nightmares about...*forgetting*. I see you and don't know your Name."

"You wouldn't be the first."

"*I'm serious.* It scares the Hell out of me. Ever since that nothingness after Avernus... I'll be fine here. I've got Nīya and have no intentions of finding adventures. The first one was almost the last."

"I haven't been myself lately. I'm sorry."

"Neither of us have. How can we be? Calli is everywhere. She even finds me in my dreams, finds a way to make me laugh. Then I wake up... It's not like we can fly away from that. I flew straight into her death... I love this life but I understand you need to go. And...I can't come with you. Both of us know the dragons refused to fly anywhere tending to east, ever since that night. Something changed for you and Īo of late. Nīya won't follow, probably because of me."

"There's no distinguishing our choices with the dragons. Not anymore."

"That's a good way to put it... But you'd better not take too long, or I'll come find you and I'll be breathing fire."

"I believe you," Nyctámēna said, with a tired smile.

"I know what I'll do, while you're gone."

"Oh yeah? What's that?"

"I'm going to learn how to fish."

"*Fish*? Now you sound like, Calli."

"Exactly. She always wanted to, but never got around to it. But she loved to watch, while she drank their beer."

"Just don't drink as much beer as she did. Actually, don't drink any of it."

"Nah. Just a little for her, every time I catch one."

"It's not that easy, you know that."

"I'll figure it out," Scylla smiled at sea foam, blown between her knees. "Then I'll be a real fisherwoman, by the time you get back."

"Want to know a secret?"

"Tell me."

"I hate fish."

"Me too!" Scylla laughed. "I just want to catch them and feel what it feels like to throw them back. Watch them swim back to those secret places of the deep, places we'll never know. Not ever."

"It's times like these I look into your eyes and see a glimmer of that forgotten place both of us must have sprung from. We never really talk about it, but there's no denying we share more than dark-bright eyes."

"I made up the stories about my mother coming from the Antipodes. For all I know, she was from one of the Sister Moons."

"Well, maybe we'll see if the dragons are up for a journey to those *Antipodes,* when I return...see something new."

"I think I'll be up for that. So you really are going?!"

"Tell me you're okay, before I go," Nyctámēna said, crouching next to Scylla.

"I'll be okay. I'm not good, but it's alright to be just okay, right? Getting better every day, I guess. Summer will be beautiful. I feel everything growing. All."

"There's so much more for you to see, Scylla. Especially, for someone your age."

"How old are you, anyway?" Scylla asked, squinting at Nyctámēna's eyes. "I've never asked you that."

"I don't know. From what I can remember," she paused and pointed at Scylla, "Don't you say anything about what I've forgotten," she smiled, before they both laughed. "I'm at least...a hundred and fifty."

"What?" Scylla cried, trying to contain herself. Then she burst out laughing, "You're older than young dirt!"

"That was almost funny. You already sound like a fisherwoman," Nyctámēna laughed on. "All that matters, is, you're laughing. There's hope yet. Want to help me pack? I'm so old I forget what to bring, so—"

"Smart ass."

After the necessities for the journey were packed, the sun was already glimmering over the eastern shore. Neither of the Dragon Weirs needed to pull up their goggles yet, so they were faced with bare confessions, through dark-bright eyes. Īo sensed her Weir's need and landed on a patch of roots, a near perfect niche for her talons. The dragon watched her Weir, with eyes beyond knowing, as Nīya flew high above them, in her majestic rounds.

Nyctámēna took a deep breath and exhaled, before she hugged Scylla with such force, it made Scylla exhale, as well, as her bare feet left the earth, in the powerful arms of Nyctámēna. Her mechanical pressed into Scylla and she welcomed the pain from one of the many pieces of Nyctámēna forged in the flames of chaos. When Scylla's feet slowly found the ground again, she realized she was crying.

"It's good you're doing this," Scylla said.

"I'll be back, long before the season changes, I promise you that. And you know the dragons are so entangled at this point, I'll know if you fly off somewhere beyond—"

"I won't. Nīya has so much less experience than Īo. It'll take her longer to open back up, anyway. She's not restless these days."

"I just had to say it."

"And you'd better not forget to take off your mechanical, before you go to sleep. I won't be there to remind you, so—"

"I'll remember. New habits don't fade that quickly, not when I'll be back before—"

"But don't feel rushed. It's your old home. I'll be good."

"If anything goes wrong—"

"*I know, I know.* I'll go straight to Yala."

"You're..." Nyctámēna began, turning her head away from Scylla. She cleared her throat, before she looked back. "*You are my daughter,* in life and love. My words are yours. *Always.*"

"You are my *mother*, in life and love. My words are us. *Always...* Took you long enough to finally say it," she winked.

They wept through the embrace, holding each other, for so long, when they opened their eyes, both of them pulled up their goggles to greet the rising sun. Nyctámēna nodded and Scylla did the same, while her mother climbed onto the wing of Īo and found her place on the dragon's back. Two minds intertwined into One. Dragon wind only blew once, before they were gone and turning into a speck on the horizon. Scylla watched them through her goggles and refused to look away, until they were out of sight. When the last vestige of their form was gone, Nīya let out a deep cry for her departing kin, in life and mischief.

Scylla was suddenly aware of the sea lapping on her bare feet, tinges of cedar in the breeze, as if for the first time. The sudden departure of her mother evoked a sense of having always been alone, a solitary soul and the haunted dragon. She took a halting breath and let it out, with great trouble.

"*Breathe*, Scylla. Just breathe. Breathe...*K*...good. Just breathe and be. It's so easy. I feel it, right now. Just coursing through me, like air. Letting go. See, Nīya! I can do this! Watch and learn! I'm letting go and just being! Just like you! Don't go anywhere! I'll be right back! Just have to see about something! Just a little walk in the woods, just like old times. Don't think you can start doing anything you want, just because Īo's gone! We're in this together!"

Scylla experienced release, as the events from Avernus came pouring back into her, like a wave of memories on the barren shore of forgetfulness. She walked, as if in a dream, towards the woods that appeared to be growing before her eyes. Scylla muttered to herself as the memories grew thicker and richer, along with the trees she was headed towards.

Just as the rising sun was finding its brightness, on the Southern Shore of Forlindea, Scylla walked into the shadows of the woods. Wherever her bare feet passed over, tiny mushrooms were already sprouting and raising their soft caps to the Forlindean morning.

End

Appendix

GLOSSARY OF TERMS

A

- **Age:** A unit of time representative of one thousand orbits (years)

- **Avernus:** Composed of Three Rims in the Tree of Avernus, also called, *Sky Realm.* Exists above the murk of the Spore Cloud

B

- **Bannus Seed:** Highly nutritious seed of Avernus, much like an almond in shape and texture

- **black fire:** A fire beyond white-hot, only possible through magical intervention of two souls working in unison

- **Blissel Lichen:** Highly nutritious lichen growing on rocks that is extremely sour, evokes temporary feeling of well-being

C

- **celium-wear:** Clothing made by a master-weaver and composed of mycelium from the Filigrees Mushroom, while sub-species replaced the superior wear after the fall of the Simmerians, who cultivated the mushroom

- **chatter:** Clicking of teeth when Ruthy is communicating through the mycelial network

- **The Churn:** Ocean surrounding the Fungal Realm, forever turbulent from the Eternal Storm

- **Conductor:** Another name for Arethūsa, in relation to Sky Tracer

- **Creepers:** Name given to the iridescent lizard-like creatures in the Labyrinth

D

- **Daphne:** Creator of Ūmfalla and Sky Realm and Goddess sleeping in the Tree

- **dark-bright:** Eyes that give off a moonlight glow and impart the viewer with preternatural night vision

- **The Dim Light:** Euphemism for Sky Tracer used by, '*The People Who Are Going To Put Out The Light*'

- **double-tongue:** Simultaneous double-language of Mēna: *Ūmfallan* and an unknown language

E

- **Eternal Storm:** Storm that has raged in The Churn for Ages unknown, making travel by ship impossible

F

- **Filigrees Mushroom:** Extinct mushroom once used to make premium celium-wear, medicines

- **Forlindea:** Wooded isle far to the West of Ūmfalla

- **Forlindean Beer:** Fermented from seagrass along the coast, extraordinarily potent and bitter

- **Fowlery:** Eatery in Middle Rim of Sky Realm, serving a wide variety of avian dishes

- **Fungal Realm:** Another name for Ümfalla and indicative of its flora

G

- **glowworm:** Maggot-sized worms that glow bright blue and eat away rot

- **Goddess:** The Ineffable One

- **greater and lesser mushrooms:** Mushrooms in Ümfalla, ranging from the height of ancient oaks to a mote of dust, many giving off bioluminescent glow

H

- **hand of (silk):** Unit of measurement in Ümfalla, equivalent to the supposed length of the ideal hand, from the base of the palm to the tip of the middle finger (roughly 10 inches)

- **Hardening:** Prophecy of the Phibians regarding the end of an Age and literal *Hardening* of the perpetually damp and soft Fungal Realm

- **Heartwood Chamber:** The innards of the Screaming Branch, place where children feed the Goddess in the Tree

- **Healer:** Those gifted in the arts of mending wounds and mental ailments, rarely useful in treatment of magics or curses

- **helm:** Space between the dragon's spikes near the bottom vertebrae of her neck, where Dragon and Weir *intertwine*

- **Hexing, building Hexes:** Hallucinatory state brought on by mushroom with a cap that resembles puckered lips

- **Hydra Mushroom:** Many-capped mushrooms that grow to tremendous heights and are ideal for climbing and conducive to growing Lantern Mushrooms on their caps

I

- **indigo:** A color indicative of immeasurable power, e.g. dragon's eyes

- **intertwine:** Act of Weir and Dragon uniting with mind and soul, a union everlasting and singular, magical at its core

K

- **katars:** Retractable blades in Briar's mechanicals, forged from Sideon ore, by the same welder who made Slender

- **Kronos Mushroom:** Extraordinarily rare mushroom that resembles a giant pitcher. A soul falling inside drifts into a sleep outside of time

L

- **Labyrinth:** Subterranean construct in Avernus used to initiate young women into the Order of the Wind Weirs

- **Lactarius Mushrooms:** Only found on the western end of the Sideon Cliffs, caps and stem exude a milky fluid ideal for motherless infants

- **Lantern Mushroom:** Resembles a pumpkin in form and size and bears a soft glow that grows bright for an extended time with a good kick (grow on Hydra Mushrooms)

M

- **mechanical:** Term indicative of metal mechanisms such as Mēna's arm mechanical or katars that retract on Briar's wrists

- **memory worm:** Ümfallan term for dementia

- **mineral-fire:** Superheated minerals in a cluster that resemble a fire, but give off no flame

- **Mires:** Home of the Phibians, marshland along the Sideon Cliffs, in the heart of the North in the realm of Ümfalla

- **mycelium:** Vegetative part of a mushroom, consisting of a network of fine white filaments (hyphae), vary in power and uses, often glow when disturbed. Every handful of Ümfallan soil contains over ten kilometers of entangled mycelium

- **mycelium tendrils:** A 'weaving' of mycelium by gifted ones who use the chord as a hub to the greater network of mycelium throughout the landscape

N

- **Nighthawk:** Nickname for the Reaper, Nyctá

- **Night Skimmers:** Tremendous black birds of prey, rarely seen in the Fungal Realm and portend the end of an Age when seen in pairs, always flying from great heights

- **Night Whisperer:** Weir who practices prostitution and uses her gifts to weave fantastical stories for the client's ear

- **Nyctá:** Ancients word for 'the long night' or 'fear the night'

O

- **Oceána:** Sea to the West of The Churn and beyond the Eternal Storm

- **onyx goggles:** Burnished onyx lenses with a Weaver Silk strap, made by master-welder, Zeffá, later by Nyctámēna for Syclla. Mandatory for Weirs with dark-bright eyes to see in sunlight

- **orbit:** One cycle of the world around the sun

- **The Order:** The name for the gathering of Wind Weirs in Forlindea

P

- **Phibian:** Resemble Ümfallans in general physiognomy, but possess gills below their ears, horizontally closing double-eyelids, webbed feet and hands, dependent on water and air, alternately

- **Proserpīne:** Goddess of the Woods in Forlindea

- **Puffball Mushroom:** Colossal mushrooms with spherical caps that burst every night, releasing plumes of spores and are responsible for a high percentage of the Spore Cloud's constitution. Without them, the sun would cook the Fungal Realm in a few turns

R

- **Resurrection Spore:** Legendary spores said to bring back the dead

- **realm-crusher:** Euphemism for a battle-hardened dragon of extraordinary size

- **Reapers:** Ümfallan warriors notorious for guerrilla tactics and merciless methods

- **red eyes:** Eyes indicative of dark magic, e.g. Ákonitē

- **Rims (Upper, Middle, Lower):** Designations of the levels in Sky Realm. Tremendous branches intertwine to compose a 'landscape' that divides and subdivides on its way up into the regality at the top of the Tree

- **Rolling Hills:** Ancient landscape of Forlindea, now absorbed by trees

S

- **Satyrs:** Hoofed and horned goat-like creatures, renowned archers and eaters of human flesh, only found on Lower Rim

- **Screaming Branch:** Euphemism for the place where children delivered on Sky Tracer are taken

- **Screevers:** Wandering traders in Ümfalla, without a shared identity or proper Name

- **Seemer:** Euphemism for a dishonest, deceitful person

- **Seeing into the white/yellow/blue:** Dark-bright eyes see on this scale, designation descending in strength from white to blue

- **Seething Falls:** Name of waterfalls at the end of the Sinel Hills, to the East, sound from afar is said to 'seethe'

- **Seven Seats of the House of the Elders:** Denoting Elders who hold the seats of rule in Avernus

- **Sideon Cliffs:** Unclimbable, unbreakable cliffs running along the entirety of the Northern portion of Ümfalla, pitch black and smooth, reflective as glass

- **Simmerians:** A people of Ümfalla who once lived in and around the Sideon Cliffs, renowned cultivators of Filigrees Mushrooms

- **Sinel Hills:** Said to have been formed by the Word of the Goddess, rolling hills indicative of sine-waves

- **Sister Moons, Three Sisters:** Three Moons that rise together and provide untold power to Weirs, the seas and the flora and fauna of the world

- **Sky Realm:** Another name for Avernus, world above the Fungal Realm and situated throughout the World Tree

- **Sky Shear:** Bird of prey in Sky Realm that work in pairs, razor-sharp wings that slice through murmurations of birds they 'herd', resemble falcons

- **Sky Throne:** New Seat of the Ruler of Avernus, crystalline chamber at the top of the Tree of the Ancients

- **Sky Tracer:** Abominable machine that follows the overarching silk tracks above the Fungal Realm

- **Slender:** Black-steel sword of Mēna, forged from ore derived from Sideon Cliffs

- **Spiders of Avernus:** Colossal spiders consisting of a Queen and her smaller male consorts, living in the Tree of the Ancients

- **Sponge Mushroom:** *'Really fucking impressionable!'*

- **Spore Cloud:** Life-giving cloud consisting of spores, covering the entirety of Ümfalla, blocks out the sun and moons

- **spore plumes:** See *Puffball Mushrooms*

- **sunborne:** Eyes unadapted to eternal darkness in the Fungal Realm, lacking dark-brightness, but fully functioning in sunlight

T

- **Temple of the Wind:** Converted temple for The Order, once a temple to Proserpīne, Goddess of the Woods in Forlindea

- **Thunder Cliffs:** Three islands to the West of Ümfalla, situated in The Churn

- **turn:** Ümfallan for one full rotation of the world, equivalent to a day

U

- **Ümfalla:** A land of perpetual darkness, The Fungal Realm, literal meaning: *Navel of the World*

- **united:** The eternal union of two souls, a vow made under the Sister Moons

V

- **Vernox Mushroom:** Noxious mushroom that replicates itself into a 'forest' of oak-sized stalks with iridescent caps, critical to maintaining balance in Ümfallan soil

- **Vescent House:** Tavern where a variety of spirits are served in Middle Rim of Avernus

- **Vescent Wine:** Carbonated alcoholic beverage made from silver grapes, bubbles particularly resilient before they pop

W

- **Wanderer:** Lone traveler in search of a particular end in the Fungal Realm

- **Weaver Silk:** Highly-prized silk made from the webs of Foam Hermit spider, a spider that lives in caves on the rocky shore of The Churn

- **welder:** Name for artisans skilled in working with rare metals

- **Weir:** (Wind, Dragon, Moon, Foam) Magical being usually tied to a specific element

- **Whispering, Whisper:** Magical words spoken by Wind Weirs, capable of controlling another's thoughts in varying degrees, deadly if words are malformed

- **be-Whispered:** A soul whose mind has been warped by Whispering, oftentimes, unbeknownst to them

- **wind-drunk:** Euphemism for bewildering effects of the perpetual winds in Sky Realm

- **World Tree, Tree of the Ancients:** Tree growing to the far East of Ümfalla whose branches are above the Spore Cloud and stretch above the entirety of murk, far below, a realm of eternal cloudlessness

Acknowledgments

Entanglement comes in many forms...

From the woods to the mountains, New York City and the sea, the whirlwind of life would be meaningless without the 'characters' who share in this world with me. Stories shaped my childhood and I've been fortunate enough to realize my own, through my family and friends, teachers and guides.

There's no beginning or end to my love and thanks to you all. To call myself lucky would be an insult to all of you. My heart beats on *because* of you. Here's to the stories we've shared and those to come, those who are here and those departed. I carry you all with me, always. I'm honored to be caught up in your beautiful Entanglements.

About Hayden Moore

Hayden Moore is the author of over fifty short stories, appearing in journals ranging from literary to scientific. He lives on a little island, with his wife and dog/dragon, in Queens, NY.

You can find him online.

www.haydenmooreauthor.com

Printed in the USA
CPSIA information can be obtained
at www.ICGtesting.com
LVHW040619210224
772297LV00066B/133/J

9 781988 034270